DAWN OF THE GREATEST PERSIAN

The Childhood of Cyrus the Great

By

C.J. Kirwin

ISBN: 1-4107-6477-X (e-book)
ISBN: 1-4107-6478-8 (Paperback)

Library of Congress Control Number: 2003093961

This book is printed on acid free paper.

Printed in the United States of America
Bloomington, IN

1stBooks - rev. 06/23/03

<u>DEDICATION</u>

This book is dedicated to my wife, Gwen, who is my love and my first editor and to Cyrus Billy Jalili Khiabani who first interested me in Cyrus the Great.

ACKNOWLEGEMENTS

I appreciate the historical advice received from Dr. Mehrdad Haghayeghi who helped me be more accurate in several areas. The editorial assistance of Dr. Mary O'Toole was both instructive and kind. Dr. Fred Marashi gave me useful historical information. Dylan Brodie helped me understand storytelling.

All errors are solely the responsibility of the author.

GLOSSARY

Achaemenes: great, great grandfather of Cyrus the Great. Began the Achaemenean Dynasty.

Ahura: beneficial religious spirits (cf. Daeva).

Andarun: the inner household of a royal residence. Place where women rule in the home. In the future it is called the harem.

Arsames: king of Bactria.

Aryenis: queen of Media. Wife of Astyages; mother of Mandane; sister of Croesus.

Astyages: king of Media. The Great King. The King of Kings.

Bagindu: prince in Anshan. Cousin to Cambyses.

Cambyses: king of Pars. Father of Cyrus; husband of Mandane.

Croesus: king of Lydia. Richest man in the world. Brother of Aryenis.

Cubit: unit of length, approximately 18 inches. The distance from a man's elbow to his outstretched fingertips.

Cyrus: called Paithi in his youth. Son of Cambyses and Mandane.

Daeva: evil religious spirits (cf. Ahura).

Farsang: unit of distance, approximately 3.8 miles.

Harpagus: a soldier in Media.

Ispitamu: a princess in Anshan. Cousin of Cambyses.

Kauklia: king of Gedrosia.

Mandane: mother of Cyrus; wife of Cambyses; daughter of Astyages and Aryenis.

Mayden: the distance a horse will gallop alone, approximately one-quarter to one-half mile.

Mitridates: Greek foster-father to Cyrus (Paithi).

Moon cycle: one full month.

Nebuchadnezzar: king of Babylon.

Necho: pharaoh of Egypt.

Oebares: a slave boy in Media.

Pagakanna: governor of Babylon.

Paithi: childhood name given to Cyrus by his foster parents, Mitridates and Spaco.

Pattmenidu: the major merchant in Pars.

Rice Rodent: a merchant in Susa.

Rusundatu: a farmer and thief in Arbela.

Spaco: Greek foster-mother to Cyrus (Paithi).
Sun cycle: one full year.
Token: a form of currency having numerous sizes and shapes.
Warohi: prince of Susa. Cousin to Cambyses.
Zatame: prince of Media. Cousin to Astyages.
Zav: Minister of Taxes and Materials in Media.

INTRODUCTION

Tales of Cyrus the Great, the fifth Achaemenean king, are most abundant in history books from Greek language sources. It is speculated that Cyrus was born between 600 and 575 BCE into the dynasty begun by his great, great-grandfather, King Achaemenes. Although Cyrus is known in history for his greatness as a conqueror and for his notoriety in biblical citations, his birth and early upbringing are shrouded by numerous fables.

In the fourth millennium BCE, Asiatic nomads from southern Russia in the Caucasus and the southeastern steppes wandered east and south to settle the Iranian plateau. King Kauimers organized nomadic tribes just east of the Persian Gulf about 3200 BCE, and over approximately two and a half millennia his leadership eventually led to the formation of the nation of Pars where Cyrus the Great became king. Descendants of King Kauimers' natives cherished their ancestry and called themselves the Aryan or "noble" people, using verbal, family training to pass on tales of heroic greatness between generations of nomadic and sedentary tribes.

Cyrus inherited these tribes while they still belonged to the Median Empire. This fictional story uses historically significant figures from that era as its foundation. Greek-derived names are used in this story to identify these personalities because such identification is in common use today. Because reference materials are inconsistent in rendering details about the youth of Cyrus the Great, this fictional story takes a guess at how the greatest man in Persian history might have started his life.

1.

Thwak, thwak, thwak!

Three arrows quivered in the footstool.

The knees of the Minister of Taxes and Materials for the Median Empire turned to mush. He dared not move. Zav knew better than to jump from his seat, step over the footstool and shout, "I will send the Great King's army for you if you refuse to pay more tribute to King Astyages."

The palace guards could only interpret such an act as a bold threat against their King Cambyses.

Zav swallowed, but his throat was as dry as a desert. He felt stupid knowing that what he had done brought the arrows in the footstool. Zav looked about and saw every bow had an arrow nocked and aimed at him. No one moved. The Minister of Taxes and Materials was sweating profusely. What a mistake! All he could do was stand perfectly still and wait.

After allowing the tension to leave the air the king flicked his hand which ordered his soldiers to put up their weapons. King Cambyses said, "Be careful, Zav! Sit and have a glass of wine with me. There is no need for excitement. Just remember who rules here."

The Minister sat studying the arrows at his feet. How foolish he had been to let his anger bring on such danger. Why threaten this minor king here in his own palace? Zav realized it was foolish to be alone challenging a king with an army at hand. He would wait until later to arrange retribution by the Great King himself against this king of Pars.

A young woman with long shapely legs and a comfortable looking bosom approached with a silver and gold tray. She wore an attractive maroon tunic. The king smiled at her with his normal politeness as he lifted a gold cup of red wine from her tray. King Cambyses intended to shift the conversation to business instead of threats by saying, "Zav, relax. Drink. You know wine in my court is diluted with cool mountain water to make it a refreshing social drink, which does not intoxicate. Sip it slowly. My wine will not interrupt your ability to conduct the Great King's business. Let's talk of his business."

The young servant woman walked down the three steps in front of the king to approach the unattractive man sitting in the chair facing the throne. Zav took a wine cup made of animal horn and silver, and smiled his appreciation for her looks more than for the wine. He was pleased that this minor king was not like the Greeks who preferred to have small boys rather than ripe women in their presence.

"Zav, you have wasted my time for two days with idle chatter about taxes, merchandise and commerce. Now, today you try to threaten me with a tax increase thinking you can enforce it with shouting. You used to be smarter than that," the king said.

Zav kicked an arrow while deciding how to continue. The minister intended to pass on orders pretending they came from Great King of Media. He enjoyed making up lies while implying he had the backing of King Astyages. Zav said, "The Great King wants the land of Gedrosia to stop insulting Media's most cherished gods with their petty wars and attacks on our temples. King Astyages also wants tariffs from Gedrosia, which their King Kauklia refuses to pay. It will take military force to change his mind.

"Cambyses, you're to invade Gedrosia to stop these border wars and subdue Gedrosia for King Astyages. You are the only close kingdom with the strength to stop King Kauklia's mischief. You can beat the Gedrosian fighters because your army understands their nomadic ways as well as their wily unpredictability."

King Cambyses tried to keep his face from showing either his surprise or anger. He was inclined to be a pacifist king who avoided letting his country get involved in war. King Cambyses knew that peace did not lead to great reputations for monarchs, but he had no aspirations to be great. Also, he abhorred the easy way Zav was able to cause international trouble.

"I remember once when you pitted two minor kings against each other," Cambyses said.

The minister sat erect, fully alert. His anxiety over being shot at had not subsided and he continued to sweat. He wiped his dripping brow as King Cambyses continued, "You once spread deceptive rumors about Parthia's king. You said he was Sythian on his mother's side of the family. Not only that, you spread the rumor in the court in Aria."

"Ah Sire," said Zav with an excited tone, "we both know when royal gossip starts it travels fast through every palace, but no one ever knows where it begins."

He lurched forward abruptly shouting, "That wasn't me!"

A resounding crash filled the air. Zav felt his chair shudder. He looked back to see an axe imbedded in the seat of his chair a finger's breadth from his spine. A soldier standing behind him had shattered the backrest of his seat. Zav began to tremble.

King Cambyses waved the soldier off saying, "Be careful how you react near me, Zav. I'm king here."

Then the king continued, "Everyone in the Median Empire appreciates how degrading it is to be called a Sythian. Even I believe they are vulgar scum living indecent lives. Every nation considers the Sythians rude, filthy, squalid people, not much better than hyenas."

Zav tried to sit back in his chair and nearly fell on the floor. Cambyses smirked. Zav said, "Sire, I wasn't involved," but his voice sounded weak and unconvincing.

Cambyses continued, "Parthia and Aria went to war because of you. Their war grew over large tracts of plain and desert. Many people died because of you"

Zav tried to compose himself as he answered, "Rumors claimed that I intercepted battle reports, which is a lie. Then rumors said I let the secondary caravan routes be affected until commerce stopped. That was a lie too. Why would I do such a thing?"

Cambyses retorted, "Because you wanted the princes to suffer significant business losses. You wanted them specifically to be inconvenienced by the war. It makes you feel powerful, Zav. We know that."

Zav said, "Untrue! But, Sire, I did convince the two warring kings to come to Ecbatana to resolve their dispute face-to-face."

The king said, "You were successful in hiding your complicity from the Great King but not from the minor kings. We know what you did, so you could take full credit when Parthia and Aria settled their argument in drunken conviviality over draughts of homa beer in Ecbatana. You contrived the whole incident just to look important to King Astyages as his diplomatic surrogate, and it worked just as you planned. And now you want me to go to war for you. Why?"

3

Zav realized he had to be careful. Cambyses was showing no signs of capitulating. What would make him follow his plan? After all, Zav thought, he must once again become a hero, a pillar of the empire for the King of Kings by stopping a war between Pars and Gedrosia. Zav believed he could use the threat of attack by Cambyses to convince King Kauklia to pay the proper royal tributes, adding piles of new silver talents to the Median treasury. Then Zav could ask Astyages for his daughter, Princess Mandane, in marriage. Zav was sure he could use Pars to add to his prominence in the royal court by diplomatically solving another controversy among the Great King's nations. That should make him an acceptable suitor for Princess Mandane, and their marriage would give him the royal status he desired so much. Zav had always believed the princess was his true path to this ultimate triumph. Her father would pick the man to be her husband. Zav intended to be that man. His ego let him dream that when King Astyages died the son of the Great King's daughter would be the successor in the Empire. Therefore when his son was the Great King, Zav himself would come into real power. Through his child he would make all the minor kings to suffer. Cambyses was to suffer the most. All this suited Zav's ambition and for that reward he must convince Cambyses to start a war. But how?

"Why not send warriors from Media?" asked the king, "Put them at risk. Let them defend their own gods."

Zav perked up. That was how! He said, "Have you forgotten, Cambyses, that you are the troops of Media, if the Great King wishes it? And he does!

"Besides, you are the very strength that is needed in this situation. I'm telling you King Astyages will reward the man who helps him gain a firm hand on the resources there, as well as get control of the Gedrosian treasury, as is his due."

King Cambyses wanted no part in this. So he asked, "And what resources are you referring to in Gedrosia? There are none! We both know that country is a sour marshland being sucked up by a useless desert. Your efforts to squeeze anything from King Kauklia are hopeless."

He looked at Zav with a stern regal glare in his eyes and continued, "There is nothing of significant value in that land. Its people are poor. King Kauklia can't pay a royal tribute. Gedrosians live more meanly than the peasants of Pars live and that is base enough for anyone. Besides, is Gedrosia even in the realm of the Median Empire?"

Zav answered, "It is because the Great King thinks so. And you are wrong. There is wealth there."

"And how much of this 'wealth' is worth the life of even one of my soldiers?"

Zav tugged at his gold braided sleeve to unstick it from his arm. His nervous sweat was making his garment feel uncomfortable. At that moment a Nubian slave began to waft a feathery flabellum at the minister. Zav noted the pressure of the breeze on his back and was pleased that someone was attending to his comfort. He felt he deserved reverence, and this was the kind of respect that was his due. After all, he was an important minister with much authority and power.

King Cambyses waved the slave away. Zav had all he could stand and said, "Cambyses, how dare you treat me like this. Have you forgotten who I am?"

The king responded, "Have you forgotten who I am?"

With an unconscious reflex Cambyses placed his right hand over the hilt of the dagger at his waist as if preparing to protect himself. In an instant a whooshing sound passed through the court. Every guard moved his hand to a weapon and every bow wore an arrow. All eyes were instantly alert, uncertain of specific danger, but convinced that their king's gesture was meaningful. Both the king and his visitor noted the reaction of the royal guards in silence. Zav stared at the three arrows at his feet and was instantly frightened again. Cambyses smiled inwardly as he removed his hand from his dagger. He looked at his guards who made him breathe deep with pride. Their muscular bodies looked as if they had sprung from the earth like his beloved mountains. These were true warriors, men of dignity and honor. They were men he would never sacrifice for Zav.

King Cambyses waited again for the tension to pass. Zav had mentioned border attacks. The king thought of how border disputes between nations were common throughout the world. The edges of nations swelled and shrank like the chest of an angry lion. Clan chiefs challenged each other with armies or with groups of bandits who stole and slaughtered. Even in peacetime ownership moved back and forth over several farsangs on national frontiers. The king could not give a measure to a farsang but he knew it was the distance a well-sighted man could see to tell the difference between light and dark colored camels. Because of Zav's comments he said, "You make me think of the poor Gedrosian peasants who move like gnats sneaking over their borders nipping with their small insignificant robberies and petty mayhem, hoping to gain something of value. They are at most a trifling annoyance to Media."

Cambyses knew this entire conversation stank of deception. He wondered if Zav had forgotten that Carmenia and Utia were located between Pars and Gedrosia? Did they need to be secured for some reason? Or did Zav just want trouble?

Cambyses asked again, "What wealth is there in Gedrosia, Zav? Explain what you mean."

Zav leaned back barely remembering there was no back to his chair. Only space was behind him. He collected his composure and said, "It isn't just the wealth that is important for you, Cambyses, it is also the increase in dominion you will gain. When I advocate for you in Ecbatana the Great King will unite Gedrosia and Pars. I will more than double your country's wealth."

"Double my problems you mean. And what about Carmenia and Utia that lie between King Kauklia and me?"

"Ah Cambyses, I will encourage the Great King to give you those lands too. Think of what how large Pars will be then."

Zav was thinking that if the war really did take place and Cambyses inherited three more countries depleting the wealth of Pars would be easy when he raised tax burdens beyond the holdings of the additional treasuries.

The king had grown weary of this conversation; he got mad at Zav's insolence. He ordered, "Don't address me by my name alone! Call me 'king' or 'Sire,' Zav. I am king here. Never forget that. And if you forget I will see the axe does not miss the next time."

This new warning upset Zav again. His mind began to wander as he questioned why the day was going so completely against him.

King Cambyses saw the vacant look on the minister's face and attacked again with a new accusation. He said, "You have stolen value from Pars in the past through your inventive tax collections. I can't prove that you have stolen from me, and I can't prove you have stolen from King Astyages, but I know you have. I suspect all you are trying to accomplish now is another opportunity to rob the kings of the realm. Am I correct, Zav?"

Zav knew he had always been clever enough to keep Cambyses from uncovering the facts of his recurring dishonesties, which kept the minor king from revealing them to the Great King. Additionally, Zav's experience in King Astyages' court let him know that anything Cambyses might say in the high court was considered irrelevant because of his minor royal status. His province was in an obscure geographical location off the main caravan routes that moved west to east far to the north. Also, Cambyses was a quiet man who never prattled over insignificant complaints or suspicions like most royal princes. He never told tales.

"Sire, I am the tribute collector for King Astyages. I answer to him alone, and he is satisfied that I am honest," said Zav.

The minister looked around the room without falling from his chair and saw Pattmenidu the chief merchant of Pars sitting as upright as his corpulence allowed. He was sprawled at the back of the audience hall listening with earnest attention for business opportunities. Zav noted there were no royal relatives in the room, only soldiers and Pattmenidu all of whom looked stern. Each soldier wore a bronze sword and half the soldiers also wore a sheaf of arrows, with an enormous strung bow in hand. The hard stares of the soldiers gave away nothing, except their readiness to protect Cambyses. Zav wondered if the guards were secretly delighted to overhear the prospect of war. They had just reacted twice with reflex quickness, like the warrior-animals they were, to a nonexistent danger. He believed they must be anxious for battle. He saw that they were tough, virile men whose skin looked like a leather hide. It was inconceivable that talk of war was anything but a delight to them.

Zav could tell Pattmenidu wanted to hear more details of this campaign because war meant the merchant's businesses must be profitably involved. Zav knew the merchant well enough to appreciate that Pattmenidu was already calculating the heads of cattle needed for beef, the number of camels needed for portage, goats for milk, copper and tin for bronze arrowheads. Pattmenidu was well prepared to estimate the materials an army on the move had to have available if they were to have a chance of winning their battles. Zav could almost see the merchant estimate the time needed to travel to Gedrosia and all the supplies needed to get there. Zav himself understood how to estimate follow-up supplies for battle time. He also knew whom he could contract with for delivery of such items. Of course Zav also knew Pattmenidu had to deal with him and his Median intermediaries to a significant degree.

The merchant and the minister had talked late into the night the evening before about the amount of business Pars was obligated to conduct with Media if a war were to develop. When Pattmenidu ask what war Zav said that it was just speculation. He did not want the merchant mentioning war to King Cambyses ahead of time.

As usual, Zav wanted to deal in illegal secrecy for his own profit with goods belonging to King Astyages, and he could use Pars to achieve it. Zav participated in governmental theft in Media, and he considered that his own affair. Zav was aware that the Parsian merchant did not sanction stealing, but Pattmenidu was willing to deal with unscrupulous outsiders as long as he could keep them from cheating Pars. This included Greeks, Sythians, and oriental caravan dealers and just about anyone from Media. Zav smirked while surveying the audience chamber and wondered if Pattmenidu questioned his distorted suppositions about increasing the dominion for Pars.

As he looked about, Zav saw that the room was plain and lacked elegant tapestries on the wall. The furniture was simple and devoid of fancy decorations. This place was a crude, unsophisticated dullness, Zav thought. After two lifeless days, how many more days must be suffered here before Cambyses is tricked into war?

King Cambyses grew weary of bantering with this tiresome man so he suddenly stood and began to withdraw from the room. Since Zav had been late for meetings with Cambyses for two days the king decided that if the minister came late tomorrow he would get a special surprise. The king said in a quiet, decisive tone, "I will think of what you have suggested. See me tomorrow at mid-morning."

When the king left Zav got furious that the strutting kinglet dared walk out on him, an important minister of the King of Kings. Zav intended to teach this minor king what true power meant and just how minor he really was when he got back to Ecbatana.

Zav started to get up and tore his toga on a broken shard of wood on the shattered chair rest. Furious about the damage to his clothing, he pulled himself free then turned and with an abrupt wave he summoned Pattmenidu to follow him as he raced like a gazelle fleeing a lion down the corridors to his chambers. Pattmenidu shuffled his bulky, overweight body with a waddle that complimented the maximum speed he could muster, without running, as he tried to keep up with Zav.

Zav spun around and almost shouted, "What is the most important food product in Pars?"

Out of breath and a little flustered Pattmenidu answered gasping, "Well, grapes are the most profitable, but rice is the most important food. We eat it daily. There are more dishes with rice than any other staple."

"Alright then. For the next three months you will buy all the rice in Pars. Sell it to me. Only me, understand?"

"Why?" asked Pattmenidu in a worried tone, "I may lose important contacts in the rice market I have been developing for ages. You could ruin my ability to deal with numerous rice merchants in the future if you get all the rice. What will you do with it?"

Zav glared at him and blurted, "I'll sell it back to you, when I decide to, at a price I will fix. Both of us will make a fortune from it."

What Zav actually intended was to restrict the entire rice supply from the Pars market and make the whole nation go without. Complaints would inevitably be directed at Cambyses who would be powerless to fix the problem. Inconvenience and disruptions at every family table would pester Pars for as long as Zav chose. Zav was going to intercept caravans from the east to purchase their rice or send rice shipments west to Babylon and beyond without allowing the grain into Pars. Zav gloated over his power! Cambyses was going to experience the leveraging influence of the Minister of Taxes and Materials! Zav dismissed Pattmenidu with a smile.

Zav spent the night eating and drinking too much. He used Cambyses' court women as if they were wanton sluts of the street. Cambyses was unmarried, but the king had an informal, inner household of concubines and princesses to entertain himself and his male guests. Zav also demanded the presence of a small prince of the court. Using boys was not to his taste, but this was his quiet way of dishonoring the minor king who dared to walk out on him. Zav wasted much of the night fussing over plans to insult Cambyses in countless ways.

Zav suffered from lack of sleep in the morning due to the abundant female company and wine he consumed. Zav lounged on the mattress lying on a carpet on the floor. His head stopped its intense throbbing by mid-morning. He tossed off his fine woven, dull colored woolen blankets and dressed with slow deliberation in pseudo-royal gowns. He adjusted jewelry with care to ensure he looked more prosperous and important than Cambyses did. It was always good to let minor kings see what true elegance looked like. Zav ordered a meal and took his time eating, while he decided that mid-day was more suitable for his audience with the king. He dawdled until he decided he was late enough for his appointment with Cambyses. Cambyses would wait for him!

As Zav strolled with a casual saunter down a corridor he was jubilant over his tardiness. At the same time, he could not help noticing the severe plainness of everything about him. The hallway had no statuary, not painted walls and no tapestries. This place could hardly be called a palace yet Cambyses seemed satisfied with it.

Suddenly Zav heard a hubbub and he was almost swept aside by a royal retinue in travel dress. King Cambyses was in the middle of the group. Without looking directly at Zav the king said with firm authority, "I have been summoned by King Astyages. I am leaving for Ecbatana now. We will have to talk later."

Zav stopped breathing for a moment. He realized in that instant that had he kept their appointment on time, Cambyses probably would have delayed his departure for the sake of courtesy and honor, while they haggled over Zav's plan. In yesterday's meeting Cambyses could have mentioned the summons from Astyages out of innate politeness, but he didn't. Had Zav known he could have raced to Ecbatana to stall Cambyses from seeing the Great King. The minister could have made it appear that King Cambyses had not reacted with proper respect to the Great King's summons, and Cambyses would have been in trouble. Now it was impossible. Zav had been so clever he had outsmarted himself.

For a king to travel from Anshan in Pars to Ecbatana took at least two weeks of royal preparation by Zav's estimation. How could

Cambyses have his cavalcade ready without a sign of it on the streets in the past few days? What trick was this? Zav suspected yesterday's insulting departure by Cambyses from the audience room was practice, leading to this greater insult. Now Zav must take at least three days to get his own travel cortege organized to leave, and he might not be able to get to Ecbatana before Cambyses to disrupt the king's appointment to see Astyages. Zav hated being outwitted by these minor kings, especially Cambyses.

2.

"I see you wear your customary filth before me," growled King Astyages, "where is your lily-white gown, your cone-shaped hat and the bush you drag to show your authority? Don't you feel you need to look clean and divine for me?"

The Chief Magus answered, "Sire, I rushed at your summons. I was more interested in your needs than in my appearance. My condition shows how dedicated I am to your welfare, Sire."

"You should have cleaned yourself, priest!"

"Sire, it is only the peasants who require my neatness. It helps them believe. The people respond better to the payment demands my priests make for religious sacrifices when they see me clean in public. You do not need such prodding, Sire."

"You don't need payments for your services. And I don't need your grime. You and your whole tribe get enough from me to satisfy you needs," said the King.

The Magus said, "Ah Sire, but there are special conditions like humans sacrifices that require selective offerings for our services to the gods. The peasants must give the demanded food offerings to feel that they have gladdened the hearts of the gods."

"So what! I suspect that your filth predicts the nature of the advice I can expect from you today."

"Sire, I am always at your service. Your spiritual health is my primary interest, always. I have been told you are plagued by a bad dream. Like always I can help," said the Magus.

"You fool! I did not tell anyone it was bad. It is just a problem to understand. You already have a conclusion without having any information on my concern. How am I supposed to trust you? You and all of your priests are becoming less useful to me every day. I should kill the pack of you like swarming hyenas."

"Never suggest that you might kill a magus, Sire. It is a serious sacrilege. Please, let me try to help you today. Obviously you are troubled. It is my task in this world. The welfare of the empire may be at stake."

"See! Again you conclude erroneously. I should have you shoveled out with the rest of my palace garbage."

"Sire, I am your chief priest. You must respect my position, my vast responsibilities."

The Chief Magus was referring to the four services performed by his tribe of magi. Long ago he had established cost guidelines for duties rendered by magi based on one's social status in the community. He supported payment scales that could be free to a peasant yet expensive for a customer in authority. To read a message, to write a short note, or to keep a record might cost a peasant a single meal. The same service for a prince might cost a sheep or two.

Another service was medical help. Long ago the Chief Magus had obligated a priest to complete three successive operations yielding complete health restoration in order to be qualified as a medical magus. If there was one failure it was failure for life. No second chance was allowed. Passing this challenge was part skill and part luck. Surgical instruments used by the magi were made of crude materials with poor design features. Inferior bronze was used to make some operating instruments because the best metals were used for military equipment. Other surgical instruments were made from the large bones of animals, but these latter tools were hard to keep clean and dulled after very little use. Clean, warm water was always used to wash a wound, but the water was applied with camel hair brushes and rags soiled from previous surgeries.

The third magus service under control of the Chief Magus was the conduction of holy rituals. These were specific religious procedures, such as the ceremony establishing the majority, or adulthood, of male and female youths after they passed fifteen sun cycles. The ceremony of funerals was another ritual service the priests conducted. They also preformed holy sacrifices of animals and humans. The latter were rare. Families offered a special blessing request to a particular god or goddess.

The final service he controlled was psychological counseling and dream interpretation. The magi could help troubled people by casting spells. The magi claimed that evil spirits caused emotional and mental problems, which priests could drive away, healing the distressed person.

Private consultations at one's home provided opportunity to discuss personal or psychological problems. Special rooms in the temples were available at an increased cost if one needed that much seclusion. The King had all the seclusion he needed in his palace, and Astyages was desperate to have the Chief Magus divine an interpretation to his dream even though he was angry with the man.

"Listen you dirt-encrusted wretch, I will describe my dream to you. For three nights I dreamed of rain. It changed in strange progressive stages. At first I saw rain falling out of season. Then it fell more heavily and became torrential. Finally, heavy sheets of water swept down onto terrain that was already soaked, but the earth did not erode away as it should have under such a cloudburst."

"Sire, the…"

"Quiet you fool. I'm not finished. By some unexplained mystery, neither thunder nor lightning filled the dripping sky. There should have been explosive claps of thunder to rattle the walls of my palace as well as life endangering lightning bolts to brighten the sky, burn the earth and singe the trees. Water was the only hazard in my dream. I thought that was peculiar. I have lost sleep and can't eat my meals. What little I eat distresses me. Why? What does all this mean?"

"Sire, it means we will have plentiful crops due to the rain. There will be fertile soil and bountiful harvests." The Chief Magus wanted to cajole the Great King into believing his dream was a good sign. The Magus stopped to let this thought sink in. King Astyages was too upset for a rushed explanation. The Magus had a unique sensitivity to the image he portrayed. So far today the King had shown no respect for him or his prominent position. His entire magus tribe could be endangered if he made an injudicious comment. The Magus had to anticipate the King's thinking to set him at ease.

"A draught will be averted, but there will be no flood that leaves disaster behind. You have dreamed a marvelous thing, Sire."

"Hmm, maybe," grunted the King as he tried to believe the Magus.

Over the succeeding nights the dream changed. The King saw water on the land. It collected in rivulets that turned into streams. Alterations in his dream progressed into more troubling sights. Streams turned into rivers that rushed where no river had ever flowed before. All the rivers flooded to endanger adjacent lands. The sprawling water smothered vast areas, and his capital city slowly disappeared beneath the wash. Still neither thunder nor lightning was present, just rain.

The dream caused King Astyages to wake in the middle of the night in a heavy sweat as he shivered with fear. Extra woolen blankets were not enough to satisfy his need for warmth and comfort. The King changed his nighttime bed wear to heavier fabric but it did not warm him. Each night the flooding increased in turbulence covering more and more of the land. From the countryside and the surrounding mountains water inundated numerous prominent places in his kingdom. It was not just Media that flooded, but far away lands that paid royal tributes to King Astyages were also affected.

"What does my dream mean now, Magus?" bleated the Great King after describing the latest details of his visions. The Chief Magus again underplayed the negative implications of the dream.

"Sire, the extensive spreading of the water signifies your great popularity in your kingdom. You touch every part of the empire with beneficial kindness."

"What else?"

"Sire, that is it! You have dreamed of your own grandeur."

The Chief Magus knew that mysticism was a significant part of the Great King's life. Decisions important to the entire empire could arise from a magus' explanation of a dream. The Chief Magus knew from experience that descriptions given to the meaning of a dream usually caused the dreamer to alter his life to ensure the magus' interpretation actually resulted. After all, the Chief Magus knew that seasonal flooding in the kingdom of Astyages was a common phenomenon. It was usually predictable by season and location in the empire. Many people in Media experienced a flood at some time in life when rainfall poured out of the mountains onto the plains and plateaus. Sometimes when the peasants were injudicious and forgot to be cautious, the floods swept away people, livestock and homes. But after the waters receded a robust crop could be grown to feed survivors with lush renewal.

"Can there be a more sinister, evil meaning?" begged the King.

"Oh no, Sire. Your fame, your wisdom and your generosity spill out over all the land."

"Why do I not find comfort in your answer, Magus? Why do I think my dreams have exceeded your meager capacity to understand them? Why do I even bother to call on you? You are useless to me."

The Magus said, "Sire, your dream means you are affecting the lives of many people in a positive way and it is desirable and good. You can be pleased that you have dreamed of your own greatness."

King Astyages continued to be deeply troubled. He said, "Magus, keep this dream a secret from the people of the court. I do not want idle talk about it until I find comfort in its meaning."

Although King Astyages tried to be pleased with the Magus' explanation the dream continued to bother him. No night vision had pestered him so much before, nor had he ever seen such strange slow-changing development with such specific continuity. Also the theme of the flooding water was a peculiar constant the King of Kings could not resolve in his mind for some reason.

Then one night the King saw his daughter, Mandane, in the dream; the raging waters did not affect her. Mandane's image sat comfortably among the torrents, and she smiled at the fury around her. No matter where in the kingdom his dream took the King, Mandane had benign safety in the rampage.

Again the Great King's agitation made him summon the Chief Magus. He said, "Magus, I have had enough of this plaguing dream! Now Mandane appears in my dream. You and your magi associates are to get together and interpret this unsettling new addition.

"My daughter is now completely surrounded by the floods, but she is perfectly safe. Why is she there? What does this mean? Go and find out."

The Chief Magus and a few priests argued for days. Finally, they agreed that the presence of Mandane could only be an undesirable symbol that must be something fearful and dreadful.

The Chief Magus told King Astyages, "Sire, your daughter's smiling face and personal safety in the dreams, while surrounded by surging floods, could only mean she is a source of danger to you."

When the King heard this conclusion he flew into a rage. King Astyages roared, "My daughter must be in danger, not me, you imbecile! Mandane is under the control of evil, daeva spirits who direct covert wickedness against her, which she cannot recognize. That is why she smiles in the dream. She is my dear innocent child and can't be a danger to me. My worry is for her safety.

"You fools! You have misunderstood every nuance of my dream, Magus, and I should make your entire tribe of magi suffer for your stupidity."

The Chief Magus squealed, "We addressed every aspect of your visions with great care, Sire. Her smile and isolation from explicit danger can only mean she is the source of danger to the kingdom, or evil spirits protect her from danger that will attack the kingdom. It is possible Princess Mandane is involved with a person who will be able to conquer your kingdom. Maybe the princess will have a child who will replace you as king of Media. We must examine her to see if someone has spoken to her of a plot against you."

The Great King bellowed, "You will not question her. I will. Get out of my sight! Before the face of the gods I will kill every one of you."

How could the soft darling of his life be such a danger? Had the evil, daeva spirits captivated her? The King called Mandane to him. She wore a pale blue gown with fine silver-thread embroidery at the neckline. She smelled sweet to him. She looked wonderful. She spoke with a hushed, melodious voice softened by respect. King Astyages recalled that she had just passed her fifteenth cycle of the sun, which led to the holy ceremony elevating her to adulthood. The King wanted her to wed, as was the duty of a young woman.

King Astyages spoke with measured caution as he said, "Well, my dear, you are a full woman now. Your adult ceremony is complete and you are ready to be a wife."

Mandane blushed and lowered her head. "Oh, Father, I am not ready for marriage. I still feel too young."

Searching for secrets the King asked, "Tell me, Little One, have any people of the court talked with you about marrying any particular man?"

"No, father," Mandane answered, "is there a man I should have known about? Mother keeps saying I should be looking for a mate before you make the choice for me. She says finding my own love is better than arranged love."

A little embarrassed, Mandane continued to speak in a subdued tone and she said, "Mother says you were the one she wanted for a husband. She picked you herself. Is that true, father?"

King Astyages smiled, feeling warm at the memory, and answered, "Yes, it is true. Her father wanted her to marry a Greek from Athens. She demanded me, and she put up such a fuss that he gave in."

"But you!" the King continued, "You always seem to associate with our relatives in the court. Is there some uncle or cousin who wants to marry you? Tell me, do they try to influence you in any way? What does our family say of how we run our palace and empire? Do the princes talk about wanting more power? Everyone expresses discontent now and then, my dear."

Mandane felt the same pang of disappointment she had experienced before when she feared no man wanted her. She said, "I do not believe any prince favors me as a wife, father. Everyone is just content and happy. You are generous to them by making their lives comfortable. Your army gives them security. The princes and princesses believe you are just and kind. Except when you order punishment, of course, but everyone usually is grateful when they are not the object of your chastisement."

Her father said, "You spend a lot of time talking with Zav. Why?"

Mandane answered in an anxious tone, "Oh father, he is always finding ways to talk to me. I try to avoid to him without being discourteous, but I talk with him because he is such an important minister of yours. At least he says so.

"He has hinted in several recent conversations that my adulthood meant that he was willing to accept me as a wife now that I am a full grown woman. Can you believe it, father? I believe he thinks he should be my husband. He seems a little dishonest to me, and he is so ugly! Oops, pardon me, father, if I have offended you," she gasped. She feared her comment might upset her father.

And so the conversation went. There was no hint of discontent in her manner or voice. The King convinced himself that she had no secret plans to damage his authority. She was not part of a plot to overthrow him. As for Zav, he was an ambitious but controllable fool. Astyages knew Zav was too cowardly to engage in a serious plot against him or the empire. The Great King had shown heartlessness before in his court, but never toward his precious daughter. However, as much as the King cherished Mandane, if she proved to be a danger to him or his empire, he was capable of forsaking her without remorse.

Still, the dream had to be important. King Astyages thought of going to Greece to see the Oracle of Delphi. After evaluating rumors of the powers at Delphi against the powers of his own magi, he decided that the journey might be worthwhile. The overland trip would be uncomfortably long because of the terrain, but for King Astyages the major problem of such a trip was the obligatory voyage by boat getting to Greece from Lydia. The sea scared him.

Long ago when he courted his queen, Aryenis, her brother, King Croesus, took him to view the sea from the shore of Lydia. Water had spread before Astyages as far as he could see! What a fantastic spectacle it was. King Astyages was astonished that the sight made him feel as if the sea went to the edge of the world. Boats rode on the water before him. Some were quite large, moving west on their way from Lydia to Athens. Croesus chuckled at the look on the face of Astyages and goaded, "Go for a swim, brother!"

Astyages walked over the rough rocks and went into the water up to his armpits. He thrashed and kicked trying to stay above the water like a boat. As long as King Astyages flailed with energetic vigor, he was able to ride high and keep his head above water, but when he stopped splashing the visiting King sank and might have drowned had a soldier not saved him. That event haunted King Astyages so much that he had trouble taking his bath that night, even with his slaves close at hand.

At the time King Astyages asked his Chief Magus, "Why don't boats sink when they stop?"

"I do not know, Sire. Maybe the gods hold them up from beneath the water."

The Magus not only didn't know, he was embarrassed for not having a suitable answer.

"You fool! I was just under that water; no gods were there. What a dumb answer. Get out of my sight."

For King Astyages to decide to go to Delphi was a very heroic decision. The sea loomed as a real physical adversary King Astyages was reluctant to contest. The Chief Magus was prompt in talking his King out of this venture. The Magus said, "Sire, Media could not do without its Great King for such a long interval. At least a full sun cycle is required to complete that journey."

"I know how long it takes. I intend to go anyway. Being away from you will be a pleasure."

The Magus knew exposure to the Oracle would undermine his own value. In secret the Chief Magus feared the Oracle just might have insights or magic that were more potent than his own. The Magus thought of scary stories that passed among the magi brotherhood about the Oracle. The Greek sage had made accurate predictions of wars, victories, defeats, births, royal assassinations, and much, much more! The Magus could not risk letting Astyages be exposed to the mystique of that sagacious woman.

The Chief Magus pleaded, "Sire, we need you here. I will have my priests give your dream a new evaluation with a more suitable interpretation."

So Astyages relented and isolated himself in a private chamber for several days. Queen Aryenis was not even admitted into his presence. King Astyages had to think. The magi were not developing comforting advice for his dilemma. Astyages knew he had to take action in order to quiet his anxiety. He trembled with consternation, but eventually, King Astyages considered calling on the magi again. Although he did not need more council on dream explanation, he thought they might settle his mind over his general mental uneasiness. They had done that too before, but not recently. He might give them another chance.

In the past the magi had exhibited skills in revealing the true nature of several problems that arose for Astyages, without either becoming involved in the matter itself, or participating in the resolution of the problem. Their counsel just made the source of the King's difficulty evident by focusing his thoughts. Even when King Astyages knew his magi had strong opinions on certain political subjects, he noted they never tried to force their own conclusions on him. His priests just helped him think so he could develop his own decisions. They were smart enough to understand how to keep King Astyages dependent on them for specific mystical services.

He concluded that the magi were unnecessary in this instance and did not call them again. Astyages contented himself with his own perfect solution. The answer was clear! He grew calm! He called the pallid keeper of records into his presence and ordered, "Search your records, magus, and let me know the name of every unmarried king. Then tell me in two days, which of them live in remote locations. Only include those most loyal to me."

"Yes, Sire," the magus answered with a weak voice.

In two days the task was done. The frail magus recited all King Astyages had asked for, ".. and finally, Sire, there is King Cambyses of Pars. His kingdom is small and poor. He is a king very dependent on you and Media."

Astyages was pleased and said, "Thank you, magus," waving him away. The King began to reflect on this minor king, recalling that Cambyses was young, presentable, polite. He was a ruler who respected higher authority. The Great King could visualize Pars, a small, weak country just south of Ecbatana. It had stalwart warriors but a small army and mediocre commerce, all of which was overseen by its king, who desired peace more than power. King Astyages thought it was impossible for Pars to sweep over the Median Empire like the flood in his dream. Its mountainous terrain inhibited swift travel, preventing its army from rushing into Media like an unexpected torrent. Therefore, Astyages chose to marry his daughter to Cambyses. If Mandane was the focal point of the mystical flood, the King was in the position to control it ahead of time by putting his princess in a poor place, giving her a weak husband who could do no harm. It also ensured the preservation of her love for him by not forcing him to be cruel to her in any way.

Normally, in circumstances like this when he wanted a minor king summoned King Astyages ordered Zav to tell whomever it was. In this instance the Great King would have revealed the intended marriage to Zav, but King Astyages thought Zav was off someplace collecting taxes, threatening minor kings or just causing trouble on his own behalf. The King liked to have Zav to do much of his royal diplomacy. He let Zav believe he could use his own creativeness. The King enjoyed manipulating Zav by making his minister feel powerful, devious or mean.

The King summoned a royal messenger and said, "Go to Pars. Tell King Cambyses I desire his presence in Ecbatana immediately!"

No reason for this order had to be given. When the King of Kings demanded one's presence, the summons was all the explanation one received. 'Immediately' in this empire meant one had to start traveling right away because traversing craggy mountains, sloppy marshlands and burning deserts from remote starting places could take several moon cycles.

In a small audience room where King Astyages could have a private conversation he told Mandane of his decision. He said, "My dear, I have chosen a husband for you."

This startled Mandane and her mouth opened in shock, unable to speak. The King continued, "You will marry King Cambyses of Pars. Your mother and I have discussed him, and we consider him suitable for you."

At first she got upset at what he was saying. Finally she controlled her anxiety and said, "Yes, father." She knew it was useless to argue with him so she capitulated then continued, "will we wed in two or three sun cycles, father?"

"No," answered Astyages, "you will wed in three moon cycles, my dear."

Again she was speechless. After her recent talk with him about marriage, which ended so pleasantly, this announcement was almost overwhelming to Mandane because it determined the rest of her life. She was not ready for marriage, at least not yet. She wanted time to think, time to get used to the idea, time to create romantic images in her mind of her ideal husband, but her father had rushed beyond all of that.

Later, alone in the garden while calming herself, she tried to picture the face of Cambyses. At first she could not remember if he was old, ugly, grouchy or mean. Slowly, his smiling face and reserved politeness came to her. The simplicity of his royal garments was a clear memory that contrasted in her mind with the richness of Ecbatana. If he proved to be as gentle as her memory recalled then maybe being his wife could be pleasant for her. Mandane hoped she was correct. She could add stylish art of her own choosing to Pars, but she was uncertain if the king would allow his wife such liberties. She began to remember that he always came to court with a soft dignity. He never seemed nervous or excited. He acted polite to everyone, even Zav, who seemed to concentrate on upsetting most of the minor royalty. She recalled that she had never seen Cambyses pushed into overt fury or anger by Zav or by petty princes of the court. Maybe she was to marry a man of contentment. Such a marriage felt promising to her.

King Astyages chose not to mention his dream to his daughter, she was so much of a factor in it that he dared not tell her. Instead he summoned the Chief Magus again and said, "Mandane is going to marry King Cambyses of Pars. You are to forget about my dreams that she appeared in, understand? Instruct your priests on this as well. Never mention it to anyone. That is an order!"

The Chief Magus said, "Sire, a record of my audience with you when we discussed your visions has already been set in clay. No one will ever see it but the magus record keepers. Your secret is safe."

The Chief Magus went to the hall of records to inspect the tablets of concern. While there he instructed the record keeper of the secrecy the record they had under their care required, as the King had commanded. The Chief Magus noted the simplicity of the deep-cut strokes of the cuneiform script, which belied the actual difficulty of understanding the nature of the syllabic sounds represented in the cuts on the clay surface. Varying combinations of characters represented sounds of text in Greek, Pars, Aramaic and other languages.

The Chief Magus knew there were no opportunities for royal citizens or the peasants to read the King's secret here, besides, he recalled that neither peasants nor royalty were taught to read. If it was necessary to write a message or deliver one over great distances his magi at either end of the message exchange could be depended upon to write and read such documents. The unique exception to this, which he permitted, involved intelligent merchants. The priest knew men such as Pattmenidu of Pars got the instruction needed to read and write from magi because secrecy in their commerce depended on being able to prepare and read private messages. The merchants were capable of increasing the speed of information transfer with their caravans. Their readable vocabulary was limited to the jargon of their businesses. In general his magi were an indolent lot who could not be induced to hurry for the advantage of someone else, so the Chief Magus only encouraged a select few merchants to be instructed in reading and writing, provided they vowed never to teach anyone else.

In a public audience the Great King announced, "My daughter, Mandane, is to marry King Cambyses of Pars. We will have a magnificent feast for Mandane and because she is my only daughter our celebration will be the most splendid of its kind in the history of Media. Every minor king in the land has to attend the ceremony or lose his head."

This announcement spread rapidly throughout the empire. All the people of Media were surprised but happy. Every minor king had to be pleased about the two to be married, because the Great King demanded it! A wife could accompany each minor king at the wedding as well as concubines, relatives who were minor magistrates, governors or other types of administrative officials. The size of the guest crowd was going to be huge. The Great King complimented himself for having such a wonderful idea. Such a grand pageant!

To his wife the King said, "Aryenis, we must invite your brother Croesus to our daughter's wedding. It will be good for you to see him again."

"That would be pleasant, but will he be able to get here in time?" Queen Aryenis asked.

"I believe he will when he realizes it involves Mandane. He has always had great affection for our daughter," said the King.

Aryenis said, "It has been many spring times since I have seen Croesus. We were always close." So close she recalled that Croesus endured the expense of war once, supporting Astyages in battle, just to ensure she was protected. She always marveled that Croesus was so wealthy he could give a gift of gold the size of an adult camel if he wanted to without worrying about the expense. The image of such a bizarre statue made her smile. It pleased her that the entire world respected her brother's wealth.

Astyages wanted his wife to plan all aspects of the wedding so she could feel important enough to strut self-satisfied before his concubines and the wives of his minor kings. His wife did not get many opportunities to demonstrate how skilled she was at managing important projects. When Astyages went to war as a young king, Aryenis ran major segments of his kingdom with remarkable efficiency. Many important royal, male relatives had resented that King Astyages allowed his queen such a privilege, but the King justified it by accusing these men of shirking their duty to the military. Some he called cowards for not going with him into war. His insults stopped their complaining.

King Astyages trusted Aryenis more than he trusted his uncles or cousins. In the chaos of supplying an army that moved constantly away from its home base, chances to rob one's King arose frequently; many princes could not avoid the temptation. Some princes were brave enough to steal straight from the palace treasury, if given the chance. Queen Aryenis had used sound judgement to good advantage by thwarting the deceitful easily, pleasing King Astyages with her acumen.

Now all Queen Aryenis had was trivial silliness to fret over. She still managed some of the business details of the living quarters in the palace. At the outset she was so successful in finding skilled under-managers to run kitchens, laundries and to purchase commodities for the inner household that her *andarun* ran itself with very little involvement from her. The Queen then placed royal family members over these under-managers to act as supervisors of various palace staffs. These assignments kept powerful princesses busy, restraining them from causing trouble in the household, the palace and the nation. At first the responsibility of the *andarun* was exciting for the Queen, but now that it was organized so well she had little to occupy her time.

The King thought this wedding was just what she needed to perk up her aimless life; he was correct. She leaped into the activities of organizing the wedding with great enthusiasm; she was far happier than she had been in many sun cycles. She laughed easily at nonsense, and she patted small children on the head that smiled at her. She spoke in gay, high-pitched tones as she organized the royal family as helpers in planning the wedding feast. Her excitement spread as princesses nearly tripped over each other trying to participate. The entire palace buzzed like a beehive hit with a stick. Everything began to happen at once. The women of the court were ecstatic as they rushed to buy fabric, flowers and jewelry, find seamstresses, hire extra cooks and sing as loud as possible. Hundreds of musicians swarmed to the palace gates wanting to become part of the festivities. Most of the musicians were too filthy to be allowed inside the opulent palace.

The queen pitched Mandane into the middle of the activity for no reason other than to boost her interest in a marriage with a man she had not chosen.

3.

Cambyses and his entourage arrived in Ecbatana where he quickly chose a clean, quiet part of the capital. He never stayed in the palace. He knew that once one got settled in the palace it was impossible to leave without creating suspicion and being followed by covert surveillance. Also, too many gates had too many curious guards that sold information to inquiring noblemen. Cambyses preferred the freedom of the city where it was also easier to set up a private meeting without running the risk of being overheard by busybody royalty looking for some small advantage to improve their personal status with the Great King.

King Cambyses first ensured his animals, servants and slaves were comfortable and fed. Then he identified his visiting schedule to the palace for his servants so they could be ready to serve him when he needed them. Past experience in this city had trained Cambyses to expect days of waiting before being recognized by King Astyages. One stood in the royal audience and waited and waited...until the Great King said to come forward and be recognized. Cambyses waited for three days. The Great King was aware of the presence of the minor king yet he forced his visitor to wait and worry over the cause of the royal summons.

Each day Cambyses entered the gates of the seven concentric, mud-brick walls the King of Kings had around his palace protecting him. King Astyages seldom left the central area where his magnificent palace stood. Early in his reign Astyages decided that the best way to control undisciplined clans and tribes wandering in deserts, marshes, mountains or valleys was to create a mystical authority. The King of Kings liked his image of a magic energy that had supreme power. The King never let peasants see him or know him as an ordinary man. He wanted them to invent rumors of his mystical attributes and embellish his image as a living god, and it had worked. Peasants were so astounded by fables of his strength that they were too cowardly to even speak of insurrection.

Minor kings knew King Astyages could be an unforgiving tyrant so they obeyed him without challenging him. Minor kings fought amongst themselves, but they never considered open rebellion against the Great King. They were too impressed with the military might the King exhibited to them in Ecbatana.

On those occasions when Media went to war the King of Kings came out of his palace dressed in silk garments covered by gold and silver armor. His horse was covered with fine linen blankets and exotic feathers. The King's saddle was made of the finest leather decorated in gold, silver and gem stones. He only showed himself at battles that Media was guaranteed to win. This constant presence at every victory enhanced his image. Now the wedding of his daughter to Cambyses was another victory, and since it was his idea alone it filled him with pride.

Each day King Cambyses entered the palace he noted that there was music everywhere outside and inside the palace. On the third day he heard reed pipes being played with lyres and cymbals. There were drums of varying timbres being vigorously thrummed throughout the courtyards, corridors and meeting halls. Small groups of men and women sang enchanting tunes at every turn, accompanied by harps and flutes. The gaiety was infectious.

Music here sounded a little different to Cambyses than at home. He liked Parsian music played on the nine-string lyre that allowed songs to be played with varying speeds or loudness. He had once noted that the event dictated how a musician determined tempo and dynamics so it fit the occasion. For him music did not set the tone of an activity; it enhanced the atmosphere. Since Cambyses was not musical, he could not assess the technical difference in the sounds he was hearing. All he knew at that instant was that everyone appeared to be erupting in melodious gaiety.

Cambyses passed from gate to gate and looked about with surprised admiration at the spontaneous frivolity. It was more natural for the atmosphere to be solemn around the palace as people stood about with serious royal demeanor. But, today even princes and princesses were laughing and cavorting in strange, energetic dances and festivity.

The minor king noticed decorations of floral bouquets everywhere. Colorful ribbons streamed from military banners adding feminizing pigments to martial somberness. Even wall hung swords and javelins were flowing with drapes of flowery lace and fresh boughs of greenery. He thought that was very unusual, because the Great King took pride in the maleness of his armament displays.

Cambyses looked at the palace pillars and walls, which were as smooth as the bottom of a newborn baby. The king knew Media had stonemasons who cut rock with perfect smoothness on every surface. This nation did not revere earth and rocks with the same fervor that his people in Pars did. His stonemasons never smooth-cut exposed surfaces like this, because it was not essential to the building process, and it offended the gods. His stone cutters would be appalled to see this. He had to admit the smooth cut surfaces did not look sacrilegious; they were very attractive.

Cambyses was finally admitted into the great presence with unusual pomp, music and happiness. It tended to confuse him because people were looking at him and smiling with silly grins. He smiled back and gave a curious nod as he wondered about the peculiar attention he was receiving. Then he ignored it and simply waited at the rear of the royal reception hall for King Astyages to address him with a direct command. It never occurred to him to think all this jovial activity had anything to do with him. He was the king of a small dominion that did not deserve any of this.

"Come forward, Cambyses, and sit here before me. It was wise of you to come so quickly," the Great King admonished.

The minor king frowned at this comment since he had been waiting so long to be summoned. He advanced with slow steps, as was expected in the royal presence. Cambyses knew palace guards viewed quick movements toward the Great King as threatening, no matter how innocent, and one could be wounded or even killed by accelerating one's pace in the audience chamber. The minor king passed Zav but did not look at him. Cambyses kept his eyes on King Astyages until he knelt and prostrated himself waiting to be told to rise by the Great King. Humility before this King was obligatory, even for the minor kings of Media. While kneeling prostrate Cambyses recalled how the Great King could be a great confusion at times. This was one of those times. The fancy reception ceremony was still unexplained and this curt admonition was the kind of inconsistency King Astyages reveled in. It kept his subjects off guard and submissive with uncertainty. When bid, Cambyses stood and sat on the ebony chair placed below the seven steps leading to the sovereign's throne.

Cambyses tried to be diplomatic and said, "Sire, I was readying myself to answer your summons when Zav appeared with a specific proposal. I had to leave him behind, without completing the business you sent with him. I apologize but I chose to honor your call with speed instead."

"Ah yes, Zav and his selective efficiency. He has returned here, worried and anxious over your presence. He also sputtered something about almost being axed to death. It was difficult to understand him through his agitated stammering. Your abrupt departure from Anshan surprised him. Did you leave with such sudden speed because he was annoying?" asked the Great King with intended meanness.

Cambyses answered, "Sire, he carries your word and I listen and obey all his sensible proclamations."

King Astyages smiled and said, "Cambyses, that was a very clever answer. Yes, Zav is useful to me in many ways and sometimes he is 'sensible'. But you are to become even more useful to me, and soon."

Cambyses nodded with submissive uncertainty. One had to be careful of this unpredictable despot. Astyages looked around his Ecbatana court. The King spotted the cloud that shrouded Zav's face, and it pleased him to upset Zav.

King Astyages continued to cast his eyes over the court and the walls of the audience room. He liked its hard stone walls. He liked the contrast of the surrounding mud-brick walls and the bright marble façade of his palace. King Astyages was also pleased with his display of wealth. There was gold everywhere and his minions were dressed in silks and linen colored with dyes from the east. The King purchased the silk as a precious commodity available only from the oriental dynasties of the Chin people far to the east because no one else had the secret of making it. The Great King was satisfied that his court sparkled with riches that he knew Cambyses could only dream about. Even though Cambyses was dressed to look regal, there were individuals in this court more ornately attired, including the King's minion Zav. Prince and princess, two-by-two, crowded in like a rainbow of loveliness to be present at this monumental occasion. This pleased Astyages too. The King of Kings should be seen to possess immense riches, and his wealth contented him, as did the noise of the music, which was so uplifting and loud.

King Astyages announced, "I want you to do a very special and personal thing for me, Cambyses."

In the pause that followed this statement, Cambyses wondered if he was about to be ordered to take up the silly war that Zav had suggested. Had Zav's return to the capital been in time for him to report to the King that Cambyses was unwilling to follow royal orders?

Looking towards his wife, Aryenis, Astyages grinned with an expansive glow. She in turn smiled covertly and blushed a little. For a moment her complexion mirrored the red in her gown with its gold brocade and lustrous jewels. King Cambyses felt more like he was trapped in a happy royal secret rather than drawn in. He nodded in respect to Queen Aryenis, a woman he admired. Her cheeks reddened again, this time in full flush.

Zav was standing nearby hoping to see the King chastise Cambyses for some real or imagined affront. All the gaiety and music in the palace of Ecbatana had confused Zav when he returned from Anshan, but his anxiety over the summons of Cambyses by the Great King caused Zav to ignore what it might mean. In the audience chamber Zav had positioned himself so he could watch Cambyses react to the rage of the King, which he hoped was coming. It was one of Zav's sweet delights.

King Astyages had talked to Zav before allowing Cambyses into his presence, but he had not informed Zav of why Cambyses had been summoned and other members of the royal family never shared casual confidences with the minister. Zav hoped to see a firm dressing down or a chastisement to the minor king that his royal tariffs were about to be increased. One thing that was strange to Zav was the obvious glee exhibited by Queen Aryenis. The Queen's normal demeanor was very stern and reserved when she knew the Great King was going to explode.

With all the authority the Great King commanded, Astyages announced, "Cambyses, you are to marry my daughter, Mandane! The wedding will be in one moon cycle. The women of my family have been working on the arrangements for ages and their plans are now developing quite fast, due to my wife's special talents," and he smiled at Queen Aryenis. She in turn blushed again.

Then the Great King continued in exuberance, "An expeditious union between you and Mandane will be a great pleasure to me. With this honor I bestow upon you, you will protect and revere my Mandane with all the respect you owe the family of the King of Kings."

When this came out of the mouth of the Great King, Zav almost shouted, "No!! She is mine." He clenched his teeth so tight they ached. His face turned beet red and his breathing became shallow and labored as he realized his magnificent future was not to be as he had planned. No one noticed of course, because all eyes were fixed on Cambyses.

Confused, Cambyses chose his words with great care. "Sire, the privilege is too great for me. There are others here in your royal court more fitting than I am to be Mandane's husband. Are you certain you wish this for me... for her?"

Astyages gave him a stern glare for a moment. No one questioned the Great King, even on such personal issues. "King Cambyses, you are our choice," said Queen Aryenis in a soft voice and she continued, "I have already planned most of the festivities and the banquet. And I will prepare my daughter for you too. You will be pleased. Any minor king would be."

With that Cambyses realized no discussion was allowed. Cambyses took a deep breath to control himself and to keep his voice from quaking as he said in a firm tone, "I do not deserve such a trophy. You honor me above my station, Sire. I thank you for this privilege. Your daughter will be the most beautiful and respected woman in my court. There is no object in my treasury that my people and I will defend with more protective care. She will have our love. I will give you grandsons who will honor you."

It was customary to present a gift at each meeting or summons with the Great King. Cambyses offered the queen a golden crocus with its six petals, plus a golden container of saffron harvested from the crocus. He said, "You have given me your most marvelous possession. I give you the Flower of Pars."

The queen received it with a deep sigh said, "How enchanting. Thank you, Cambyses."

Mandane was not allowed in the court for the marriage announcement. Her mother did not want her precious princess embarrassed before the full court if Cambyses had been fool enough to refuse the daughter of the Great King. Had the minor king done so, he would have died on the spot wearing a hundred arrows. Mandane, therefore, did not hear the pretty speech of acceptance from his own lips.

Cambyses pictured Mandane in his mind and recalled a sweet, attractive beauty, a youth more pleasing than most women. He felt a sense of warmth as he recalled talking with her on previous occasions. She was intelligent and interesting, yet she respected the authority of the minor kings. He felt the two of them had always been agreeable acquaintances, if not friends. Maybe this could change to love since they had never developed any specific relationship in their prior meetings. Having been independent for so long in his own kingdom, picking his own female companions and never getting attached to them with anything more than casual, romantic emotions, he thought of himself as an unattached ruler. Until this audience he had thought of Pars as separate from Media, but now he had to admit his country was the unquestioned property of King Astyages. As king of Pars Cambyses had allowed his country to meld many of its laws and its economy with Media, mostly under the pressure of Zav. It was not a topic he thought of often or was proud of, nor was it something he thought he should regret at the moment.

Cambyses had requested to see his prospective bride before the royal audience ended. It was arranged for them to meet later that day, and Queen Aryenis told her husband the betrothed couple must be allowed to visit together without escorts. The Queen felt her daughter and the minor king had to be trusted to respect each other.

Later that day after dusk Cambyses and Mandane walked in one particularly pretty palace garden lit by olive oil sconces. Flowers were in full, fragrant bloom, and the splendor of warm evening breezes hovered about them. Not touching, but close, they strolled in slow, almost romantic accord.

Mandane gazed at him and was pleased at what she saw. He was tall and handsome. His dark hair was combed and neat, complimenting his full beard. He smelled clean and his eyes were clear and alert. His tunic was simple but elegant even with its pale dun pigment. There was no outward attitude of deception about him. He was not acting as if he had just gained a long desired goal. Instead the king was modest about his circumstance and seemed deferential to her. Mandane did not feel Cambyses gave her attention solely because of her exclusive importance as daughter of the Great King. Instead, when he spoke Cambyses made Mandane feel like a person he respected. He was so different from Zav, who spoke as if he already owned her as a wife. Mandane wondered what had made her father settle on Cambyses. To her the choice felt correct. Mandane found comfort in this king's company. She wanted to put her hand on his cheek to ensure herself everything was going to work out just fine, but in her innocence she was too embarrassed to touch him.

Cambyses felt he needed to comfort them both and said, "I can do nothing to change your father's decision. Mandane, I am sorry if you had desired a different life for yourself. Anshan is small and unsophisticated. We have far less art than you are used to, and our comforts only meet the bare essential of royal living when compared to Ecbatana and this elegant palace.

"We are far poorer than anything you have ever lived with. I want you to understand that I will provide you with anything that will make you happy. Mandane, has your father told you why he picked me? Maybe you should convince your father he has made the wrong choice." He was getting confused, and he stopped talking.

She giggled and said, "Cambyses, you have just brought up a number of issues all at once and all I know is what you know. Father intends us to marry. Mother is pleased because father is pleased. I am a little scared, but not of you. The idea of marriage itself concerns me more than thoughts of being your wife. Gradually, the more we talk, the more I come to believe it is an agreeable match, maybe even a nice idea."

She gazed up into the sky and countless stars sparkled just for her. Would the gods be kind to her and give her sons and a happy home? A woman with that much was perfectly satisfied. A happy marriage and children completed life for any woman, even the queen of a minor king. Then she prayed in silence, "Dear gods of the sky and the night, give me a sign confirming our future happiness, please."

She continued to look at the night ceiling of flickering lights when a falling star streaked across the sky. Was that her sign? She sighed and asked, "Does a falling star bode good or bad, do you think, Cambyses? I think it must be good because the star is so pretty in its way to disappearing."

Cambyses answered, "I have never been sure. Sometimes I think of a falling star as a sorry moment when a light of the gods falls out of its place and dies. For the person who sees it there might be sorrow."

He turned toward her and tripped on a stone, stumbling. She laughed out loud and they both stared into each other's eyes and knew life was going to be fine. He leaned over and picked a small, red rose bud, the color of her dress, and placed it in the lace near her breast. The touch of his fingers on such an intimate place sent a delicious chill through her. From that moment onward the evening became an enchantment for her. Love began to bud in her heart, like the rose.

//

After the King's audience Zav erupted from the court in vengeful anger. He rushed through corridors to his tax record room. He brought with him a large draught of homa, beer fermented from specific exotic weeds and emmer. He raised it to measure the quantity left in his cup with a quick glance. He wanted to be intoxicated so he drank several cups of the foamy liquid. Cambyses was on his mind, and Zav stared into his cup, recalling that in Pars homa was used as a curative and in ceremonies for the dead. He smirked, thinking that death was the correct symbol for today as he continued to drink until he was good and drunk. In his unsteady, inebriated state he was uncertain if death referred to his own future or that of Cambyses. He quaffed another drink in several swift gulps and screamed for more. Servants and slaves rushed in to whisper that more homa was coming. They were anxious to stop his shouting because it never fared well for them when he was in such an excited temperament.

Zav reached for a whip and swung it at the nearest slave. He began to beat the poor wretch without mercy. Zav took several swings that caused instant bleeding when a eunuch of the palace came in and took the soggy whip from him. Zav spun to confront the eunuch who was twice Zav's size. A servant arrived with several cups of homa and Zav muttered a series of drunken obscenities at the man as the minister reached for another drink.

A young soldier, named Harpagus, came rushing in to investigate the noise. He waved the eunuch out of the room and told the servants to get the injured slave to a magus surgeon without delay. He began to control the room with the skill and authority of an army officer. Zav looked at him with contempt and said, "Well, master soldier, what do you think of the big announcement today?"

Harpagus wanted to ignore him and leave but chose instead to remain still. Zav said with menace in his tone, "I'll tell you what I think. Cambyses has set the stage for his own destruction. See those clay tablets? The record for taxes from Pars is going to change dramatically. Everyone in Pars will rue this day! Revenge will be mine."

He almost mentioned Mandane too, but Zav was fortunate to remember he was talking to a soldier of the Great King and to mention the King's daughter in a fit of anger and hatred was likely to be a painful error.

Harpagus frowned and said in a growling voice, "You should be more careful in the future to ensure a beaten slave deserves such treatment. The princes allow their slaves to be marked but only when it is an absolute necessity. Body damage reduces the value of a slave in the market.

"Remember, Sir, that these slaves and servants belong to the royal house and they are only loaned to you to complete your official work," and with that Harpagus left the room.

Zav fumed again, realizing that a very new adult had just taken him to task, and there was no punishment the minister could extend to a soldier, even one who was not an officer.

"That fool will never get anywhere in life if he keeps interfering in the affairs of important ministers," Zav said as he flung his cup against a wall and grabbed another and drank with a deep gulp. He sat down and tried to plot a reprisal that was equal to his loss today, but his drunkenness forced him to sleep instead.

4.

The next few days passed by like the speed of a racing chariot for Cambyses. He asked Prince Zatame, a distant cousin to King Astyages, for help with having marriage garments made. Prince Zatame who was about his age was a friend, and Cambyses knew Zatame had a deep familial affection for Mandane. Cambyses was pleased that the prince had never expressed a desire to marry his cousin Mandane because that might have strained their relationship now that Cambyses was to be her groom. The king accepted marriage between cousins, nephews and aunts, or uncles and nieces in a royal family as common and desirable. It held the royal household together and kept sovereign power in the family structure where it belonged.

Zatame found the best tailor, the best silk and the best linen in the city for Cambyses. The minor king was grateful for the help and friendship the prince shared with him. The special excitement of the wedding preparations was bringing the relationship between the king and prince closer.

Cambyses spent his daytimes with Mandane. He spoke to her about himself and his countrymen. He wanted her to understand how different Pars was from Media. Gods, diets, customs and clothing styles differed. Cambyses wanted to make her understand the magnitude of the change she was about to experience.

Mandane was eager to hear everything Cambyses had to say. She asked intelligent questions convincing him she truly intended to accept her new station with all its authority and responsibility. She was not coy or child-like. She looked straight into his eyes as if to challenge him to be accurate and forthright even though she knew his Parsian upbringing made honesty his most noble trait.

These conversations helped solidify their feelings towards each other. Cambyses described his gods, and Mandane tried hard to follow what he said. Cambyses was pleased with the way his future bride questioned his explanations.

King Cambyses said, "The earth is respected in a religious way by Parsians. The very material of the earth, its dirt, rocks, plants and trees are worthy of worship and reverence. Gods oversee the mystical provision of these materials for man's use and in this sense the full embodiment of man himself is reflected in the earth. The substances that make man come from these sources. Therefore, we are obligated to acknowledge this endowing contribution. People of Pars seek within themselves to honor the gods of earth. And I mean everything, not just the soil, stones and rocks, but all vegetation and animals."

Mandane gazed in deep pensive thought and did not speak for a couple of moments. Finally she raised her eyes and caught his uncertain stare. She said with a speculative air, "It's hard for me to comprehend how a whole nation of people can understand the value of the earth this way. In Media we never think about man's relations with all these materials in such detail. At least I haven't heard of it, and I haven't been taught to think that way."

She hesitated a moment and carefully added, "I understand your gods, Cambyses, as you explain them, and I can accept them without question, but please remind me of this again when we are living in Anshan. I want to get this concept about the earth clear in my mind, and maybe I can begin to believe as deeply as you do. I want this as much for you and me as I do for your people, whom we will share together."

Mandane did not know how her comment touched his heart. Cambyses was delighted with her sentiment. The king appreciated that she desired to understand and nurture trust in the holy beliefs of Pars for the sake of the nation. He knew Mandane would be a true queen of Aryan people if she continued this open-minded thinking.

For Mandane it was not a fake expression of concordance. To her a new nation should bring new ideas, and she was willing to accommodate a fresh approach to life. It was the teaching of her mother that gave Mandane this insight, because her mother was always fascinated by the ideas ambassadors of the minor kings brought to Ecbatana. Queen Aryenis received new ideas with understanding and open curiosity. Mandane thought some of this attitude had to come through her mother from Uncle Croesus, the king of Lydia.

Her father manifested selfish power and prudish disinterest in foreign affairs. Mandane knew that King Astyages accepted the superficiality of Media was the perfect example of how to live. Her father had never taught her understand the external world. All he wanted was to make her feel like his little girl. She was his protected little dove. She was his healthy little baby doe who was going to breed fawn after fawn. She found this attitude endearing, but she had always hoped he might include her in important international matters. He never did.

When Cambyses talked with Mandane about fashions she helped to make the conversation uncomplicated. Cambyses said, "Anshan has no deliberate fashions. Simple materials, like flax, wool and camels hair are woven into yarns that are dyed undramatic colors from vegetable sources. The women of Anshan use woven cloth to make simple, smooth hanging garments.

"Only ladies in court try to outdo each other in dressing and grooming because I encourage female competition. I give compliments sparingly and this makes the female courtiers fret over which styles please my tastes the most. It is a small game I play."

Mandane said, "I suspect there is more fashion than you realize. Men never notice the important things," and she looked down at her yellow, silk sheath with its gold tasseled waistband. The sash bound about her midriff was decorated with blue and violet embroidery, representing a floral splay entwined in green foliage. Her shoes were speckled with gems. Raising her hand to her head she gingerly touched the gold and lapis pin which held her silk veil in place with its delicate emerald and ruby studs. Mandane turned her face to Cambyses and looked into his eyes with uncertainty. She asked, "Is my dress suitable for your game, Cambyses?"

"For you there is no game. In Anshan you will go into the city to shop and greet people, and I expect you will not isolate yourself in the palace," and he extended his hand toward her as if pointing, "dressing this fancy. We have fewer stone paved streets and far more dust. Your pretty garments will get soiled, if not ruined in our markets."

Cambyses reached forward and touched her cheek and whispered, "Maybe I am confused. It may not be your clothes but your beauty that is too elegant for my marketplaces."

Mandane glowed and nuzzled against him saying, "We will make adjustments in my garment chests in Anshan. I will enjoy shopping in your stalls, if you insist that your queen must go out and buy for herself."

Cambyses wanted to make a kind suggestion to her. He said, "I prefer that you do, for a while at least. It will give the merchants an opportunity to quickly spread rumors of your true loveliness across the entire country. You will be a legend in an instant. Then you will have peasant-support that my relatives in court cannot ignore.

"At first my princes and princesses might be inclined to reject you and make things difficult for you even though our marriage is the order of the Great King. They always expected me to marry a cousin or niece."

Mandane observed, "So with me the line of royal succession leaves the protection of your family." She said this simply with no hint of challenging him.

Cambyses said, "Well, yes it does, but you are of Aryan decent too and that must be respected by my family. Mandane, I think you are going to be the best choice of a wife that could have made for me. You are more beautiful than an angora goat standing in snow in the mountains. Even more gorgeous than a mare sweating in the mid-day sun after a tense victory."

Her mouth dropped in astonishment at his comparison. Instead of being offended Mandane realized in an instant she had a lot of work to do to make this gorgeous brute see her differently. After their wedding bed if Cambyses compared her to anything less than the unseen goddesses of the bluest sky she would be disappointed. She saw herself telling mother about his comments and Mandane feared their laughter might never end.

The look on her face made Cambyses realize that he had said something that required an apology. He said, "I am sorry for how unjust that comment was to you. Your beauty is so overwhelming today that I have trouble thinking of an accurate compliment for you. Please forgive me."

She turned from him slightly, just enough to appear to rebuff him. It was an innate female response intended to keep him on edge. It never hurt to confuse a man, and keep him off guard.

A moon cycle was beginning to feel like eternity. They both knew there was to be no intimate touching or physical satisfaction of their surging love for each other until their wedding night. King Astyages still wanted the couple to be accompanied at all times, but Queen Aryenis insisted on leaving the young couple alone. The queen knew this was the time for the betrothed couple to establish mutual respect for each other. This was the interval of biding. Biding time, biding dignity and biding courtesy towards each other. The Queen put unfair stress between Cambyses and Mandane for their own benefit.

Sometimes the betrothed couple sat on a bench in a garden trembling when their thighs touched. Cambyses had to force his leg away from hers. Mandane was grateful for that because her virginal purity was yearning to be conquered by this beautiful man. At those moments she turned crimson and Cambyses gave her a silly, screwed up grin that made her burst out laughing in erotic delight that only helped to upset them both even more.

What a delicious time this was for them. Anticipation of their wedding bed caused the two to have the most scandalous dreams. Once in her innocence Mandane began to describe her latest dream to him. She stopped as it came to her that her virginal inexperience caused her to dream of feelings and flowers, perfumes and colors more than the physical aspects of love, with which she was still unfamiliar. She felt like a child, but he put his arm around her shoulder and said in a whisper, "Our life together will be a dream we will create each day. When as many sun cycles pass, as there are stars in the sky, people will still recite the legendary love story of Mandane and Cambyses."

Her heart lurched in her chest and Mandane moaned sweetly as she melted against him. His arms encircled her as a warm, engulfing breeze. His beard brushed across her cheek as he bent his head to kiss her. Her lips trembled at the light, stirring touch. She took his hand and for the first time placed it on her breast. She wanted him to be aware of the intimacy she was feeling. His beard was beginning to feel like soft linen threads to her, like those in delicate cloths that she enjoyed dusting across her face for comfort and warmth. His tender caress of her breast was a warm delight she welcomed like a hot drink in winter. Love rushed over her, making her loins feel sensitive and vulnerable.

Days passed with slow agony while Cambyses mingled with princes and princesses in and around the palace. He wanted to establish selective alliances within the palace to make future dealings with the Great King easier. He needed to find individuals he could trust to buffer the iniquity of Zav. He needed royal intermediaries throughout the domain of Media like Prince Zatame who was a good natured, perceptive ally. The prince had contacts everywhere and he became useful in introducing Cambyses to important Median royalty. Prince Zatame knew relatives of Cambyses from Bactria that the Parsian had never seen. Cambyses expressed his gratitude to Prince Zatame when the prince introduced the minor king to his extended family from the east.

Cambyses knew the Bactrians were a line of Aryans descending from his grandfather, Teispes, and his own father Cyrus had a brother Ariaramnes who ruled in Bactria, leaving Pars to the first King Cyrus. This eastern family Cambyses was now becoming acquainted with ranged into the countries of Arachosia, Parthia and Aria. These relatives were elevated to a kingship only in Bactria, but their prince and princess kinsmen were widespread.

Cambyses was pleased to find amiable relatives from these far off lands who teased him about having well developed sisters and even mothers within the family who were eligible for him to marry. Cambyses recognized their suggestions as the 'us versus them' attitude which grew from normal upbringing within clans and tribes. Cambyses remained polite and non-committal as he used his diplomatic skills to evade rash promises about future marriage alliances between their families.

One Bactrian cousin joked that his mother was a sister to the wife of Cyrus, and this cousin claimed his own sister was the perfect first-cousin family match for Cambyses. The prince claimed that a more intimate kindred relationship was hard to find. The prince told Cambyses to tell the King of Kings to join the evil daeva spirits and take his daughter Mandane with him, because there was a family match far more suitable for the king of Pars!

Everyone present laughed self-consciously at this comment. They were all aware of the fate of any man who made fun of the Great King, talked back to him or refused the King's wishes. To get only a hand cut off would be a mercy.

Through all this, Cambyses continued to solidify his affiliations with strangers who wanted to get to know the Parsian better. Some suggested business ties as a way to develop their relationships in the future. Cambyses himself joked that he felt like a wayward ram meeting up with strange herds of sheep willing to share their pastures and ewes with him. He let them know he appreciated their conviviality.

41

Since Cambyses was off the major caravan routes in his kingdom, making firm commercial deals with these men was impossible at this time. The secondary caravan routes were dangerous and bandits were everywhere. Cambyses was unsure of how business transactions might be protected to the satisfaction of all involved, but now the minor king had names of princes he could instruct his merchant, Pattmenidu, to contact. The products Cambyses had for exchange were not something a minor king decided, but his business managers did. Safe delivery and bartering of goods was the domain of smart businessmen and in Pars that meant Pattmenidu.

One day at dusk while waiting for the evening meal King Cambyses wandered through a market as the heat of the day was pulled away by the disappearing sun. A man dressed similar to a magus, but somehow different in demeanor, came up to Cambyses and inquired, "Are you King Cambyses of Pars that everyone is talking about? The man of great fortune who is to marry the Great King's daughter?"

Cambyses smiled politely and said, "Yes, I am. Who are you?"

The stranger said, "I am Zarathustra from across the Araxes River to the northwest. I am pleased to meet you. I am travelling about, trying to understand more about the gods and their proper places amongst themselves and amongst man."

Cambyses joked, "And I thought worrying about marriage was difficult."

Zarathustra chuckled and said, "Although I have not yet settled my own thoughts about the gods, I do believe that if you and your wife-to-be keep the gods foremost in your relationship all will be well for you. I wish you great happiness, Sire."

Cambyses nodded his appreciation and said, "Where are you going next, Sir?"

Zarathustra was pensive for a moment and sighed; then he smiled with benign amusement. He said, "I will wander throughout Media until the gods fix me a direction to travel. They must have a deliberate plan for a man said to be born of a virgin."

Cambyses exclaimed, "So you are that man! I have heard of you. Being born to an untouched mother is strange. It is impossible, yet I see no profound difference between you and me! Your story must be an ancient fable that was mistakenly confused with your birth; do you believe it yourself?"

Zarathustra looked directly at Cambyses and said, "That question is the reason for my wanderings, to find out. I need to learn if I am different from other men. Sire, would you not want to search yourself and others to confirm your sameness or separateness, if stories said you were born different than every other man?"

Cambyses inquired, "Do the people of your tribe believe they are special? Is that why they spread rumors of a cousin from an impossible birth?"

Zarathustra answered, "My people consider themselves quite ordinary, but I am more philosophical so they spread the story you have heard about me. They cherish my mother but only as an old woman who needs to be protected and cared for."

The king asked, "What gods do you believe in?"

Zarathustra answered, "I am not sure any more. I think there might be only one god or one truly supreme god, but I have to think about this more."

Cambyses asked, "Do you think anyone will agree with you? Only one god? That is a strange idea, sir."

Zarathustra smiled and said quietly, "I know. That is why I wander and think."

They talked for a short while until Cambyses felt the need to move on.

One man Cambyses sought out without hesitation was Kauklia, the minor king of Gedrosia, a nation of nomads who made their way through life like scorpions in the sand. He located Kauklia by stationing a servant at the gate of the first wall surrounding the palace. Each minor king, upon arrival, was obliged to present himself in bent obeisance before Astyages, if the Great King chose to admit him. When Kauklia's man announced the minor king's arrival at the first gate the servant of Cambyses rushed over and arranged the meeting.

Cambyses led Kauklia aside to a private eating place that had a small, rough stone alcove cut into a hillside rock. They could talk without being overheard. Cambyses had inspected the ceiling, walls and floor of the cave to ensure its integrity. There were no cracks or holes for conversations to pass through to the ears of strangers. The dirt floor and crude, adz-hewn furniture fit the atmosphere of their clandestine meeting. A lovely wool rug to keep the dust down rested on the floor beneath the cushions the two kings rested on. The food, homa beer and wine were excellent. Long ago Cambyses had discovered this place during an unusually hot summer when he sought a cool place to rest and eat. Each time Cambyses came to Ecbatana he made sure he ate here at least once. The owner knew whom Cambyses was and what he liked best to eat, and the proprietor always served the king himself. The owner never let servants near Cambyses. This king was his own personal prize.

King Kauklia was an enormous, beefy man who seemed to always stink. His gaze was stern and unyielding. He was an authoritarian despot among tough, nomadic men. Cambyses related to King Kauklia how Zav said the Great King wished to stir up a war between Gedrosia and Pars to gain Kauklia's total capitulation to full Median sovereign authority. This authority included the dictation of tax burdens.

Kauklia said, "I am proud of not paying tribute to King Astyages without alienating him enough to create war. Your news convinces me that Zav is a fool, and I prefer peace to war, at least for the moment. If your Parsian army did come over the mountains fighting we would match you blow for blow and win. You are no challenge to me."

Cambyses did not press the point because the Parsian knew how well his own army fought. He answered, "Maybe, Kauklia."

The groom-to-be continued, "I am only talking to you about this because I wish to avoid the war Zav, the tax collector, wants to precipitate between us."

Kauklia bellowed, "I will surely not go to war for him, and I would accept many inconveniences just to foil that ugly half-woman."

Cambyses asked solicitously, "Would you be willing to give a token tax payment to Astyages while you are here, now?"

Kauklia chortled and said, "For you, you poor trapped daeva, I will do it."

So once again Cambyses was able to thwart Zav and frustrate the minister's effort to cause trouble.

5.

The Great King had ordered Cambyses to marry Mandane in one moon cycle, and that was hardly enough time for Queen Aryenis and her *andarun,* or female household, to complete essential preparations, but her bevy of princesses were doing well. Marriages held in Media had no bearing on the annual season, particularly this wedding. Only the wishes of the Great King mattered for his daughter's nuptial ceremony. However, in Pars the turning of the spring season was when couples married. The population of Pars recognized spring was coming when daylight lasted longer as the sun rose more directly overhead each day. Young men and women passed from childhood into adulthood, and marriage allowed young couples to start their own families and gardens. Crops were made ready for planting. Newlyweds could also begin breeding goats, cattle and other domestic animals they received as marriage gifts. Spring was a time of festivals and joy in Pars.

//

Messengers began arriving in Anshan from Ecbatana with the news about Cambyses and Mandane. Several women in the Parsian court swooned with exasperation for they had been trying assiduously for ages to please Cambyses. They had wanted to capture his affections and win the right to be his wife and queen. One princess grabbed the first available prince, and her erotic leg embrace locked him to her until he agreed they should wed. Another became the wife of her brother.

Prince Bagindu, a close cousin to King Cambyses, assigned several eunuchs to establish an *andarun,* or inner household, which would be the official residence of the king's wife, concubines and unmarried palace princesses. The palace at Anshan had never developed a true inner household for King Cambyses. His concubines and princesses were well cared for, but their rooms were not isolated in the fashion of a true *andarun.* Living area in his palace had never been set aside for the exclusive use of women. Prince Bagindu knew the king's new wife would require such an arrangement to protect her

45

privacy where she alone ruled. The queen needed a large room near the king's bedroom with a private passage between their suites. All other doorway passages and corridors had to be sealed or guarded to protect the safety and modesty of the queen. It was exciting for the Parsians to plan Mandane's sanctuary. She needed serving ladies quartered near enough to her rooms to give her comfort and convenience.

Planning space for future concubines could wait till later. Right now the eunuchs used the queen's bedroom as the focal point and studied space around it to ensure it could expand; the queen would want her *andarun* to grow.

Everyone expected Cambyses to let his wife have total control over running the female household. There were two important aspects of this responsibility. The first was the physical space dedicated to it. It included rooms for women and children, bathing areas, laundries, larders, kitchens, sewing and entertainment rooms, gardens and receiving rooms.

The second feature was more significant. It was the ownership atmosphere of the *andarun*. It belonged exclusively to the queen and her women. Men were invited guests and had no privileges in this area. Eunuchs dedicated to the inner household responded to orders from women only. If any man entered, uninvited by a woman, he was escorted out with polite force. It did not matter whether he was a king or a peasant. The *andarun* was a female stronghold. No man dared to violate its space.

The eunuchs decided to locate a room for the queen's use that allowed access for magi, who had to act as her scribes and correspondence readers, without having them pass directly into the inner household. If the room was not needed later it could be put to other uses, and the door to the women's area could be sealed.

The princesses were afraid to anticipate the adornments a sophisticated princess from Media might want so the queen's personal rooms were left plain and undecorated; the sole exception was the queen's bedroom where servants placed the bed that had belonged to Cambyses' mother. The princesses felt it added a link with tradition the new queen should welcome since it was the bed where Cambyses had been born. The princesses also placed for the new queen's convenience the toilet articles used by Cambyses' mother, such as her tub, her 'seat of eliminations', her large bronze mirror and other personal items. They prepared themselves to react to every demand from Mandane when she arrived.

Prince Bagindu summoned the merchant Pattmenidu to the palace. The prince assumed the right to organize purchases for the new queen. The prince wanted the merchant's advice on acquiring fabrics for drapes, curtains, bedclothes, personal garments and selected furniture items for common areas of the *andarun*. Pattmenidu was flattered by the summons and the royal family appreciated the merchant's ability to find goods and materials from suppliers throughout Pars. The merchant wanted to offer the new queen items made by citizens loyal to King Cambyses, if she was willing to accept them. Since Pattmenidu had traveled broadly he understood the vast difference in living styles and quality between Media and Pars. Craftsmen in Pars were no less skilled than artisans of Media, but the peasants from Pars spent more time with essential tasks, and they put less effort into time-consuming artwork.

Pattmenidu could go to Zav later and acquire Median goods, if that was the queen's wish, but the merchant made his purchases inside Pars since losing confidence in Zav during their last meeting. Zav had been mean and antagonistic towards the Parsians and referred to them as crude and inferior. Pattmenidu knew his own business acumen was far superior to Zav's. The tax administrator used power and threats where Pattmenidu used his wits and craft. Pattmenidu always feared Zav's power might be used to forbid Pars to conduct business with Ecbatana for goods essential to Anshan markets. The merchant constantly had to devise ways to placate Zav's anger and willfulness. Pattmenidu was unaware of the hatred Zav had recently developed for the king and the new queen of Pars.

Dealers for every conceivable product began pestering Pattmenidu. The whole nation wanted to provide something for the new queen. Tribal people living in the mountains and in valley pastures began making all sorts of metal, wood and fabric items as gifts for the palace. New carpets that took several moon cycles to weave were started. Mountain dwellers were more generous and open than city dwellers, since robust commerce was less important in remote high places; spontaneous hospitality was more natural in their small domains. Mountain people chose to share their meager resources with the new queen, just as they did with friends, strangers and family members who passed through their mountain territory. City merchants on the other hand were more interested in selling goods to the palace rather than giving gifts. However, the city people did encourage craftsmen to enrich the quality of the materials being used to ensure the products to be sold to the queen were worthy of her.

The soft, delicate hair closest to a camel's hide was used for making elegant garments that would touch her skin. It was also woven into outer garments she would need to appear elegant. Its velvety smooth feel was most desirable. To supply their new queen, camel herders began to collect the hair in large, unclean piles until entire herds began to be laughably bald. Normally camel owners reached beneath the coarser outside hair and plucked the finer hairs over a long period of time. The animals did not appreciate being plucked, but they tolerated it. Also, the camel owners plucked on a seasonal basis when the hairs were full-grown after winter, but were a less essential insulation in the springtime and summer seasons. However, since it was heralded that the new queen desired garments made of this valuable hair many camel herders shaved their animals, and bales of blended hair were arriving at the shops for washing, carding, separating and yarn spinning.

Copper and tin mines were being worked overtime to provide material to make bronze lamps, bowls, and cooking utensils for her *andarun* as well as armaments for the inner household security force of eunuchs.

Pars did not have gem mining of the most precious stones that Pattmenidu wanted, except for lapis and turquoise. Pattmenidu and his colleagues solicited for sapphires and rubies that had already arrived from across the Indus River in the east and for pearls from the Chin, very far to the east. The merchant could not wait for delivery of new gems because they were dangerous to transport across the caravan highways menaced by thieves, making delivery unreliable. Gold and silver already processed and purified were provided by the merchant's usual sources. There was not enough time for Parsian metal workers to purify ores for new metal goods. Pattmenidu inadvertently avoided problems by not dealing with Zav for these precious materials. The

Tax and Materials Minister would have made delivery promises without keeping them.

Prince Bagindu kept inquiring about the more exotic materials to get, such as the precious stones, precious metals and silks. He appreciated rich quality and focused his attention on these goods. He was anxious to please Cambyses because he loved him as a brother and wanted to show his king Pars truly cared about the sensibilities of the new queen.

Objects of art, such as statues, gold gilded oil lamps and sconces, Corinthian designed columns and pedestals, and multicolored marble tables were not objects that the population of Pars acquired because such items were too expensive. Also, they were frivolous nonessentials, which did not increase the efficiency of living. Peasants considered them unnecessary accessories. They were scarce in Pars.

Musicians began creating what they thought were enchanting new musical works worthy of a queen. Lyres, cymbals, drums and pipes were all used to varying degrees in the compositions. Much of the music included rich poetry designed to accommodate singers. There were groups of people everywhere wanting to sing to her highness as soon as they could get access to her, in the streets, in the palace, anywhere. The learning process to get the tunes correct by the instrumentalists and the choral ensembles produced a hilarious cacophony. Everyone, even people normally irritated by noises, accepted it with good humor and sometimes chimed in to make matters worse.

Unexpectedly, the priesthood of magi became infected with the happiness. They abandoned their normal seriousness and smiled more as they prepared stores of unused clay tablets and animal skins to record the most important event for Pars in many, many sun cycles. They hummed while grinding pigments for their inks and sharpening stylets for carving their cuneiform figures in the clay sheets. They practiced their vocabularies of Parsian, Greek and Aramaic with an occasional chuckle. They began to exhibit an unnatural politeness toward each other when they tutored and corrected the less experienced. They joked about taking baths or washing their grubby garments to give the queen a positive first impression of them.

The entire country was mobilized to welcome the queen. Joy was everywhere. War was the only other event that had ever mobilized the entire country so, but now marriage, royalty, richness, unity and dedication to splendor had gaily invigorated everyone.

6.

Zav began the process of restricting rice deliveries into Pars. He called a scribe magus and said, "I will give you a message that is to go to every kingdom in Media. Make certain my message goes to the major countries of Susiana, Bactria, Parthia, Gedrosia, Aria and Sagartia. However, send it to all the minor kingdoms as well."

Zav did not ask anyone to stop dealing with Pars, because that might cause some of the more rebellious areas to snub his note and increase support for Cambysis. Instead, Zav advised, "Media must centralize the distribution of rice to protect areas needing rationing within the Empire due to regional draughts and famine."

Zav was able to make his message sound logical. If he could get administrators of the provincial nations to alter distribution systems before the minor kings returned home from Ecbatana, where they were attending Mandane's wedding, Zav might succeed in hiding from them what he had done at least for a while. The kings would not discover his intrigue until Pars was suitably punished. Even then the minor kings probably would not revert back to normal market dealings. They were unlikely to understand the hardship caused to Pars households, and the minor kings might never know of the food-supply dilemma he had caused.

All excess rice was to be shipped to Ecbatana, giving Zav complete control of its price and its distribution as he sold most of the available rice to passing caravans going west. He decided to send token profits back to the provinces to make it appear that the new way of managing rice was beneficial. He even intended to sell some rice back to all the provinces at fair prices, with the exception of Pars. There the price had to double at first and as the pinch began to become evident at the average household table, Zav would triple the cost to make rice appear even more dear. Pattmenidu might complain, but since he acted in concert with Zav at the beginning of this escapade Zav believed the merchant would never go to Cambyses to reveal his own involvement in the rice shortage. Zav had once again created a foolproof system of hurting Cambyses. The Minister of Taxes and Materials was thrilled at his own cleverness and thought how ironic it was that the very wedding ceremony he resented the most had made this scheme possible. The kings were all assembled in Ecbatana, well beyond their own borders, and Zav had the power to intimidate minor administrators to do his bidding.

Zav's hatred for Cambyses had developed over a long time because the king always argued about royal tribute increases and frequently accused Zav of stealing from Pars or the Great King. Numerous threats and counter-threats between these two kept them from being amicable. Now, Zav's hatred overwhelmed him and became directed at Mandane too. Somehow he would make the princess pay personally. If there were some way to keep her from bearing children he would find it. Zav consulted with a surgeon-magus who understood female sterility methods and Zav asked, "Can sterility be brought about by surgery?"

The magus answered, "Yes."

Zav asked, "By herbs?"

"Yes," said the magus, "well, not herbs, but certain plants, however, it is not permanent. Only the loss of one child occurs when the plants are administered during pregnancy. The surgery is permanent."

Searching for details Zav requested, "Tell me how the surgery is done, please."

Zav and the magus discussed the procedure, and the minister realized a magus seldom performed this operation, and no magus could be induced to perform this horrible procedure on Mandane. She was too important and too well known in the realm. Zav wondered if he could to do it himself after listening to the magus. He could knock her unconscious with drugs or a club. Zav could butcher her and make her barren, but he could never keep her alive, and Zav wanted Mandane to live so she could suffer the fate of conceiving no children, no heirs.

His next idea seemed more achievable. Zav could kidnap her before the wedding and have a magus cast a spell over her. The magi did this often to help protect the sick from pain. A well-trained magus could somehow make a patient's mind go to a different place. It was an unrecognizable domain to the patient. Zav knew the magus could make the mind of a person stay there as long as he wished. The mind could not free itself and later, when the magus brought it back, the mind could not remember where it had been. While in this other domain the magus could fill the unrecognizable vacancy with instructions the patient had to obey later when he appeared to return to normal. To a limited extent the magus made the patient perform deeds the priest suggested with specific words. It was a great mystical skill, and Zav decided to use it.

First, Zav had to find a magus he could bribe who was skilled in mind suggesting, which was easy to do, except the magus must also be susceptible to threats and frightened of royal retribution. Also, Mandane had to be a stranger to the magus. The magus and Mandane must never have seen each other. Zav traveled outside the environs of Ecbatana to find his priest.

Zav said, "A female was going to be presented to you at a place you will learn about later. You are to send her mind away. I will instruct you beforehand about how her future is to be controlled. Understand?"

The magus nodded and said, "Of course you realize this might not be completely successful. Sometimes the mind does not accept our bidding."

Zav was irritated as he handed the magus a small lump of silver and said, "You are to do the best you can."

The magus looked at the payment, smiled and said, "I will not fail you, sir."

Before the wedding Zav planned to abduct Mandane and have this magus put her mind elsewhere. During that time Zav intended to steal her virginity which he felt was his right, then under the power of the magus convince her that no man should ever touch her again, ruining her marriage.

A few days later an outdoor play was being performed in one of the private courtyards of the palace. Zav knew Mandane was going with her servants but without King Cambyses. It was the perfect time for Zav to execute his conspiracy. On the day of the play Zav noted what Mandane wore when she was outside. A slight chill hung in the air because a strong breeze blew, and Mandane wore a green cape with an attached hood to protect her from the breeze. This garment was the cue Zav needed to locate Mandane in a crowd from which he intended to coax or wrestle her away.

When the play started all eyes were on the players. Mandane had stood in the rear of the audience to allow her servants to stand close to the players. Unknown to Zav, Mandane had loaned her cape and hood to a servant girl who complained of the chill. Zav made the mistake of hitting the servant with the hilt of his sword, then he caught her as she fell and whisked her into a cellar, thinking he had Mandane. The magus was waiting there to cast his spell on the girl who was delivered to him. Zav laid down the body in a heap. The green hood covered her face. The magus asked, "Why is this woman not conscious? She needs to be awake for this procedure to work. I cannot control the mind of an unconscious person."

Zav said, "The woman became nervous, and she fainted."

The magus turned the girl on her back and removed the hood from her face. Seeing the wrong face Zav growled, "We will forget our agreement. Here, take this silver locket as payment for you time. You may leave, magus."

When the magus left, Zav in a fury killed the unconscious servant on the spot. As Zav exited the cellar a eunuch saw him leave, but paid no more attention to the minister.

By surprise, Cambyses arrived at the play and went to Mandane. She said, "Oh Cambyses, you came just in time. Help me find the servant who is wearing my green cape. I am chilly."

Mandane and Cambyses searched the crowd with swift, abrupt glances. The eunuch mistook their actions as looking for Zav and he whispered, "Sire, I saw the Minister of Taxes and Materials come out of that door, if he is whom you are looking for."

They were surprised at this and Mandane could not resist mischief as she said, "Cambyses, we must go into the cellar. I can get out of this wind, where it will be warmer" and seductively she added, "with you."

There they found the dead servant lying on the floor. Mandane fretted and wept over the poor dead girl. She almost fainted as Cambyses steadied her. Cambyses understood at least part of what had happened. Zav had killed the servant for some reason. The king wondered if Mandane's cape meant she was the intended target? Cambyses became alarmed at this thought and said, "Mandane, you must stop crying before you leave here. Please try not to cry in public over this girl. You can return to your rooms with the eunuch outside, and then weep all you want."

Mandane looked at him with pleading eyes, whimpered and said, "I will try, Cambyses, but she was such a lovely, little girl."

The king said, "Mandane, do not speak to anyone but me about this. It is very important for this to remain a secret for now."

Mandane straightened her shoulders, nodded and heroically caught her breath as she exited the cellar, walked directly to the eunuch. They marched off together. Cambyses was proud of how Mandane got control of her emotions after such a shocking discovery. The king looked about for a religious magus and brought him to the cellar. Cambyses said, "Magus, take this body to the Tower of Silence and prepare her for her funerary presentation before the gods."

The magus saw the girl's wound and said, "Sire, if she has been murdered we must inform the guards."

Cambyses answered, "I will take care of that. You conduct your holy ritual for this poor child but do not leave this room with the body until the crowd outside is gone. I will pay for your services tomorrow when I visit the body."

Now Cambyses had a murder to hold over the head of Zav but the king knew he needed to comfort Mandane before he confronted that wretch. At the evening meal Mandane could not eat. Cambyses sat by her and took her out into a garden when it was allowed to leave the royal dining room. There he soothed her wounded spirit, convincing her she was safe. Cambyses made up stories to distract her. He kept her from associating Zav with the incident. He wanted Zav to himself.

Cambyses could not kill Zav without compounding the crime. The only way the king could attack Zav legally was by trial before the Great King, so he chose not to report Zav's misdeed to anyone. Cambyses wanted to use this murder to intimidate Zav later to his own advantage. Here was an opportunity to gain control over the minister of Media. It was a unique situation that favored the king of Pars. For two days the minor king searched and asked for the whereabouts of Zav, but no one had seen the minister anywhere. Cambyses hunted throughout the palace and the city of Ecbatana. He thought either the coward was hiding, or Zav had left to cause trouble in another city or country, expecting no one to relate him to the dead body when it was inevitably found.

Cambyses sent a message to Anshan that said, "Administrators and my family are to reverse all policies instituted under the recent direction of Zav. Any new orders from the Minister of Taxes and Materials are to be ignored. Pattmenidu is to do no business with Zav until I return and oversee the dealings."

Pattmenidu was thrilled to get this news! He returned a message in an instant to Cambyses saying, "Zav developed an order to have all rice raised in Pars sent to Media to his stores. You can appreciate the economic burden and the extent commerce would be affected if his rice plan were actually implemented. I wonder if merchants in other parts of the Median kingdom had been instructed by Zav to restrict rice sales to Pars. Do you have the time to investigate that possibility, Sire?"

Upon receiving this message Cambyses went to the Chief Magus and asked him if any of the scribe magi had recently written any record or message from Zav about rice. The magus who had sent the rice message to all territories of the empire of Media came forward with his record. Cambyses realized the Chief Magus could do nothing. He and his tribe of priests provided several services but they had no authority to act or reverse the dictates of the King's ministers.

Cambyses moved about the palace of Ecbatana comfortably blending naturally into its royal society. He made his way among elite patrons of the court and the visiting sovereigns without discomfort or stress. He found some visiting minor kings by using court chamberlains. He held casual meetings with several potentates, one at a time, in gardens and fruit groves where he told them of the rice plot. Some were amused and considered it a minor annoyance. Others were outraged, offended that such a thing would be executed in their country while they were away. Slowly, the situation began to reverse. The minor kings sent immediate instructions to cancel the rice trades Zav had instituted. Some even discussed challenging the King of Kings face-to-face. King Kauklia of Gedrosia encouraged confronting King Astyages. The rice plot and the aborted war plan with Pars had been too much for him. The minor kings admitted that questioning the Great King was heroic but suicidal. King Astyages always reacted with vicious retribution when challenged, and besides, they reminded Kauklia, the Great King's army was at hand and their armies were not.

11

Zav had indeed left the city only far enough not to be found, but so he could return in time for the wedding. As much as he loathed the idea, Zav knew he had to attend the abhorrent marriage or risk the wrath of King Astyages. Zav's personal messengers began bringing him information of how his plans to control the rice market throughout the kingdom were being thwarted. This sent him into a new rage. What kept him from killing the messengers was the absence of information about the dead girl. It was impossible for a murder to take place in the palace without an uproar. Had no one found her yet? Could he go back and remove her body himself? No, but Zav could and did send a messenger into the cellar under the guise of wanting to use that space for storage. The messenger returned and said the cellar was empty, not even a wine jug was in there. Now this was a strange mystery Zav could not comprehend. What might have happened to her? Zav affirmed in his mind that there was no way anyone might connect him to the dead girl so he stopped worrying.

7.

Over the three moon cycles since Queen Aryenis first began her plans for the wedding, her arrangements matured at a rapid pace. A very large courtyard had been set aside for the ceremony and the celebration. It was an undeveloped, stony area large enough to hold hundreds of people. With miraculous speed gardeners harrowed and fertilized the soil as they planted citrus trees along one wall opposite the major gate entryway. The princesses of the palace supervised the work with great enthusiasm. Boulders were removed and ground was leveled. Olive trees and fig trees were placed in a mixed pattern down the two sidewalls. It was always the preference of gardeners to blend in edibles with decorative plants. Good soil was dear and not to be wasted. A well designed, flowering landscape, devoid of consumables, was considered to be as valuable as an arid desert; just prettier.

The princesses saw to it that a large arc of mixed flowers and vegetables was planted in front of the citrus trees. They planned for this arc to set the boundary for the head table, before which the Chief Magus would perform the wedding, and where the Great King and the newlyweds would recline during the banquet festivities.

After measurements were taken for table placements and lounging areas throughout the courtyard for the guests, pomegranate trees were planted in rows producing a rectangular feel to the courtyard. The enclosure was so expansive that even the large empty area left in the center for entertainment and dancing did not interfere with this rectangular pattern. One princess wanted apple trees raised along the walls where the entry gate was located. She liked apples. Small spaces were left for musicians between the trees, flowers and vegetable plants.

The women agreed that garlic plants were to be deliberately avoided due to their unique odor. Grapevines were unattractive with their wall of sticks, hemp ties and stunted seedlings and therefore grapes were not planted. No grains were planted either. Oats, emmer, barley and rye looked attractive, but large fields of grain were needed to make growing them economical. Small patches in this yard had no kitchen value either. Beets, cabbages, lettuces, cucumbers and radishes were added. Melons were placed to add variegated color. Lentil and pea plants were dispersed at random also.

One princess suggested placing a pond for watercress in front of the royal arc and the women agreed that was an exciting addition. The Great King's table was placed behind the pool and in front of the planted arc. The pool set him off with authority from the crowd. Later, fish were added to the pond to ensure that an ugly green mat did not form over the surface of the pond.

Poles standing fifteen cubits tall were raised beside pomegranate trees. Queen Aryenis ordered multicolored banners strung between these poles to create intermittent shade as the sun rolled past the earth each day. Garlands of flowers hung on the poles to enhance the appeal of the court. Plenty of aisle space was left between the guest eating tables so attendees could visit each other without congestion. The princesses were satisfied that their plans allowed adequate space for food servers to race up and down the aisles while carrying food trays and cleaning materials. The women discussed how guests got drunk, overstuffed and sick after days of celebration so they planned for sanitation ahead of time.

No effort was made to pretend King Astyages could create a garden rivaling the magnificent Hanging Gardens of Babylon that Nebuchadnezzar was developing. If rumors of the terraced gardens were true, the Babylonian had forests of exotic trees from all over the known world. The king of Babylon also had interspersed vegetables and fruits from foreign lands among his trees. King Nebuchadnezzar was developing his magnificent gardens to please his wife, Amytis, who was a princess from Media. She longed for gardens reminding her of the mountain glades of her homeland.

In comparison, King Astyages had his modest courtyard for a single event that his women transformed with loveliness. The Great King of Media had considered inviting his neighbors in the west to the wedding. King Astyages could really impress the world by having both Croesus and Nebuchadnezzar enter Ecbatana together. What a splendid sight that would be! But when he accompanied Queen Aryenis to the ceremonial yard Astyages realized it was far too small for three Great Kings. Also, Ecbatana was not able to house the combined entourages of servants, slaves, guarding soldiers and the family members accompanying two important visiting kings, plus the hundreds of extra camels and horses that would strain his available grain stores and stable facilities.

King Astyages knew that his brother-in-law Croesus was already on his way and that was enough. King Croesus had been invited as soon as Astyages had conceived his solution to his troublesome dream, before he even ordered the presence of Cambyses to Ecbatana. Croesus could be relied upon to keep the size of his contingent small enough to be handled by the merchants and stables of Ecbatana. Astyages knew Croesus was always solicitous of his sister Aryenis and himself. A more supportive and compassionate family member could not be found on earth.

Astyages knew that when it came to King Croesus running his own kingdom and increasing his control over commerce between Greece, Egypt and the vast lands to his east, the king was a different man. Croesus was stern, perceptive, crafty and infamous. Anyone in the known world wanting to do business in large volume and with frequent transactions had to do business with him at some point. The merchants knew Croesus extracted high profits from them, but his seaports and his international contacts made the cost worthwhile. He accumulated more wealth than any other regent on earth did because King Croesus commanded the best seacoast harbors, and his slaves built vast storage buildings designed for the sole purpose of moving merchandise with efficiency.

Astyages knew Lydia was the extreme western end of the mighty caravan route that traversed from west to the east where the mysterious Chin people kept the secret of silk production. Any valuable spice, wood, ore, fabric, food or produced commodity like rugs, lanterns or statues on that route were all part of King Croesus' commerce. The Lydian was an unavoidable focal point. He was the very breath that sustained business everywhere.

Astyages told his Queen he wanted decorations in the streets outside his palace where King Croesus would enter Ecbatana. The King planned the parade route from the caravan highway to the palace because he knew King Croesus loved to be an ostentatious spectacle whenever he entered someone else's capital. Streamers were hung on poles and fruit trees were transplanted from orchards to the streets. King Astyages planned to place camels and riders on both sides of Croesus' path. The riders were to be decorated in various colored uniforms, with peaked hats and plumes, and the animals were to be clean and groomed so their hair was sleek and attractive. Small hats with brass bells were to be placed on the camels' heads. Necklaces of flowers and bells were to be hung on the camels so when they turned their heads the bells must chime, adding melody to the drums, reed pipes and lyres of musicians along the way.

It was not necessary for the King to force the citizens of Ecbatana to line the route. Peasants were always anxious to be involved in pageantry. They would adorn the route with shouting, singing and whistling and for a short time the poor could escape from their ordinary dull routines filling their lives with happy excitement.

This pageant was a perfect addition to the legends the Great King of Media encouraged people to invent about him. The wedding festivities were going to establish new allusions and fantasies. The pageant King Croesus created was going to leave the population buzzing with lies about what they saw and what they imagined was happening behind the seven walls. Fictitious legends suited King Astyages.

Cambyses was astounded at the expense the wedding was incurring. He could have fed Pars for moon cycles with the silver and gold that exchanged hands. He could have leveled mountain glades and created new farmlands for hundreds of peasants and he hated being the object of so much waste. With each declaration of new spending he wanted to shout, "Enough!"

Cambyses said, "Mandane, can you please request a reduction in the expense of our wedding plans? Better still, can you ask your father to give Pars the equivalent in silver as a wedding gift, or reduce our annual tribute to him."

The king continued in an anxious tone, "Mandane, I could have used all this gold and silver to far greater profit by spending it on the peasants of Pars to make their lives easier."

Mandane was pleased at his fervent concern and dedication to the welfare of his subjects. Mandane was determined to make every effort to become a proper queen for Pars. She answered, "Father is not in a mind to listen to such a request, Cambyses. You know that! He intends to make this ceremony the biggest event ever. However, as your wife, I will always support your decisions to allocate resources to benefit your people... our people."

As Cambyses associated with the vast aggregation of minor kings he began to hear desires to go to war in various regions. The king of Parthia talked of going straight north to conquer the Sythians living just east of the great northern sea above Ecbatana. The land there was less mountainous and very fertile.

King Arsames of Bactria talked of warring with the Massagetae far to his north, which was not part of the Median Empire. He made an impressive sight when he roared at some fictitious injustice from Massageta that he took personally. King Arsames said, "All I really want is to give my army something to do."

His great bulk shivered and his mighty arms seemed to swell as he made threatening gestures in the air. He was very demonstrative and emphatic. Cambyses thought his cousin King Arsames was fun to watch and listen to.

The Sogdianan king, who was between Bactria and Massageta added, "I do not relish the thought of your Bactrian army passing through my land to get to our northern neighbors. We have enough trouble managing that border. It was a trivial annoyance, but it takes up enough of my attention already."

Cambyses stayed out of the blustering. He did not appreciate war, certainly not just for the sake of activity and distraction. Cambyses was always quick to use his military to protect Pars when necessary, but he never fought for fun.

King Cambyses was making new friends and acquaintances, and he wanted to protect these new relationships. Being amiable toward everyone was easy for him because of his polite personality. Cambyses feigned loss of attention about the subject matter when arguments became heated. He used the excuse that he was the intended groom and smiled with a sheepish grin. That always brought laughter and cooled tempers. His passive demeanor had a calming effect on the other more belligerent potentates.

Frequently, Cambyses changed the topic of war to address the efficiency of commerce. There were many minor kingdoms in Media that were south of the major west-to-east trade route. He suggested ideas to bring more caravans through the countries of Pars, Carmania, Utia, and Gedrosia. The kings of Parthia, Aria and Bactria who had direct access to the major caravan route were sympathetic but were unwilling to make changes in established business practices. They were doing well and did not want to give anything away, even to a friend.

King Kauklia of Gedrosia blustered that maybe he would just force the issue to realign the route by force of arms in the future. Everyone looked at him and wondered if he was joking or predicting war.

Substantive matters of internal and external importance were seldom spoken of with such openness and candor among these kings. They found it refreshing to see if they could get away with telling egregious lies. The kings encouraged discussion of complaints and strategies with each other. Everyone benefited by reassessing perceptions of each other. The great kingdom of Media seemed to be coming together more cohesively than if Astyages had demanded it.

8.

Mandane's excitement swelled as her wedding day approached. She kept after her tailors and servants. She wanted to make certain her clothes chests were filled by the time she left Ecbatana for her new home with her husband. Her servants had selected a vast wardrobe of garments for her to take to Pars that were fresh, colorful and novel. All these clothes had to last Mandane for at least one sun cycle. Her tailors could not imagine garment makers in Pars being able to produce suitably resplendent clothes for their precious princess in less time. In fact the servants and sewers agreed among themselves that poor Pars would never supply her with adequate garments.

Every kind of seasonal wardrobe was planned; including winter sheaths of warm wool along with short shawls and jackets to fend off drafts. Everything had to be decorated with beautiful, tasteful simplicity to prevent the royal court of Pars from being overwhelmed with her elegance and beauty. She was the demure flower of Ecbatana that was about to blossom in these clothes before the eyes of others. Her servants were so jealous of Pars that they wanted to demonstrate to the inferior Parsians the proper way to outfit their Median treasure. Only the finest yarns and materials were used for their darling princess who was about to be someone else's queen.

Summer frocks of light linen and silk with gay embroidery and delicate jewels were designed and fitted to her. The Medes wanted to present her as a royal vision without equal, their inspiration to the world of how a queen should look. They even made a few outfits for Cambyses to match what Mandane was to wear to make certain that his handsome and regal appearance complimented her in the Anshan palace.

Her Median servants agreed amongst themselves to be ready for Mandane to return in the future so they could replenish the contents of her garment trunks with splendid new outfits. Mandane was not being given up, just loaned.

Mandane talked frequently with her mother about being a queen. The princess said, "Mother, I want to appear natural, yet have proper deportment that compliments my new position. How is this?" and Mandane began to dramatically mimic the exaggerated walk and bearing of an aloof woman. She swung her shoulders vigorously back and forth as she sauntered with deep knee bends and swaying hips.

Her mother laughed and advised, "My dear daughter, just be 'Mandane' and you will be fine. You have never acted self-important or pompous and please don't start now," and the queen giggled again.

Mandane was not self-conscious about her new status, but she wished her mother had a special secret about being the primary companion to a king. The princess said, "Mother, you are always the perfect queen. You have such natural regal demeanor and authority, yet you have compassionate consideration for your subjects. You never complain. You never judge minor kings or their representatives in the reception rooms of the court. You never contradict father in anything."

Queen Aryenis was surprised and pleased with this unexpected evaluation from her daughter, but the Queen knew how sometimes in the solitude of private conversations with Mandane, Aryenis said how she wished certain people of the court were more circumspect. The Queen revealed privileged confidences to her daughter when she thought certain princes needed to develop more polite traits in their relations with peasants, and sometimes that included the King. Mandane knew her mother spoke to her on these occasions with complete trust. Mandane understood that she had to have a trustworthy companion in Pars, as well, someone she could share her privileged opinions with. Mandane knew she was going to need a female to talk to about matters that vexed her periodically. Mandane thought that finding such a companion might be difficult in a place where she was likely to be resented.

//

Mandane's uncle, King Croesus of Lydia, arrived and when she was presented to him he gushed, "Ah Mandane, you are more beautiful than a quality mare that has just won an important chariot race for me."

Everyone present laughed, including Mandane. King Croesus continued, "You are a truly gorgeous princess, my dear. Your posture, your elegance and the sparkle in your eyes give you the look of a goddess."

Croesus was kind as he smothered her with more compliments. She could not help loving this man whose flattering comments predicted her inevitable success as a queen. King Croesus added, "My dear, you will be as beautiful a queen as my sister."

Croesus was so proud of his sister that he openly let everyone know it. He continued to everyone's pleasure, "Mandane, I vow to share my wealth with you if ever you need something Pars cannot afford. You need only ask."

Croesus was a man of confidence and achievement who was in a position to share his success with her. He never bragged about himself; he just accomplished what seemed like the impossible every day. He flourished where others floundered because he worked hard at personal achievement, not at being important.

King Croesus spoke in Greek, which Mandane spoke with ease because her mother, Queen Aryenis, had always spoken in Greek to her as part of her education. The Queen was better at seeing to Mandane's teaching than King Astyages, who did not believe his daughter, or other females, needed to be knowledgeable of the world.

King Croesus counseled, "Even a queen must work hard to be a true queen. You must show you love the peasants as well as soldiers and sailors." Then he chuckled and said, "Ah, will you have sailors in Pars?"

"I do not believe so," Mandane answered with uncertainty, "at least Cambyses has not mentioned ships. If he has a navy it probably requires minor attention from our palace. It is more likely a commercial responsibility."

Changing the subject Croesus said, "You must be diligent to balance fairness with firmness, Mandane. At times, you will be tempted to expect glorification and fame but do not let your ego demand fame. Hard work should be your glory, my dear."

She turned her beautiful face toward him and teased, "If what mother says is true, you work very hard at being famous. I saw your entrance into Ecbatana as well as your face at the reaction of the crowds. You look more pleased with yourself then with the shouting."

Queen Aryenis snickered and blushed as Mandane began to laugh. He roared with gusto saying, "Maybe you saw something I did not know I was feeling. My fame made the people shout so I had to accept their adulation to be polite. After all, I am your guest, my sweet, but it was uproarious, was it not?" and he laughed again saying, "When you are the king of a country as successful as Lydia, fame is unavoidable. I am well known because the whole world comes to me to do business. I am famous because the world makes me richer than any other king. I am lucky Lydia is where it is."

When he had entered the city his entourage was so long, it took half the day for his parade to pass any single spot on the road into Ecbatana. Croesus said, "I made sure I was not accompanied by a large contingent before I left Lydia. Here I just ordered my animal drivers to spread the beasts of burden in a thin line to give the appearance of a large escort. I wanted your peasants to be entertained as much as I wanted the minor kings of Media to appreciate my wealth.

"I liked the way my parade of carts and chariots were decorated with banners and flags. I had my camels dandified with braided hair locks, combed tails, and gorgeous multicolored blankets with golden tassels just for you, Mandane."

Mandane said, "I liked their silver bells and the soft soothing tinkle."

He asked, "Did you like my musicians? I wanted music to herald my approach to entertain your citizens."

Mandane chuckled as she said, "Uncle Croesus, I was enthralled by the golden helmets and golden breastplates of your guards. Even their spears were as sheathed in gold as your chariot! I have never seen such splendor. People are going to explode with new myths and untruths about you."

Croesus beamed at her comments. He said, "Mandane my dear, let me give you some advice. Don't concentrate on worrying about appearances, you must become the lioness of Pars, protecting the pride."

She liked that expression because Cambyses had said that the lion was the symbol of Pars, and it was indeed the lioness that hunted and protected the pride. King Croesus turned and snapped his fingers.

"And you shall do it from this; I have your wedding gift."

Slaves entered carrying two large boxes made of exotic wood grown only in the east by the Chin people. The wood had a rich, dark reddish-brown finish. The slaves opened the front face of the boxes and inside were two golden thrones. One was smaller than the other.

Lioness heads, sculpted on the ends of the arm rests of the small chair, looked with fierce intensity at Mandane. They complimented the lion heads on the arms of the larger, matching chair. She was thrilled that Uncle Croesus had thought of her as a protecting lioness even before this visit.

The backrest of the larger throne had a large crown interlocked with a smaller crown and both were cast above a full-bodied lion. The crown figures had a simple cylindrical design. The decorations on the sides of the crowns were geometric. Croesus had avoided putting gems in the crown figures, although he almost added precious stones just to impress everyone. His own crown had gems. Mandane was pleased at how her uncle had intertwined the crowns above the Lion of Pars since it symbolized her joining with Cambyses.

The backrest of her chair had a picture of a palace positioned below mountains. She did not realize it was a replication of Anshan where she was to be queen.

Everyone in the room gasped. Mandane was stunned. "Why, Uncle Croesus, you have created my fame and glory already!"

He smile was expansive because he was quite pleased with himself. He knew no one could give her a present to compare with this.

For her everything was developing into a perfect wedding; all she needed now was confirmation that Cambyses was as satisfied as she was. She prayed to the goddess of love and fertility and the god of happiness that he was. She did not see Cambyses on the last two days before the wedding. The time of biding had come to an end. Their next meeting was to be the end of her bridal entrance procession. She held her breath when she thought of it. Mandane's heart stopped when she tried imagining their first moment of love making. Would her servants undress her, would Cambyses undress her? Would she go to Cambyses naked, or in a shift he would remove from her? All this would be revealed to her in these last two days. Queen Aryenis had promised to explain to her how the most intimate moment in Mandane's life would be her most precious memory when she grew old.

Mandane was resolved to make Cambyses a happy husband, a happy father and a happy king. She was determined to learn how to be his perfect wife. When other women came along as his concubines

Mandane quietly vowed to allow the choices Cambyses made seem naturally satisfying to her, for his sake. If she ever got jealous she vowed to hide it from her husband. He had promised her he would never take a second wife.

Mandane called for a scribe magus and told him to write on a lambskin the following, "Remember to be the lioness, not the peahen. Remember to be the crocus, not the rose."

She could hardly read at all but she was never to forget what her lambskin told her. When she looked at it later it would remind her that her uncle had advised her to protect and guide, not just be a figurehead of beauty. She decided she needed to be like the flowery source of saffron, so valuable to Pars, and not just a pretty, fragrant rose while wearing a coat of thorns. She hoped these sentiments might help stabilize her in her life as queen, anchoring her allegiance to Pars. She thought that if ever her deep-seated love of her king and country should be thrown into confusion or anger she could emerge from it with heartfelt familial love with the help of her lambskin.

9.

The day of the wedding finally arrived. All the gods of fire, earth, water and air came together for the king of Pars in an explosive clash of interests, infecting everybody with love, energy, sin, drunkenness, compassion, aggravation, sensitivity, patience, dishonesty, sorrow, gladness. Every man, woman and child in Ecbatana became enmeshed in celebrating with maximum exuberance and gaiety. It was almost impossible to walk the streets because a massive tangle of people clogged all the available outdoor space; no one remained indoors. For days the energy of the citizens had been surging with anticipation of the great wedding. Now it was permissible for every person to fling off all personal inhibitions as they joined with the singing, frolicking crowds.

Love conquered the day and love focused all its magical powers on the two betrothed; the swain and his beloved; the king and his new queen. Everyone else was there for the party, the melodrama, and the spectacle.

Early in the morning the minor kings assembled to begin a parade through the streets of the city. Median soldiers had to march before them clearing the way. The soldiers had to heave drunk, dancing folk off the road. Soldiers marched beside the minor kings with their accompanying retinues to keep ebullient peasants from clutching the kings, their mounts or their royal family members, who rode behind, all dressed in costumes of the region where they lived. It was pure delight in Media to see many-pointed hats, conical hats, flat hats with colorful veils, round hats with shields over the neck and front-veils to seductively cover the features of the females. Puffed sleeves, overlapping coats, waist sashes as wide as a man's foot is long, plus jewelry glistening in the brilliant sun entranced the viewers.

A few local camel riders from the city barged into the parade ensemble to ride with the kings. The crowds laughed at the antics of peasant camel herders cavorting with balancing tricks on the backs of their animals, while the camels rebelled with their own silly, angry dance of insubordination.

It was amazing how the minor kings were able to display their regional glamour and ethnic elegance when they had not come

70

intending to do so. Their tour of the city lasted beyond mid-day even though it had not been planned that way. The night before the minor kings had contrived to do some little thing of their own to keep King Astyages from stealing all the glory the next day. They wanted to set the excitement of the day with a spontaneous event, so epic stories could recall their magnificence in the hosting city too. They ordered their minions to prepare the animals and their accompanying royalty for the parade, which worked far better than they could have hoped. The show of unity gave everyone a sense of togetherness, delight in the unfamiliar, plus a feeling of empire.

When King Astyages heard of the parade already underway, he was angered at the insolence of his minor kings who were interfering with his own magnificent plans for the day. But as the day progressed his ministers reported the success the minor kings were having in helping to control the people and keep order in the streets so the Great King's wrath eased as he presumed their parade as a sign of reverence to himself. He decided the minor kings were wise enough to know they should do such a thing to help their sovereign. The minor kings were completely surprised too, but it pleased them to see how they had controlled the mayhem that might have developed into real riotous trouble in the streets. Later they congratulated each other with zest for their intuition. The minor kings compared themselves with merry good humor to clairvoyant magi.

The Great King looked lovingly at his wife and said, "Aryenis, is our daughter ready?"

"Oh yes, Astyages, she is nervous, but very anxious. We had a long talk yesterday about the marriage bed and she is impatient to get started," said the Queen as they laughed together talking in sweet remembrance of their own wedding bed.

Astyages had been observing Cambyses and his guards all the while he was in the capital. The Great King felt comfortable about his choice for a husband. The groom was calm, hard to upset and tended to negotiate rather than argue. The guards Cambyses had brought were rugged, but controlled. None had gotten drunk since they arrived. They were as careful as Cambyses was about conceding arguments to avoid upsetting belligerent rivals. Cambyses understood the difference between emphasizing important issues or just being manly. He could joke his way around controversy with ease.

71

Cambyses could pick out troublemakers then dodge their antagonism using diplomatic humor.

However, King Astyages noted that when the groom decided a topic was significant he was able to develop his argument with a strength that could convince and sway men who expressed contrary opinions. Cambyses could be persuasive when necessary. He seldom raised his voice and never trembled in fury. If his face turned red it was not from rage, but from embarrassment.

King Astyages, recalling his dreams, decided that no surging flood was going to swamp his precious Median Empire because of this man. Certainly no engulfing army from Pars was about to march against the King of Kings while Cambyses ruled there. Even though Mandane had been in the horrifying dream, all was safe for his empire now because Astyages had his daughter sequestered far away with a good man, a good husband who was a weak, minor king unable to create a rebellion.

King Astyages decided to ease up a little on taxing and pressuring Pars. He chose to let Pars fish the Great Sea to its west without paying the established tribute-per-boat to Media. The Parsians only had a few boats and fishermen anyway. Because of their small fleet, King Astyages wondered if Parsians were as afraid of vast bodies of water as he was. Zav had suggested the fishing tax, which Cambyses had questioned before the Great King. It did not sound unreasonable at the time so Astyages ordered it, but the amount of silver which fishing in Pars generated was not enough to half-fill a freestanding wine amphora. To Media that was nothing. As a wedding gift the King decided to cancel this tax to appear magnanimous. King Astyages smiled as he reflected on how being the Great King was so easy!

Queen Aryenis was dressed in a smooth hanging linen shift dyed with a rose pigment. It had gold thread with flower designed embroidery on every edge. She wore a purple sash with delicate, geometric designs in at least six different colors, and tassels of gold decorated the ends of the sash and hung to her knees. The Queen's black hair was allowed to hang straight to shoulder length. Her cheeks were made up with a sparing touch of violet rouge that was almost lapis colored. Around her eyes she had a different shade of violet to offset her dark eyes. The Queen's lips were crimson. The makeup consisted of fine ground pigments blended into fresh vegetable oils and soft wax. Poorer individuals might use animal oils for makeup and the heat of the day, plus body heat, made their oil stink.

Queen Aryenis reflected on how face painting in Media followed the Egyptian fashion where it had been the practice for eons. She liked the way it added attractiveness to the women, especially as they aged. The cheek paint obscured wrinkles and sags. Women loved it! Queen Aryenis wore dozens of very thin gold bangles on each arm that rose as high as the width of her hand. She also wore a gem-studded necklace that hung past her full bosom. It was the gift she received from King Astyages at their wedding ceremony. She hoped wearing it was a favorable omen for her daughter Mandane. The Queen had almost gone to a magus to ask if the necklace could have powers to impact her daughter's future. The more Queen Aryenis thought about it, the more she was afraid a priest might think that her notion was silly.

The Queen looked elegant beside the tall King Astyages garbed in a violet wool tunic that hung to the top of his knees. It was woven from special thin yarns spun just for him. The pigment was crushed lapis lazuli stone that was blended into cleaned, carded wool fibers from angora sheep that lived high in the mountains. The Great King's garment hung loose in soft undulations, not in sharp darts or pleats. The hem was higher on the right side than the left, giving the garment a stylish look. He wore no sash or belt. He wore no sword. Today the King of Kings exhibited his confidence in being safe in his own palace in spite of foreigners everywhere by not wearing a weapon. Absence of his sword was a symbol of his power. Normally, the gold sword he wore was his symbol of strength, even though the soft gold made the weapon a useless ornament. The King had a sturdier bronze sword he used in his audience room to personally strike victims when it suited his fancy.

King Astyages wore leather sandals, topped with red and green gems that came from beyond the Indus River, past the eastern edge of his kingdom. He wore matching gold bracelets on each wrist with his own image embossed on each one. The Great King's long black hair and full black beard were both combed and trimmed to perfection. He also had very thin black lines of charcoal in oil outlining his eyes that sharpened his facial features. He used this mixture because it washed off easier than the black made from walnut bark.

The Great King and his queen started off together to take their place at the head table in the nuptial courtyard after he decided everyone who had been invited should be there. The bride and groom were to arrive last. Upon entering the yard all the noise of joy the King and Queen had heard as they walked through the corridors of the palace stopped as a sign of reverence. Hundreds of people in the yard, regardless of their status, knelt on the ground stretched their arms above their head and bent touching their forehead to the soil. He glanced at the head table to see King Croesus was lounging but not bowing. With a casual sweep of his arm Astyages had them rise. He was careful to guide Aryenis away from the table of honor to pass through the crowd. He wanted to greet his subjects personally, asking if they had seen two or three people that he named. In this way he was able to identify the absence of people he had 'invited' to attend the wedding ceremony. He was not anxious to discharge cruel punishment on the missing today, but he would use them later as examples for discipline when he emphasized to the world how very important this event was for him.

In his stroll he commented to Queen Aryenis, "I see the trees are healthy, some have full, fragrant blossoms. The vegetables were growing nicely in robust clusters and rows. Your banners and streamers were colorful and gay."

She smiled as music filled the air without being too loud. Groups of guests sang together and seemed to be beguiled by their own talents. The King noted servants and slaves racing up and down aisles serving or cleaning with neat efficiency. The sun was shining without being too warm. He could see the long strips of shadow cast by the overhead cloth runners protecting the guests from the direct rays of the sun. He was pleased the wedding feast had started well.

In the middle of the court in the cleared entertainment area the King saw jugglers tossing and acrobats leaping with flawless dexterity. From every side bursts of laughter assaulted his ears. He smiled at the frivolity.

A jester wearing funny mismatched clothes and a skewed floppy cap advanced toward the King and Queen, carrying a gold tray with two gold cups on it. The clown stumbled in ridiculous skids staggering like a drunk. He even rolled on the ground in a somersault without spilling the contents of the cups. This brought laughter and hand clapping from the royal couple and the crowd. The jester bowed from the waist extending the tray before him. The royal couple each took a cup of red wine then Aryenis patted his arm in jovial gratitude. The King said, "What a pleasant day!"

Silliness prevailed everywhere. Food was served without stop. Breads of every grain were always on the tables. Fruits previously placed on tables were replaced with yogurts. Raw and cooked vegetables followed the yogurts. Several different rice dishes with exotic spices were served. Trays of candies and cakes followed the meats and fish. Then it started all over again. The smart guests did not drink or eat to excess at the beginning of the day. They spent their time socializing, sharing joy of the entertainment. The unwise ate or drank too much and were quick to become ill, even before the Great King and his Queen arrived, which King Astyages noted as a personal insult that must be punished later. He led his wife to the head table so she could lounge by her brother.

As the day progressed the sun rolled toward the horizon causing the crowd to begin murmuring for the start of the marriage ceremony. The women wanted to see what Mandane was wearing, how her hair was fixed. The minor kings wanted to see if Cambyses looked uneasy or trapped.

Finally the Chief Magus entered. He looked impressive in his sparkling white garment; his hair and beard had been cleaned for this public appearance. He was presiding over an official ritual. There was no evidence of ancient food or past meals in his hair or clothing. The Chief Magus did not smell; both his face and hands were clean. His toga hung in graceful ripples to his toes. The Magus wore leather sandals in good repair. There was no sash about his waist. He wore a peaked hat that he always donned during religious rites. The priest carried a branch that was a symbol of his priestly status. Around his neck was a silver chain from which hung a medallion. On the medallion were specific irregular forms that represented the unseen, formless gods of the water, earth, sky and fire. A small grotto in one corner of the courtyard, prepared by the magi, contained a Parsian sacred fire to show all those present that today was a spiritual day as well as a festive day.

The Chief Magus walked in short, solemn steps to the fishpond and faced the royal table. In the center were two empty chairs. On the right sat Astyages and the primary wife of Croesus. On the left sat Croesus with Queen Aryenis. The Magus knelt, extending his arms as he touched his forehead to the ground. It appeared as if even the gods had to bow to King Astyages in his kingdom.

The Chief Magus turned to the crowd, his back to the royal table and began to chant a holy poem. He begged the gods to bless the day as well as the people present. Specifically, his poetic plea begged the gods of love and fertility to protect the devotion of the couple being married. The holy prayer was not long but it seemed so, due to his toneless chanting, yet the Chief Magus was impressive as he commanded the full respect and attention of his audience.

Finally, Cambyses entered the large gate, making his way by the most direct route to stand before the Magus. The groom wore a simple yellow silk sheath that was loose fitting except where a colorful linen sash adorned his waist. Thongs that held his sandals were wrapped above his ankles and tied in a simple bow. No ornaments or engraving were set in the leather. His black hair and beard were trimmed, combed and curled in an elegant Parsian style. Cambyses wore no sword to show his trust at being protected in the presence of his future father-in-law. Around his neck the groom wore a linked-gold chain, shaped with unusual delicacy. A central gold ribbon, crisscrossed by thin filaments of gold rods, twisted into tiny roundels. The rods elevated and depressed the gold ribbon, giving it a shape that glittered brilliantly in the sun.

Cambyses looked confident, content. He marched forward with the smooth glide of an athlete. There was no swagger or brusqueness in his gait. He stood before the Magus firm and tall. He knelt in fitting fashion before the King of Kings then rose to wait for Mandane to make her entrance.

In an instant all the music stopped. It took a while for the guests to notice the absence of music, but eventually the crowd was quiet too. The hush created a very dramatic moment. A single lyre began to play a soft melodious tune. The audience began to look at each other in muted excitement. Mandane appeared to float through the large portal as if on a cloud. Her gait was smooth and feminine. She moved in a breathless calm. Her gorgeous rouged face shined above the perfection of her bleached white costume. A long flowing dress completely covering her legs was tailored to reach the tips of her toes.

The gown wafted in delicate, silent ruffling. One could barely see her jeweled sandals or colored toenails, which were painted red. The pomegranate pigment was held securely in place by dried tree resin. Mandane's black hair was swirled up to create a sort of crown on her head. The absence of hair around her face gave her a more radiant glow. A series of veils draped in uncluttered lightness from the gold Parsian tiara she wore. A single diaphanous veil spread across her face from her nose downward, but it hid nothing. The lips of the princess were ruby and her virginal smile was evident to everyone. Older women wondered if they had looked so perfect when they were wed. Her eyes glistened with happiness. Mandane carried a bouquet of crocus flowers to honor her groom and Pars. Cambyses smiled as if he was already her proud husband. Once she saw Cambyses she never looked anywhere else. Her trust in her own nascent, blushing love propelled her forward.

The actual ceremony that bound them in marriage was swift. The Chief Magus chanted poetic oaths and prayers in an overly loud drone. The Magus reminded them of their obligations to honor sacred fire, earth, water and sky. He challenged them to find comfort in each other in times of pain and difficulty. The Chief Magus declared them wed! Through it all the enraptured couple could not see anything on the face of the earth but each other. If eternal love could be established in a single instant, it was so for them.

As Cambyses guided Mandane around the pond and into the arc of flowers to their places in the center of the royal table he whispered, "I'm glad that is done."

Mandane murmured, "Me too, but I don't think I feel married yet."

She pulled his hand up to her bosom pressing it against herself. Her tiny hand squeezed his as if in desperate need for comfort. He enjoyed touching her warm, yielding cushion of flesh. Cambyses touched his lips to her ear sighing, "Tomorrow we'll both feel different. This night alone will change everything for us."

Mandane peeked at him from the corner of her eye and saw his simple smile. Something in her loins made her tremble. It exhilarated her. The roar of approval rushing from the crowd was deafening. Dozens of musical instruments began to play. People danced everywhere shouting congratulatory greetings to the newlyweds.

Zav had forced himself to return to the city to attend the ceremony. Although he smiled, deep-seated hatred smoldered in his chest when he marched before the royal table and said, "Sire, your highness, congratulations." Zav could say no more; his gesture was only to ensure the Great King saw that he was present. When Cambyses recognized Zav the groom almost leaped up, thinking of the dead girl. However, Cambyses got control of his negative emotions, smiled and nodded in benign disinterest. Cambyses could ignore this scoundrel today while enjoying the magic of his new wife. When Mandane saw the minister she was inwardly delighted that the unattractive minister had not become her husband; also she was so enthralled with her wedding that she did not recall the murder of her servant girl. Mandane smiled with sweet triumph at him and said, "Thank you for your kind greeting, Zav."

Hearing Mandane say his name made Zav quiver with fury as he raced away from the head table. His angry mood did not sour the enjoyment of anyone at the wedding.

The celebration, which was planned to go on for days, went long into the dark of night. People danced everywhere. As was the custom, men danced with men using steps that consisted of hops and skips. They did not glide or sway. Women danced with women, also hopping, skipping and twirling to the music. Torches were lit while food, wine, and music never stopped coming. There was one special excitement, which involved a dance in the center of the court.

Before this dance began, slaves entered the court carrying torches they placed in elevated holders bordering the center area. Other slaves extinguished about two-thirds of the lamps and torches throughout the entire assembly area. This cast a dark shadow over the guests, but brilliantly lit the center entertainment area. The noise turned quiet. A single drum beat a passive pulsing rhythm that hushed every other sound. A perfectly formed young man in a short skirt and flowing blouse, as white as the garment worn by the virginal Mandane, entered the center ring while stepping with delicate precision to match the beat of the drum. He walked the perimeter of the area once, stopped in a corner then turned to face the royal table. Then he turned again and faced the great gate entrance. A beautiful, petite young girl wearing a short, provocative, bleached white gown entered and sauntered to the center of the court to the pulsing beat of the drum.

She also moved in slow, short steps creating a sensual air while gliding toward the young man.

The two youths faced each other then began to circle one another in a chaste, non-touching dance. Arm movement, body movement, head and leg motion all kept time with the haunting drum sound. Graceful, fluid steps brought them tantalizingly close only to move them apart again. It was bewitching to see. Every eye was fixed on the dancing couple as if a magus had mystically shrouded the crowd in a spell. As the dance developed the virginal purity of the white apparel gave the suggestion of erotic nudity. Inexorably the pace of the drumbeat increased, as did the dance. A feeling of passion intensified in the crowd.

Men began to breathe fast and shallow. The women almost swooned in romantic delight. Everyone began to give off an erogenous heat. They were completely caught up in the moment as they watched the seductive flow of the girl's hair when it gently brushed the arm or face of the young man. The audience felt covered with a static tingle as when lightning strikes too close.

With one loud slam on the drum and a skillful leap, the girl flew at the young man! He caught her in his arms; he spun so they both faced the royal table. Magically her dress was transformed to a vibrant red color. Red streamers hung beneath her. Everyone understood the symbolic loss of virginity. A startled gasp rose in the yard at this dramatic climax.

Mandane looked at Cambyses. He was blushing. She was also, but his expression delighted her. A sob of pure joy caught in her throat.

Queen Aryenis signaled that it was now permissible for the bride and groom to leave and they did. A chorus of cheers accompanied them, as the dancing started anew.

Cambyses led Mandane by the hand to their wedding chamber. He waved off her maids and his servants. The groom had every intention of ensuring that this was to be their moment, unaccompanied, unshared and unforgotten.

In their room Cambyses and Mandane stood facing each other. He reached to remove the veil from her face. He put his arms around her brushing his beard against her cheek. He whispered into her ear, "I shall never be happier in my entire life as I am right now."

"Oh, I hope I can make you happier, Cambyses," she said with breathless passion.

He kissed her with soft, pliable lips. Gradually, the kiss became an urgency for them both. Cambyses began to remove her tiara and veils. He removed her clothes with slow, experienced hands. Mandane was grateful she only had to stand before him. She was afraid to move. As he removed her last garment he looked at her with wide, intense eyes. His gaze seemed to trace her every line and curve. He stared with heated desire at her upturned breasts, her perfect sloping thighs and her tiny waist and erotically sweeping hips. He was busy taking off his own garments. She was stunned at the sight of his manhood. She wanted to touch him, but she could not make herself move. Both were naked as Cambyses lifted his bride onto the bed, slid his hand over her breast; her nipple swelled at his touch. His hand glided with practiced ease down her stomach. His lips engulfed her nipple. His hand reached the puffy thatch that hooded her untried virginity. Muscles in her stomach and thighs convulsed with expectant delight. And thus began the love that was to spawn a magnificent future for Pars.

10.

The return to Anshan trekking over the mountains went well. Cambyses was concerned for the safety of his new wife on the rocky elevations with their steep risings and precipitous fallings. He had two special carriages constructed in Ecbatana. Each had a long, wide floor and walls just high enough for a person to sit comfortably. The wheels were large, solid wooden disks as thick as the length of a sword hilt, for strength. On the rolling edges were brass bands with solid metal nodules that bit into the ground to limit sliding and side slippage. Horses were harnessed to the front to pull and harnessed to the rear to slow downhill speeds. Cambyses had thought to use donkeys or even bulls to pull the carriages, but for controlling a heavy load on the mountain paths he wanted the strong, agile legs of horses.

The carriages had windows covered with thin, shaved sheets of mica that let in light while keeping out the bitter cold mountain wind. Several women and three eunuchs rode in one carriage during the day with Mandane to provide body warmth. A stove inside the carriage was too dangerous in a moving wagon on the mountain passes. At each meal an outdoor fire warmed the passengers.

The second carriage was the sleeping quarters for the king and queen. Its floor was covered with heavy wool rugs with patterns designed and woven by talented Parsian women. Goose down blankets plus large, puffy pillows were everywhere. Looking inside the cart for the first time one thought of having a comfortable sleep, but the newlyweds used the carriage for heated love play.

The passage in the mountains rose almost to the melting snow at times where it turned bitterly cold. The barren rocks and sheer stone walls were frigid, hard and uninviting. Sharp edged protuberances were capable of piercing the skin of passing animals if riders or guides were not careful with their mounts. Camels were selfish beasts fussy about comfort and with every new bruise or scratch they became harder to move or handle. The dusty dangerous trek was tiring. Cambyses was proud to note that his soldiers were almost as strong as the animals when it came to climbing or doing a day's work. The soldiers certainly had the will to struggle without complaint or giving up. Many of his soldiers were born in the mountains and expected hardship. The mountain men set the example for others as they all worked side-by-side pulling, heaving and tugging to advance through the unforgiving terrain one cubit at a time.

They progressed to within three days north of Susa, a major city in Pars, when they heard a commotion coming from a mountain gorge high above them. Looking up they saw nothing but stone. The hubbub could be heard as an echo, reverberating on the steep limestone walls. A strapping young warrior flew from his horse then began to scale the wall with the agility of a goat, grabbing overhangs, standing on almost nothing as he jammed his hands into holes above him to pulling himself up the rock face by his fists at incredible speed. Others followed. The warriors swarmed like voracious ants after a long sought victim.

Their thin leather skirts and thick jerkins with bronze buttons on large leather shoulder flaps were designed to protect the soldiers from arrows, swords and javelins. Now these sturdy garments warded off knife-sharp edges of rock. The bow and sheaf of arrows slung over the backs of the men did not interfere with their climb. The bronze sword that hung from the waist, with its scabbard tip tied to the thigh, did not impede the climb either. The soldiers seemed to fly up the wall!

Sagartian nomads had wandered too far into Pars raiding highland villages looking for food and plunder. The noise of the skirmish overhead had caught the attention of Cambyses' soldiers who pounced to protect their countrymen. It was a stalwart military reflex.

Mandane came out of her carriage to watch soldiers spread across the face of the mountain wall; they climbed with unspoken strategy. She had never seen such a sight, nor did she realize the degree of heroism that was being displayed. The Parsians began disappearing as they climbed to enter clefts in the rocks. The mountain men knew how to surround a band of pillagers to prevent their escape. The soldiers intended either to capture and enslave, or to kill every one in the group. Once in place the Parsian warriors shot arrows, as accurate as a hunting eagle, to pick off the Sagartians. The battle had the foreigners trapped between the village and the climbing archers. The fight ended swiftly. The villagers sent food and water down to the caravan as a gesture of thanks.

Early each evening Cambyses patrolled as his camp was being set up. Then he visited his wife so they could eat together. A soldier delivered supper to the sleeping carriage of the king and queen, unless it was so cold they had to sit by a fire. After the meal Cambyses left to inspect his camp once more, leaving no doubt in his mind that the campsite was secure. His soldiers reported their plans for the next day to him each evening. On an expedition such as this Cambyses took the role of a military leader in lieu of his king's role, preferring the close association with his men when he could act as one of them.

Cambyses and Mandane snuggled together every night in the cold reaches of the mountains under soft fluffy blankets. His touch always made her yearn for more. His lips on her breast made her shiver. Some nights she did not sleep at all as their lovemaking became more exciting in its variety. Frequently she encouraged him to duplicate a performance in spite of his weariness. And when she slept most of the next day her servant girls made sport of her in her slumber. Mandane began to feel that lovemaking with Cambyses in these mountains, in the midst of his soldiers, was like a drawstring, pulling the nation of Pars closer to her.

Cambyses knew he had to go into Susa to stay for a few days even though he preferred to go straight to Anshan without delay. Susa was the most important northern city in his kingdom. It was closest to Media where the major west-to-east caravan routes passed. In Susa his royal family was the principal focus of commerce in northern Pars as well as the delaying defense against military attacks which could come from the north and west. King Cambyses had to ensure that his rapport with his family was intact. Mandane needed rest as much as she needed to be introduced to the royal relatives who administered the welfare and protection in the northern extremity of his country.

Cambyses noted that Susa was still smaller than Anshan as his caravan entered the city. No clear pattern to the street layout was evident. It looked like the city was a web of camel trails. The king recalled that in ancient times the city naturally formed around such trails as hillsmen and valley dwellers moved about the area to trade and barter.

Mandane looked out of her carriage after ordering the windows to be uncovered. She saw that many homes were built of jagged, rough stones, having no evidence of smoothing or polishing. They looked as if rocks that fell off a canyon wall had been picked up and incorporated into buildings with no stone cutter's dressing at all. It was something Mandane expected to see in a mountain village, but not in a developing city.

She asked Cambyses about it. Cambyses grew pensive for a moment then answered, "Recall when I told you the earth is sacred, dear. We are obliged to use the rocks, boulders…whatever the gods wish to share with us, in the form that the stones are given. We use them as we find them, just as they fall from a cliff. When a rock is too large to move we can smash it into portable smaller pieces, but we never shape stones the way the Medians smooth them.

"We have made slight changes in our attitude over the ages. We do trim extremely sharp edges from rocks now. It makes brushing against a wall safer. Our small children are in less danger of being injured in the home. Also we build our homes with a modified technique now. Masons flatten the sides of stones that fit adjacent to one another. We used to just fill the gaps between unfinished stones with clay mortar. Now we use less mortar because the stones fit closer together, due to the smoother surfaces."

Cambyses asked his wife, "When you get a gift do you change its shape? Do you dent a cup because you only want it to hold a small amount of wine?"

Mandane decided to tease Cambyses and said, "Well, I have changed the shape and size of gifts. I altered this dress to fit me!"

Cambyses smiled and said, "Ah, a very feminine answer, your charm delights me, my dear, but our soil and rocks are special. They may be used to enhance the welfare of man. We can only use them for essential purposes. Plowing the soil to plant crops is acceptable interference of soil's integrity. On the other hand, knocking down or moving a pile of dirt or a stack of rocks just to make an area look different is an abomination against the gods. Moving rocks to improve the defense of a village is righteous, however."

Mandane challenged him by stating in an insightful manner, "But, Cambyses, to make a city like this one requires removing rocks."

The king said, "Maybe not so much removing stones as using them in the construction of a home, a barn or a defensive wall. Putting earth to work as a benefit to man is fine. Just moving it about is not right. It insults the gods who placed it here. Sacred rain from the precious sky is a gift that the cherished earth accepts. If too much rain moves the earth, we must leave the flooded soil where the water has pushed it. That is how we show respect to the gods."

Cambyses was very patient with her. Mandane was beginning to understand the Parsian religious beliefs, which pleased the king. He noted that his caravan had arrived at the interior of Susa where his relatives were expecting them. The royalty of Susa had already heard of the mountain village rescue so they rewarded his soldiers with a sumptuous feast. Protecting, giving, rewarding. These were inherent responses of how Parsians shared their bounty within tribes as well as between tribes.

The building where they stayed had adequate facilities to sleep, bathe, eat and socialize, but to Mandane it was hardly a palace. The family of King Cambyses was spread throughout the city in large, yet unpalacial dwellings. The prince who acted as their host owned a large, simple home. Several royal cousins and their families lived together.

The local princes asked Cambyses, "Sire, what is happening with the rice crop? Are we to sell it all to Pattmenidu or to Media? Are we forbidden to purchase rice from caravan merchants? Is that true?"

Cambyses explained the origin of the rice plan revealing Zav's part in the scheme. He told them, "That problem no longer exists. I want you to be cautious if Zav tries to force the issue. Also, if any new orders come from Media in general or from Zav be careful. Check with me before you agree to do anything that might have a negative impact on your business or Pars. You may conduct all your commerce as usual."

The princes were relieved and promised to warn him of future problems with Media.

Mandane enchanted the royal family in Susa. They loved her beauty and her soft consideration for strangers. If ever she sought allies in the future, she could find them in this city.

Some princes and princesses of Susa had traveled to Ecbatana living for short periods in the elegance of that beautiful city. They knew how rude their city must look to Mandane in this first visit, but the queen did not mention how different Susa was from what she was accustomed to. She made no disparaging comments about its smallness or its rougher living conditions. Mandane refrained from making her new relatives feel like second level kinsmen. Other Median royalty always treated the Parsians with dismissive rudeness in the capital city of the empire, but here the princes and princesses were grateful to Mandane; they appreciated her civility. After a few days stay Cambyses and Mandane moved on.

Only one dismal, dangerous day arose when a thunder and lightning storm with very high winds hit the mountain wall they were crossing. They were traveling high in the rocky peaks of Pars when the sun became masked by unexpected, gray-black storm clouds with the speed of a lightning flash. There was just enough room on the trail for the accompanying soldiers to unhitch the horses from Mandane's carriage before the horses had a chance to bolt in fright. The wheels of the carriage were secured with boulders. Soldiers surrounded the carriage to tie large hemp ropes to rings on the base of the carriage then around themselves. They were the anchors preventing Mandane from being thrown off the mountain by the high winds.

During the storm Mandane prayed out loud to help keep her servant girls calm. Praying also kept the queen's mind occupied. The enormous eunuchs were scared, but stunned at tiny Mandane's apparent composure. She prayed, "Oh majestic gods of the sky, please stop throwing gifts from the fire god to the earth god. Oh gods of water, please stop feeding the snowmelt that had already wet our trail. Dear gods of the sky, please stop sending the wind that shakes our carriage with such violence. You scare my friends."

Mandane was unaware of the danger to the soldiers whose lives, like the men themselves, were tied as moorings to her carriage. Had she seen the bravery of the soldiers, on her behalf, she most assuredly would have prayed for those men.

The storm raged for a full half day abating slowly, removing the danger. Except for numerous bruises on the soldiers no one was injured or killed. Cambyses had stayed outside to observe the degree to which the storm threatened his entire entourage, as well as his wife. Throughout the storm he moved up and down the column finding places for the men, horses and camels to huddle against the wall to secure the greatest safety. The king had his people place themselves between the mountain wall and the wagons that carried wedding gifts and supplies so they were protected from the chilling force of the wind.

The clay content of the soil turned the dusty, hard-packed ground into a slippery, slimy danger. Cambyses had to dismount to walk on foot with extreme care as the storm developed. He needed to protect the most precious part of his caravan, his new queen, his people and his animals. The goods the caravan carried could always be replaced or forgotten. Cambyses would even forsake the matching, golden thrones from Croesus for the safety of his people.

The king knew that if his highland tribes found valuable debris strewn over the mountain cliffs after a storm they would return it to him. The peasants of the mountains only kept materials from shattered goods that could not be repaired. They would return to him all the items that were intact, plus the items repaired by mountain craftsmen. They were honest. If nomads from other countries were to stumble on lost gifts then all was lost. It was fortunate that the storm passed without carts being flung from the cliff.

Mountain peasants saw his passing caravan from cliff tops and glades. They did not rush down mountain slopes to crowd around him, but their exuberant cheers expressed their loyalty to Cambyses and Mandane.

The travelers arrived in Anshan tired, dirty, hungry, ready for rest, but Anshan was ready for celebrating the arrival of their new queen. The citizens shouted, "King Cambyses is coming with our queen!"

Runners had been arriving from the hills for days, reporting almost cubit by cubit the progress made by the king's train. Exuberance almost described the feeling that filled the hearts of his citizens in Anshan. They bristled with love, energy and need for their king. They always felt more comfortable when he was home in his palace. His absence was like the separation of a family member.

Prince Bagindu, the king's cousin and close friend who lived in the palace, had difficulty controlling his own excitement as he organized a parade route lined with palace guards to protect Cambyses from being smothered by his adoring citizens. The prince marched a contingent of mounted warriors out into the lowlands to meet the royal caravan, because people were riding into the small hills outside Anshan trying to be the first the greet Cambyses and Mandane. Had King Astyages witnessed this he would have seriously considered executing Cambyses out of jealousy.

The soldiers Prince Bagindu sent out also included a contingent of powerful slaves who carried a gold, horseless, silk hooded sedan on long poles decorated with brass shoulder rests and brass filigree that had been made just for their new queen. Hanging silk curtains could be retracted or used to block the sun and dust of the road. A soft bed of goose down covered the inside for comfort. Puffy pillows, encased in gorgeous dyed linen and variegated tassels, let occupants of the sedan sit up to comfortably view the surroundings. In this instance the pillows propped up the king and queen so they could be seen.

In the sedan Mandane asked, "Cambyses, are you always greeted by this much noise?"

He smiled, "This is not for me. It's for you. In Pars we always make visiting beauty welcome, but you are not a visitor…this time we get to keep the beauty, which is you!"

She touched his dusty, sweaty beard with her hand in a loving caress and her gesture sent the crowd wild. She jerked away astonished while Cambyses beamed saying, "It's alright, you please them and that pleases me."

He took her hand in his and kissed it, which started the peasants screaming again. They both laughed. The king and queen were tired, weary of travelling, but they found pleasure in the welcoming procession.

Inside the palace Mandane was surprised at its small simplicity compared to her father's palace in Ecbatana. The columns holding up the ceilings were coarse surfaced, unfinished stone. The ceilings were only twice the height above the floors as the head of a tall man. Walls were made with the same unpolished texture. No furniture was placed about which served as a decoration; every item she saw seemed to have a purpose. If a table stood in a corridor alcove there were always chairs lining the walls, as if the alcove were an open business area. Statues were rare. Only a few wall-hung rugs were visible in corridors. Sconces for holding torches were plain and utilitarian.

Mandane was not offended or disappointed. The new queen had hardened herself to expect a serious change in living accommodations and here it was. Mandane knew she had to adjust to these surroundings and as long as Cambyses was near to give her help, she would make it her home and her country.

Queen Mandane was determined to take over the management of this palace, just as her mother did for her father. The queen decided she must begin by identifying the royal relatives that were responsible for overseeing each area of the *andarun* and talk with them first. Her starting points were to be food supplies, wine supplies, water supplies, then heating materials, in that order. Later she wanted to look into the fruit, vegetable, sheep and cattle farms owned by Cambyses. She had to become familiar with the slave and servant quarters and the kitchens. Mandane decided not to presume or demand too much at the outset. Asking the princesses how various sections of the *andarun* were controlled would be smarter than making demands so she did not appear to be domineering at the outset. It was not in her personality to be overbearing. Once she possessed the information she needed her inquiries could begin in the areas her mother said were the most common palace domains for the princes to steal from a king. She would make step-by-step changes, if necessary. Cambyses had told her not to expect dishonesty, just minor incidental problems.

Two enormous Nubian eunuchs appeared at Mandane's side to usher her into the *andarun* chambers. They were to be her protectors. Cambyses said to his hovering relatives, "After a bath and a nap I will be honored to present you to our new queen. Prince Bagindu, please clear the reception hall. I want something changed."

With that he took the prince aside explaining about the thrones from King Croesus. The prince was not to let anyone see the thrones until he and Mandane were seated on them.

Later that day after a rest and a light snack of fruit, pistachio nuts, and wine Cambyses and Mandane sat on their new thrones. Cambyses nodded to Prince Bagindu who waved to the guards to open the doors. Dozens of men, women and children rushed in creating a dull hubbub. In their haste they pushed and shoved each other to be first to bow to the king and queen. Stunned, the people in front skidded to a stop. The sight of the queen and their beloved king on the golden thrones, wearing garments of Pars, threw the crowd into silence. This picture of Cambyses and Mandane in matching outfits previously made in Media would later cause one prince to begin calling the king and queen the Mirza Twins. The royal residents could only stare at the lovely sight. Mandane overcame her uneasiness at this first introduction to the court of Anshan by saying in a soft tone, "Please, do not forget to pay homage to your king."

It was spoken with such a sweet voice that the princes looked at her with adoration while bowing toward her touching their foreheads to the floor. The princesses also bowed, but toward the king. The women saw the flash of light in the eyes of their husbands and cousins and knew Mandane was going to be a success with the males, but maybe not with the princesses.

During the course of the introductions Cambyses reached across to touch the arm or hand of Mandane several times; she did the same. Each touch pulsed with commitment and love between them. When the most elegantly dressed princes were introduced Cambyses stroked Mandane's arm. Mandane touched Cambyses when the loveliest princesses were introduced. They were feigning signs of jealousy. It became a delightful little game between them. When an exceptionally stunning princess, such as Princess Ispitamu, came forward Mandane squeezed the arm of Cambyses. This squeeze suggested an increased level of anxiety about the affect such beauty might have on the queen's lover. It was utter foolishness, but fun. With these little signals Cambyses and Mandane began to develop an unspoken, yet clear, communication scheme which they would use throughout their lives together.

Cambyses was pleased that the first introduction of his queen was a success. He was proud of how Mandane received this mob with quiet politeness. The king realized it would take time before Mandane got to know his family as individuals so Cambyses decided to invite small groups of relatives in the future to small, intimate dinners to help his wife make their acquaintance.

//

Princess Ispitamu was a cousin to Cambyses and on more than one occasion had been his nighttime bed partner. This tall, well-proportioned woman had deep olive skin that was a compliment to her rich black hair. Of all the princesses in the palace she was without doubt the most graceful and eye catching. Her facial features were flawless. She did not aspire to be queen but supported female relatives who did. For this reason she was offended that a Median non-relative was now the wife of her king. Princess Ispitamu decided that her task was to make the new queen as unwelcome and as uncomfortable as possible. If Mandane was going to take the wife-opportunity away from the female relatives of Cambyses, then someone had to take revenge.

Earlier when Princess Ispitamu observed the arrangements Prince Bagindu had made to establish the inner household she got involved immediately. She arranged for inept slaves to be assigned to the queen. These bumbling individuals would perturb the new queen in her unfamiliar palace while Princess Ispitamu kept Mandane from developing confidence in her new station as queen. Princess Ispitamu knew the servant and slave girls in the palace, which made it easy for her to choose the most clumsy, most unintelligent chamber help. She also picked a few attendants unable to speak any of the local languages.

On one occasion Prince Bagindu had entered the *andarun* to inspect the development of its arrangements. The only reason he was allowed to enter without invitation was because it was still being designed. He beckoned to a slave and said, "Move that table over there."

The slave girl just stared at him, then knelt and bowed. He commanded her again but she still just stared with a confused look on her face. The slave did not understand the Parsian language. Prince Bagindu turned to Princess Ispitamu commanding her, "Removed that slave from the queen's service."

The princess smiled and said, "Yes, Bagindu, I will take care of it."

The slave had remained assigned to Mandane's serving coterie. The princess intended to place herself very close to the queen to enjoy the show when problems arose. As Mandane's closest companion she would be asked to find the queen better servants. Princess Ispitamu already had replacement help available, just as lean-minded as the first group. She chose servers who would do nothing more than create fresh difficulty for the interloping queen.

91

11.

After an absence of over two full moon cycles Cambyses busied himself getting back to overseeing countrywide administrative activities. Mandane contented herself with accepting piles of gifts that arrived each day at the palace. She had fun with the princesses as they placed the gifts in the 'proper' places throughout the palace to accent the attractiveness of each item. She appreciated the way the nation had begun to greet her. She was also happy to solidify relationships with the princesses as they giggled in playful games to keep her from getting lost in the palace. Many of the women who wanted to hate her fell under Mandane's charming spell.

It was late springtime when business picked up as usual for Cambyses as a wide variety of important events developed. The confusion and randomness of kingly duties was an expected routine for Cambyses. Prince Bagindu and the dominant businessman, Pattmenidu, had kept operations from going astray while the king was away in Ecbatana being married. But the season had changed to the time for winter grains to be harvested. Grain storage bins had to be cleaned as old grain was sold. Cambyses contacted his relatives in Susa to coordinate the sale of winter crops of barley, emmer and oats to passing caravans.

In southern Pars fruit trees had blossomed, and trees would soon be ripe with apples, peaches and citrus. Cambyses had to validate that exchange contracts for the future harvest were still in effect and that merchants from different clans were still willing to do business with each other as agreements dictated. Cambyses had to reinforce the cohesiveness of family, clan and tribal communication to keep his people from drifting from each other for some petty reason.

King Cambyses sent trained soldiers on rounds to inspect his borders. The soldiers had to rescue villages and pasture land that had succumbed to serious levels of banditry or military invasion. The king's warriors took adequate armaments to pursue and slaughter invaders. The soldiers of Pars were reputed to be the fiercest fighters in the empire of Media. They were the most disciplined, most accurate bowmen on earth. Mounted on horse, camel or donkey a Parsian bowman could hit a mark on a tree from well over five hundred cubits away. Most warriors from other lands could not even string the bow of a Parsian warrior, let alone draw and shoot an arrow with one.

With the soldiers bringing a renewed peace the season became a time for festivals that brought national activities back into concert. Cattle and sheep stocks belonging to King Cambyses had already been released from their winter pens for herding into royal breeding pastures where animals also fattened themselves. It was not too early to anticipate sheep shearing or the selective slaughter of the older, less fertile cows.

Fields were plowed and seeded. Flowerbeds were planted. Crocus fields were started so the saffron spice crop was large enough to satisfy Pars, yet still provide plenty more for selling to the caravans. The crocus beds were many meydans long and wide. Farmers recognized a meydan was the distance a riderless horse galloped on his own before stopping. For gardeners this was a sensible measure that outlined a manageable space. The cubit was too short and the farsang was too distant a measure to be useful in defining a farm field, or a farm village.

In the mountains where small flat areas were suitable for a family to begin a village settlers made the outside protective rock wall of the village one meydan by one meydan square. Inside this area peasants then built homes, barns and animal pens. The fire altar, surrounded by a stream of sacred water, was always constructed first inside the barrier wall and dedicated to the beneficial heavenly spirits before homes were built. Parsians honored their gods. Every city, every village had a sacred fire burning at all times. Women made certain their cooking or heating fires in the home were lit from the sacred fire of the village. The central village fire altar had a magus or another attendee who had the responsibility to reconstitute the sacred fire to keep it burning. These central fires were always placed on altars of stone with a large rectangular base that rose up to a tapering rectangular peak several cubits high. A stream of clear, potable water flowed just below the level of the fire and fell into a cistern or well which the villagers were careful to keep clean because the whole village used this water for cooking and bathing. Their water came free and pure from generous holy spirits.

Home fires rekindled from the sacred one ensured conjunction with the spirits but also ensured unity within the community. Holy fire also tied them to King Cambyses who always honored their gods.

//

Cambyses chose to remain in his capital of Anshan all that summer. He delegated numerous duties to trusted princes who acted as his ministers traveling around the country keeping order. Since most of the minor kings of the Median Empire had been to Mandane's wedding ceremony not many foreign visitors came to Anshan. Cambyses' relatives who lived in Pars did visit Anshan. These people had to see this wondrous vision everyone chattered about so enthusiastically. Princes and princesses came ready to be enchanted, and they were.

Mandane began walking through the markets of Anshan to shop, as Cambyses had suggested during the time of their biding. A small cluster of eunuchs, servants and princesses of the palace always accompanied her. Sometimes she invited royal visitors to shop with her. After her excursions she enjoyed holding hands with Cambyses in private while she told him all that she had seen in the city. The queen loved sharing her adventures with her husband. Mandane could enthrall him with her excitement; frequently he would lean to kiss her cheek numerous times during her narrations. At first several military guards, plus her eunuchs went into the city with her to keep the mobs at bay. As time went by she became a more common sight; this permitted her to reduce her retinue while she enjoyed a safe saunter about the markets in the cooler parts of the day. When the queen saw a weaver or metal worker skilled with a unique style or pattern she ordered a magus to send a message to a cousin or two in Ecbatana describing the craftsmanship. Mandane always tried to help local Parsian tradesmen increase the range of their markets if it was possible for her to do so.

The very servants considered inept by the dazzling Princess Ispitamu, because they could not speak local languages, came in handy when Mandane could not talk to foreign tradesmen selling goods she found interesting. As the queen watched her girls haggle on her behalf in a strange tongue over prices she began to pick up snatches of their languages. This helped Mandane learn to talk with her own slaves and servants. Having come from such a cosmopolitan capital as her father's, Mandane was not naïve about languages. Foreign tongues were less of a challenge to the queen than they were for isolated Anshan princesses. Princess Ispitamu saw quickly that her game was not as inconvenient to Mandane as she had hoped so she schemed to revise her tactics to interfere with the queen's comfort.

Confusing events did occur in the *andarun* that delighted Ispitamu and met her expectations for embarrassing the new queen. One situation the princess enjoyed was the time a slave escorted a visiting princess from the south to the "seat of eliminations" instead of to lunch. On another occasion a slave girl had rushed a surgical magus, operating tools and all, into Mandane's reception room when the queen had asked for a dish of yogurt.

The most vicious trick Princess Ispitamu played on Mandane was a religious insult to all Parsians. Mandane had gotten ill. Nothing critical, but an upset stomach with accompanying nausea had persisted for two days. One of the princesses suggested giving the queen a draught of homa. This fermented drink made from a special plant, plus emmer, had several uses. It was a social drink; a medicine believed to have spiritual curing power and also a libation used at funeral ceremonies. The latter use required a sacred portion of homa, called *draonah*, to be set aside for male use only. Females were forbidden by religious restriction from consuming this special aliquot of homa.

Princess Ispitamu arranged to have a draught of *draonah* delivered secretly to the palace by a religious rite magus after she promised him sex. Intimate relations were a forbidden privilege between a royal princess and a priest. It was more a social restriction than a religious one, but Ispitamu did not care. She could keep it secret if the magus could. The princess hid her involvement in the acquisition of the sacred drink when it was delivered to the *andarun*.

Queen Mandane had the drink in her hands ready to swallow when one princess asked in innocent curiosity, "Where did this homa came from?"

Another said, "I saw a magus bring it to the palace. I was wondering why a priest delivered it."

Princess Ispitamu commanded, "It does not matter who delivered it. We must introduce our poor, sick queen to its healing power."

Mandane agreed saying in weak agony, "I'm tired of this misery. If spiritual help is in this cup as you claim then I am ready for its healing power."

Princess Ispitamu silently tensed at the pending disaster Mandane was about to create. The princess could almost taste the homa herself. She did not want to insult Cambyses, but she saw no better way to truly wreck the queen. As Mandane raised the cup to her lips one of the princesses standing nearby pulled the cup from her. Everyone gasped.

"You shall not drink of this, highness, until we know why a magus brought it," said the princess with a rebellious challenge. The magus was located and admitted into the reception room of the *andarun*. After confused questioning by the many royal women in the room, he lied as he said, "I brought sacred *draonah* by mistake."

He furtively glanced at Princess Ispitamu hoping for help. She ignored him. High pitched squeals leaped from every throat. The princesses all looked with new admiration at the heroine princess. The young girl could not have been more pleased with herself.

Princess Ispitamu was furious. She had almost succeeded in tricking the innocent queen to commit an unforgivable sin. Shame would have enveloped Mandane like soot from a pitch fire.

Mandane never complained about the troubles she encountered in the *andarun*. The inner household was her responsibility, and Queen Mandane frequently thought of the words of her Uncle Croesus she had paraphrased on her sheepskin, which told her to work hard at being queen. She chose to believe this included solving her own difficulties.

It is impossible to have problems in a palace without rumors getting to the king. Cambyses listened to some stories about the inner household; he was pleased that he never heard about them from his queen. The king never heard the *draonah* story. He would have been obligated to investigate the event and issue a royal order of execution if he had. Most assuredly, the deliberate complicity of the magus would have been revealed. The Chief Magus would have decided his fate. King Cambyses would have been obliged to execute palace residents involved in the deceit, namely Princess Ispitamu who violated a sacred trust. Princess Ispitamu had conducted an extreme act of folly. She was fortunate not to get caught.

//

Mandane discovered that a supplier of wine was cheating Prince Bagindu when she got into the details of how the palace was managed. The wine merchant had the Prince count the amphorae of wine in his cart each time he made a delivery before unloading the cart. The prince presumed all the wine went into the palace storage cellars. However, the wine merchant always tossed his large cloth over one-third of the wine containers during the delivery process. He made it look like a cloth bundle stuffed in the cart while he hid the containers. Mandane watched this man perform his deception on two occasions. The next time she made Prince Bagindu watch with her as another prince counted the amphorae. She asked, "Does he deliver the same number of filled wine containers as the empties that he removes?"

"Yes," said the prince.

"You never count the empty jugs he takes away?"

"No, highness."

Mandane asked, "Is this man a citizen of Pars?"

Prince Bagindu answered, "No, highness, he is a Babylonian. They produce better wine than our vineyards can. They have more rain and their soil is better."

The prince and the queen watched from a window as a prince came out, counted the containers on the cart, turned and left. Then the deliveryman covered several amphorae on the cart with his cloth. When the cart was reloaded with empties, the man simply pulled the rag over the empty amphorae and readied himself to leave with several full jugs of wine standing on the cart bed. Prince Bagindu was amazed. He never expected anyone to steal like this. The prince said, "I'm going to bring this Babylonian thief before Cambyses on Reconciling Day."

That day was the time when crimes or personal disputes were judged and settled by the king. Mandane asked, "What will happen to the wine merchant?"

The prince said with an air of menace, "He will at least lose a hand. He might be beheaded since the wine he steals belongs to the king."

She said, "Can you change wine merchants? Is there a Parsian who has access to Babylonian wine? We could even begin to drink our own wines. The palace probably won't notice the taste difference since we dilute our wine so much."

"But this criminal must be punished," said Prince Bagindu as he passed final judgement. Mandane made a demand of the prince with unusual decisiveness in her voice. She said, "Banish him from Pars as punishment."

"That is too lenient. It sets a bad example," but he did not press his disagree with her. Later with quiet efficiency he made the change as she suggested without involving the king. There were very few adjustments like this for Mandane to make because the general conduct of palace business was efficient and honest.

Mandane's citywide excursions caused her to ask Cambyses where their fish came from. She seldom saw fish in the market. What they ate was not the river kind that the queen was familiar with, nor were they the kind that came from the great sea north of her father's capital, which had the wonderful fish eggs.

Cambyses took his wife on a special trip to the great Erythraean Sea to the west to show her where these fish came from and let her view the western edge of her own kingdom. They stood side by side, holding hands, nuzzling each other, smelling the fresh, briny fragrance of the sea in the hot summer air. Mandane was impressed that the body of water before them was so large that one could not see the other side. In fact fishing boats could sail out of sight with their inverted triangle sails. She pecked her husband's cheek with a kiss of joy upon seeing the fishing dhows sailing on the water. Cambyses pressed her hand in his as a reflex response to her kiss.

Cambyses said, "My dear, we should not stay here too long because mosquitoes were thick in these marshlands along the coast. It is lucky we are wearing light-colored clothing because local fishermen tell my guards that mosquitoes prefer attacking people wearing dark colors."

At the shore of the Erythraean Sea Mandane said, "Fishing does not seem to be a significant industry for us," and she wrinkled her nose as she said, "and it must be uncomfortable to live in this heat and humidity."

Cambyses said, "Yes, we have two illnesses that are common here. Some people get fits of chills that make them shake for days at a time before the discomfort goes away. The fits always return, but our medical magi don't know what causes these episodes or how to cure them. The magi have observed, however, that at elevated terrain levels to the east, where it stays cooler longer this danger does not seem to exist.

"By the sea the illness is so debilitating that only the most committed fishermen chose to live near these marshes. Something here must cause the disease. Worm infections are another disease common in our marshes. I am told worms get inside people here and make them sick enough to die sometimes. The magi have no medicines to prevent that either."

King Cambyses continued, "We have stayed by the sea long enough. I want sons, many sons, and I do not want you to get these life-threatening illnesses, my dear."

They left for Anshan. Upon arrival in the capital the royal couple discovered that Governor Pagakanna of Babylon was visiting. Cambyses had Mandane sit on her throne beside him in the audience chamber to receive this politician. It was the queen's first official audience with a foreign dignitary but she controlled her excitement. Cambyses admired her regal demeanor when she sat on her throne. He appreciated how her presence complimented his importance. Mandane was dressed in a light green shift with a wide, pink sash. The sash was a routine garment worn by both men and women of rank. She reached across and glided one fingertip over the back of his hand. It was her signal meaning she was ready to support her husband in all things.

King Cambyses said in a kind voice, "Governor Pagakanna, we welcome you."

Pagakanna advanced and completed his bow of homage. "I come from King Nebuchadnezzar. My king sends his love and wishes of good health to you and your new bride. It will be my greatest pleasure to tell my king how striking you are, Queen Mandane. The gods are most kind to allow me to cast my eyes on your lovely countenance.

Please accept this gift as a token of joy Babylon wishes to share with you."

The governor placed a silver flower vase covered with gold filigree on the bottom step before her. A court guard picked it up inspecting it for safety, without appearing to do so. Then the guard held it before Mandane for her to see. Queen Mandane did not touch it but she smiled her benign gratitude and said, "Thank you, sir. Please give our kindest regards to King Nebuchadnezzar for his thoughtfulness. You are most kind to bring us such a precious gift. How beautifully it expresses Babylonian wealth and craftsmanship."

The visitor was obliged to give a gift to the visited. Pagakanna came prepared! The exchange of compliments continued as part of the common diplomatic practice. His experience helped him pretend his offering was a prearranged Babylonian wedding gift, but the governor had been in transit for many moon cycles not realizing Cambyses was a newlywed. Pagakanna discovered the marriage upon his arrival in Anshan, yet past dealings with royalty helped him pretend his king was aware of the wedding. King Nebuchadnezzar knew little of current events being away from Babylon involved in his war with Judah.

The governor was very hopeful of getting King Cambyses to assist Babylon in its war and he said, "In his greetings to you, King Cambyses, King Nebuchadnezzar wishes you to know that he compliments you on the grand reputation your army has in many lands. He knows you are at peace because it is your personal leadership that makes Pars such a powerful nation."

Cambyses answered, "Please tell your king his praise is gratifying. I am only a small sparrow in a flock of eagles when compared to his greatness."

Pagakanna said, "My king wishes you to accompany him on a great journey. He believes you are a most worthy companion for this venture. He is fighting to keep the Egyptian horde on its own barren sand dunes. The Syrians and Jews are rebelling against King Nebuchadnezzar.

"If he had the Lion of Pars at his side the Egyptians would stay at home quaking while the Syrians and Jews returned to peaceful acceptance of Babylonian control due to their fear of your warriors.

Your army would be a comfort to my king, Sire. Egypt and Babylon have been feuding over Syria and Judah for a long time."

Cambyses said, "Yes, I know."

Pagakanna continued, "Then you know, sire, that King Nebuchadnezzar won the last contest just a couple of sun cycles ago, but Pharaoh Necho is threatening to push back into Judah with a fresh army since we ran him out. The Egyptian is trying to induce Judah to revolt against Babylon by sending emissaries to stir up the Jews. King Nebuchadnezzar told me to recruit allies to help him against this new Egyptian challenge.

"I went to King Croesus in Lydia but he is not interested in our plight. If our borders are attacked he will help. His only concern is the safety of Babylon on the trade routes. He has ships he could send south to Judah where it is possible to trap the Jews and Egyptians between his soldiers and ours.

"Of course since King Croesus will not help, neither will King Astyages. But you, sire, have the most respected warriors in the world. They are known to be the world's best riders as well as legendary bowmen. Even I know the weakest Parsian soldier can toss a lance further than the average Babylonian."

With polite but firm words Cambyses turned him down. Mandane reached across to glide one finger over the back of her husband's hand, her sign of agreement; the king smiled at her.

The king said, "Prince Bagindu, please escort the governor out."

As they left Pagakanna muttered, "This is a serious insult to King Nebuchadnezzar. One day your King Cambyses is going to be sorry for this."

Prince Bagindu said, "I doubt it. Besides your Babylonians have defeated Pharaoh Necho by themselves in the past. Your army will pacify Judah and Syria again," but Prince Bagindu could not help thinking that he might be wrong.

Cambyses was again settled into being king after the trip to the western sea. Only now he intended to share his duties with his adorable wife. Mandane preferred to stay out of direct national business by waiting until they were alone before she helped him recall specific details when affairs of state got complex. She smoothed conflicts over petty matters that arose around him among his family members. Her commitment to Cambyses was so complete she willingly sacrificed her own needs for his.

12.

Prince Zatame came from Media in the autumn to see his friend Cambyses. The king was pleased to see the prince and Mandane had special rooms decorated with items she had purchased herself in the local markets just for him. She was so excited to have a visitor from home because she wanted to hear all the news of Ecbatana. She made Prince Zatame feel as if he were her favorite brother. Her attention flattered him.

"Your father is well. Your mother was ill for a short time, but the Chief Magus cured her. In addition to having severe headaches she couldn't always catch her breath. The Chief Magus sent her mind to a secret place where he discovered the Queen was upset because you were gone. She misses your gaiety. She says her life is somewhat ordinary without you. Queen Aryenis gets so wistful at times her handmaids worry about her. I believe she will get over her loneliness if you have a magus send her a message, Mandane. Tell her you miss her too. It will make her happy again."

"Thank you, Zatame. I must do that. I'll send one to father also. I miss them both. Cambyses keeps me so involved with the court and the *andarun* that I forget to take the time to send messages to mother and father."

As Cambyses touched her arm she gave him a funny, crooked smile. For a moment he was afraid she was going to cry. She had such a tender heart.

While casually strolling about the palace one day with Mandane, Prince Zatame noticed Princess Ispitamu. It was more than that. The instant he saw the princess he coveted her. Ispitamu had made certain that their paths crossed by placing herself so he could not miss seeing her. She had dressed in a bright lapis colored gown that had a sloping front that accentuated her cleavage. The wide sash was drawn tighter than usual, to stress her narrow waistline. Her shining black hair was piled in a spiraling twist. Although she was statuesque with her perfect posture, her hair made her look even more striking. The prince asked Mandane to have the Princess join them at the evening meal. Princess Ispitamu was in his presence and in his bed every night thereafter. The princess asked questions about Ecbatana, especially about Mandane's youth. Prince Zatame told the princess how snakes petrified Mandane. He also revealed that Mandane could not drink much wine without getting drunk and how she had always wanted to learn to ride a horse, but had never been allowed on one. This was useful information to Princes Ispitamu for her campaign of revenge against Mandane.

When Prince Zatame was alone with Cambyses and Mandane he reported, "Pharaoh Necho wants to drive King Nebuchadnezzar from Judah, and he seems to want King Nebuchadnezzar out of Syria also. King Astyages received a message from King Nebuchadnezzar accusing you of being insubordinate by refusing to help Babylon. The message stated that if you had shown proper respect for a higher king by doing your duty as a minor king, Babylon's effort to keep the peace in Judah would be easier. King Nebuchadnezzar says you need to be punished. The Babylonian requested the right to attack Pars after his battles with the Pharaoh and Judah were settled."

Prince Zatame cautioned Cambyses saying, "King Astyages at first announced his intention of allowing the Babylonians to attack Pars because you have not acted with the proper example of a minor king toward the Great King's allies. Military leaders in Media recommended against allowing Nebuchadnezzar to assault Pars.

"They asked, 'Why let Babylon invade a Median country?' and Astyages relented. As long as Babylon addressed Pars, you were in trouble, but when the generals said, 'Media' it caught Astyages off guard."

"Yes," said Cambyses, "the Great King will always protect himself as his foremost interest. You may tell him I said that if you believe it to be seditious. It is only the truth."

Mandane was instantly pulled between loyalty to her husband or her father and said, "Father has always put his minor kings at risk to set examples. He does not wish them evil, but it is how he instills discipline and control."

Zatame agreed, saying, "I have seen it many times, but here we are not speaking of treason. Our frank honesty keeps our discussion in perspective, Cambyses.

"As an alternative, King Astyages thought of allowing, even requesting, Greeks or Lydians to invade here. His affiliation with

King Croesus would modulate the severity of the attack but still ensure you were chastised while Media avoided involvement."

Mandane tried to explain her father by saying, "Father always thinks of alternatives. He prefers to choose the path of minimum effort on his part to avoid acting on complex problems whenever he can. Allowing King Nebuchadnezzar to attack would require father's involvement to control the magnitude of the war."

Cambyses smiled at her as he patted her arm. She was telling her husband a risk of attack was unlikely from King Nebuchadnezzar's perceived insult.

They decided to shift to more pleasant topics as Prince Zatame asked, "Are there any direct family connections between Princess Ispitamu and me? It would be nice if she was a cousin of mine. She would make a splendid in-family wife."

Unfortunately he finally concluded that as a Parsian she was an outsider to his family so he began to lose interest in her though she continued to meet him each night in his bed.

In shuffling through his belongings one day the prince came across a forgotten javelin blade he had brought with him. The prince thought of it as a curiosity more than an important weapon since he was a poor soldier. While showing it to Cambyses they noted the metal was iron, not bronze. Cambyses struck it with his sword, which marked his own blade.

"In Media do your soldiers have such iron to make weapons, Zatame?" asked Cambyses.

Zatame responded, "I don't think so. This came from the east by caravan with an accompanying lump of red ore. They were presented to the Great King. He is interested in finding such metal, but his metal craftsmen say they do not know how to process the ore to make a reliable weapon. Every time they process the ore to form a blade it comes out brittle and cracks easily. They have never made one as strong as this one."

Cambyses said, "I have heard of red ore in Utia to the southeast of us. Maybe I should have my metal workers get some to work with. If there is a way to make a blade this strong then they will figure it out for me. May I keep this?"

Prince Zatame said, "Sorry, Cambyses, but no. That javelin belongs to King Astyages. I only borrowed it… well I stole it, but just

105

long enough for you to see. I must return it when I go back to Ecbatana, or lose my head."

Cambyses said, "It is a powerful weapon to own, Zatame. A surface that will dull a bronze blade is a marvelous thing. I would love my sword to strike your lance with the force of a warrior's strike just to see how much better your stolen blade really is. But if I dented the javelin, it might cost you your head, and it is such a pretty head."

They laughed patting each other on the back like brothers. Later, Cambyses did send two metal workers with several soldiers to Utia to see if they could buy some of the red ore. The craftsmen were instructed to ask pertinent questions about purifying the ore to make implements. As it turned out the Parsians saw much ironwork in Utia, but no weapons. There were items like amphora stands, olive oil lamps, but mostly household implements. The price on these products was quite a bit higher than for comparable bronze ones, indicating to Cambyses' craftsmen that red ore processing must be expensive. The Utians were guarded about their methods of handling the ore. It was a valuable mongering secret worth a lot to them and their merchants who sold iron goods. The contingent from Pars did succeed in returning with a large amount of ore. The Utians had sold them the poorest quality ore available to discourage the Parsians from coming back. Cambyses did not demand that his metal workers solve their problems when they complained about the red ore.

Zatame suggested that they take Prince Bagindu to go hunting in the mountains. While they were gone Princess Ispitamu arranged with a groom in the stables to let the queen ride a horse. She wanted to apply her newfound information about Mandane to see if she could manage to get the queen injured. Not killed hopefully, just hurt. The groom thought it was forbidden to let females ride royal horses. No woman had ever ridden. The splendid Princess Ispitamu offered sex as his reward; he relented immediately. Also, the Princess said, "It is your queen's wish. You can't refuse her! After all, the queen can have, or do, anything she wishes."

The groom was intimidated by this claim, yet he knew only one model existed for the saddletree, forming the shape of the saddle. It required the rider to straddle the horse, gripping with the knees. Men learned from childhood to develop control of their seat and the horse with body strength. He questioned whether the queen would have the essential strength to control a horse.

Princess Ispitamu was unaware of these details that worked in her favor. The queen was naïve about them also. In the *andarun* the servants and the slaves got very excited about the prospect of the queen riding a horse. Princess Ispitamu ordered them to stop talking about the ride. The fewer number of people that knew before the ride the better. The princess did not want another failure like the one with the homa, where an alert princess took the cup away. One of the eunuchs heard about the plan and began to watch the activities of the queen with deliberate care. He was such a poor rider it let him understood the danger for the inexperienced. He was apprehensive about Mandane's safety. The eunuch was noble enough to be more concerned for the queen's neck than his own. When the eunuch saw the queen modeling a pair of balloon shaped trousers gathered at the ankles, he knew the ride was imminent. The eunuch found a military officer and revealed the gossip he had heard in the *andarun.* The officer paid covert attention to the route from the queen's chambers to the stables so he could not help seeing Mandane, if she went near the corral. When she and Princess Ispitamu entered the stables the officer was behind them, unseen. The soldier waited for the queen to make a full commitment to her folly before he intervened, just in case the queen changed her mind and declined to ride. A groom brought out a fine brown mare three sun cycles old. The horse was spry and raring to go. The groom positioned the horse near a gate the queen had climbed to ready herself to mount the saddled mare. While Mandane was still balancing on the gate the officer stepped forward.

"Your highness, you must not do this," he advised with polite caution.

The queen was startled. She gathered her wits saying, "I have seen many small boys do this. I believe I can ride if they can."

The soldier begged, "Please, your highness, wait until His Majesty returns. Allow him to help you if he wishes. He is a very skilled rider."

Mandane demanded, "Do you ride, sir?"

The officer answered, "Yes, your highness."

The queen ordered, "Then you will instruct me."

With brave determination the officer said, "I am sorry to refuse you, your highness, but I cannot. I must see to it that no one assists you until His Majesty is back. Please forgive me, madam."

Mandane relented and with the officer's polite assistance the queen climbed down from the gate. He instructed the groom to return the mare to its stall. The queen turned and left the stables. Princess Ispitamu was beside herself with frustration as she followed behind the queen. It was another defeat for her.

The hunting expedition had been sportive but not very productive. The two princes really just wanted to just get out of the city to breathe the country air. Cambyses did too. They almost cornered a bear, but none of them had the enthusiasm to put forth the effort required to take the bear without endangering themselves. They chased it, got it to rear up; then they left it alone. The hunters saw elk and predatory cats from a distance, but they did not pursue them either. The food the hunters ate consisted of hares or fowl that they shot.

They visited several mountain villages where peasants received them as guests, not royalty, but only after everyone had bowed, forehead to the ground, when they first set eyes upon King Cambyses. These visits were the king's way of renewing peasant loyalties. He asked about the military training of the local young men as he examined the quality of their weapons. Cambyses thought of the iron blade and speculated on how much his hill people could use such a weapon when these peasants had to contend with marauding nomads.

Being in the mountains was always a pleasure for Cambyses. It was getting cold with the approaching winter. In the areas where there were large fields, the king liked to check on the planting schedule for the winter grains. Winter grains were very important in the crop cycle. He called his visit a hunting trip but it was also a king's information gathering venture. Prince Bagindu made in-depth inquiries about fur, lumber and metal ore supplies intended for market in Anshan or the caravans north of Susa. It was data Pattmenidu the merchant needed.

No one had to ask the king if he wished to hunt a lion. They already knew that the Lion of Pars had made his kill as a young man. Every citizen of Pars knew it was required of royal males to go out alone and come back with a lion. Of course a young man could not carry the dead animal by himself. After his kill the prince had to seek the help of hill or mountain dwellers in getting the lion back. This immediately spread the word through the hills and mountains of the successful kill by the hunter.

The mountain people only helped if the weapons taken on the lion hunt were hand held. The bow and arrow were forbidden. A young man was too well trained at shooting arrows. The distance an arrow allowed between the hunter and his prey made the lion hunt a slaughter instead of a skillful kill. The hunter had to complete his catch with hand weapons. A javelin was acceptable provided the hunter did not toss the javelin. He could hold it before him when the lion charged. A sword, a dagger, or axe were also acceptable. Some young hunters used a net to ensnare the lion to reduce his feline quickness and the range of his movements. A thick heavy leather jerkin and a thick leather apron or skirt had to be worn to protect the hunter from the vicious power of a lion's paw swipe. It was rare for a young prince to be killed, but it happened sometimes. A careless slip, a fall, a clumsy defense during a charge, all these were reasons for a fatal loss. If hillsmen saw a young man being bested by a lion they never interfered. They always took the lion after he killed the hunter, however, to consume its power.

A victorious prince saved his lion skin as a personal trophy, but it was the skin of a leopard a prince wore in battle to look impressive. The king wore his leopard skin strung over his left shoulder, leaving the right arm free to draw and swing his sword. Cambyses wore his leopard skin when he went to war.

When the king and the two princes returned to the palace from their hunting excursion the officer explained the horse-riding incident to Prince Bagindu. He roared with laughter and rushed to tell Zatame and Cambyses. Cambyses did not appreciate the humor of the incident like the two princes did. He promoted the officer on the spot for his intelligent courage at refusing the command of his queen when it obviously was essential for her safety.

Cambyses ordered Prince Bagindu to locate a very old, very slow mare having the energy of a sloth. The king allowed his queen to ride in secret while he walked by her side, leading this rusty, old mare. No one observed Mandane riding, and the queen was never allowed to ride alone, only with Cambyses. The king did not know that by teaching Mandane to ride safely he was adding another insult to Princess Ispitamu.

109

After a very enjoyable stay Prince Zatame prepared to leave for Ecbatana, carrying Mandane's messages to her parents. The prince wanted to get home before winter hit the mountain passes so he made his departure.

The big event that truly excited everyone in Pars that winter was the pregnancy of the queen.

13.

Mandane knew it was the duty of a wife in Pars to bear many children. As a queen she had to produce the future successor to the throne. All the princesses said that her proper function in life was to have a son for many reasons. The family set the pattern for how royalty and peasants viewed the world. The concept of "them versus us" spread from the family group of husband, wife and children. This unit looked inward for support before considering assistance outside. Solidifying family relationships with children was the responsibility of every married couple.

The princesses instructed her in the traditions of family development by saying that once children grew up and began new families the central focus shifted from the old mother-and-father family to the new husband-and-wife family. Mandane knew nothing was written down for peasants, yet they passed on knowledge inside the family by telling stories. Only the great school of magi wrote to preserve historical information. Only the magi had direct access to that written record or could read a written record. The one minor exception was a handful of mercenaries who read, but their reading skill was limited to their business vocabulary, not historical data.

Mandane learned that anything known within the family had to be memorized. Rhymes and poetry were rhythmical expressions of information they found easy to remember, easy to recite. Every child of Pars was taught prayers or simple poems that any toddler could learn. The sentiments of the first learned prayers had to do with parents and immediate family. Cambyses had told Mandane that children were not taught to pray for themselves. Personal welfare came second to 'us'. Wishing or praying for the welfare of people outside the family was a remote concept as well, until the spread of the family grew large enough to create a village. Cambyses once recited a simple family prayer to Mandane:

Mother bears our children
Keep her healthy for our sake
Make the milk within her breast
Fresh and pure, to help us grow

Mandane was touched by the sentiment knowing it was a wish the gods could grant, because there was no 'me' or 'I' in the verse. As a cluster of families produced a village, prayers included the broader relationships asking for protection of 'us' against outsiders. The unity of the clan or the tribe always retained a cohesive, internal solidity. One poem she appreciated was:

Gods of every part of life
Protect our clan and tribe
Preserve our homes and land
From every outside threat
Grant peace among our loved ones
Give us strength against all others.

When Cambyses married Mandane some of his royal relatives thought he threatened the linear continuity of true Parsian stock. One prince, Prince Warohi of Susa, felt this way. He did not wish Cambyses and Mandane evil the way Princess Ispitamu did, however, he had his own ideas about preserving the ancient Aryan line. The prince wanted changes that prevented Mandane's male child from becoming the king of Pars and Zav wanted to reinforce his attitude. The minister did not go into Pars as far as Anshan. He was happy to avoid Cambyses for the time being. Zav also had enough of traveling over the mountains in snow and sleet. After stopping in Susa he planned to go west to Babylon to give his regards to Governor Pagakanna. He and the Babylonian had done business together for a long time augmenting their personal fortunes by the affiliation. Some of their dealings were honest. Some were not.

In Susa Zav spoke with Prince Warohi about commerce that was mutually important. Neither of them knew yet that Mandane was pregnant. She was still keeping that secret until she was absolutely certain. The minister and the prince talked in general terms of royal succession. Zav was careful to hide his true feelings about the king and queen, but he deliberately tried to upset Prince Warohi on the subject of succession to the throne. At first Zav asked, "Do you want the son of a Median princess to be your future king? To degrade your royal lineage?"

Prince Warohi answered, "No. I prefer pure Parsian ancestral connections. National purity demands the best for our kingship."

Zav made a subtle suggestion to influence Prince Warohi as the minister asked, "Help me remember, Prince Warohi, who is a suitable substitute as king to follow Cambyses, now that he has ended the proper connection with Aryan ancestry?"

The prince corrected him by saying, "Queen Mandane is Aryan, but not Parsian, and I am not certain who is the best successor to Cambyses. I have to get a magus to look into the bloodline records for that information. It is possible that several princes, including myself, might have the most appropriate family connections."

Zav was not above fomenting a revolution as he said, "You can take over. You'd make a very good king, Prince Warohi, just assume you're eligible."

The innocent Prince Warohi was concentrating on genealogy as he said, "For me to be king is not as important as restoring our lineage to a proper heritor. I sometimes wonder why the gods allowed this marriage to happen. Are we doing something in Pars that angers the holy spirits? Have the vulgar daeva begun to take over the earth and the sky, replacing good with evil? Our magi have said nothing. If magi receive divine messages decrying our shifts in piety, no magus has come forth to help us understand our mistakes."

Zav replied, "It is strange. I also ask why the gods are being so mean to you. I pray it will not spread to other segments of our kingdom."

Zav left it there. He knew the seed was planted. Zav could depend on Prince Warohi to think deeper about the situation and investigate while worrying himself about the future of Pars. Later the prince could be influenced to consider rebellion, or the murder of Mandane's child. Zav did not care who followed Cambyses as long as Mandane's son did not. Whatever the gods chose to do in the immediate future, Zav wanted to help them along in the direction he preferred. From Susa he moved on to Babylon.

//

In Anshan Mandane finally decided to tell Cambyses he was to be a father. She knew that later in her advanced state of pregnancy her intimacy with Cambyses had to stop. She regretted the thought of knowing how lonesome she would be for his touch. The gods left to

113

men, in sacred trust, the obligation of purity in marriage. Sexual contact late in the bearing time was an unclean act that polluted the woman, insulted the developing child and offended the gods. She knew sexual abstinence was a religious obligation.

Mandane put on warm clothing to protect herself from the cold winter drafts that slipped into the palace. She donned a light, dun colored, woolen shift over which Mandane wore a heavier angora coat that hung to her toes. The coat was woven from yarn dyed orange from the plum tree. The yellow collar and wide upturned cuffs were woven of yarns dyed by pomegranate rinds. The queen painted her face sparingly with light blue eye lines and pink cheek rouge. The blue came from eggplant skins. The pink was from a touch of beet color in a large quantity of olive oil. Now that she was certain of her pregnancy she worried about retaining her attractiveness to her husband, who complimented her so often about her beauty.

Cambyses was in a meeting with military men who had just returned from the south. The soldiers reported on minor problems with nomads from Utia. Invaders had burned a few farms while stealing animals and equipment. It was winter when hunting was made difficult when small animals hid in their burrows. Nomads found it easier to steal than hunt or work. The soldiers not only caught the vagabonds, but they located their camp capturing the men, women and children. The Parsian peasants had lost valuable grains, and farm implements had been burned. Goats, sheep and camels had been either stolen or slaughtered. The soldiers returned confiscated goods to the Parsian peasants. They also chained the hands and feet of the nomad captives and gave them as slaves to the peasants as recompense for their losses.

The soldiers convinced King Cambyses that the situation was not severe enough to warrant going to war. On their return to Anshan they reported that they had marched up the eastern border of Pars settling a few additional marauding problems. Again these were no more than policing troubles. The soldiers convinced Cambyses that Pars was at peace.

When Cambyses ended his meeting Mandane came into his audience chamber. Cambyses saw her radiant face and stood with excited devotion. He went to her to kiss her eyes, cheeks and mouth. She swooned in his embrace. His charm filled her with love. He placed his hand over her breast with a light touch where she felt her nipple respond by swelling beneath her shift. His gentle caress sent waves of thrills through her thighs. She pulled him closer pressing herself against his solid body. His male part thrust itself to her with its own urgency. Then Cambyses released her realizing this was the wrong place for such tender intimacy. Mandane's mind swirled in lightheaded desire. She felt him release her as she tried to cling a little longer, wanting his warmth to envelop her.

Mandane finally remembered the small, private lunch she had arranged for them and she said, "Follow me."

She led him to a tiny room overlooking a flower garden where the fig trees and olive trees stood leafless in the winter breezes. The flickering fireplace added heat to the room while heavy drapes blocked puffs of wind from the leaking windows. The room was cozy and warm. Olive oil lamps cast a romantic glow around the room. The low standing table was covered with food waiting to be eaten by hand. Blankets and pillows were fluffed about the table, lying on a velvety, thick, camel hair rug. The couple reclined on the pillows around the table then fed each other fruits and meats. Each teased the other with seductive, sensuous, lip-tickling portions.

Cambyses said, "My love, you are so clever at forcing me to act very unlike a king. I must relax my inclination to press my zeal for you," as he raised up on an elbow after caressing her; he moved away from Mandane slightly. She said, "My Sovereign, why stop what the gods intend? Your embrace has already opened the gate to my heart. Why delay invasion?"

He smiled at the lewd suggestion that had become common between them. They enjoyed trying to invent poetic, sexual phrases that should only pass between a husband and wife.

Cambyses said softly, "You make me tremble with need to devour you. But, why are we here, my love?"

Mandane said, "I have a special secret for you."

The king was intrigued and asked, "Ah, you will fill my day with a private confidence. Must I keep it secret?"

Mandane snickered and said, "If you can, you may. You will not be able to though, my darling."

115

C.J. Kirwin

Cambyses looked at his wife with a quizzical gaze and asked, "So, not only a secret, but a mystery I will feel compelled to share as well. Is it as sacred as the mysteries of a Great Magus?"

She laughed. "You are to have a prince of your own."

He lurched upright and knelt before her. "Is that true, my little crocus blossom? When? How long must we wait?"

"Slowly, dear, we still have many moon cycles. It will be late summer before your son puts you on the path to being an ancestor."

Cambyses chuckled, "I must make the announcement right away," and he started to rise.

Mandane took his hand in hers rubbing it with languorous ease, placing it on her stomach and asked, "Can we wait until tomorrow? I prefer that only you and I share our secret tonight."

They went to bed early that night sleeping little as they celebrated their good fortune with love. The next day Cambyses told Prince Bagindu to assemble the extended royal family in the palace in the largest audience chamber at mid-day. Everyone worried over whether it was good news or war. Several princesses were put out because they had intended to spend the day wandering about the markets. A few of the princes had intended to go horseback riding to hunt small game for sport. The inconvenience of the meeting made them grumble amongst themselves. As the royal relatives, servants and slaves crowded into the room Cambyses and Mandane were leaning towards each other head to head paying no attention to the assembling throng. The king and queen touched one another as much as possible without becoming intimately entwined. No one was able touch their foreheads to the floor no matter how hard they tried because of the crush of bodies stuffing themselves into the room.

Mandane had been able to keep her secret from even her personal attendants up till now. So this announcement was going to surprise everyone. Cambyses waved his hand to stop the whispering buzz. Speculation was interrupted by his signal. Prince Bagindu was jammed in beside Princess Ispitamu near half a dozen other cousins. If the prince wanted to move he would have to push someone aside, everyone was packed so close. Princess Ispitamu was annoyed because she could not position herself away from the crowd where all the eligible princes in the room could see her. She always envied the way Mandane was exhibited on her sparkling throne. It had been tailored to fit Mandane's size as if it were a gown. The queen carried herself with her usual regal grace looking so perfect beside Cambyses that it inflamed the irascible Princess Ispitamu.

Cambyses waited for every sound to cease. He then announced in a loud, sturdy tone, "We are pleased to inform you that Pars is to have an heir to the throne."

A thunderous applause shook the very stone walls of the room. Servants began to cry, princes cheered, princesses shrieked and Princess Ispitamu almost fainted. She caught hold of the arm of Prince Bagindu to hold herself from collapsing as her knees weakened. She had prayed for Mandane to be naturally barren. Now the princess needed to get out of this crowd; she must think of a way to end this pregnancy before the birth. Prince Bagindu misunderstood her touch, presuming the princess wanted to share this moment with him. He gazed at her with foggy, amused eyes, seeing nothing but his own inner joy.

Cambyses smiled with a grin as wide as the Choaspes River. He dismissed the mob so they could rush to the magi to send messages throughout the land. The king had already ordered the Chief Magus to send a messenger to Ecbatana to inform the King of Kings and his Queen of their daughter's happy condition. Cambyses had intended to have the Chief Magus conduct a small rite to pray for a safe, successful birth, but the exultant chaos changed his mind. His most significant duty now was to protect the health of his wife for the sake of his son.

14.

In Babylon Governor Pagakanna had continued to develop the Hanging Gardens that the king had ordered for his queen. Zav was astonished at the magnitude of the project. His eyes scanned the gardens built on terraces with walls of sundried brick. Stairs and ramps led to higher terraces so visitors could stroll about on various levels of elevation. The view of the gardens on entering Babylon was stunning! The magnitude of the project was unbelievable. Outside the walls blue ceramic decorations over the arches of the gates had greeted him.

He noted how the gardens were placed at the end of the city closest to the Euphrates River. The river, the outside wall and the mounds of earth in the gardens provided a thick bulwark of protection to that sector of Babylon. The base of the gardens was nearly half a farsang in all directions. Zav could not discern the color of the flowers at the other extremity of the garden they were so far away. The terraces were not built on a natural hill; they were completely man-made constructions. The tiers reached higher than any human-built structure Zav had ever seen. The earliest spring flowers draped over the edge of each level in bundles of blossoms. Each landing was accented by fruit trees blossoms or flowering vines of all colors. Benches were spread throughout every balcony so visitors could sit in small garden areas to rest, contemplate or talk. The gardens were a perfect place for Zav and Governor Pagakanna to sit to have a business discussion.

Zav's eyes traced sand and gravel paths that wound over the terrain of each balcony. He said, "I count four terrace levels."

Pagakanna said, "At least seven tiers will be built, maybe more."

In his enthusiasm, Zav promised, "I will send you crocus plants from Pars and trees with delectable tasting figs from Media as a present from the Great King."

Up till now Zav had never been able to get Pattmenidu of Pars to sell him any crocus plants or bulbs. Pattmenidu used the excuse that the crocus was indigenous only to Pars. The merchant claimed that crocuses were too fragile to grow elsewhere. Pattmenidu did not know if that was true, but he liked to believe it might be. It was not a

Parsian lie, just a presumption. Zav did not understand plants so he did not question this 'speculation'.

Pagakanna changed the conversation by saying, "The war over the influence of Pharaoh Necho in Judah is not going well for King Nebuchadnezzar. Our Babylon warriors have been driven out by the Jews into Syria by a very determined army."

Zav asked, "Do the Egyptians continue to supply the Judeans? I wonder if Egyptian merchant ships deliver supplies across the sea to the coast of Judah. The Egyptians were successful with this strategy before."

Pagakanna said, "Yes, and King Nebuchadnezzar has Syrian merchant ships but he does not know how to use them well. Naval warfare is a stranger to him. King Nebuchadnezzar only understands land operations."

He continued, "In Syria a Jewish land force, not as belligerent as the force in Judah, supports the war of Judah. It appeared that together these forces are defeating us by driving our army deep into Syria almost to ancient Chaldean boundaries."

After a thoughtful silence the governor said, "King Cambyses refused to help us and King Astyages won't let King Nebuchadnezzar attack Pars after the war with Judah is over. However, King Astyages suggested he might allow Greeks or Lydian, under King Croesus, make the attack on behalf of Babylon."

Zav said, "Yes, I heard that in Media."

He was pleased this possibility was still an active story. He left Babylon very happy.

The minister returned to Susa again intending to tell Prince Warohi of the Lydian danger to Pars. As he veered south away from Ecbatana he felt enough time had passed for Prince Warohi to come to a conclusion about revolution. Zav was determined to reinforce discontent. Zav intended to taunt the prince with suggestions of insurrection. Zav invited the prince for a private conversation at a secluded eating hall he was familiar with. Zav believed the place was a safe place to discuss any topic. Zav relished insulting peasants or lowly merchants when it suited him. Zav greeted the proprietor, "Rice Rodent, we wish to be served your finest meal. And keep your thumbs out of our food."

Even Parsians addressed the owner by that name. However, he was able to ignore Zav's uncomplimentary remark about putting his fingers in the food. He smiled and said, "It is my humble privilege to serve you, sir. Come this way to my most private room."

The proprietor showered them with compliments he knew Zav enjoyed hearing over and over. Serving a meal to Zav was so profitable it kept the proprietor's hatred of Zav in check. The Rice Rodent led them to a small rocky cave with a curtain over the entrance, giving the allusion of privacy. Olive oil lamps lit the room. On the ground rugs covered the dirt floor. The air in this underground cavity was cool and dry. Pillows surrounded a low, ornate table. The two men reclined in luxurious comfort as they began to snack.

The Rice Rodent did not personally serve in this room. The wall contained a hard-to-detect cleft, which cut through to another small cave. This was where the Rice Rodent hid listening to private conversations. The proprietor had become wealthy after listening at this secret place to Zav's business plans by selling details of Zav's business transactions to Pattmenidu the merchant from Anshan.

When the Rice Rodent left them Zav opened the conversation by asking, "Well, Prince Warohi, have you given more thought to overthrowing Cambyses?"

The Rice Rodent shivered with fear on his secret side of the rock wall. Prince Warohi answered without hesitation, "I cannot even consider such a thing. After thinking of your suggestion I completely discounted it. Cambyses is my cousin, my king, and for me to go to war against him is a severe dishonor to our Pasargadae tribe. In all our history there is not a single story of intratribal warfare that went so far as to unseat a king. No Achaemenean king has ever had to suffer the insult of personal revolt from his own family. I could never do it."

Zav was disappointed but not defeated. The minister tried to sound encouraging as he said, "Yes, but now the situation is different than ever before. You will begin to dilute the Parsian royal line because his wife is a Median. Does that not make you hate him?"

The prince said, "No, I don't hate him. At least half the blood of his son will be our blood. Maybe that will be enough. And if his son marries a Parsian woman then those sons will be more Parsian than the father. With time full noble blood may be restored to our kings. Besides his wife is with child now."

Zav jolted up from his reclining position choking on the piece of fig he was chewing.

Prince Warohi continued on, "I did have a magus check the line of inheritance. I'm one possible prince who could succeed Cambyses should anything happen to him. But I'm his relative, a leader of his administration and an officer in his army. I'm loyal to him."

Zav saw the moment to shake this commitment. He said, "Babylon wants to attack Pars now that their Judean war goes against them because Cambyses will not support King Nebuchadnezzar. King Astyages might let King Croesus attack Pars. It appears that war is inevitable for you. Susa is the first stronghold in northern Pars. You could yield it to the Babylonians or the Greeks with negotiations for your own succession as king."

The Rice Rodent had been relaxing a bit when Prince Warohi made his pretty speech about loyalty to King Cambyses. Now the prince was silent, and the Rice Rodent tensed again.

Zav qualified himself by saying, "Well, there is no need for you to commit yourself to me. I have nothing to do with this. Think about it for yourself. Let's eat. By the way tell me more of the pregnancy of the queen."

Their talk became general, and the Rice Rodent went on with conducting his business. He had to tell Pattmenidu about Zav and Prince Warohi at the first opportunity.

//

In Anshan Princess Ispitamu, still shaken by the news of the pregnancy, went to a magus to talk about medicines. She did not desire something to calm herself; her need was more insidious. She asked the medical magus, "Do medicines exist that protect people from poisons?"

She was coy about talking around the subject that interested her most by appearing to want curative information. She said, "I have heard of a honey that can be dangerous to people. If bees make honey exclusively from oleander flowers, the honey causes the same illness that the oleander poison itself causes. I think it troubles the beating in the chest. Is there a medicine to prevent it?"

This sounded to her like a food that might be ideal, but the princess had no idea about where to get such a product. How could one make bees buzz the oleander and leave every other flower alone? It sounded impossible.

The magus said, "You are correct, but no one I know of has ever been able to harvest such a honey intentionally. We also have no medicine to prevent the problems that arise when someone accidentally encounters such a honey."

She began to bring up illnesses for discussion that led her to pregnancy issues. The magus said. "Silphium both prevents pregnancy as well as it stops an existing pregnancy."

The princess found this to be too good to be true. She asked, "Are medicines available to stop silphium from acting?"

The magus said, "No. Vomiting after eating it helps occasionally."

Princess Ispitamu asked, "Is this silphium available?"

The magus said, "Only medical magi have access to it in Pars. It is very expensive because it comes by sea from far away, west of Egypt."

If Ispitamu could get this substance she could not only abort Mandane's pregnancy, the princess could prevent future pregnancies. What a wonderful material it must be. Princess Ispitamu left the magus very pleased with herself. The magus was pleased that the princess gave him a few pieces of silver plus a stone token valuable enough to purchase a ram.

//

People in the palace began to act silly over the queen's pregnancy. The princesses tried to keep Mandane from walking too much. They tried to prevent her from climbing stairs. Servants did not let her carry anything. They forced the queen to don too many clothes to ensure she never got chilled, which kept Mandane slick with sweat. Slaves built fires in the middle of the room when Mandane bathed. Making the queen choke on smoke was better than letting her catch a cold.

Cambyses almost tried to carry her up the three stairs to her throne. Mandane was so pampered that she got a little testy at times. She wanted to be left alone; the queen yearned for privacy. Doing nothing was boring for her. Mandane demanded to go walking through the markets and she insisted that Cambyses allow her to ride the mare, at least for a few minutes each week. She truly enjoyed the latter activity. Mandane thought her riding ability was really improving, and she was disappointed when Cambyses refused to let go of the horse's halter. As soon as her belly began to swell the king refused to allow her to ride any more. Cambyses promised to give her much more riding exercise after the birth. That placated her a little.

When spring came weddings were planned everywhere. A couple of princesses married their cousins. One widowed aunt married her nephew. Everyone grew active and fresh in the sunlight. The days got longer and planting began in flowerbeds in the palace. Vegetables were interspersed among the fruit or nut trees with maximum efficiency. Herbs were planted near the kitchen entrance. In the hills the animals were driven from their winter pens into the pastures set aside for them. Other fields were reserved for planting grains and vegetables.

All types of nut trees had been pruned although walnut and pistachio trees were the most common. Orchards of apple, pomegranate, plum, fig and date trees began to blossom. Everything began to look alive and healthy. Springtime festivals were held everywhere. Dancing and singing could be enjoyed almost every day. Young children who had been taught to play a musical instrument, like a lyre, a harp or one of the reeds or whistles, made their first public performances in the spring, and the children were so proud that they almost played well. The aspiring musicians were always cheered on by the immediate family as well as by the extended family residing near by.

Zav was in Ecbatana conducting his normal duties when he decided to travel to Anshan. He stopped in Susa to see Prince Warohi but nothing had changed with the prince's attitude. The prince had decided he could not rebel against Cambyses. In Anshan it was impossible for Zav to arrive without being noticed. He set himself up in a very comfortable set of rooms in the palace without asking. He had a view of the rolling pastures that ran right up to the forest that grew at the base of the steepest snow-capped slopes. Mountain snowmelt drained to the forest in cascading waterfalls. It was a very attractive sight.

Zav told Prince Bagindu he wanted an audience with Cambyses. The prince asked him if there was any special topic to be discussed. Zav told the prince there was to be an increase in the royal tribute paid by Pars. Zav did not tell him it was going to double, that piece of news he saved for himself to tell King Cambyses.

Cambyses told Mandane that Zav had arrived. She began to tremble and whispered, "Please send him away."

She became overwhelmed by the memory of her murdered servant girl. She dropped her head to weep. Cambyses knelt before her taking her in his arms. He whispered hushed tones to comfort her. The king did not let her go until she had stopped crying. He lifted her chin and said, "It is times like this that make you a queen, my dear. You must forget the past and live with today. You and I together will face this man. Zav is no danger to us. Today you and I will win our ascendancy over Zav forever. Do you believe me, Mandane?"

As Mandane looked into his eyes she recognized his commitment to be completely honest with her in all things. She had seen this look many times before, and she had come to trust it. She whispered, "Yes, Cambyses," as she leaned against her husband.

When Mandane and Cambyses sat in their golden thrones they looked as if they commanded the world. All of Pars knew of the special thrones, especially how beautiful their king and queen were when seated on them. This mental picture was growing into a legend as the most fabulous image ever in the history of the Achaeminid dynasty. Today Cambyses ordered the chair of Zav to be placed to his right, not in the center of the room. This was a deliberate insult to Zav, and the entire court knew it. The chosen chair was also too heavy for one man to lift, so Zav could not place it where he wanted once he spotted its rude location. Cambyses had Mandane on his left. He had placed himself between the queen and the vermin as symbolic protection for his queen. She squeezed his arm with grateful appreciation when she realized what her husband had done.

Zav made his obligatory bow. It galled him to have to prostrate himself before such a paltry king. He tried to keep his anger under control when he had to sit off-center in the room. Zav recognized the insult. Several princes and princesses rushed into the audience room when the story of the chair circulated in the palace. It pleased them that King Cambyses had the courage to insult this most unpopular minister of the Great King so openly.

King Cambyses said, "We welcome you to Anshan, Zav. We hope you will give our kindest and most respectful greetings to the Great King."

Zav said, "Thank you, sire. I bring you the greetings of King Astyages and Queen Aryenis. They are very pleased at the message that your queen is pregnant."

Cambyses smiled and said, "It is our happiest news. We will have a son!"

Zav presented his compulsory gift to the king. Zav said, "This is offered as the first sword of your future heir, sire."

It was a small dagger made of bronze. However, it was more tin than bronze with very plain decorations. It was unworthy of a royal prince. All in attendance recognized it as a cheap toy found in any market. Zav felt he had exchanged with equal measure insult for insult. It made him feel warm.

Cambyses smiled struggling to be polite, "Thank you, Zav. Is there a special reason for your visit? You seldom come to Pars for the social life in our quiet kingdom. You have such important errands to run for the Great King we hate to delay you."

Cambyses knew how to exchange insult for insult if necessary. He was making Zav sound like a common message runner, but Zav knew he had the ultimate victory coming. The minister said, "The Great King has chosen to increase the annual tribute from Pars. It will be doubled this year!"

Zav was very satisfied with the gasps he heard from the princes and princesses who had to bear the greatest portion of this expense. He forced a grin to hide his malice. Then Zav noticed that Cambyses did not react with surprise or anger. The minor king appeared almost disinterested. Cambyses asked in a subdued tone, "Are you certain the Great King wants to put this burden on his only daughter? Are you sure this tax is not just a symbol of your own greed?"

Zav stirred in his seat, because he had not expected this type of response. He was prepared for fury, confusion or capitulation. A calm retort that challenged was too much from this fake king. Zav kept his calm and asserted, "Say what you will, sire, but the tax will be assessed."

"Zav, this tax will never be paid," Cambyses stated without wavering.

Zav almost jump from his seat with joy. Cambyses was trapped! In his excitement he said, "Sire, such a statement is treason. To refuse tribute to King Astyages makes you his enemy."

After saying that Zav realized he was in jeopardy if Cambyses was determined to make himself an enemy of Media. King Cambyses could keep him prisoner since it was customary to imprison emissaries from one's enemies. Surprisingly, things had turned on Zav.

Cambyses growled, "Have you forgotten the green cape and hood? If you remember them you may leave, now! Do not return to Anshan."

Mandane reached over and stroked the back of his hand with one finger, acknowledging her support for what her husband had just said. Her gesture was also her thanks to Cambyses. She fought to keep her face calmly emotionless as she visualized the writing of her lambskin in her disturbed mind. It reminded her to be a lioness not a peahen. She had to protect Pars and her husband the way a lioness protected the pride.

A look of dread fell over Zav's face. He turned as white as a mountain ram. Mandane was happy to see the change in his countenance. She stared at Zav as her face tensed. The queen's eyes were hard, revealing nothing but her righteous resolve to exude authority, the lioness prevailed.

The audience around the room was confused by this reference to a cape and hood. What could it mean? Why was Zav trembling? Clearly Cambyses had won the exchange of insults, but the audience wondered how?

Zav knew no one could have seen him kill the servant girl in the cellar. He was alone in the cellar with her. But now Zav understood at least a little of why no rumor of the murder had buzzed throughout the court in Ecbatana. Somehow, Cambyses had learned of Zav's complicity and gotten involved. Mandane had too. As impossible as it seemed to Zav it had happened. The king and queen stared at him with unwavering eye contact seeming to peer straight into his evil heart. Zav stumbled to his feet to stagger from the court crushed, defeated, and confused. He felt as if he might never get over this.

Princess Ispitamu rushed out to follow Zav to his rooms. She said, "Zav, here, take this message. Can you get me any of the material described on this sheepskin? It is called silphium."

The minister did not look at her; he just reached out his arm to grab the message then push her away as he said, "Leave me alone. Go away!"

He did not hear what she said. His eyes were so clouded by confused anger that he did not recognize her, even though he knew her well. In his rooms all he could do was grab a cup of wine, order his servants to prepare to leave immediately as he collapsed into a hypnotic trance of total failure. Princess Ispitamu was so stunned by his reaction she worried immediately about their affiliation. Zav was her only hope for acquiring the silphium, and she feared he might never have the presence of mind to know the message came from her. She had been afraid to have the magus sign her name to the note in case it got intercepted somehow.

Back in the audience room, Cambyses stood before his throne extending his hand to Mandane. She took it with smooth grace as they left the chamber under a cloud of mystery. In a small, private room Mandane finally gave in to her feeling of tension. She closed her eyes and released a deep, anguished groan.

Cambyses leaned, kissed her cheek and said, "Today you became a true queen, my darling. You held your passions in check without wavering during that tense meanness. When Zav reflects back on today even he will be impressed with your strength. You were a queen, my darling, not just a woman. I am proud of you, my sweet."

Mandane opened her eyes to look at him, admiring how he had kept his calm while speaking with firm, modulated tones to Zav. He had referred to the worst moment in her life, the finding of the dead servant, as if it were just another piece of business. But it was business that gave Cambyses the upper hand over their enemy. She could not tell whether she wanted to cry, or just sleep for a while; she was so exhausted. The strain of not breaking down had depleted her strength.

She wobbled toward a couch, pushed some of its many pillows aside and collapsed onto it. He walked over, knelt and said, "My darling, with you beside me today I was able to say precisely what was needed. Did I say too much? Did I reveal too much?"

Mandane said, "No. You gave him the hint of your clue to his murder, no more. I do not believe the assembled courtiers understood the implications of your comments. I saw how they were stunned by Zav's reaction. He was crushed."

Cambyses said, "Well, we will never go through a scene like that with him again. It will be surprising if he ever comes back. He knows we are aware of something, but he is not sure of how much. If he had intended to kill you he believes we know it. He will fear us forever. He'll have trouble playing tricks on us again. You were so marvelous out there."

As the king leaned over her his beard rested on her neck when he pressed his cheek against hers. She touched the back of his head with a gentle caress, drawing him tighter to her. He rested his hand on her waist sliding it down slowly over her hip. She moved to lie flat on her back and he moved his hand over her thigh. She became alive with new energy. All the heavy exhaustion weighing her down just a moment ago was leaving her. New vitality, aroused by his erotic touch began to inflame her. Mandane felt his hand glide with slow determination between her legs and caress her with soft, delicate intimacy. She moaned in anticipation of new delights. She twisted her face to his to kiss him with full desire and wanton need. All the suppressed passion of the last hour rose up in her as she lifted her hips to force herself against his searching hand.

As Cambyses began to remove her clothing she wondered if this feeling of intensity was because of his touch or because of the high energy demanded in the audience hall during their victory over the daeva. If it was the latter, let there be more such struggles, soon!

15.

Zav returned to Susa more intent than ever to cause a catastrophe in Pars. This latest, bitter defeat from Cambyses was just about all he could take. He recalled the previous occasion when Cambyses had left him behind in Anshan with rude forethought while the king of Pars answered a summons from Ecbatana to learn of his obligatory marriage. Now Zav mumbled, "This puppet has not only stolen the woman who could make me powerfully royal, but Cambyses has also managed to discover that I committed a murder, and he tossed it in my face like a smelly fish!"

Zav promised himself that if Prince Warohi did not decide to go to war with Cambyses this very day the prince was going to suffer because someone would pay for this insult immediately. Zav met the prince at the Rice Rodent's place again where they were led into the same cave-room. Prince Warohi noted that Zav was agitated.

The prince asked, "What has you so uneasy today, Zav?"

Zav snared and said, "News, bad news. The Babylonians have decided to ignore King Astyages and definitely attack Pars after their western war is finished. It will not matter to the Babylonians whether they win or lose Syria and Judah. King Nebuchadnezzar will seek revenge against Cambyses for his failure to act as a friend towards him. Your Susa will be utterly destroyed. Only you can save your family or your country."

Startled, Prince Warohi asked, "How did you come by this information?"

Zav lied, "Governor Pagakanna told me. We are friends with mutual business interests that need protecting. He was quite explicit. You must take action to overthrow Cambyses. Then you can placate King Nebuchadnezzar to preserve peace. Pagakanna assures me King Nebuchadnezzar is willing to accept you as a substitute for Cambyses. You must go to war with Cambyses now!"

The prince said, "I can't. It is too great an insult to my king. Maybe I can go to explain the situation to Cambyses in Anshan. You and I could go together. He'll listen. Maybe an apology will soften Nebuchadnezzar."

Zav said, "Nothing but the destruction of Anshan with the body of Cambyses buried in rubble will satisfy the king of Babylon."

This was terrible news to Prince Warohi and he said, "But to bury a dead Parsian is a defilement, just as cremation is an abomination! Burial pollutes the holy soil and rock. Even more important, burial is a severe insult to the gods of the earth."

The prince knew the earth could never be cleansed, leaving a stain of vulgar impurity for all time. The place where the body was buried could never be used again, or at least until all living men forgot about the burial. Prince Warohi said, "The only respectable way to dispose of a dead body in Pars is to leave the corpse out on a high hill to allow animals and birds of prey to pick the bones clean. This ensures the sacred matter of the body returns to nature in a way that honors the gods. The clean bones could than be laid in our sacred ossuary."

"Yes, I know all that Prince Warohi, but you must do something swiftly."

The Rice Rodent was horrified at the suggested burial; such an abomination was all too real to him. The Rice Rodent appreciated how Prince Warohi had wanted to resolve this incident with negotiation because of his loyalty to Cambyses. The proprietor also noted Zav's intent to create revolution leading to the downfall of Cambyses. The Rice Rodent had to get this news to Pattmenidu. The great merchant would be able to get Cambyses to do something to stop Zav from causing insurrection.

Prince Warohi fretted and thought for a moment. "Zav, leave me, please. I must think. There has to be a way to keep peace in Pars. An agreement with Babylon will help, but I need to find a way to prevent Susa from being forced to revolt against Anshan. How can I go to war with Cambyses just to save Susa? I will have to tell Cambyses ahead of time. It will be a greater disgrace if I attack my king unannounced. Leave me, Zav. I must think."

Zav was pleased because he had clearly upset Prince Warohi. Now he needed to send a message to Pagakanna encouraging him to feign war with Anshan in communication with Prince Warohi. Zav could ask Pagakanna to tell Warohi that Babylon wanted to deal solely with the prince of Susa for peace, otherwise war was unavoidable. If Warohi thought he was to be the savior of Pars he might invade Anshan. That would satisfy Zav's desire of revenge. It did not matter if Cambyses defeated Prince Warohi. The minor king would be forced to kill his own family members creating a vulgar legend staining the memory of Cambyses forever.

Zav returned to Ecbatana. As he was getting settled he came across the message from Princess Ispitamu. He had a vague recollection of receiving it, but he could not remember who had given it to him. He called a magus to read the message to him. It requested a large quantity of silphium. He had heard of this plant. It came from the west in the Greek colony of Cyrene, west of Egypt. Zav recalled insignificant dealings with its monarch, King Battus, over minor business adventures.

The magus could find no name on the message. Zav was about to ignore the whole thing, but decided to order the plant anyway. He recalled it was a medicine used by the magi for some female illness. He could add it to the apothecary stores.

Zav requested an audience with the Great King. Zav asked about the possible war between Babylon and Pars. The Great King waved it off as folly saying, "I have stopped it."

Zav was disappointed that the issue was so easily dismissed and continued, "Susa was about to attack Anshan, Sire."

The Great King said, "I don't care. It is probably a family squabble, but Cambyses better protect my daughter, or I will have his head. She carries my grandson."

King Astyages looked forward to messages from Mandane. He was pleased to discover she was a happy queen, a satisfied wife and a gleeful, expectant mother. The Great King's plan, as protection from his dreams, to isolate Mandane seemed to be successful and this Susa-Anshan thing better not endanger her safety. He made an unspoken vow to slaughter the entire nation if a single hair of her ebony locks was ruffled.

The Great King began to have renewed dreams of his daughter. He saw her as a playing toddler. Her pregnancy report from Anshan had stimulated his memory to recall their past together. It was a comfort to dream of his lovely child while he slept. Mandane had given him many moments of happiness with her stumbling run and bouncing falls. He had often sat with Aryenis worrying that Mandane might fall or be injured, but the King and Queen had laughed together watching her jiggle along playing in complete innocence.

131

His dreams included her adult life where in his slumber he saw her wedding over and over. Gradually she became isolated from any other object or person as she began to appear in his dreams alone. She floated among the clouds. She floated across the sky then vanished as the gods of the sun blocked her from his sight. The brilliance of the sun was harsh but not uncomfortable to his sleep.

Soon Mandane seemed to take on a light of her own. Over a couple of moon cycles Astyages realized a progressive dream was developing again, as before. He called the Chief Magus to a private meeting. He described the little bit he could remember of his new dreams. They sounded harmless enough as he spoke of his nighttime visions to the Magus. The Chief Magus said, "I am not alarmed. Mandane's pregnancy had made you nostalgic. It is nothing to be concerned about."

Astyages changed the room he slept in, thinking a new bed or new room would alter the nature of his dreams, or even better, stop him from dreaming altogether. It was unfortunate that his heart and his head accompanied him with their contents of memories about Mandane. Astyages stopped nighttime visits from Aryenis and began to sleep with his concubines, thinking his wife might somehow be the source of his dreams. The dreams continued. He changed to new concubines who had never seen cr heard of Mandane, believing the complete removal of her memory might help. It did not. The dreams continued!

King Astyages called the Chief Magus again telling him of the changes he had made in his evening habits. The King asked, "Why are the dreams persisting? I find them so disturbing and undesirable."

"Hmmm," the Magus had no good answer. He made one up saying, "Sire, you must realize that your daughter is about to deliver to you your first grandchild. It is wholesome for the Great King to dream of his succession. It will keep you in this world forever. You will die, but simultaneously, you will live for all time."

The answer sounded plausible but made up. Astyages again began to think he should take the dangerous trip across the sea to Delphi to solicit the prophetic words of the Oracle. The Greek enchantress might give him a better interpretation, covering a fuller meaning of his dreams. She might not dictate the need of a specific course of action, but neither would his Chief Magus. King Astyages put off planning the actual trip because his fear of the sea exceeded his fear of the dreams, yet he lacked the confidence to accept the dreams as insignificant; they made him too uncomfortable.

As the dream-daughter appeared more isolated, she took on a greater degree of radiance. She began to shine like the moon. The light seemed to originate within her. Then she began to shine with the brilliance of the sun. Astyages started to wonder just how bright she might get. A glow radiated from within her.

Then the dream changed with a radical twist. Although the brightness persisted with the same intense glow, a strange new phenomenon arose. A large green stem, with small leaves began to grow from Mandane. The Great King worried that this might be the most significant part of his dreams. Astyages consulted the Chief Magus again. As much as the Great King wanted and needed the help of the magi, he distrusted their skills when it came to this unique problem.

The Chief Magus advised, "Your daughter is growing a new line of descendants for you. It is good for you to dream of your future family."

This helped the King a little. But as the plant grew with each succeeding dream it spread all around her. Even though it looked dangerous, she seemed unaffected. The Magus continued, "Sire, your descendants are being depicted as healthy and prolific."

But a radical shift in the significance of the dream developed abruptly. Astyages began to see his beloved palace in the dream. Mandane with her growing greenery hovered over the palace. Slowly, the shrubbery spread into the palace. Astyages jerked up from his sleep in a cold sweat. Now the dream was exhibiting clear danger of some sort. The King could not get back to sleep. He trembled. He shivered from cold fear. He tried to tell himself it was foolish for an important king to fear a dream. As nights went by the green growth continued to be widespread over all of Ecbatana. Then it spread over the adjacent provinces until it covered his entire empire and other nations too.

King Astyages feared something valuable was being revealed to him in this mystical way even though he wished it to be a preposterous nonsense. In the disturbing dreams he had prior to this one Mandane had been comfortable above the flood. Now she was the actual source of the dangerous growth. It was a remarkably healthy plant that appeared to expand across the entire world. Was a great conqueror or a series of conquerors coming from her pregnancy? Was Astyages seeing his descendants as successful vanquishers of established kingdoms everywhere? Since the vine started by engulfing his palace did it mean he was to be overthrown by a conqueror who would spread new power from Media to the rest of the world? Was it a good sign or an evil premonition? King Astyages had to think.

He again isolated himself for several days. If he could just devise a course of action for himself, he could make the dream stop. He thought of assassinating Mandane, then dismissed that foolish idea. There must be a better answer than killing his darling girl. It never occurred to him there were ways to stop the pregnancy. Killing the father now that the pregnancy was a reality made no sense.

The King smirked over the religious nonsense of Pars that obligated discontinuance of sexual contact between a man and woman after a certain point in the pregnancy. The King decided to order Mandane to Ecbatana for the birth. Alternatively, he thought a strong suggestion might look more loving and family-like than a direct command. He had medical magi and midwives with superior birthing skills than those in Pars. He might convince Mandane that she and the child would be safer in Ecbatana than in Anshan when the birth came. At that time he could contemplate his next step while having total control of Mandane and the child.

The next day King Astyages sent a message to Anshan, telling Cambyses of the superior health protection available in Ecbatana. He also suggested, man to man, that it was no hardship for Cambyses to send Mandane to Media when the pregnancy obligated them to stop sexual coupling for Cambyses could take up with his concubines. Astyages asked them to plan to have her travel north at the appropriate time.

16.

In Anshan life had grown quiet and stable. Peasants worked through the late spring planting and weeding. Peace reigned in Pars. Showers came to nourish the crops. Flowering trees blossomed heralding the bearing of fruit. Lush, large apples, figs, oranges, pomegranates, plums, lemons and nuts of all kinds were ready to flourish.

Merchants in the city made contracts with peasants from the hills for sheep, goats and donkeys as newborn domestic animals began to thrive in the fields. The hill dwellers bartered with the high mountain dwellers for goat and camel hair in exchange for fruits, vegetables and game meat. Fine, soft animal hairs grew better on animals raised in the colder high elevations. There were no large herds of camels deep in the mountains, but the few camels living there had finer healthier hair.

Fathers began to teach their very young sons the value of honesty and truth. Honesty was the national emblem one encountered everywhere. Lies, deceptions and thefts among the young were dealt with harsh discipline. As acts of dishonor continued punishment of a youth became progressive. The lesson was learned rapidly.

Boys were given their first bow and set of arrows five sun cycles after their birth to learn the critical skill of shooting. As boys grew, they were expected to make their own equipment; additionally, older boys had to make new bows that were increasingly harder to string, harder to draw. Each lad had to keep up his strength to work the new bow. He was not allowed to reduce the power of the bow to match his strength. The father set the pace his son was obligated to rise to.

The youths were taught that being the best bowmen in the world was their national glory. It was reinforced in them that they had to ensure only the strongest warrior outside Pars could string and shoot the bow of the weakest warrior in the army of King Cambyses. The nature of the wood used to make a bow changed as a boy aged, from supple softwood to stiffer woods. Boys had to learn to spin hemp used to string a bow until later when animal sinew replaced the hemp.

A young boy's arrows were made of light wood, easy to nock and shoot. If they got lost or broke it did not matter. At first the tip of an arrow was nothing more than the sharpened end of a stick. Later, as the boy aged, a tin point was added. Eventually, bronze was used to make the arrow the projectile of a warrior as the shaft was made of straight hardwood. Every boy learned to carve perfectly straight arrow shafts after climbing trees to select specific branches. The length of the arrows grew as the arms of a boy grew.

Feathers used to stabilize the flight of an arrow came from birds that boys shot. Hitting fowl on the wing came after children developed accuracy hitting stationary game birds. Picking one's first bird out of the sky was a moment for great jubilation. It was a forecast of the need to hit a moving enemy, who might be running, jumping, falling or riding.

Honor and arrows. Bravery and bows. Skilled riding was taught later. These virtues were the heart of the nation that every man strove to be best at over a lifetime of effort. No young lady accepted a groom who refused to live for these endowments. No man helped another man who did not carry national dignity in his heart. To fail at shooting arrows, telling the truth or riding was to fail utterly.

No festivals were celebrated in Anshan during the hot summer. Peasants found it best to stay out of the sun when possible, and remain in a room with cross ventilation that allowed breezes to pass through.

Trying to keep clean in the heat was difficult. However, at all times Parsians kept as clean as possible. Clothing and the body were cleansed often. A Parsian never washed garments in a lake or river. One never walked into a lake or river to bathe. To maintain the sacredness of water and soil, water was always removed from a large body of water, a well, or a cistern then carried in a clay pot to the place where cleaning activities were conducted.

Men on the march never allowed their mounts to stop to drink from a river. Water was always dipped out of the river and carried to the animal. Soiled water was splashed on the ground to let the revered water and soil replenish each other. Together these materials decided how to purify one another thus honoring mutual divinities. The deliberate soiling of water with human or animal waste was an unpardonable offense against the gods, which every Parsian made an assiduous effort to avoid. If it occurred by accident one had to stop the soiling without delay. That could require one to remove a camel or donkey from a river with urgency. Crossing a body of water with animals was planned so the animals moved as fast as possible across points where the edges of the water were closest together.

During the summer of her pregnancy Mandane was prepared to be uncomfortable, but clean. Her slaves bathed her every day with loving carefulness. Her bath was in a very warm room with no moving air. Everyone was afraid she might catch an illness from a draft of blowing air. However, Mandane did manage to take the outside air most days to maintain her health, even against the protests of the princesses of the palace who protected her excessively.

After a long business morning Cambyses nestled in cushions on a roof at the top of the palace with his wife. They sat in the shade out of direct sun light. A constant breeze blew keeping them cool. Unseen below them three musicians with lyres plucked slow, soft melodies to suit a quiet afternoon. The king and his queen were sipping red wine from golden cups. It was so pleasant to have time to enjoy each other.

Cambyses watched her lick wine from her cup. When they were alone she found ways to tease him with little erotic gestures, like licking her food while staring straight into his eyes. It always made him squirm. But today he asked, "Do you know the fable of wine, my dear?"

Mandane answered, "No. Is it a long story? I need to lie down to nap a while. My condition with this heat makes me weary."

Cambyses began, "There once was an ancient king of the Aryan tribe who one day was watching his warriors practice archery. He saw a bird flying over head with a snake around its neck. The snake was choking the bird. The king told an archer to kill the snake, but not to harm the bird.

"You know, dear, that in Pars the birds of the air come as a gift of the gods of the divine sky. Since these spirits are the ahura, or beneficial gods, the birds are good too. They spread seeds they eat helping to keep the land covered with foliage. Snakes come from the daeva and are evil.

"The archer with a single shot killed the snake. It dropped to earth. The bird flew away. Later the bird returned to the feet of the king, placing several seeds on the ground before him. No one had ever seen such seeds before. The king ordered the seeds planted and grapevines, which also no one had ever seen before, began to grow.

When the grapes ripened on the vines the king was amazed, as was his entire court. All the princes and princesses were familiar with plants that grew poisonous berries so no one was willing to eat the grapes. The king ordered a slave to eat one. It was difficult for the slave to know which he was more afraid of, the king or the grape. He ate one. He told the king in a weak, frightened voice that the grape tasted good. After several minutes of waiting nothing happened. The king ordered the same man to eat several grapes. Nothing happened. After waiting several days to ensure the slave did not die by some strange, delayed device all the grapes were picked for the whole court to sample to their delight.

"The king ordered the slaves to crush the grapes so the vast amount of liquid hidden under the skin was released. The liquid was placed in capped amphorae. The king drank the sweet liquid often but a few moon cycles later a slave tasted the liquid and told the king it had turned bitter. The king put a finger in the liquid. He was astonished that the sweet flavor had changed so much.

"The king thought it had turned to a new form of poison so he kept it because poisons were sometimes useful to a monarch. They helped end disputes or rid the kingdom of troublemakers.

"A favored princess in the palace began to experience a vicious pain in her head nothing would relieve. The magi tried everything to no avail. In an attempt to kill herself, she drank the grape fluid that had gone to poison, or so she believed. After falling into a deep sleep she awoke with the headache gone. She rushed to tell the king what she had done. From then on fermented wine has been called 'the king's medicine.'"

Mandane laughed at his story. The music from below had added an enchanting touch as he spoke. She was pleased when he told these fables to her. She felt a little closer to her new country when she learned a new story. She resolved for the future to think of the diluted palace wine as a healing gift from Cambyses to his guests. His stories made her feel that her husband was sharing his innermost being with her to make them both one person. She surveyed his handsome face in bliss, noting its perfectly groomed, full beard. He did not curl his beard or hair like some men. He allowed it to hang in a natural way that developed a slight twirl at the ends of each hair. She enjoyed tracing the small twists with her fingertips.

Her condition was fast approaching the time when she no longer was able to receive him inside her. She had started creating new opportunities for love making causing sex to last as long as possible. She let Cambyses rest only enough to keep him going. Her swelling belly was getting in the way but that just left room for discovering new positions to enjoy. She began to feel clever. Her antics at bouncing to and fro, her newfound touches that made him thrust harder, were a personal achievement. She had lost her original innocence, replacing it with luscious enjoyment in her new world of sexual adventure. She was going to miss his touch as well as his surging energy heavy against her.

She began to feel tired and said, "Darling, I must lie down for a while. Will you come with me?"

He saw the lines of exhaustion on her face and answered, "No love, get out of this heat. Rest as long as you like. You must save your energy for our son."

She kissed his lips then disappeared into the palace. Cambyses had not mentioned the summons from her father. He knew they had to talk about it soon enough. Cambyses could not accompany her on the trip because there were too many regal duties requiring his attention. Cambyses was obliged to sit in the ceremony to promote new officers in the army. He had to help Pattmenidu with negotiations for bartering the coming harvest so he went to meet with the merchant.

In a small gathering room Pattmenidu rose from his bow of respect to the king to recline on pillows close to the food. He grunted as he dropped his vast sweaty bulk to the floor. The merchant picked up a cup of wine drinking it with deep satisfaction. The summer heat always made Pattmenidu thirsty. The wine was well diluted with mountain runoff water making it taste very refreshing.

Pattmenidu said, "Sire, I have startling news. I was with a business associate in Susa. You have heard me speak of the Rice Rodent before."

"Yes," said Cambyses, "he's been an excellent source of information for you… for us, in the past. What wonderful news has he for us now?"

Pattmenidu said, "Not wonderful, Sire. It is misery! Zav, the scoundrel, has been fomenting revolt in Pars."

King Cambyses jerked up straight and barked, "What! How? What does that fool think he is doing? No Achaeminid will participate in insurrection against my family. Who would even discuss it?"

"Well, Sire, Zav has spoken to Prince Warohi. According to the Rice Rodent, the prince listened with unusual attention to Zav's suggestions."

Cambyses grew alert wondering if his cousin might consider the heinous prospect of revolution and said, "Warohi knows better than that. He knows Zav; how could he listen to what that idiot says?"

The merchant said, "Zav told him about the Babylonian anger towards you then he said that Nebuchadnezzar will invade Pars through Susa. Prince Warohi believed him. The Rice Rodent says Warohi mumbled something about contacting you before he revolted against Anshan. There is still some honor left in the prince."

Cambyses called for a scribe magus. The king wasted no time in sending a message to Prince Warohi explaining that there was no invasion threat from Babylon. The rumor of invasion by King Croesus' army was too remote to be credible, as well. He demanded that Prince Warohi come to Anshan to talk. Next, Cambyses sent a message to Zav telling him to stop trying to create trouble in Pars. He reminded Zav that he had not forgotten the green cape hoping this would scare Zav again.

Elsewhere in the palace Princess Ispitamu was getting nervous about her inability to interfere with the queen's pregnancy which threatened putting a foreigner in line for the kingship of Pars. The princess had a magus prepare a message to Zav asking whether he had been able to acquire her 'medicine'. This time she risked adding her name.

Princess Ispitamu thought it took a long time to get silphium because she knew Cyrene was far away, although she did not know precisely where it was. She needed to terminate the undesired pregnancy soon or risk having to plot the murder of the newborn baby later, which was far more dangerous for her. Her message went to Ecbatana with the one from Cambyses.

In Ecbatana Zav received both messages at the same time. He went into a raging fit when the magus read the message from Cambyses. The magus wondered what the green cape reference meant, and why Zav reacted with frantic violence upon hearing it. The priest wondered if it referred to some significant national event, but the magus could not remember any specific details about a green cape. Zav made the magus write a message to Governor Pagakanna. He reminded the official of their previous conversation about 'influencing circumstances' in Pars without giving the magus a clear understanding that he was recommending invasion.

The magus next read the message from Princess Ispitamu. So, thought Zav, it was she who wanted the material. He asked the magus what one used silphium for. The magus said, "I am not physician-trained, but it sounds like the substance that alters female matters in pregnancy. I could ask a medical magus if it is important to you."

"No," said Zav, "the princess probably wishes to prevent herself from getting pregnant. She is not married yet."

Zav began to wonder if the princess might become an ally against the hated king and queen of Pars. He dictated a message to Princess Ispitamu stating that her medicine was on its way. He asked if Mandane would be pleased to know the princess would have the silphium in her possession in about a moon cycle. Zav thought that if they had the same enemy Princess Ispitamu would understand his real question, since she was fully aware of his past controversies with Cambyses. He waited patiently for a response from the princess. Zav believed that in all probability he was going to lose Prince Warohi as his dupe. It would augment his plans to perfection if the princess became a new ally inside the palace in Anshan!

Later a message came back from Princess Ispitamu to Zav. She had received the silphium and was forwarding a silver carafe to pay for it. The princess added that she did not believe the queen would be at all pleased to discover the medicine was in her possession. Worse still, the princess said the queen was about to experience its affects soon.

Zav began to dance with spins, hops and skips. This was better than any plan he could have thought up. From now on he would provide Princess Ispitamu with any weeds, herbs or medicines that she desired. She might even make a critical mistake that killed the queen or the king. This was the perfect revenge for him, because someone else would be taking all the risks. All he had to do was stay in the background supplying the princess with her weapons. What a faultless way to get even.

Princess Ispitamu did not actually know how to prepare a potion to abort a pregnancy. She stared at the bush that had obviously been pulled out of the ground, roots and all. She wondered if one ate the bark, the stalk or the leaves? Should the leaves be crushed and eaten or blended as a mush in a liquid? She could not go to a magus to get answers because a priest was sure to remember such a conversation after Mandane aborted and report Princess Ispitamu to the Chief Magus. The Chief Magus in turn would inform Cambyses and Princess Ispitamu would be in fatal trouble. She had to be careful to keep the possession of the plant to herself. She needed, also, to discover the correct way to administer the part of the plant that worked. Additionally, she needed to practice on someone who was pregnant other than Mandane. This was going to take stealthful planning but the princess felt she had enough time to practice this new art before the birth.

One day Cambyses took Mandane aside in a small room with rugs strewn over the floor. They sat in chairs by a window where a breeze blew. It was easier in her condition for Mandane to get up from a chair than from a reclining position on the floor. They began to review their relationship with loving care. He started by saying, "Darling, you are so far into your time with the child that we need to think of stopping our love making. I have to honor you and your condition. We need to respect the restrictions placed on men toward pregnant women. It will be a desperate separation for me. You are the greatest excitement I have ever known. Just thinking of your naked body makes me swell. I have no control over my need for you. It is such a relief for me to be able to surrender myself into your arms forgetting the world. Seeing only you, feeling only you, loving only you."

Mandane sighed, touched his cheek and said, "Oh, Cambyses, I know! I have been so afraid of this. I worry that we will be changed because our lovemaking is interrupted. Will we ever be the same after the birth because we have to discontinue our physical love? Will we be able to continue just as we have up till now? Our love has grown to be perfect for me. I love you so much. I depend on being touched by you, feeling your wonderful strength lunge against my frail desire."

Cambyses wanted to calm his wife and said, "Darling, this time of separation will make our need for each other just that much more dear," he laughed as he continued, "and there is nothing frail about your desires. They are as real and powerful as mine."

Mandane answered in a plaintive tone, "You know what I mean. Your loving strength gives me the support I need to be a proper queen, as well as a lover, for you. I could not be a queen without you. And I need you inside me to make me complete."

Cambyses laughed and said, "Now you have stirred me again, darling. See how my toga stands?"

"Oh Cambyses, please give me the thrill of your power once more," Mandane pleaded. He lifted her out of her chair and carried her to the center of the room where pillows were piled high. He was kissing her lips as she held his face with her hands almost in desperation. It was to be their last union for a long time. Many moon cycles would pass before he could feel this urgency in the muscles of his arms again.

He placed her on the pillows with gentle concern and began to stroke her breasts, swollen with the milk of life. They were harder than ever before but that did not reduce his ardor to touch them. He slid her gown off gazing at her nakedness. He lowered his head to lick her nipple before he took it into his mouth, almost in reverence. He rested beside her after removing his toga. Her fingers hungrily searched his nakedness. He rolled his hand over her bulging stomach to the cleft of her legs. Their slow deliberate stroking and kissing of each other had to become an important memory for them that must linger for many moon cycles.

When their passion was spent they stayed reclined on the floor engulfed in the soft, smooth shelter of the cushions. Cambyses said, "My love, your father wishes you to go to his palace for the birth of our child."

"Our son, dearest," she corrected, "but why? I can deliver him here."

Cambyses cautioned, "The medical assistance in Pars is very poor. Many women die because our magi are not very skilled; frequently new babies die, too. I hate to have you go but your father is correct; you will have better help in Ecbatana."

Mandane whined, "But Cambyses, there are children born here every day. Why should I be different from any other mother?"

Cambyses touched her cheek and said, "You are different from any other mother. You are my wife. You are the queen. You are the daughter of the King of Kings. Need I say more?"

Exasperated Mandane said, "Oh, you know what I mean. I am just another woman doing what women have done since the beginning of time, having a child!"

Cambyses stroked her arms, neck and face and said, "Darling, we both know it is best for you to return to Media at this time. Please do not resist."

Mandane admitted that leaving for Media was the correct thing to do, but she preferred to have Cambyses near so she could present her son to him. She knew full well that he had to stay behind in Anshan. She would be alone without her greatest strength at the time of the birth. Even though her parents were with her, she would feel isolated without Cambyses. They talked of advantages and disadvantages of going, travelling over the mountains, plus leaving each other at such a precious time. Cambyses brought up the danger of not following the desires of her father. They cried, petted, made love then agreed that Mandane should leave for Media soon. They decided that she should depart as soon as travel arrangements could be made. It was their safest solution.

17.

Princess Ispitamu traveled to Susa. She had heard of a pregnant princess who was not married. Taking the silphium with her, Princess Ispitamu rushed to experiment on the girl with her treasure. Princess Ispitamu had tried various parts of the plant on pregnant cats, but they just got sick. She did not use dogs because in Pars dogs were given respect almost equivalent to sacred fire. This was because dogs protected man with no thought to their own safety. Dogs were uniquely unselfish. The princess also respected the fact that dogs had a ritual importance in funeral rites.

She could not wait to discover which part of the plant had the effective components. She took the entire bush with her. She also felt she had been wasting her prize using it on cats. The princess needed to save the plant for Mandane. After interrupting Mandane's current pregnancy, Ispitamu intended to use the plant to prevent the queen's future conceptions. The princess knew Zav could always get more for her, but she wanted to have plenty on hand instead of worrying about getting more delivered. The princess knew shipments of goods were unreliable. She also realized that all too often no delivery was made. Boats sank in storms; bandits attacked caravans or merchants lost things. She intended to have plenty of the poison to use against the queen after returning from Susa.

Princess Ispitamu decided it was best to give the princess in Susa a little bit of all parts of her plant, roots, stem and leaves, crushed together in a liquid broth. Getting the quantity correct might be important, but she was not sure if the amount mattered.

In Susa Princess Ispitamu was very solicitous to the girl as they spoke alone. Princess Ispitamu told the girl of the plant that could abort her child. Princess Ispitamu talked like a concerned cousin, worried about the young girl's honor. The father of the child was a Greek emissary who left for Sparta, after seducing the girl, without returning to Pars. The young girl got worried as she listened to Princess Ispitamu talk about the treatment in vague terms, so she demanded that a medical magus be consulted. The youngster was afraid the plant might kill her. She was willing to protect her honor but not at the risk of her life. Princess Ispitamu tried to talk her out of having a magus involved, but the young girl trusted the godly protection a magus could give her.

The magus chosen told Princess Ispitamu he would prepare the potion needed from her plant. He was familiar with the bush but had none of his own. He was happy to participate in this secret to protect this young girl. He confirmed that the discomfort was minimal and everything was going to work out to the princess' advantage. Grudgingly, Princess Ispitamu agreed to let him prepare the potion, provided she could watch. It was very educational for her. The process involved picking, cutting, trimming, and grinding. Then there was boiling, cooling, pouring off and boiling again to evaporate. Finally, the liquor created was diluted in wine for the unfortunate young girl to drink. Princess Ispitamu was able to ask, as if disinterested, if there was any difference in the preparation of the potion just to prevent a conception. She discovered that the quantity of the material used did matter. The magus volunteered precise details. She had all the information she needed for her future adventures.

After a couple of days of illness, the young princess felt the physical evidence of her pregnancy leave her body. She recovered rapidly and the girl's thanks gratified the visiting princess. Princess Ispitamu was also elated over the information she had from the magus about using the silphium the exact way to ensure its effectiveness. Now for Mandane!

While Princess Ispitamu was away the preparations for Mandane's trip to Ecbatana were completed. The final parting was very touching because all the women in the palace cried. The young princes looked upon Cambyses with sympathy. They knew how he felt. At least they told each other they understood his feelings. His face crumbled with remorse as he stood watching Mandane's small parade of wagons, servants and guards disappear into the hills to the north.

So many cushions and pillows had been stacked under Mandane by Cambyses after she climbed into her carriage that she was only able to move with exhausting twists. The servant girls fussed while simultaneously shouting out windows ordering the drivers to go slower and avoid all the bumps, which everyone realized was impossible. The servants in Mandane's wagon fidgeted over the queen's comfort. They watched her the way a hawk watched a mouse. Mandane got a little uncomfortable being constantly stared at by her companions.

One very serious incident occurred going over the mountains that scared Mandane and all her women. In Media a band of wandering bandits attacked their caravan. Vagabonds had blocked the path with felled trees then dropped rocks from cliffs above onto her carriage and her military escort. The Parsian guards struggled to break through the debris while boulders showered down on them. The path was flush against the mountain wall, so there was not enough room for her guards to step back to get a good bow shot at the bandits. The Parsian soldiers had to scale the wall to fight hand to hand.

The explosive bang of large boulders striking her carriage made Mandane so frightened she began to have cramping pains in her stomach. Her servants started to scream compounding the queen's fear and discomfort. The shouting soldiers along with the petrified grunting of the animals just added to the confused cacophony Mandane had to tolerate inside her wagon. Mandane was afraid she was losing her child as she began to breathe in deep, slow gasps. With a sudden jolt the carriage moved forward. The pounding on the top of the carriage stopped. Mandane's wagon was traveling at a very high rate of speed, but it felt safer to her than being a still target.

Gradually the carriage slowed to a stop. She gave a weak smile to the girls about her while trying to catch her breath. She said in a tiny voice, "I think everything is going to be fine."

The girls continued to cry as they tugged at blankets or cushions around her. They did not know what to do. She gave them small instructions to move this, change that, just to keep them busy with something besides crying. She asked for water. She asked for a small piece of bread.

The captain of her guard opened the carriage door to look inside. He asked in a high, excited voice, "Your highness, everything is safe now. Are you hurt?"

"I am fine. We are all well, just scared," Mandane sighed bravely as she winced in pain at a cramp.

The captain wanted to put his wounded men in her carriage, but after seeing her obvious distress he made other arrangements. Her bravery was infectious and the women began to calm down. The captain said, "We will send a messenger ahead to get help from The Great King. These were his people that attacked you. His soldiers may be able to tell from the dead where they come from. Meanwhile, I will have men scout the path well ahead of us so this does not occur again. I am sorry, your highness, I have put you at risk. Please forgive me."

Mandane smiled benignly and said, "We are safe. I will see that my father does not make you suffer along with the ones that attacked us."

Her remarkable generosity in such a stressful situation impressed the women and the soldiers. If ever she could do something to win loyalty, this was it. She now had protectors for life.

The caravan moved on, at a slow, steady pace. The women checked her often to ensure that she had not lost the child. The queen had a few more cramping episodes but she settled down at last in a fitful rest.

As they approached Ecbatana large columns of soldiers seemed to fly past Mandane's caravan. Median soldiers not only found the tribe that attacked the daughter of the Great King, they brought them back to the capital where the entire tribe was killed in public execution at the order of the Great King. Men, women and children were all exterminated like a nest of snakes even as they pleaded ignorance of whom they had tried to rob.

On her arrival, Mandane was not even allowed out of her travel carriage before being swarmed by a midwife hoard. They poked, prodded, felt, sniffed. They examined every speck of fiber on her garments. Midwives gave reports to medical magi standing outside who rushed news to the King. Her mother, Queen Aryenis, was in the middle of the mob in the carriage asking questions, demanding answers. The ordeal in front of her father's palace eventually ended to the profound thanks of the victim.

Mandane was lifted onto a palanquin carried by four enormous eunuchs, who rushed her into the palace to a cool, airy room. There she napped in total quiet for the rest of the day. When she woke she ate a small amount of fruit, bathed then returned to bed for the night.

Queen Aryenis went to the King of Kings to inform him Mandane was going to be fine. Mandane had requested that the captain of her train be considered a hero for saving her life. Although King Astyages was inclined to execute him for putting his daughter in danger, he relented for his daughter's sake. Instead the Great King promoted the man. Even though the soldier was from a different army than that of Media, the Great King's every order was accepted as final throughout all his lands. The soldiers from Mandane's caravan slept well that night, grateful to her that they did not die in Ecbatana by royal decree.

//

Meanwhile, Princess Ispitamu had returned to Anshan elated that she had the material as well as the knowledge she needed to make Mandane suffer. She slipped into the palace to prepare her little potion. It took her a while to find a place where she could heat water as needed. It also took several hours for her to complete the process. She had to locate cups, pans, and firewood, then sneak it all into her workplace, unseen. Her entire activity had to be conducted in total secrecy. She hid the final liquid material in her room then left to find Mandane.

Princess Ispitamu went wild with rage when she discovered the queen was gone and was not coming back until she had her child in her arms. The princess was as uncontrolled as a disturbed hornet. She would have beat a slave or a servant if there were a whip handy, even if her swing had no more bite than the slap of a butterfly. Once she got control of herself, she addressed the astonished princesses around her pretending her reaction was severe disappointment at having left Anshan, only to miss wishing the queen a safe journey. She expounded about her concern for Mandane's safety and asked very female questions about Mandane's welfare. Pretending to be satisfied she returned to her room. There she could only stare at the now useless silphium liquid. She did not know if the fluid would stay effective until Mandane returned. She wondered if she could send it to Zav. Maybe he could get it administered to Mandane. In an abrupt fit of frustrated temper she tossed the liquid out her window.

The princess was careful to hide the remaining bush of silphium so the plant was neither lost nor discovered. She wrapped it in a silk cloth then stuffed it into a plain, bronze vase, having a narrow neck with a tight fitting lid. This container was a decoration in her room that was never used for anything. Slaves never touched it except to dust the outside. The bush could be safely hidden there. Then Princess

Ispitamu turned her thoughts to plans for killing the child. She did not know how to go about such a thing. She had to concentrate over the next few moon cycles to come up with a plot that did not implicate her. Maybe if Zav came to Anshan before Mandane returned she could talk with him. He should know a way to kill someone without being caught. She would have reveled with gay anticipation at these thoughts if she had not been so angry about missing Mandane.

18.

Sythian bandits wandered down from the northeast into Hyrcania. They attacked farms belonging to the Great King and his relatives. They killed peasants and whole herds of animals as if the animals were of no value. This was their summer time sport more than it was the plundering of important resources. The Sythians did not need new herds of cattle, sheep or goats. They had all the camel, goat and cow milk their people could use.

Young Sythian men were being taught to fight an enemy and destroy property. Learning what to ravage or obliterate was educational for young boys. Simultaneously the youths learned what had value and raids like this taught them to recognize what was worth stealing. Older Sythian warriors instructed the young men to spot equipment that was significant for the care of orchards, cattle, sheep or fields of crops. That was what they were to destroy. They were taught how to pull up small trees in orchards and how to burn larger trees. Contaminating water supplies with dead animal carcasses was an important lesson too. All these things interrupted an enemy's supply lines in a real war.

Forcing the young to ride at full speed on camel, mule or horse while putting an arrow through a peasant at a distance of a meydan or more away was good practice and good sport. Hitting smaller targets, like children, was also good practice. Children were always running and to hit a small moving target was a sign of improving skill. A fatal shot at a moving target was always celebrated later with singing, backslapping and wine.

The invading party was not just a small band of cutthroats. It was a surging mass of dozens of dusty gritty troublemakers. They intended to do as much damage as possible to ruin summer crops and kill newborn animals that were the future flocks and herds. Several lakes were ruined.

The young men had to learn to drive one-horse and two-horse chariots while firing arrows at the same time. It was a tricky skill that required quick reflexes. Speed with the eye, arms and hands was essential to develop controlled riding as well as accurate bow work.

This season the young learned how to cripple the property of an enemy. Their rampaging became so fierce that the major caravans stopped trying to pass to the west. Caravans going east realized they saw no traffic coming from that direction so they reported this to Ecbatana. The Great King sent out ten soldiers to investigate. They were to report their findings to him on their return. Only three wounded soldiers returned and one of them died upon entering Ecbatana. Astyages was furious. He called the young soldier, Harpagus, into his presence. The Great King said, "I hear you are showing great progress with your military capabilities. Do you wish to be an officer in my army as well? If so, why?"

Harpagus answered, "Sire, I believe it is my duty to be as good a soldier for you as I can be. Also, my wife is to have a child in two moon cycles and I will require more to keep them fed."

The King of Kings said, "I can abide developing skill in my army, but I will not abide cunning or profiteering in my army. The latter is something I do not trust or tolerate. Is that what you just said, young man? Do you aspire to a position where you can rob? Where you can intimidate others for your own benefit?"

The soldier said with a strong voice, "Sire, I only wish to be an officer for you. I want to have you lead me to great victories that preserve the kingdom of Media for eons to come."

The King smiled and said, "Good. You will start on those victories now. You will take command of three hundred warriors in chariots, on horseback and camels to drive out the Sythians plaguing my family farms in the east. Make certain you use horses. They are swift. I want this over quickly. You are to kill as many Sythians as possible. Do not take them prisoner because Sythians make poor slaves. They try to escape at the first opportunity so I have to cripple them and even then they are more bother than use. Kill them, do you understand?"

Elated Harpagus answered, "Yes, sire. Thank you, sire."

With that instruction from the Great King, Harpagus prepared to leave. He took more camels than usual. He did not explain why to the more experienced officers. The Great King said to take horses so he took some, but very few. Camels travel slower, but he wanted to try a new fighting tactic.

Several older officers, who were relatives of the King, were annoyed that this young whelp had been put in command. This had never happened before, and they did not understand why this young man was being favored. To their knowledge Harpagus was not a relative of the Great King who deserved such an honor. They did not realize this was the very reason he was chosen. King Astyages planned to cultivate new loyalties in the army. He wanted men with no family ties to him. Later, he could play military relatives against non-family officers, if necessary.

Harpagus expected the Sythians to be spread over many farsangs in the hills. He used his horsemen to flank the Sythians to force them into a consolidated group. He knew they were too fierce to run from what appeared to be a small military force. He wanted them to assemble into a cohesive corps on the plain below the hills, where the Sythians could expect to slaughter the pursuing soldiers of Media.

Harpagus hid his camel-mounted warriors from the Sythians behind the hills. His strategy was to send them over the crests to gallop down into the vast field below where the Sythians were congregating. He had already committed his horsemen as a visible threat behind the invaders. The Sythian leaders drew their chariots; horsemen and camel-mounted fighters closer together ready to charge in force. Both opponents approached his hidden camel troop with the invaders trapped in the center. The Sythian commanders shouted their offensive strategy as they moved unknowingly towards Harpagus.

The Sythian horses were grouped close together in front of their own camel and mule riders. Harpagus rushed his camels over the top of the hills straight at his enemy's horses. It was normal in battle for horses to outrun camels so that horses confronted horses in a charge. But in this circumstance Harpagus had planned well to surprise the enemy's horses with his braying camels.

Once in the past Harpagus had been mounted on a war-horse that turned from a group of charging camels; he was unable to keep control of his stead. At the time he did not understand why his horse reacted the way it did. He never forgot that situation and now he was willing to charge with camels to see if it had useful military application. He was hoping the Sythian horses would be disrupted by the frontal attack of his camel horde.

153

It worked! The Sythian chariots ricocheted uncontrollably against each other as the horses panicked. Horses tossed their riders as confusion turned to chaos. With more troops and more control Harpagus pressed his attack against the muddled Sythians. His victory was as decisive as it was swift. Just as the Great King ordered, his men viciously slaughtered all but a few Sythians who escaped.

The Median soldiers had never maneuvered like this before. They knew it was different, but they did not understand the strategy was significant. They saw the confusion in the Sythian ranks, but thought their superior number of soldiers was the cause of the disorganization of the invaders. Harpagus decided to keep his secret to himself and accepted congratulations in humble silence. Harpagus returned to Ecbatana a new hero where he was promoted to the officer ranks. He had the confidence of King Astyages. His military career looked bright.

//

Prince Zatame went to Mandane a few days after her arrival in Ecbatana to welcome her. They talked of Cambyses and his welfare. Mandane said, "I am a bit concerned, Zatame. My husband has had a disagreeable meeting with Zav."

"That's no novelty," said Prince Zatame with disgust. "Most people who meet with Zav consider the meeting disagreeable. I only speak with him when it is essential because he is so fond of making trouble even when problems are not justified.

"For instance, last month my farm to the northeast was utterly destroyed by a Sythian invasion. All my orchard trees were either burned or ripped from the ground. The vegetables in the fields were trampled. All my equipment was destroyed. There will be no harvest this autumn from that farm. Zav told me that he heard of my misfortune, but then he added that my taxes were still due. I argued with him about it, but he did not rescind the tax requirement. I had to go to your father to beg for relief. The King granted my request. Zav then told me the tax on that farm would increase in the future to make up for the tribute loss."

Mandane said, "He lacks compassion, as we all know. Is he still allowed to tax independent of royal family oversight?"

154

"Yes," said Prince Zatame, "I wish your father would put a prince in charge of Zav, then we could get control over the tax process to make it a bit more fair."

Mandane commiserated but answered, "I am not surprised. I remember father saying once that Zav is his way of ensuring that the royal family does not cheat the kingdom. Father admitted to mother that it is better to have only Zav stealing from him than the whole family. Father will never put Zav under a prince, because he distrusts most of them. In Pars Cambyses trusts his family without reservation. In turn, they do not steal from him or from each other; it could not be more different than it is here."

"Yes," Prince Zatame chuckled, "although I never steal from your father I know several princes who do, but their theft is against Zav more than it is against the King. Some princes just need to feel they are getting back at a minister who is too sly and too powerful. I understand their feelings."

Mandane said, "I am concerned about Zav. Cambyses sent him out of Anshan and out of Pars; it was a virtual banishment. I fear Zav will attempt to take revenge against us."

"He will. At least he'll try. What happened?" asked Prince Zatame.

Mandane did not tell Prince Zatame about the murder of the servant girl. She did tell him about the attempted tax increase, she said, "Cambyses refused to accept it, then he told Zav to leave, never to return. Now I am afraid Zav will tell Father that Cambyses was unwilling to pay his royal tribute. Zav will make it sound as if Pars will not pay any tax. If he can make it sound like treason father will be furious. Cambyses will always pay fair taxes."

The prince said, "I will talk with the King about this. Do not fret my little cousin. Now, tell me, precious one, when is your child due to be born?"

Mandane answered, "In about two moon cycles," and they continued to speak of family matters.

Later in a royal audience, Prince Zatame bowed before King Astyages and the King asked, "Well, Zatame, what do you want this time?"

"Nothing for myself, sire," the prince said as he saw Zav in the audience ready to report to the King. "I have been questioned by others about the tax obligations this sun cycle. Are you doubling or tripling the taxes?"

Zav jerked back. He did not want this subject discussed without being involved. He rushed forward to bow. He blurted, "Sire, I am prepared to report on that along with several other topics. You might not wish to discuss it with Prince Zatame right now."

The amount of money was not as important to King Astyages as the tribute. It was the homage the money represented that was important to the King of Kings. Zav wanted to use this distinction to make King Cambyses look like a traitor who refused to honor King Astyages; the minister was determined not to lose this opportunity.

King Astyages said, "Zav, be quiet! Zatame what is bothering you? I told you your tax on your farm in Hyrcania would not have to be paid because of the Sythian invasion. Do you want more? I will make it two sun cycles. Are you happy now?"

"Oh, sire, yes! Thank you," stammered Zatame. He had to get back to his intended topic to help his friend Cambyses. "Sire, I have been told by your daughter that the tax in Pars is being doubled. Will all taxes throughout the realm be increased?"

The Great King glared at Zav wondering what his minister was up to. King Astyages said, "The tax against Pars will not increase. I declare that because of my daughter's pregnancy, I will reduce the Pars tribute one-third for the next three sun cycles."

Zav gasped. Why did everything go wrong for him? Why did Cambyses win every challenge? He felt that he had made careful deliberate plans, but somehow Cambyses thwarted him before he could present his scheme to the King. Princess Ispitamu was disappointing to Zav also because she had failed to eliminate Mandane's pregnancy. He began to wonder if Cambyses had the greatest magus in the world. Did that minor regent have some mystic that could keep the evil daeva at bay? Was there a new magic at work? What was going on that favored Cambyses so?

Zav needed to trick the Great King into commanding him to go to Pars. With such an order Cambyses could not uphold his ban on the minister's official return. Zav chose to work on that later. It should not be hard to accomplish and then he could visit Princess Ispitamu to aid her in any mischief she was perpetrating.

Prince Zatame returned to Mandane after the King's audience to tell her the good news about the reduced taxes to Pars. He was pleased to say, "It is your doing since you accomplished it with your pregnancy."

She smiled appreciatively as she summoned a scribe magus to send a love letter to Cambyses telling him she was still in perfect health, but she missed his touch. She added a short tale of how their tribute had been reduced substantially. Her note made her so happy!

King Astyages began to ponder his own situation. Now that Mandane was in Ecbatana under his watchful eye he needed to spend his private time deciding what was to be done about her and his dream. He had two moon cycles before being obliged to act.

He enumerated the possibilities to come. If she had a female child there was no need for him to do anything. Girls were never a threat to a king. Maybe it was to be her second, or third or fourth child to whom the dream referred. Maybe this child would not be born alive. If she had a son he might be crippled or have mental instabilities. Maybe if she had twin boys he could convince the weaker son to kill his stronger brother later on. As much as the King hated the thought, he would force himself to kill his own sweet daughter if necessary to preserve his empire.

No decision was needed right now; the King still had time to protect his future. King Astyages wondered about which royal cousin, nephew or uncle he could use to help him later. Prince Zatame would not be willing to harm the family of Cambyses and if Zatame heard of a plan to harm the Parsians he would raise a loud noise to rebuff it. Astyages knew this had to be a secret plot and that was where the Great King excelled.

157

19.

Pattmenidu was not having difficulty doing business now that Cambyses had stopped Zav's nasty tricks. The merchant began developing new contacts from Bactria that Cambyses directed for him. There was opportunity to purchase gems that came from beyond the Indus River more profitably as well. It included blue sapphires and red rubies. Buying from Cambyses' relatives in Bactria instead of from intermediaries in Media reduced the cost to the Parsian market. Gems had never been a big business in Pars since few people could afford them. However, Pattmenidu could now sell less expensive gems further west in Egypt, Judah, Syria, or in Lydia yet still make a substantial profit.

There were iron lamps and wine stands coming from the east the merchant could market. Iron ore still was not in demand in Pars because iron continued to be too difficult for metal craftsmen to process effectively. Everything iron was either brittle or soft when they cast it or forged it. The metal workers told Pattmenidu they thought they were not getting all the impurities out of it. It required very hot temperatures and the fuel was too expensive for them to buy on a routine basis. Until Pars craftsmen could figure out how to make high-heat fuel for the iron furnaces they stayed with copper, tin and bronze which were good enough for them. It also satisfied Pattmenidu's market as well.

Rugs from across the Indus River were plentiful, as were rugs woven in Pars. Pattmenidu knew the rug differences were reflected in both the quality of yarns and the designs. Yarns from the east were inferior, and the patterns were less intricate than Parsian creations. Pattmenidu noted that the colors were also different. Pars used more vegetable dyes that had a flat, earthy look. The eastern weavers used crushed lapis lazuli stone to get a blue that was a different shade from the indigo plant. The easterners also tried using turquoise to get greens but the stone grit did not impart pigment well into the yarn.

Pattmenidu preferred to sell rugs made by weavers from Pars. The weaving knot they used, plus the finer spun yarns, allowed more knots to be tied per finger length of rug. This gave a lighter, tighter, sturdier rug that lasted longer. The vegetable dye colors were bright enough, and the Parsian patterns were far prettier than any other patterns the merchant had seen coming from elsewhere.

In Pars animals or plants were replicated on carpets with surprising detail. Some clever weavers were even able to depict Parsian fables in their weavings to educate children. Some patterns on floor mats allowed children to play counting games or image identification games with the designs, which made these rugs teaching aids in addition to being a way to make a living.

The timber business was important to Pattmenidu. Forests were very thick and full at the base of the mountains. The trees extended up onto the hills, yet in some places rocky peaks rose above the tree line. This timber was first used by the hill dwellers for their homes and villages. They settled in small, hidden dells throughout the mountains where the land was almost flat and water was plentiful. All excess trees provided an industry for the peasants. They sold logs; sold wood for fuel; shaped pieces of wood for making home furnishings or kitchen utensils. They bartered with Pattmenidu for enhanced profits. It was difficult to move tree trunks over long distances, but there were many places in Pars and in Media where trees did not grow. Populations living in those places bought wood. So, logs of varying sizes were carried to markets by carts pulled by bulls, oxen and mules. Pattmenidu involved himself in the organization of this business too.

Most of his businesses expanded in the east as his business in Babylon fell. Pattmenidu understood that Governor Pagankanna had to show loyalty to King Nebuchadnezzar over the controversy of military support and reducing Babylonian contacts with Pars was one way for the governor to do that. The rebellious Jews in Judah were beating the Babylonian army so tensions grow for the governor causing him to blame Pars openly and to reduce commerce with Pattmenidu.

The governor had been trying for ages to get crocus plants from Pars and on this product only did he continue to pursue commerce with Pattmenidu. He said he needed two thousand bulbs for his queen's Hanging Gardens. Pattmenidu realized the value of the saffron trade and he refused to sell crocus bulbs to anyone outside Pars and that included the governor of Babylon. Pattmenidu also had to be careful to support his own King Cambyses while tactfully protecting his business interests with diplomacy so he gave the governor concessions in trade he granted to no one else. However, he restricted his crocus commerce to saffron and never negotiated away the precious bulbs.

//

With Mandane gone, Cambyses thought of her often. He recalled one conversation with Mandane when his wife told him Pattmenidu had refused to ship hundreds of crocus bulbs to her mother, Queen Aryenis. Mandane wanted her mother to plant the bulbs in the courtyard where she and Cambyses had married for sentimental reasons. Pattmenidu used all his tact in refusing her. He described the high commercial significance the crocus had to the country of Pars. The flower was protected for Cambyses by the gods because it was the source of saffron. Saffron was such an important spice that it brought a livelihood to enormous numbers of Parsians. He could sell the spice anywhere in the world. When he told Cambyses of this conversation he begged the king to make the queen understand how precious the crocus was to them.

Cambyses enjoyed recalling the subsequent conversation he had with Mandane. In a diplomatic sequence of questions Cambyses had asked Mandane one day when they were eating a yellow rice dish spiced with saffron if she enjoyed the dish. She said, "Yes. It is very tasty."

He then asked her as he peeked out the side of his eyes, "Is such a meal served in Media?"

She said, "No, I don't recall ever tasting this there."

He then dared to ask her, "Should I give away this treasure to another country? Since the spice comes from the crocus, should I give it away?"

She was startled at first then answered, "No, we must keep it to ourselves."

"Will you be upset if we do not send crocus bulbs to your mother?"

Now she understood what they were talking about and she laughed at his circumscribed way of getting at her request to Pattmenidu. She leaned toward Cambyses and kissed him. The matter was settled. The crocus continued to belong to Pars without controversy.

In spite of his loneliness Cambyses was able to conduct normal national business. In his diplomatic communications with Bactrian friends far to the east they confirmed that new business arrangements with Pattmenidu were satisfactory and profitable. One negative point they always brought up was the remote location of Pars relative to the northern caravan routes. It bothered Cambyses too. He told his Bactrian contacts that alternate caravan routes were being developed that ran southwest from Bactria over the deserts and through his mountains. He told them he needed their patience while trail possibilities were explored. He advised his eastern relatives it was going to require time, sacrifice and labor. He promised them a success, because the result would reduce dependence on Zav's Media contacts for everyone involved.

Cambyses lived for the arrival of messages from Mandane. He sent message after message to her telling his wife how much she was missed. He invented new ways to say he loved her. He tried his hand at creating a poem because poems were used so much to tell fables. He wanted her to think of their love as a beloved legend. He did not know she laughed at his naïve poetry attempts or that she was enchanted by his effort to impress her. One poem truly touched her heart when he wrote:

> Now the flowers dress the trees
> And birds begin to chirp in glee
> My thoughts are caught in a single trap
> Like a newborn bee in its crowded hive
> The gods make me yearn for your sweet kiss
> They rob me of your touch and gaze
> No magus can help my buzzing mind
> No magic can still my nervous hands
> Only you can help and serve my need
> Return to feast on our bloom of love

His attempt to make the busy bee the theme of his poem came from observations of bees he saw in a garden while he labored over his verses as he longed to still his anxiety with her body and her love.

Cambyses was surprised as he realized how exclusive his love was for Mandane. He felt even closer to her when he read her message explaining her part in the tax reduction. She gave full credit to Prince Zatame, but Cambyses wanted to think it was all her doing. She made a great joke out of Zav and his unsuccessful attempt to quiet the prince in the royal audience.

King Cambyses dreamed of Mandane at night and sometimes requested to be allowed to spend time in her rooms, to the amusement of her servants and the princesses. The king walked around touching her jewelry, her garments, and her crown. He looked so pensive the servant girls snickered behind his back. If he heard them he did not react. She was his missing treasure, yet safely sequestered with her parents, the two most powerful, most protected people in the entire empire.

Cambyses began to think of stories about the origin of Pars that he needed to tell his son later. He would let the boy know that although his mother was not from Pars she was of Aryan descent. His son may not be a full-blooded Parsian, but he would be a complete Aryan.

Cambyses recalled the old tales he needed to tell his son of how pastoral Aryan tribes had moved with their cattle from plains far to the north to settle east of the Indus River. Some of these people were believed to have reached the southern Erythraean Sea where they took the coastal route to move westward entering the bottom of Pars along with their cattle.

He thought of other more warlike clans who preferred to wander into dangerous places. They crossed mountains and deserts with easily herded sheep and goats, but no cattle, and entered the northern reaches of Pars. Some of these same people stopped along the way to settle in Bactria, Parthia or Media. As they moved they vanquished the indigenous populations then established new Aryan tribes. Cambyses recalled some of the local names like the Caspii and Hyrcanii who settled where they pleased. Cambyses was proud of his own tribal origin, the Pasargadii.

The wanderers continued west all the way past the Caspian Sea and overcame the Armenii who had lived in western Media. They all were the 'noble' people. His son would be taught to take pride in his noble ancestry. Cambyses would dilute the significance of his mother's Median background by emphasizing her Aryan origin for the boy.

The king could tell the boy how these tribes began to develop city-states with palaces and protecting warriors. Their farms began to produce more than was needed at the same time the forests gave them more wood than they could use. This abundance allowed the city-states to begin a bartering commerce that still existed, which his son would rule some day. Cambyses planned to tell his son to minimize war between tribes so the nation of Pars could prosper.

Cambyses would introduce his son to the two large cities of Pars, Anshan and Susa. He intended to describe innumerable small townships and village communities that had not yet developed into cities as well as the mountain strongholds that were not yet townships. Cambyses wanted to create large cities with successful caravan markets for his son by guiding the small, self-governed townships to expand their trade contacts.

Cambyses would explain to his son how he had sent various princes to the small townships to develop concentrated trading organizations that used Pattmenidu as their focal point. So far the presence of the royal family prevented the townships from starting wars or attempting to gain full independence. It had forced them to expect prosperity only through the established royal organization. Cambyses was proud that this process had started already. It was his attempt to reduce the power of tribal groups around his country to enhance unity, but tribal control still predominated in too many areas of Pars. Pars did not have the national sophistication or reduced tribal influence that Media had already established. Cambyses intended to make it change so he could show his son how to create an impressive nation.

Cambyses believed Pars was a small nation of vigorous people. Their survival was precarious in the swampy, marshlands of the west and in the mountains and deserts of the east. There were still many places where people tilled gardens or farms by stabbing the rocky ground with a thick stick. Hard work made his people tough; his son would learn to respect the stalwart peasants who made up his nation.

Rocks, dirt, barren salt plains and deserts were interspersed between fertile, level grasslands and farms. The harsh mountains provided lifesaving water from the snow. The eroding mountain walls gave mineral rich soil to the farms and forests. The salt plains were mined to yield salt essential for human survival as well as salt for sale to the caravans. His Parians were durable people who took advantage of a rugged geography to live independently. They cherished their Parsian nation more than their place in the Median Empire and fought valiantly to keep it. He looked forward to explaining that to his son.

Cambyses would talk of ancient Aryan conquerors that formed the great Pars nation. He would talk of individual warriors, like the great, fabled Rustam who slaughtered monsters in mountains and caves with his brutal sword to save his king.

Having a son was going to be a great joy. Cambyses vowed to keep peace so his son could travel about safely discovering how wonderful the world was. It would be fun to teach him honesty, archery and riding. Cambyses would make a true man out of his son. His boy would be tolerant, fair and kind; he would never make war; he would be the paladin of peace. His son would be proud to have his own sons preserve the Achaeminid dynasty for eons to come.

His son would surround himself with honest family members who worked to make Pars a legendary paradise. The women of Pars would be worshipped as the most gracious and charming wives on earth. Everyone would revere the gods by offering sacrifices in thanks for being the best nation in the world.

Cambyses believed it was both an honor and a duty to be the best king possible in the best nation in the world so his son would respect his duty as a leader later. His son would continue the bloodline to preserve the noble heritage started by the ancient kings. Cambyses planned to tell his son of his own great, great grandfather, Achaemenes, the man who had taken Pars away from the Elamites in war. Here was a man who knew how to unite tribes into a great fighting nation. This ancestral man was a paragon of war and organization. Cambyses was a man of organization and peace. His son was going to be a man of peace and prosperity. To Cambyses his son already represented the most magnificent legend of all time. He had to have a son!

Cambyses began to plan the return his wife and son from Ecbatana by the safest route. They could travel best in the late summer or early autumn when the weather was cool but comfortable. Cambyses had heard of the attack on his wife's cavalcade going north. When she was ready to come home with his son Cambyses resolved to provide so many warriors as guards that even Babylonians would not attack her train. He had almost sent his army into southern Media to punish their mountain dwellers for the assault when he heard how endangered she had been. If Mandane had lost her child, he would be at war with Media right now. It was fortunate for King Astyages that the Great King took immediate action. If he had neglected to punish his own mountain people, Cambyses would have done it for him, and much, much more. Cambyses loved peace, but he could fight with relentless determination for his wife, his child and the honor of his nation.

Meanwhile in the capital of the King of Kings, Astyages had begun to be bothered by his dream again.

20.

Palace life in Ecbatana was once again quiet now that Mandane was home. Everyone was thrilled that she was pregnant and healthy. The King was pleased his nation was at peace. Within his own family intrigues were minimized by Prince Zatame, who interfered in arguments between princes that might have otherwise led to fighting between city-states in Media.

Zav conducted his business in a reasonable manner without causing new bickering or name calling, at least not at the moment. Zav appeared to be spending the summer acting so polite that people had to talk about it and marvel at his good humor.

However, in the palace bedroom the dream came back to King Astyages with troubling frequency. Mandane was still the center of the dream. The green vine was still growing out of her covering his entire kingdom. She was still smiling. She was still unaffected by the vine's presence or growth. The vine continued to grow east and west well beyond the boundaries of Media.

King Astyages started to fret again. He woke at night in a cold sweat, unable to calm down. He became unusually agitated with everyone and everything. He kept the reason for this abrupt change of behavior to himself. He did not consult his Chief Magus this time. The King believed the reason for his anxiety was beyond the superficial skills of the magi to understand. He had to resolve the burden of these dreams himself, somehow.

Mandane was to have her child any moment, and he still had not decided what he should do about her, the child or the dream. His self-esteem began to drop. He was afraid he was becoming ineffectual and weak. He needed to change his attitude or his perception of his problem to improve his temperament. He had helped himself before when no one else could by marrying off Mandane to Pars; now he believed that he could do it again. Whatever he did had to be explicit, resolute and conclusive.

//

Mandane was so bloated with child that she was having trouble moving about. She knew she should be getting at least a little exercise. Midwives told her that exercise made the birth easier. She tried to walk in a garden every day. Some days it was just too much to even eat, let alone walk. Her tiny body was bravely suffering through this pregnancy that got harder to bear every day. She needed to remind herself she was carrying the future king of Pars to keep from ordering the medical magi to end her suffering with a premature delivery of some sort.

She looked at her servants and said, "I feel a little better today. I'm going to stroll in the garden alone for a short time. Go find something to do," she ordered, "I'll be fine. I'm not experiencing any pains or dizziness."

She walked down a corridor in solitary quiet to a flight of stairs she had to descend. She held onto the handrail and took one step downward. This caused her to bend at the waist with her weight thrust forward. Her supporting arm went limp when an abdominal cramp hit her. She pitched forward gasping in air; she was unable to scream. She toppled, rolled, twisted and twirled down the stairs. She became unconscious as her head bounced off the edge of a step. Blood spurted from the cut the stair made. Blood also streamed from scratches and numerous cuts produced by her fall. When her poor, frail body came to rest, blood began to flow from between her legs.

It was several minutes before a eunuch became anxious about her and went to see if she needed help returning to her rooms. He saw her at the bottom of the stairs where he wasted precious seconds staring in disbelief. Blood was everywhere. He wasted more time trying to decide if he should pick her up or get help. The eunuch rushed to find a midwife and carried her in a race to Mandane. After a quick inspection the midwife instructed the eunuch on how to move and lift the injured queen.

News of this tragedy flew like a hawk through the palace. Queen Aryenis rushed to her daughter. Every midwife allowed into the palace ran to Mandane's rooms. If there was any way to help the young princess-queen the midwives wanted to do everything they could.

King Astyages ordered the palace guards to kill all her daytime servants and slaves. It was done instantly. Then he instructed a eunuch to report to him right away when it was known if his daughter and the child were going to live. The King did not wish to send a message to Cambyses until this crisis reached the point where the fate of his daughter was evident.

King Astyages sequestered himself in a small room to worry over Mandane and his dream. What if she and the child both died? If that occurred then there was nothing to fear in his dream, but that outcome would give him grief since the loss of his daughter could only bring heartache.

What if both lived after Mandane gave birth to a daughter, or if it was a male child and it died? His dream might portend problems because her next child might be the creeping 'vine.' Mandane alive was the source of his misery. King Astyages still had to face an unpleasant decision eventually.

What if she died and the child lived? He could kill the child. It was a fitting revenge for causing Mandane's death. If they both lived, what might he do? That was the hard question to which he needed to find an answer. He could kill the child and suffer the consequences when Mandane found out. He knew the look in his daughter's eyes was going to devastate him and living with his wife would be traumatic also. He might have to go to war with Cambyses, but that was a minor bother.

The King could let a male child live while he monitored what it was taught. If Cambyses began to instruct the boy in revolution, the Great King would know of it. He could have Cambyses killed, which was not much of a loss, and that would give the Great King time to re-educate the boy to be loyal to Media.

The waiting took almost two days. Mandane did not wake up. She only groaned in unconscious pain. Everyone around Mandane wished they could take her agony from her. There was discussion among the midwives about calling a surgeon magus to abort the baby. Some agreed this was the best course to take. Queen Aryenis disagreed. She wanted to wait because Mandane's condition was not getting worse.

Contractions and heroic assistance from the midwives produced a live son. Mandane still did not wake up but she was alive. The *andarun* tried to be happy about the birth, but Mandane's condition still distressed them. A eunuch rushed to tell King Astyages of the live birth of the boy and his daughter's continuing unconsciousness.

The King made an instantaneous decision and sent the eunuch to find his young military officer, Harpagus. This was the young man that had carried out his orders to perfection against the Sythians. Every task this young man got was completed with mature perfection. The Great King appreciated his extreme loyalty in doing his duty.

Two moon cycles ago the wife of Harpagus bore a son that kept his father in a state of glee. His wife did fine nursing the boy. His son was growing fast and his tiny body was proportioned the way a healthy boy should be. The King knew this complimented the military manliness Harpagus felt. The soldier was able to provide a larger home for his family because his success in the military kept gaining him promotions. He was rising fast among the middle ranks of officers. Several officers of higher rank made it a point to help him recover from military errors as they tutored him in specific tactics and strategies. Military life suited Harpagus.

The officer walked into the presence of King Astyages and bowed, waiting with his head touching the floor to be told to rise. The King let him stay in obeisance while still formulating his royal plan. Finally King Astyages said, "Rise, Harpagus."

The young man got up but dared not move beyond standing erect. He wore a sword at his waist. The end of his military scabbard was tied to his leg to allow his weapon to be drawn with lethal speed if the need arose. A eunuch and two guards had entered the room with Harpagus. The armed guards never let anyone in unescorted to see the King.

The King waved Harpagus to a chair to sit. Then the King waved the eunuch and the guards out of the room. The soldiers looked at each other with concern because the visitor was still armed, but they were afraid to refuse to leave. One guard started to reach for Harpagus' sword, but the King waved him away and said, "Close the door as you leave."

The guards and the eunuch did as they were told, but they stood outside as close to the door as they could, ready to bound back into the room at the slightest hint of noise or call for help.

King Astyages asked, "Harpagus, how do you feel about your career in my army?"

Harpagus with perfect military bearing answered, "Sire, I am extremely pleased. You and your officers have helped me progress faster than I ever expected."

The King asked, "Do you wish to continue in the military?"

"Yes, sire," Harpagus answered uncomfortably. He worried that something was about to jeopardize his career. He held his breath as he sat transfixed in uncertainty.

In a contented tone the King said, "You did quite well when I sent you to battle the Sythians in Hyrcania."

Harpagus said, "Thank you, sire. I appreciated your kindness to me at that time. Your gift of the promotion was wonderful. Several other officers were jealous."

The King observed, "Several other officers would not have won so decisively. You did well, Harpagus. You followed my orders like a good soldier. That pleased me!"

Harpagus, still a little uneasy, said, "Thank you, sire."

King Astyages said, "I am told you just had a son. How is he doing?"

The soldier said, "He is well, sire. He grows every day. Some day he will be ready to serve you as I do. I am looking forward to helping him become a soldier for you."

King Astyages said, "I trust he is important to you."

Harpagus answered, "Sire, he is my most prized possession." The soldier was becoming a little concerned about the trend of this conversation. Normally, the Great King looked at his subjects; told them what he wanted then sent them on their way. He almost never talked in such a casual or personal way, and indeed never to a non-royal subject of unimportant status in the empire.

King Astyages finally said, "Harpagus, would you kill the son of another man if I told you to?"

A little shocked, Harpagus answered, "Yes, sire. I do that all the time when I kill someone in your defense."

A simple 'yes' or 'no' was all the King expected. King Astyages realized this man was a deeper thinker than most military men were so the King decided to be careful; he said, "If I told you a baby boy was going to grow up to be a serious threat to my kingdom would you be willing to kill him?"

Harpagus answered, "Yes, sire." Then he thought for a moment and worried that the conversation about his own son had significance here. He began to stir uncomfortably in his chair.

The Great King said, "There is a child I want you to kill for me. How will you do it?"

Harpagus touched his sword and answered, "Swiftly, sire."

King Astyages looked at him thoughtfully for several moments. Harpagus waited, praying he did not have to kill his own son.

King Astyages took a deep breath then said, "I will tell you how to kill this boy. You are not to kill him by your sword or by any other weapon. You will take him into the mountains and leave him for the wild animals to eat. You will return to where you leave him to bring me his bloody clothing so I know you have done my bidding. Do you understand?"

"Yes, sire," Harpagus answered intending to be an obedient soldier to his King.

The King demanded further, "Also, you are to tell absolutely no one and I mean no one! No one is to know where you are going either. You are to show no one the bloody clothing. I want this to be the greatest secret of your life. Do you understand, Harpagus?"

"Yes, sire," the soldier answered.

The King needed certainty and asked, "Can you do this?"

"I can, sire," answered Harpagus, as he grew confident.

King Astyages asked, "Will you do it, just as I command?"

"Yes, sire."

The King said, "Then, go to the palace nursery where you are to take the son of my daughter, Mandane. Tell the midwives you are bringing the child to me. Do not let any one accompany you as you leave the nursery. Bring the child here to me."

Harpagus asked, "But sire, how can I get into the *andarun*?"

The King looked confident and said, "I have already gotten permission for you to enter from Queen Aryenis."

Harpagus was relieved that he had not been commanded to kill his own son. He wondered if the Great King was going to command the death of his own grandson with deliberate absence of emotion. How could this strange pattern of murder be ordered with such disinterest? Harpagus marveled at the complete absence of familial love in the heart of the King. Is this baby the threat the Great King had mentioned a moment ago? What was behind all this? The soldier decided he had to do what he was told so he left to fetch the child.

King Astyages contrived to tell the court that the child had died in his arms and in his grief he had chosen to send the child to the Tower of Silence for an immediate funeral. As more of his plan, the Great King was going to order everyone to stay out of the Tower of Silence claiming he wanted to save people from the added grief of seeing the dead prince. It was enough for the palace to loose a prince everyone would mourn for. By the King's own command all of Media was to mourn. King Astyages decided to tell his daughter himself that her son had died.

The Great King called for a scribe magus to send a message to Cambyses telling him his wife was doing well, but the son had died. Now that the King's plan of action was underway the details came quickly to him. He presumed that the peace of mind he was feeling since his grandson was to be killed would also allow the dream to disappear. He was back in control of his own destiny. He felt improvement in his mood, felt his self-confidence began to return. Telling his wife and daughter about the death was no longer worrisome for him. He was the King of Kings again. Nothing could faze him!

Harpagus entered the suite with the baby boy in his arms. It was wrapped in a royal purple blanket. Harpagus began to put the child down on a bench, covered with a plain linen coverlet, so he could bow to the King. Astyages waved him to stop and said, "Give me the child."

Harpagus handed the baby to the King. Harpagus knew the Great King could not go through with this murder after he looked at the boy. The King looked down at the baby. Then he pointed to the bench and said, "Harpagus, take that spread. Cover the child so no one will know what you are taking from the palace."

Harpagus spread the dun colored linen wrap over the sleeping child. Then the King said, "Remember what I said. Be certain the child dies and do not let anyone know of this. Also, be certain to show me the baby's blood stained garments and this wrap later," as he touched the blanket. "Now go," the King commanded in his most detached, regal voice.

Harpagus left. He was very surprised that he was not only allowed to go, but he was also expected to carry out this wretched scheme. The King went to his daughter's room to tell her his vicious tale. Inwardly, King Astyages was smiling.

21.

As the news of how the tiny prince died spread throughout the palace of Ecbatana, mourning hovered like a storm cloud in the air. Zav absorbed the news of Mandane's accident with glee. He wanted her to die. The news of the dead son was beyond belief. He was so ecstatic he could hardly contain his need to shout or cavort like a child. He was bursting with excitement for the way his hatred for the family of Cambyses was being avenged. The minister felt like a conquering general who had done absolutely nothing to achieve victory. He had instigated none of this. Without lifting a finger his conquest became a reality. Zav was in awe at the thought of how mysterious the actions of the gods were when they performed their best works. They had just conspired a most amazing turn of fate.

He remembered the efforts of Princess Ispitamu to get a poisonous plant that could force the loss of an unborn child, just like this death. It was so ironic. Zav was curious about the plant he had gotten her. Did she know how to use it? Was she going to need more, or would she need a different poison?

In Anshan Princess Ispitamu received the news with stunned excitement. She was a little disappointed that this death was not achieved by her own efforts, making it her success. She wondered if Zav had somehow managed to accomplish what she had failed to do. Did the queen fall because of the effects of an abortion? Did Zav have the plant too, and was he able to use it with the good advice of a magus as well? The curiosity of the princess did not shadow her elation about the suffering of Mandane. The princess prayed for the foreigner to die from the fall on the stairs or an after-birth illness; the princess was just not certain of what god or gods she was praying to, but her prayers were futile. Mandane lived.

Princess Ispitamu made sure there was plenty of silphium to ensure the surviving queen never had another child. The princess began planning how often to give the poison liquid to Mandane to prevent another pregnancy and birth. Once every two moon cycles should do it. She could give the liquid to Mandane during the full moon. It was best to keep a specific moon interval in mind to ensure she did not forget.

Now all Princess Ispitamu had to do was schedule a periodic meeting with the queen to give Mandane the poison in her water or her wine. The princess planned to disguise the meetings as private condolence sessions with her mourning sovereign. The princess would claim to want an heir for her king as much as the queen needed a child for herself. Princess Ispitamu glowered with sullen meanness as she planned to remind the queen during these meetings about her inability to become pregnant. The princess was going to psychologically upset the queen while she perpetuated the physical reason for the queen's emotional discontent, and that combination was going to fill the queen with grief and guilt.

//

Elsewhere in the palace Cambyses was devastated by the message from Astyages. Cambyses had lost his son. He anguished over his loss. Cambyses was unable to sleep or eat. He ordered a horse to be saddled because he intended to ride to his wife without delay. Mandane must need him.

Prince Bagindu made more deliberate arrangements and prepared to go to Ecbatana with Cambyses when he realized his king was not in the proper emotional state to make the trip, or to return with Mandane, safely. The prince arranged for two midwives and a medical magus to ride in a carriage filled with cushions and blankets. Cambyses became impatient over the delayed departure. Princess Ispitamu demanded to go with them. She insisted that Mandane needed a close personal female friend with her. Cambyses allowed it.

Prince Bagindu had heard of the attack against Mandane on her way to Ecbatana and he was determined to prevent a repeat of such an assault on the way back. King Cambyses said, "We have too large a guard retinue. We will not be able to travel fast enough."

Prince Bagindu said, "Sire, we need a military guard so large that only insane bandits will accost us. There is no advantage to going fast if an unfortunate circumstance caused new difficulties in our family."

As the caravan passed through Susa, Prince Warohi with several of his local relatives joined Cambyses. They were heartbroken at the loss of a first son. Prince Warohi thought the lineage question Zav had suggested was now inconsequential; it was time for everyone to mourn for the parents. Cambyses was too distraught to remember he had insurrection issues to discuss with Prince Warohi. The prince anguished with the father who had lost his first born. The men hugged as they prepared to travel on from Susa to Ecbatana.

The atmosphere in the capital of Media was nothing like the atmosphere at the time of the wedding. Even a man deeply engrossed in his own problems could not avoid noticing the general quiet that prevailed in the city. People whispered in small groups. Very little shouting or boisterous hawking of goods was done as the minor king passed. However, children squealed and laughed out loud while they played, as they always did. People in the streets who knew King Cambyses by sight pointed and buzzed as he passed. All this added to his sadness. He longed to hold Mandane in his arms. He felt he needed her as much as she must need him.

In the palace his passage through the seven gates of the seven walls was swift. He rode without stopping. If any man had challenged him the man would have died with his next breath. The seven gates were positioned in a staggered pattern. A man on a horse or camel was unable to careen straight to the palace. There were several obligatory turns to get through all the gates. It was a brilliant defensive construction. Cambyses made the turns with such ease that he appeared to be accelerating instead of slowing at each corner.

In the palace he knelt beside his wife who had recovered consciousness a few days before his arrival. They both cried with deep anguished sobs. Cambyses was not too proud to show such emotion to the woman he loved. They shared their mutual sadness with tender affection for the heartfelt loss to each other. Cambyses promised Mandane they would have other children; one of which would be a son they would make the most magnificent man of his time. She vowed to bear a son as handsome and caring as his father was. They sealed each other's wounded spirits by clinging together with their unselfish love.

The servant girls in the room were overcome with sadness and affection for the minor king who expressed love for his wife so deeply. They left the room crying. The women already knew that Mandane was going to be fine. The surgical magus had pronounced Mandane capable of having more children. She bore no physical damage to prevent future pregnancies. This was the sole piece of good news Mandane could share with her husband.

Cambyses touched each little cut and scratch on his wife. His fingertips glided over the cut on her head and asked, "Does this cut hurt, darling?"

"Not now," she answered.

On a man Cambyses thought her injuries would hardly be noticed. On his wife her wounds seemed like dismal retribution from the perverted daeva because she tried to conceive him future king. Cambyses wondered why the corrupted gods did this to Mandane? What had his wife ever done to make this terrible accident necessary?

While they spent their time comforting each other, Princess Ispitamu searched out Zav. He was surprised but pleased that she had come. Zav ordered a servant to bring them food and wine as he took her to a small room. They reclined on cushions and comforters around a low table. Zav noted her toga had a deep cut neckline that revealed her ample breasts. He had difficulty taking his eyes off them. She allowed the hem of her garment to ride up above her knees to exhibit her well-formed legs to enhance her desirability. She was aware of the effect she was having on this ugly man. If Zav hated Mandane as much as she did then she intended to seal an alliance with an endorsement of sex, because that was her favorite method of concluding a negotiation.

The princess said, "Thank you for being so quick to get more of the plant for me. Unfortunately, by the time I knew how to use it, Mandane had left Anshan."

Zav was almost salivating as he said, "It was my pleasure. You will have your chance to use it from now on. I believe we are of one mind about Cambyses and Mandane."

The princess looked confused for a moment. She said, "I have no interest in hurting Cambyses. I would be very hurt if something happened to my cousin. I feel bad that he had to be affected by the death of the prince, but he will get over it with time. I only want to hurt Mandane."

Zav hesitated for a moment. He suddenly realized he had to be careful to make his hate appear to be directed towards Mandane alone. He said, "Well, maybe I misstated myself; Mandane is my intended target, yet I fear that Cambyses must be unfortunately hurt as we strike at her. Do you agree?"

"Yes, my cousin will be affected, but I have to use that plant to ensure *she* does not have another child. You must be ready to get me more next summer. We must make certain that Mandane never produces a half-Parsian heir to our throne," Princess Ispitamu promised with a deep venomous growl.

"Ah," said Zav. He loved conspiring. "You can prevent the queen from having children? That is wonderful! Will she suffer a misery with each lost child?"

The princess looked sharply at the enormous nose on his face wondering how a woman as beautiful as herself had ended up sharing crime with a man so unattractive. She answered, "No, but she will never give birth again. At least that is what I understood from the magus I spoke with in Susa. Does that suit you, Zav?"

Zav said, "Oh yes. That will be just fine. I am glad we have this interest in common. I will be pleased to help you. If you need any new poisons that will add to our mutual pleasure, please contact me. I will be happy to help you acquire them. I can personally deliver anything you want when I come to Pars again. How will you be able to poison her without being discovered?"

Princess Ispitamu answered with confidence, "It will be easy. The queen believes I'm her best friend. I'll be in her presence very often and every two moon cycles we'll meet alone when I'll give her the potion in her wine. It will be simple enough to do.

"But, Zav, Cambyses sent you away, forbidding you to return. If you enter Pars again he will either hold you as a prisoner or have you beheaded."

Zav said, "I can get a written order from King Astyages telling me to go there when my ministerial duties obligate me to go. Cambyses will not contest such an order will he?"

"No, that would mean war, which Cambyses will avoid at all costs," said Princess Ispitamu as she picked up a peach and gave it an erotic lick as she stared into Zav's eyes. He squirmed and smiled. She asked, "Do you think my legs are attractive, Zav?"

Zav's eyes bulged and he said, "They are extremely lovely, princess. May I touch them?"

She teased him by spreading her knees and saying, "If you think it will amuse you."

He began to caress her calf and her thigh. He simultaneously wondered why the gods had given him such a stunning ally. The princess smiled, pushing her neckline open a bit more. Her breasts were half exposed. He looked at her chest and licked his lips. She reached behind his head to pull his face to her bosom. Their wretched affiliation was ratified.

Elsewhere, Prince Bagindu went to find Prince Zatame to inquire about the details of this terrible event that made Queen Mandane suffer so. Prince Zatame said in a pained voice, "From what we could discover it was an unfortunate accident. Mandane just fell down the stairs. It was reported from the midwives that she began to have cramps or contractions. The difference is a mystery to me, but the pain made her fall."

Prince Bagindu revealed his suspicions about the rumors he had heard regarding the baby boy when he asked, "And what about the child? How did he come to die?"

Prince Zatame related what he had heard. He said, "The Great King had requested to see the child, and it died in his arms. Only a soldier was present. The Great King called a magus to order the child taken to the Tower of Silence. The body laid in rest for the required three days. The King ordered everyone to stay away. No one was allowed to look on the dead baby."

Prince Bagindu asked if he could speak with the magus who stood over the body. Prince Zatame said, "No. The Great King had the magus executed. As you well know, it is a grievous offense to injure or kill a magus. However, in this case the deed was done before the Chief Magus could object. Also, because the King's agony was so profound, the Chief Magus did not conjure a spell on King Astyages for his repulsive offense. However, the priest cautioned the King to never do such a thing again. He went on with such vituperation that I am surprised the King did not kill him."

Prince Bagindu asked, "Do you think it strange that the Great King would kill an innocent magus over the death of a prince? Could the magi have had something to do with the death or with Mandane's fall?"

Prince Zatame said, "I had not thought of that, Bagindu. I do not know if I could even investigate that possibility now that the man is dead too."

Prince Bagindu asked, "Can we talk with the soldier who was present with the King?"

Prince Zatame answered, "I already have. He is a young man named Harpagus. He just had a son of his own. He would be very careful handling a baby. He had already gained a little experience holding his own son when he got involved in this incident."

That seemed to close the issue; however, the questions Prince Bagindu asked made both men curious because the details were not at all clear. The princes agreed to talk more in the future about the details of this situation, encouraged by a mutual trust in their friendship.

When Mandane was well enough to travel, Cambyses left Ecbatana in a slow parade with his relatives. This time Cambyses rode in the carriage with his wife. He still worried about her health since she had lost weight and her complexion was pale. Mandane had lost the healthy pink glow in her cheeks; also, her eyes were sad and heavy. She still believed the fall on the stairs that caused the death of her son was her fault, and it was going to take a long time for the queen to forgive herself.

Cambyses felt their loss was his fault. He believed he should not have allowed her to leave Anshan to return to her parents. Mandane might have had a safe childbirth in her own palace. He told her this, wishing to take the blame and shame from her. Together they tried to heal each other with tender love.

The royal cavalcade arrived home safe but sad. The royal pair worked to reestablish the closeness they had felt before their tragedy. It took a lot of effort by both of them, but slowly the old comfort they had nurtured together returned as their lives were renewed. But guilt gradually strained their relationship.

22.

After taking the live infant from the Great King, Harpagus left the palace without anyone seeing him, except for a few slaves who saw nothing wrong with an army officer carrying an unidentifiable bundle from the palace. The slaves bowed out of fear for his authority, not for the man. Harpagus took empty corridors to pass through doors that were seldom used. He went home to change his clothing so he could be more comfortable on his ride into the mountains.

While he was home the tiny prince woke up crying. His wife heard the baby and thought it was her son. She was amazed to discover it was a different child. Harpagus said, "You are never to mention this child to anyone. Do you hear?"

Harpagus said it with such severity he shocked her. Her look told him she expected an explanation. He said, "This child is being moved in secret for the sake of a palace princess. That is all you need to know."

She said, "The baby is soiled and hungry. Let me care for it for a moment."

With that she did not wait for his approval. She cleaned the boy then fed him from her own breast. She said, "I hope I am not depriving our son of a meal," as she smiled with maternal sweetness at the baby in her arms.

"There was a second child born that died today in the palace. Queen Mandane's recent accident produced a dead boy," said Harpagus as he lied to his wife. She accepted his statement with a disinterested nod, since she was busy concentrating on the child in her arms. Harpagus waited for her to finish with the baby who had fallen asleep again as soon as it was full. The officer wrapped the child just as the King had instructed and rode into the mountains with the sleeping infant snuggled against him. Harpagus rode to the northwest towards the western edge of the Median kingdom.

Harpagus was equipped to travel until he found a secluded place. He did not want any passing traveler coming to Ecbatana to stumble across the royal garments and make the mistake of bringing them into the court during a public audience. His wife had given him goat's milk to feed the child. As he rode to higher elevation levels in the mountains he noticed what he thought was evidence of wild animals. He was not a woodsman who could recognize signs of life in a forest. The soldier missed most of the animal footprints, leftover bones of a scavenger's meal, and he seldom heard the rustling of predators moving out of his way. He could feel the temperature dropping as his horse climbed up the steep slopes. The chill in the air made him shiver. He wondered if the sleeping child was cold.

Harpagus crossed vast fields of farmland that the Great King owned. The King's vassals worked the land raising domestic animals for slaughter. Harpagus slept one night in a clean barn loft owned by King Astyages. He hid the baby's purple cloak then ordered the wife of a slave to care for the child for the night. She kept it comfortable till morning. The officer left when the sun rose. The peasants did not know who the man with the child was. They did, however, recognized his accoutrements as valuable military gear, but they dared not ask him questions.

Harpagus came to a clearing at dusk on the second day of his travel. He decided to camp there for the night before leaving the child tied to the base of a tree. It was a place he could find without difficulty later when he returned to recover the garments. He slept well, except for when the child cried. He got up to feed the boy when he could not ignore its crying. At dawn the bleating of sheep woke him. He was surprised. He thought he had climbed high enough on this mountain to avoid people. He did not expect anyone to be living at this elevation. He could not remember if sheep roamed wild in the mountains. He had never heard of it.

The officer mounted his horse with the child in his arms and slowly rode along the edge of the forest toward the bleating. He came upon the shepherd. The man was startled to see a man on horseback here. The shepherd bowed from the waist and said with a nervous tone, "I am you servant, sir."

Harpagus was annoyed that the man was here and he demanded, "Why do you run sheep on this mountain?"

The man answered, "This land belongs to the Great King. I tend his animals for him. Lower down the mountain I tend cattle and his orchards."

The farmer waited for Harpagus to say something but the horseman just sat astride his mount looking pensive, so the farmer said, "Sir, may I have my wife feed you?"

Harpagus was hungry so he said, "Yes, and take this child for me."

The shepherd was amazed that the bundle was a sleeping baby. Today was already turning into a very strange day and it was just barely the break of dawn.

The shepherd's wife took the child. Harpagus saw the light of a mother shine in her eyes. She undertook the cleaning and feeding of the child with eagerness while Harpagus ate. During his meal he observed the couple. They appeared to live alone here. He asked, "Who else lives in this house, on this hill?"

Together they answered, "Just us, sir."

"You have an accent. Are you Greek?" asked Harpagus.

The man answered saying, "Yes, sir. We are Greeks but we come from Lydia. King Croesus sent us to be servants to your Great King as a gift. I am a free man, not a slave. We think the two kings are related. My wife is Spaco and I am Mitridates, sir."

Harpagus asked, "Have you been here very long?"

Mitridates answered, "Yes, sir. It has been many sun cycles."

"Then you are familiar with these mountains," exclaimed Harpagus.

Mitridates said, "Oh yes, sir."

"Are there other people who work up here with you?"

Mitridates said, "Not up here, sir. There are slaves in the valley below us. They live down there caring for cattle in a field and the orchards that are growing below. They never come up this high. Just we live here. We tend the sheep, but I also supervise the slaves below to make certain they care for the King's property well."

Harpagus thought for a while. It was possible that this man might be able to help him accomplish his mission, so the soldier said, "I charge you, farmer, with a specific task that you will complete for me in secret. Do you understand?"

The farmer said, "Oh yes, sir. I understand."

"Does your wife understand, Mitridates?" asked Harpagus.

The farmer answered "Oh yes, sir. She understands. Spaco, you do understand," and the farmer looked at his wife. She agreed with an affirmative nod. They had no idea of what was expected of them but they were ready to agree to anything this powerful, young soldier wanted.

Harpagus said, "You are to take this child higher into the mountains and tie him to a tree. You will leave him there until he dies or the animals eat him. You are to bring his wrappings and any parts of him you find back here. If none of the child remains I expect to see blood on these garments. You are not to talk with anyone about this, nor is anyone to see the wrappings. Do you understand?"

"Yes, sir, but when the animals of the night eat him there will be no child or clothing to bring back," pleaded Mitridates.

Harpagus said, "I will return to recover whatever you can find. Tie the garments as well as the child to a tree. You will save what there is for me to take."

Mitridates said, "Yes, sir. We will do as you say."

With that Harpagus mounted his horse for the ride back to Ecbatana. He intended to return after spending a few days at home. He wanted to spend time holding his own son before going to the Great King with the salvage of this miserable task.

When he returned home his wife asked, "Where did you take that baby, Harpagus?"

He lied, "To its relatives in the south."

Harpagus held his sleeping son and wondered what emotion could motivate King Astyages to have his own grandson killed. What quirky motivation could possibly drive the Great King to commit so vile an act as to order the death of that baby? How could the King do such a thing after holding that guiltless tyke in his arms, or after looking at its beautiful face? If King Astyages could order the murder of a completely innocent baby, what other dishonorable acts was he capable of committing? Harpagus began to question his loyalty to the Great King. He wondered if he should leave the military to take up another occupation, if more of this type of duty was in his future.

He looked about his home at the large living space. The officer saw the neatly arranged kitchen with its fireplace beside the oven built into the brick that his wife was so excited to have. He had a stable for his war-horse. His armor and weapons were of the highest quality. His career was developing well. These things were only possible because of his dedicated service to the Great King. Maybe other duties the

King gave him in the future might be less bothersome so Harpagus chose not to think about this particular episode too much. The officer put his son down. Later on he would return to the mountain where he was to recover what he could to show the King.

//

When Harpagus first left the home of Mitridates and Spaco they were both very scared. Besides being frightened to see a soldier on their mountain, his instructions petrified them. They took turns holding the baby. Spaco began to cry and said, "Mitridates, the gods have sent this child to us. We must keep him."

"We can't. That soldier is coming back and we have to give him back these wrappings. He expects to see blood on them. Remember he said to tie the child to a tree so forest animals could eat him."

"The gods have put this child in my arms. I will not give him up!"

"Please, Spaco, do not make this difficult for yourself or for me. We need to do what we have been instructed to do. Tonight I have to go high in the mountain forest and leave the boy. Tomorrow I will pick up whatever remains. Our obligation will be done."

"But, Mitridates, we lost our own child just days ago and this one came to us. I can keep this baby in its place. It is the will of the gods. I can't give this baby up too. Please..."

"Our baby died at birth. That was the will of the gods. You are healthy now. That is the will of the gods. You will have other children, Spaco. That is the will of the gods. The gods must have made that soldier understand their wishes, as well. We must do as he commanded."

"Mitridates, I will not let you take this baby from me. Wrap these garments around our own dead child and leave him in the woods. Return tomorrow with whatever the animals leave. You will have satisfied your duty to that soldier who will never know the difference."

Mitridates thought for a while. Their child's dead body was still in a small room in the barn. They had decided to consider that room their Tower of Silence where their deceased baby could lay for three days. Today was the third day. They had satisfied their obligation to the gods. Maybe Spaco's idea could work. If he needed blood to soil the baby's garments later Mitridates could get it from a sheep, or even himself. He could hide the live boy below with the slaves until the soldier left with his bundle.

It took all his strength to let his very own child's body be ravaged by the animals of the forest. Human sacrifice was common practice when conducted by a magus in a religious rite. Mitridates begged the gods to accept his child as a special offering, a special sacrifice. The farmer climbed into the forest high above his residence with the body of his child wrapped in the designated garb. His wife cried as he left. He had no intention of visiting the place he climbed to again after this episode was over. He wept when he placed his burden on the ground. He took hemp from his pocket to tie his dead baby to a tree. He tied the garments to the tree using a secure farmer's knot so they could not be carried away because the clothing was the evidence of his obedience to the soldier.

The following morning he returned to pick up everything he could find, including a couple of tiny bone fragments. There was not much blood because the body had rested for three days after its death. He soiled the wraps with a sheep's blood. Too much blood might look strange since the baby had such a very small body, so Mitridates smeared just a few tiny streaks on the cloth. His duty was done.

It worked precisely as Mitridates planned. The live baby was hidden when the soldier returned. Harpagus said nothing. He just held out his hand to receive whatever Mitridates had recovered. Harpagus inspected the lot and rode away. It was ended for Mitridates and Spaco. They had a live, healthy son! The gods have strange ways and this time the Greek pair were favored.

Harpagus took his packet home and hid it in the stable because he did not want to bring it into his house. He was afraid his wife would ask questions if she saw the bundle. He was also bothered about other things. The most powerful man known to the officer had sent him on a cruel errand with two firm royal instructions. The first was to see the child killed and the second was to tell no one. As an officer he had no trouble carrying out orders but in this episode he had violated a serious trust by not following either command the King had given him. The officer was in danger because he had given the job of performing the murder to a total stranger. Secondly, he had involved three other people in the task, his wife and the two Greeks in the hills.

Harpagus prayed for the gods to protect him. He wondered if his prayers went to the beneficial gods of the sky, the ahura, or the spirits of damnation, the daeva. A prayer is a prayer and the soldier knew that where it ends up is the business of the good and evil spirits. Man presents the prayer then he becomes a bystander in its fate. Harpagus felt the godly domain that received his prayer would to be quite evident when he next met with King Astyages.

//

The King smoothed over the entire disaster in the palace. He lied to his wife and daughter. He forced another man to commit murder for him. He executed a perfectly innocent magus to add compounding mystery to the baby's death. The magus was a rites-magus but there were plenty of those, the King did not consider him a substantial loss. Additionally, there were plenty of army officers, and if Harpagus made the mistake of not following royal orders then executing an officer was just another insignificant matter.

Harpagus carried the dregs of his crime in one hand as he was ushered by a guard toward a room where the Great King waited. The guard said, "I must inspect what you have in your hand, sir."

Harpagus answered, "Come into the presence of the King with me. Examine it there."

In the presence of King Astyages the guard reached for the bundle, but the King waved him away saying, "Leave and close the door."

The King looked at his officer bowing before him, wondering if the secret was still safe. He said, "Rise, Harpagus, and tell me what you have done for me."

Harpagus rose then tried to hand the King the bundle. Instead of looking at it King Astyages just waited for the officer to describe his actions. Finally Harpagus realized he had to speak. He said, "Sire, I did as you commanded. I left the palace without being seen with the child. It slept without drawing attention. I rode to the northwest into the mountains."

Then he lied and said, "I tied the child to a tree. Later I retrieved those," as he pointed to the clothes.

The King asked, "Did you tell no one, as I commanded?"

Harpagus lied again and answered, "I kept the secret, sire, it was easy to do."

"I am pleased with you," the King said, "open the bundle."

Using his fingertips, Harpagus did as he was told. He was reluctant to touch any more of the bloody cloth than he had to. He showed King Astyages the stains of blood, plus the two small bones. The King smiled saying, "I had thought of having you executed for what you have done. You committed a murder against my descendant. You insulted the whole royal family. However, I forgive you. I am pleased to find a person I can trust. You will be protected from now on."

The King looked at Harpagus and said, "Destroy these. Burn them."

"Yes, sire," said the officer and left the room.

Harpagus breathed a sigh of relief as he left. He was out of the presence of the King and alive. The King's last barrage of senseless accusations was bothersome, just as the entire episode had been disturbing. The soldier wondered if the King was going crazy. Harpagus felt uncomfortable but safe because he was not facing a death sentence. He burned the final evidence of the King's scheme. Now only the soldier and the Great King knew what had happened, and Harpagus thought he was the only one who knew the true details of what had happened.

23.

"Our son died a full sun cycle ago, Cambyses, yet I have not become pregnant again. What do you think is wrong?" asked Mandane. The anxiety in her tone was evident.

Cambyses said, "I do not know, my love. The medical magi tell me there is no reason for us to be childless; after all we are not ill. This isn't your fault or my fault. The midwives who were present at the birth say you do not have any injuries that prevent you from conceiving again. Our midwives in Pars cannot identify any damage to your body either. It may just be that we both have felt a strain over our loss."

Mandane gave him a concerned look and said, "I enjoy when we try to have another child, darling, but why doesn't our lovemaking produce a child? There must be a spell on me, which I am not able to overcome. Should I have a magus search my mind? Maybe I should go to the Greeks at Delphi. They are renowned for understanding strange circumstances."

Cambyses felt a twinge in his chest because of what his wife said and he whispered, "There is nothing wrong with you, Mandane. You must stop worrying. The gods will intervene at the proper time to help us conceive an heir."

He took her hand as he led her to a garden in full bloom. Rose bushes and various kinds of lilies decorated soft, fine sand paths. They strolled hand in hand among the flowers complimenting each other and speaking of love.

Suddenly Mandane said, "Darling, take me to Ecbatana so I can see my parents. I miss them."

He answered, "I can't go. I am too busy with official affairs."

Mandane said, "Then I will ask mother to come here," but she knew Queen Aryenis no longer traveled. Her mother was hidden behind the seven walls with King Astyages who refused to leave his palace. Mandane knew her father's image, as the occult enigma, was valuable to him so he never jeopardized it by appearing casually before the peasants, even in a royal caravan. When the King of Kings came into public view outside his palace he was always dressed as a conquering war hero in his gold and silver armor. Mandane had to visit Ecbatana or be content in her loneliness.

//

Elsewhere in the palace Zav had arrived to see Cambyses. This was his second visit since Cambyses had banned him from Anshan. The minister still had in his possession a letter from the Great King ordering him to go to Anshan. This time Zav was to look into the development of the alternative caravan routes that were starting to reduce the flow of traffic through Ecbatana. Cambyses had not allowed Zav the opportunity to visit in the public court assembly; he just passed Zav off to Pattmenidu instructing him to minimize the significance of these trade avenues. The merchant was working assiduously to expand them, but he refused to admit their growing success to Zav. The gem trade was increasing. Marauders to the north were used to gems coming by established west to east routes. These robbers were not industrious enough to travel across the salt desert to intercept the new routes, making them safer. There were large tracks of barren wilderness around the trails taken by the caravan drivers across the salt desert and no one but a few nomadic tribes wandered these wastelands. Unfortunately, commerce traveling these new routes was much slower.

Pattmenidu had difficulty convincing caravan drivers to across the salt and sand deserts east of Anshan. A camel's hoof could pound through the crusty layer of dried salt, leaving a sharp edge on the salt sheet that cut the animal's ankles. This made the animal angry and difficult to drive. The pack-train drivers claimed they were losing an entire trip each sun cycle because the animals moved slow, reluctant to walk through these hazards. Pattmenidu worked hard to convince the drivers that as the salt path was trampled the trail would be safer and faster to use.

During his investigation Zav asked, "What kinds of goods are moved over your new route? And in what volumes?"

The merchant answered, "Would you like to inspect the records?"

Pattmenidu wanted to escape from Anshan as soon as possible to get away from Zav. He pretended the whole subject of the salt desert trade was incidental.

Zav said, "Of course," but there were no good records for Zav to inspect since only a few clay cuneiform tablets described the commerce even existed. A moment later Zav said, "Never mind. I'll look into this later."

Zav recognized that having a Parsian magus track down the tablets took a lot of time. Normally, the minister enjoyed searching the clay tablets of Pars as much as a bore enjoyed snuffling in a mushroom patch but today the delay annoyed Zav. He was anxious to finish his business so he could visit with Princess Ispitamu.

Zav was beginning to think he might join the royal family by marrying the princess. He still aspired to reach the ranks of royalty through marriage. He hoped the Great King would make the official designation nominating him a prince, even if it had to be a prince of Pars. As much as he hated Cambyses and Mandane he would accept becoming a prince by marriage while living in Ecbatana. Zav intended to rise to the level of king some day because he believed he had the capacity to rule a nation. Zav was smart enough not to suggest marriage yet to Princess Ispitamu, but he had started to entertain that possibility in his mind. This visit was be the third occasion for him to sleep with Princess Ispitamu. He did not understand how naïve his thinking was.

The princess wanted to have as little to do with Zav as possible because he was so obnoxious, but she had to keep on his good side because he provided her with the poison that she needed to plague Mandane. The liquid she gave Mandane in her wine during their 'friendly' meetings together appeared to be working since no new pregnancy had developed and Mandane never showed signs of being sick after drinking the secret silphium. It was very easy for the princess to blend the brewed liquid into the queen's cup on regular intervals. Princess Ispitamu also managed to keep the queen on edge about not getting pregnant. The princess did not accuse the queen of being the source of the problem, but her subtle innuendoes made Mandane believe she was either barren or cursed because Cambyses did not have an heir. The princess was very pleased with herself. She was preventing pregnancies while mentally traumatizing the queen at the same time.

The princess' affair with Zav continued as a tolerable inconvenience. For such an ugly man he was remarkably well endowed and a lion on the cushions. He had no trouble satisfying a woman repeatedly. His visits might be worth looking forward to if it were not for his looks and his personality.

Zav in Anshan was an annoyance to Pattmenidu, so the merchant went to Susa. Pattmenidu preferred to avoid answering the weasel's questions. Pattmenidu hated Zav's pushy assertions about how Pars was obligated to do business with Media. Also, going to see the Rice Rodent was a pleasure because the proprietor always had important information for the merchant. The Rice Rodent did not believe it was an offense against the Parsian code of honor to overhear conversations. To lie about what he heard was dishonest so he was careful to avoid that.

The food the Rice Rodent prepared was always excellent. It helped Pattmenidu keep his portly figure. The merchant experienced difficulty with breathing due to his bulk, but breathing was not a problem when he ate. Long ago he had developed a technique of alternately chewing and huffing so he suffered little discomfort while delighting in large meals. Pattmenidu always looked forward to trying new dishes the Rice Rodent served.

It had been an entire sun cycle since Cambyses had refused to help King Nebuchadnezzar. Over an enormous dinner that Pattmenidu ate with wanton zest the Rice Rodent said, "I hear Pharaoh Necho's help in Judah is defeating King Nebuchadnezzar."

Pattmenidu was startled and asked, "Is the Pharaoh conquering Babylon?"

The proprietor said, "Oh no, but he is encouraging the Jews to push out of Judah to the north. They probably will not chase the Babylonian army to Aleppo. They have done enough damage to Nebuchadnezzar. I hear King Nebuchadnezzar no longer possesses Judah and maybe not even Syria. We will have to make direct contact with Jewish and Syrian ministers in order to trade there if the Babylonians are truly out."

Pattmenidu said, "I will send gem dealers to Judah first to establish good will."

The Rice Rodent said, "You had better send someone to Babylon without delay to investigate their mood. You recall they were angry with our king and wanted to attack us after their war. I am not sure

King Astyages will prevent them from punishing us if they decide to come here."

"Yes," answered Pattmenidu, "I will go myself to talk with Governor Pagakanna in Babylon. I am anxious to see those splendid gardens he was developing for his queen. Maybe King Nebuchadnezzar will be too tired after, what, three or four sun cycles of war? He will need a rest. I may have to promise him a caravan full of gifts to soothe his anger but it will cost less than a war."

The Rice Rodent loved to spread rumors and said, "I hear the robbers in the mountains to the east are realizing that you have begun to ship goods across the southern deserts. The rumor I hear is that the mountain people are reluctant to move to the unlivable salt desert just to rob your caravans. You should continue your efforts; you may have a real success there."

Pattmenidu said, "Thank you, that is good news, but the caravan drivers do not like that route either. It is very hard for me to make them go that way."

The two men talked long into the night. It was beneficial for them both to exchange information. The Rice Rodent was developing a trading business, and he was ready to attempt to be in the caravan business. He had traded for a camel herd he now wanted to use to ship goods himself for the first time. Pattmenidu said, "With my knowledge I would be happy to take your first pack train to Babylon, if that is agreeable to you."

Delighted, the Rice Rodent said, "Oh Pattmenidu, I would be so grateful if you would. I need the confidence of having a success the first time. You can instruct my driver to do my bargaining. I do not know how to train a camel sitter. Even worse, I can not tell if he is as experienced as he claims. Maybe you will help me understand his skills, or lack of them, as well."

They agreed on what the caravan was to carry as well as what the personal profit for Pattmenidu was to be as payment for his training efforts. Pattmenidu agreed to instruct and to evaluate the driver for the Rice Rodent. The cavalcade was to travel to Babylon and back to Susa with a full load in both directions since that made the greatest profit. The Rice Rodent identified the types of goods he preferred to have come back from Babylon.

In Babylon Pattmenidu arrived safely and saw what he expected in a war-weary nation. Most of the army was still in Syria but those men who had already returned had arrived without booty. As the retreating party, the Babylonians had to leave behind all the plunder they acquired during the previous occupation of Judah when they ruled the lands they now lost. He observed the poverty and misery of beaten warriors as he traveled through the streets. Whole families were begging in the streets. For a man to come home empty-handed after four sun cycles of absence was devastating to the peasants.

Babylon was still rich because of its location on the west to east caravan route but only the royal family, successful merchants and bankers shared in that wealth right now. The peasants could fare better after the warriors began to make their way back to the farms and pastures to take up working as vassals for the rich again. That is, except for the men the king ordered to march off to fight again.

Pattmenidu went directly to his acquaintance Governor Pagakanna where he negotiated an exchange of goods for the Rice Rodent. Pattmenidu had a heavy, valuable load for the return to Susa. It would provide a nice profit for him and his friend. Pattmenidu was pleased with the skill of the caravan driver. It would be a pleasure to tell the Rice Rodent he could depend on this man for efficiency, but the one feature that could not be assessed at this time was the honesty of the driver. Pattmenidu could give the Rice Rodent clues on how to evaluate that in the future. Pattmenidu felt good that he could encourage his friend to commit himself to this risky yet profitable business.

Governor Pagakanna was excited to show the merchant the progress being made on the Gardens. Pattmenidu counted seven levels now. The dull, sundried bricks only made inlaid multicolored marble designs appear more fabulous. The marble depicted animals and geometric shapes. The blue ceramic decorations on the outside walls of the city were elaborate. The lush greenery among the sparkling flowerbeds could not have been more impressive. Each level had stairs or ramps leading to higher plateaus of exotic foliage. Strange plants never seen in Pars or Babylon were vividly exhibited. The multicolored floral designs of the gardens were magnificent. The governor had succeeded in collecting unusual, lovely trees and bushes from far off lands.

Governor Pagakanna said, "When the King returned from Syria he was in an evil state of mind. He shouted, whipped everyone in sight; executed slaves for almost nothing. Queen Amytis was not able to calm him.

"But these gardens, oh, how they delighted him. I was the one citizen in the kingdom that was safe. But, if I had not made such excellent progress with the height and planting of the gardens, I probably would be dead now."

Pattmenidu said with honest admiration, "You have built with incredible speed. These gardens are the highest structure in the city. I was able to see the top level even before I saw the city. And the way you have made the blue ceramic on the outside walls blend with the flowers above is startling, my friend."

Pagakanna said, "Oh really! I ordered it done but I never went outside the gate myself to look. Was it truly as pleasing as you say?"

"More than pleasing. It was exciting, a marvel! There is nothing to match it in the world. The Gardens are high, so high! So large! I must admit I could not see the color of the flowers that clear the top, but the vines with their runners falling over the wall of each level seem to be suspended in air. It is a miracle of design, my friend.

"How is it watered, Pagakanna? Do you depend exclusively on rainfall?"

The governor said, "No, our engineers have constructed pumps that draw water from the Euphrates River. The gardens were placed close to the river for this purpose. Each level has its own pump connected to an irrigation system.

"Pattmenidu would you like to climb to the top with me? May I show you our ingenious system?" begged the governor, elated by the merchant's compliments.

The governor continued, "You will be able to see the entire city. You can almost see the Tigris River. If the sky is clear enough you can just barely see the Erythraean Sea. I guess this structure is a marvel. I am very proud of these gardens."

The portly Pattmenidu said, "Ah my friend, I could not climb that high in less than three days. It would be a folly for me to even try. I will take your word for it, but I promise to tell others what you say about the view. I'm proud of you. You've made a monument men will admire for eons."

The governor scheduled an audience for Pattmenidu with King Nebuchadnezzar. The king sitting on his elaborate throne was still in vile spirits about Judah and the war. A royal purple canopy hooded the king's throne. The canopy was held up by four, gem-studded pillars that glistened in the rays of the sun that streamed through the windows. Everything in the audience room shrieked of opulence. Pattmenidu saw that this king had a very large ego.

Nebuchadnezzar said, "Well, Pattmenidu, I see you have eaten well in Pars while my army suffered in Judah. It angers me to see you so fat and content."

Pattmenidu began to fear he might be made a prisoner. On this visit he was an official representative of Pars which made him vulnerable to the practice of keeping messengers and ministers of enemy nations hostage or prisoner for long periods. It appeared that Nebuchadnezzar still considered Pars his enemy.

Pattmenidu squealed, "Sire, I bring you greetings from King Cambyses. He is disappointed that Babylon has so much trouble in the land of Judah. My king feels your governing was good for the Jews as well as the shipping trade businesses. King Cambyses appreciates your benefaction to the people of Judah. He is disappointed they do not accept it. My king extends his wishes for your good health."

King Nebuchadnezzar retorted, "Your king is a coward. If he had fought at my side I would not struggle so in those lands the way I do. While you travel in my dominion of Chaldea you will hear grumbling against your Cambyses, don't let it surprise you. Cambyses may suffer yet for his unfriendliness as well as his insulting behavior towards me."

Pattmenidu answered, "King Cambyses wishes you to know that it was King Astyages who refused to assist you. His kinsman by marriage, King Croesus, also refused to help you.

"As we say on the caravan trails it is the lead camel that holds us up, but it is the last camel that gets whipped. King Cambyses begs for your understanding, Sire. Also, he believes you will win Judah back."

King Nebuchadnezzar thought for a moment and said, "Hmm, that was well spoken, merchant. Maybe your Cambyses is not my problem."

The merchant said, "Sire, King Cambyses wishes you to know he has dedicated his foundries to making arrow heads, javelin tips and swords instead of lamps and wine stands. He would be pleased to give a caravan shipment of these weapons to you for your next conquest, provided it is not against Pars."

Pattmenidu held his breath, waiting in sweaty fear because he knew this was a dangerous statement to make to an angry king. With a subtle innuendo, Pattmenidu knew he had just threatened King Nebuchadnezzar. The merchant had said Cambyses was preparing for war with the production of arrows and javelins he would use against Babylonians if they decided to attack.

The king laughed and said, "You have more courage than I expected, merchant. The very fact that you are willing to talk to me such as you do amuses me. Tell your Cambyses I intend to return to the coast of the great Erythraean Sea to settle my ownership there for all time. I will look forward to receiving his gift. If he changes his mind about delivering the gift I will kill him with my own hands. You may go."

Pattmenidu was thrilled to escape with his life. Overall, it was not a bad trip for Pattmenidu. Now all he had to do was convince King Cambyses to agree to the production and delivery of the weapons.

24.

A man named Rusundatu lived in the province of Arbela about one day's travel from the Great King's property that Mitridates and Spaco managed. This man was a lying thief. Rusundatu once had worked on a farm, and as time passed Rusundatu acquired wealth by stealing sheep from his employer, the farm owner. Rusundatu noted that the farm was not far from the major caravan trail. He could use the farm as a well-placed base to rob passing caravans so he began to plan a way to take the farm from the owner.

On one trip into Ecbatana when he delivered wool to the market for his employer, Rusundatu went to the office of taxes to ask Zav if the farm he worked on in Arbela was recorded as owned by anyone. Zav had no record that taxes were being paid for the farm. Rusundatu asked if he could pay taxes for one year as a way to assume full ownership of the farm. Zav agreed and had a magus prepare a lambskin as deed to the property giving it to Rusundatu. Thus, he became the property owner of the farm by legally sneaking it from the previous owner. On his return to the farm Rusundatu showed the farmer his deed. The man howled in anger, but he was now a laborer not an owner. He got nothing for the property except a new job.

This new ownership was a fortuitous boon for Rusundatu. He hired pickpockets and highwaymen for his farm who willingly stole from adjacent properties. Rusundatu visited Zav on several occasions during which time they made a pact to bind their mutual dishonesty. Occasionally, Rusundatu got information from Zav about small caravans going west that his robbers could raid. He developed a working relationship with Zav where Rusundatu shared profits from his plunder with the minister.

Rusundatu made occasional excursions through the nearby countryside to recruit individuals to help him rob. On one occasion he came upon Mitridates. Although strangers, they talked while Rusundatu recognized how productive Mitridates' farm was. He said "Mitridates, do you own this lovely farm?"

"No, the Great King owns it. I manage it for him."

Rusundatu asked, "How much are you able to steal?"

Mitridates said, "I do not steal from the Great King. My family serves King Astyages faithfully."

In a quiet, conspiring voice Rusundatu said, "I could help you make yourself wealthy using the King's resources. For instance the harvested wool could be separated into two bins, a large bin for him, a small bin for you. I will buy your portion so you are never seen selling wool in the markets of Ecbatana."

In a self-righteous tone Mitridates answered, "I refuse to consider such an arrangement."

Rusundatu was not put out by this harsh dismissal. The visitor said, "I know people who make a great profit by robbing caravans. They never get caught because, like you, they are securely employed on local farms. Are you interested in being included in that enterprise?"

Mitridates agreed to get involved because he would be stealing from merchants, just not from the King. The Greek went on several caravan raids. When they were alone Spaco complained, "This new business of yours scares me. I don't think it's safe. It might endanger our son. Besides, the boy is becoming aware of activity around him, and I don't want him to grow up knowing his father is a thief."

She was a simple woman who wanted nothing more than a healthy family. Mitridates did not listen to her. He was impressed with the wealth that accrued so easily. It was simple for him to leave slaves tending the sheep while he was away robbing.

Mitridates was no warrior. In the attacks on the caravans he never shot arrows to provoke fear or surrender. His strength was his eye for value. Back in Lydia there had been vast wealth in the highest quality gems, silver, gold, ivory and fabrics. Mitridates had been trained by a merchant to barter for profit. He had no training in stealing goods, but he could assess the value of materials by feel and sight. In a full moon, for instance, he could see a difference in value in three bronze pitchers by noting weight differences and engraving differences in the metal that made one worth more than the other two. His skill helped the highwaymen take only a select few precious items on each raid so they could escape without lugging cheap heavy items that might slow their return to the farms they worked on.

Rusundatu began holding regular discussions with Zav about the best merchandise to steal. The worth of the plunder was in the resale value, something Zav understood quite well. The minister gave Rusundatu the schedule of those caravans leaving Ecbatana carrying expensive goods. Zav sometimes even identified specific objects he was willing to purchase from the bandits for himself. Zav bought much of the stolen property to keep or sell at a profit. It made Zav very wealthy.

Sometimes Zav took gold and silver; other times he agreed to take tokens the camel drivers carried. He taught Rusundatu to recognize stone and metal tokens of varying shapes that bore inscriptions designating specific purchasing power. Rusundatu had seen a few stone and ceramic tokens but Zav showed him new kinds that were round, flat or spherical; some were cone shaped. Zav talked of the specific value assigned to each kind. Rusundatu learned which tokens allowed one to buy animals, grains, or precious metals such as gold and silver. This education made Rusundatu a more effective robber.

One day Zav came to the Great King's farm with Rusundatu where the minister met Mitridates, Spaco and their son. The small boy entertained Zav with his stories of how he had taken command of the farm animals and the small children of the slaves. Zav liked the boy because at his tender age the child already understood authority and power; the two virtues Zav cherished the most.

Mitridates had accumulated such a large store of stolen bulky objects that he was having trouble hiding it. After evaluating the boodle Zav agreed to pay a token having the value of twenty-five sheep for everything. Mitridates was very pleased. That one token alone made him rich. He could save it for when his family returned to Lydia where he intended to buy his own farm.

Zav and Mitridates became very well acquainted over a meal. With unspoken admiration, Zav appreciated how Mitridates seemed to pick only the best merchandise as his portion of the stolen items. Other members of the band took larger fractions of the stolen property than Mitridates, but they did not realize the Greek never complained when they took more because he always walked off with the most expensive goods. Zav began to understand the difference between these two men. Rusundatu was the organizer he could depend upon to schedule robberies. Mitridates was the man Zav needed for choosing quality. Zav told the farmer he was sending a camel driver to pick up the goods with the understanding that the band was not to steal them from him. They laughed together.

Mitridates felt good about the positive impression he made on Zav. Such an important palace contact could help Mitridates keep his good reputation with the noble princes who oversaw the running of the King's properties. On regular excursions, noblemen from Ecbatana came to the King's farms to inspect the efficiency and honesty of the managers. The profit Mitridates was able to provide to the King always drew compliments from the visitors. He kept labor costs low while keeping the yield of the property's output better than most farms. In spite of his dishonesty toward others Mitridates was loyal to the King he had never seen.

Mitridates' status as a thief who robbed the caravans was a perfect contrast to his farm position. As the manager of substantial assets for King Astyages, the King was not just the sovereign of Mitridates and Spaco; the King was his family patriarch. These free Greek employees were extended-family members to the royals. The farmers were incorporated into the patriarch's tribe by assent, not by blood. The patriarch protected Mitridates through the noblemen that came to inspect the farm. They arranged for guards if necessary to protect the herds, crops and laborers. The princes protected Mitridates as long as he made the farm profitable. The Greek understood this so he was careful not to let Rusundatu get too close to him or his management privileges. Rusundatu had made suggestions about taking over the farm duties to allow Mitridates to spend more time raiding. The Greek ignored his suggestions.

Mitridates was careful to ensure his foster son grew up properly. When the boy misbehaved he was disciplined without delay but punishment was never excessive. They had named him Paithi. The wife, Spaco, began to realize the boy was a very fast learner. He did not require a lot of instruction to grasp the essence of a lesson. Paithi looked with a concentrated stare at the person talking to him to take in every word. When he began to talk he did not make many mispronunciation mistakes. Spaco thought he was quite amazing and he was. Spaco marveled that the boy never tried to say anything his vocabulary could not handle. He learned new words rapidly. He was learning Greek and Aramaic from his parents. When Paithi heard slaves or noble visitors speaking Median he picked that language up just by hearing it spoken around him.

The boy related to Mitridates and Spaco as if they were his real parents. They never suggested otherwise. He was a happy child who loved to play outdoors. Paithi began to give orders very early. He was just able to walk without falling when he decided the sheep had to do his bidding. He stood in the middle of a flock of sheep waving his arms, shouting commands. He had one sandal on while the other sandal trailed behind his foot, tied loosely by a string at his ankle. His toga would hang off one shoulder and its hem sagged to his feet. His black hair was so curly it was impossible to tell if it was messy. The sheep just gnawed in the grass around him occasionally nuzzling against him without tipping him over. He never got angry or frustrated. He gave his futile commands to the entire flock until he decided to chase a new lamb that needed his training.

Life for Paithi was enjoyable. He liked the changes of the seasons. In winter he was bundled up in warm woolen garments covered with an animal skin outer shawl. He played in snow. He ate ice. Once in the winter he stuck his tongue to a bronze pole and Spaco soaked it off with water after she stopped laughing. When she told Mitridates that night they enjoyed laughing together and were so happy they decided to try to have another child, but they were never successful.

Paithi was strong and healthy when he reached the age of five sun cycles. This was the time when a boy made the transition from being a baby to learning how to grow into being a man. His parents made him learn to read. It was the way of the Greeks. Reading was not the way of the Parsians. If Paithi was with his real parents reading would be left to the magi or the merchants while he was taught to use a bow and arrow instead.

Mitridates could read and write in cuneiform better than his wife so he began to teach Paithi. Mitridates made the boy spend more time reading or writing than the youth appreciated. Lesson time was a struggle for the father. The boy was not a poor learner; he just preferred to be out with the animals, walking in the forest or climbing the nearby mountains. Mitridates thought this was probably why his son caught on to his studies so fast. Paithi could escape to the out of doors quicker.

Paithi was taught to shoot a bow and arrow. He was not pushed to increase the pulling power of the bow the way boys in military families were, but the boy knew his father expected him to hit a target when he and the target were stationary. He began shooting at moving targets on his own and his accuracy improved very rapidly. Soon he began to bring home a rabbit or a squirrel for Spaco to prepare for supper. She always gave Paithi the first cut as Mitridates sat waiting for the second cut. A boy of five sun cycles hitting a moving target was an amazing feat in the experience of Mitridates. He wondered where the intense concentration came from in this small boy.

25.

King Arsames, the ruler of Bactria, sat pensively as he said, "I wish to review two things, the status of my citidel and the trade developing with Pars. Tell me about my citadel."

A general stood and said, "Sire, it is positioned where you ordered to the west of Bactra between here and Ecbatana. The walls are several cubits thick. They are also 20 cubits high so ladder assaults can be repulsed easily. The whole structure on the outside is stone. We did not use firebrick like so many structures in Babylon. There are no external wood surfaces that can catch fire by flaming arrows. The arms rooms are full of bows, arrows, axes, javelins, and lances. Although we have hundreds of stalls no horses are stabled there yet. Your throne room is organized so military reports can be made safely. We can house thousands of soldiers and citizens during a siege and still feed them for at least two sun cycles. Wells beneath the citadel have plenty of water."

King Arsames nodded and smiled. This fit his plans perfectly. He intended to stop paying tribute to the King of Kings. Why take taxes from royal relatives only to forward them to Ecbatana to make the Great King richer? Also, he did not want his son, Hystaspes, to be a vassal of Media; he wanted him to rule an independent country.

The king looked in a different direction and asked, "How are the discussions with Sogdiana, Aria and Arachosia coming along? I intend to have them use my capital city Bactra as a focal point of commerce. We have regional control of the major trade route and they should be willing to do business directly with us instead of Zav. I also directed you ministers to centralize the businesses coming in from east of the Indus River, especially the gem trade. How is that progressing?"

A minister wearing a very elaborate toga with matching sash stepped forward and answered, "Sire, Sogdiana to the north and the two southern countries are in agreement with us. They will stop trading directly with Ecbatana as soon as they are convinced it is safe to do so. As for the eastern trade rearrangements, that is completed. We have eliminated several caravan stations that Zav controlled personally. He has made many threats about it but never acted. We suspect the caravanserai we closed were places he used to steal from King Astyages so he can't really take action without revealing his dishonesty."

"Good," said the king, "and how are those new caravan routes to Pars progressing? Are they profitable? Are we moving more products with each new caravan? I like that man Pattmenidu that King Cambyses sent us. Also, I want you to realize that King Cambyses is my cousin. His father, Cyrus, was my father's brother. They split our two kingdoms long ago, but I wish to maintain good relations with King Cambyses."

His minister of trade said, "We are making good progress there. The number of caravans traveling southwest has not increased as fast as we hoped, sire. However, we do send more packed camels with each run."

The minister looked at the princes seated around the audience chamber. Some of them stirred uneasily. The king's relatives had been giving false reports about the profitability of these trading ventures because his noblemen did not want to appear inefficient. They were afraid he might think they were poor business managers and make changes at their expense.

King Arsames said, "I believe I will send a message to my cousin to ask for his opinion."

His princes became even more agitated, and King Arsames noted their discomfort. He continued, "I also want to ask him if he will support me in battle if I have to defend Bactria against Media. My intention with our changes in trade and my new citadel is to stop paying Media tax tributes and to move our business contracts from Ecbatana to Pars with my cousin."

Several men in the room nodded affirmatively. This was just what they suspected had been their king's plan. It meant revolt, and war was profitable.

"I also want a new citadel built to the east," he spread his arms toward his princes and added, "Two such structures will help me protect you better. An attacking enemy will not know in which fortress I hide you. We might have to fight two or three sun cycles but two citadels can hold enough supplies."

King Arsames called in a scribe magus. In addition to the trading question he included a cryptic statement that suggested his intent to separate Bactria from Media without actually stating it. Cambyses would read between the lines to understand his intent. King Arsames asked if Cambyses was prepared to support him against the Great King. Pars was an important ally for King Arsames.

In Anshan Cambyses called Pattmenidu into the audience room. Cambyses and Mandane sat on their gold thrones. She wore a small crown that was a replica of the one cast in the backrest of Cambyses' throne. It was small with a crisp geometric design that was hand-carved, not cast.

Mandane was very pleased because her crown looked exactly like the one her uncle, King Croesus, had designed in the throne. It gave her a sense of connectedness with her immediate and extended families.

The king and queen looked like a matched pair. Both wore shoes with long pointed toes that curled up and backward, with a gold tassel on the end. They each wore a red toga with a royal purple sash about the waist. Cambyses had a crown that also replicated the one on the back of his throne. Mandane planned for them to be dressed alike on numerous occasions. It gave her pleasure to know they were joked about within the palace as the Mirza Twins.

Pattmenidu had listened to the message read by the magus from King Arsames. The merchant said, "Sire, the path through the salt desert is developing but at a slow pace. Its profits are erratic. It only brings a fraction of the trade we need to support our nation. It is useful nonetheless. Certain products like gems, fabrics and metal goods travel well on that hot, dry route. We ship metal lamps, pans, drinking vessels, ladles and other kitchen utensils. We also send clay pipes, clay amphora, and clay water jugs.

"Foods do not travel well over the desert. Even cheese travels poorly, as do some spices and herbs that dry out too quickly and need to be moistened, but we are unable to depend on the caravan drivers to keep them wet. They prefer drinking water to dampening herbs."

Pattmenidu continued, "The path is still rough and our camels continue to cut their legs because the salt is not yet packed down. The drivers coming from Bactria still complain of the slowness of travel. It will get better, but it will take at least two sun cycles to match the efficiency of the northern route. The salt desert does have one advantage. It is less dangerous. It has far fewer nomadic pilferers."

King Cambyses thought for a moment and said, "Pattmenidu, I want you to keep shipping goods over the salt desert. It may be of critical value some day. If King Arsames rebels against King Astyages, as he suggests, we will be in a very uncomfortable position. I will have to decide on allegiance with my wife's father or my cousin."

He looked pleadingly at his wife who caught his eye. She said, "Cambyses, I will support you in any decision you make regarding your loyalty for I am steadfastly yours alone," as she traced one finger over the back of his hand.

Cambyses was grateful for her comment. He said, "My fidelities must compliment yours also, my dear."

Pattmenidu asked, "Sire, please consider sending a message to King Arsames telling him we will continue to use and develop the desert route. I intend to increase the number of our cavalcades soon."

Cambyses looked at Mandane and said, "I will, Pattmenidu, after the queen and I talk."

Cambyses stood and took Mandane's hand, and they left the audience chamber. Cambyses led her to a small sun parlor. It was a little alcove with several small windows covered with shaved mica that let in plenty of light. Bright colored cushions and blankets were spread on the floor beside a low table. A servant came in without being called and placed a glass container of wine beside the gold cups on the table and filled the cups. A tray of bread, yogurt and fruit was brought in next. The servant opened a door leading to an outside balcony, then left the room. This let in a warm breeze. The king and queen reclined on the cushions, which were customarily heaped on the floor. Cambyses said, "King Arsames is going to stop paying his taxes to your father. It will mean war. I can stand behind your father or my cousin."

He took a spoon of yogurt and spread it on a piece of bread and fed Mandane a bite. He ate the rest of the bread himself.

Mandane said, "If you support your cousin, Cambyses, it will mean Pars is at war with my father."

Cambyses said, "Yes, what would you have me do?"

The queen asked, "Can you remain my father's ally without fighting King Arsames?"

Cambyses picked a few grapes from the bowl and fed them to his wife slowly as they both concentrated on their situation. Cambyses said, "No. Your father will order me to fight beside his army against my cousin, just to shame me."

He leaned to Mandane and kissed her. She responded by placing her hands on his cheeks, touching his beard. She held his face before her own trying to see his thoughts by peering into his eyes. She could see he was troubled. She said, "I think you are more afraid for your cousin than for Pars."

Cambyses nodded. Yet it was never easy to confront King Astyages. The Great King was so vindictive he punished any act of disloyalty without hesitation. She felt Cambyses tracing circles on her breast. She smiled. Their conversation was over. He was ready to be a husband instead of a king. Mandane said, "We need to have another son. This time I will be more cautious. My friend, Princess Ispitamu, meets with me now and then to caution me about how careless I was before when I was pregnant."

He was pleased that Mandane had a friend, but it struck him as odd that a friend accused her of being careless. It sounded like the princess was making his wife feel guilty about the loss of the child. He wanted to think about this as well as his problem with King Astyages, but only after they caressed enjoying the delight of their love.

The next day Cambyses called for a magus. He sent a message to King Arsames that said, "Pattmenidu is increasing the volume of cargo going to Bactria by way of the salt desert. We intend to increase your profits there.

"Commit yourself to the safety of your citadel and prepare to fight King Astyages. King Kauklia of Gedrosia might be an ally for you since he does not relish supporting Media with tribute either."

Cambyses continued, "I will follow the orders of the Great King and go to war against you. However, not only will my Parsian force be kept small, no Parsian arrow will hit the entry gate of your Bactrian citadel. Also, no Parsian arrow will fly over your citadel walls. My soldiers' arrows bouncing against the stone wall of your Bactrian fortress will be no danger. You need only use your marksmen against the warriors from Media and Parthia."

//

The war went just as planned by Arsames and Cambyses. King Astyages did not come out of his seven-walled palace. He promoted Harpagus and sent him with Median, Parsian and Parthian armies to fight Bactria. King Cambyses was true to his word. He protected his wife and kingdom by going with Harpagus to attack the citadel west of the city of Bactra.

The fighting lasted a short few moon cycles instead of several sun cycles because the attacking army was not equipped for a long siege. Although warriors from the non-Parsian armies tried hard to kill Bactrian archers on the walls and tried without success to set fire to structures inside the fortress with flaming arrows, the battle went poorly for Harpagus. The archers under the command of King Cambyses appeared to be fighting aggressively while honoring the agreement between the Aryan cousins. Warriors from Parthia were ordered to use ladders to scale the walls. Cambyses volunteered to provide the ladders. Cambyses ordered them to be made wobbly so the rungs broke as the Parthian soldiers climbed them. Several ladder assaults failed. Cambyses and Arsames were subtly tricking Harpagus in this battle without the Median officer realizing it.

Harpagus held strategy sessions every few days to review the situation of his army. It was agreed that the attacking army must be committed to a very long siege if it was to wait for supplies inside the citadel to be depleted. Cambyses convinced Harpagus the citadel could not be breached. He also agreed when the Parthian general suggested attacking the city of Bactra and seizing its spoils to satisfy the Great King. Harpagus left the Parsians at the fortress to prevent the Bactrian army from attacking them while they sacked the city.

When Harpagus and the Parthians left, King Arsames invited Cambyses into his fortress, where he fed and bathed the Parsian warriors. King Arsames told Cambyses that a large army of Bactrians and Gedrosians were protecting the city. Cambyses was not shown very much of the inside of the citadel by his cousin out of sound military caution. In the future an unexpected circumstance might make Bactria and Pars adversaries and important, vulnerable points like the food stores and the water supply were hidden from the Parsians.

King Arsames told Cambyses that Harpagus might get a little booty, but nothing of significance. Arsames anticipated the Median army attacking his city so he had planned for his ministers to load a small caravan of camels with gold and silver for this eventuality. The camels were placed so it was easy for Harpagus to take them. The camel load was equal in value to one sun cycle of Bactrian tribute. King Arsames was disguising his last payment to the Great King as war booty. The Parsians left the citadel to wait for Harpagus to return. As they approached the citadel Harpagus' soldiers looked as if they had lost the battle in the city. There were many wounded soldiers. The entire rank was dirty, and their mounts were spotted with blood. The animals were sweaty and panting. Harpagus had been forced to run from the city. He ordered a strategy meeting and said to Cambyses, "We were met by a large force of Bactrian and Gedrosian fighters. They were fully prepared to defend the city. We were successful in capturing a herd of camels loaded with gold, silver and some trinkets. We were not able to wrest any supplies to help us remain here any longer."

Exhausted, Harpagus gazed at Cambyses and his warriors and noted how fresh and neat they were. In a petulant tone he said, "Why are you so clean? Did you take a rest while we fought in the city?"

Cambyses answered with caution saying, "We could not assault the citadel alone so I had my soldiers bathe and rest so they would be prepared to help you in any way necessary, Harpagus, when you returned."

The officer was so tired he was partly mollified yet partly annoyed by this answer.

"Did the gold you captured amount to enough to keep the Great King from thinking he lost this battle?" Cambyses asked.

"I believe so," answered Harpagus.

"We can return to Ecbatana with our army looking as if we have fought with valor. Not many warriors have died," said the Parthian general.

"It would be better to go home now and return here later with a larger force and more supplies, if that is what King Astyages wants," agreed Cambyses, "We can't fight and be victorious over both Bactrians and Gedrosian with the forces the King sent us here with."

Harpagus was too tired, too sore, so he agreed that this battle was finished. He saw no way to capture the citadel or the city with his small army. They had fought per the King's bidding. Anyway, this was an issue of taxes that mattered to Zav more than to the army. It was more of an administrative issue than a tactical military concern. Let Zav worry about it. Harpagus commanded his officers to prepare to return home. The Parsians were the last to march away, and without turning around Cambyses waved goodbye to his cousin.

26.

Mitridates acquired enough wealth from his caravan theft ventures to buy three camels of his own. He also had a small herd of sheep. As his herd grew he periodically sold the older animals to accrue tokens he could use later to live on when he, Spaco and Paithi returned to Lydia. His personal wealth was growing faster than it should, based on his compensation from the Great King. He hid his tokens in a secret hole the same as he hid sheep and camels on a remote pasture to keep them out of the view of the visiting noblemen representing the King. It was easy for him to do.

Paithi asked, "Why don't the noblemen ever look at our animals? They are as splendid as the King's."

Mitridates said, "I keep our animals separate because we sell ours regularly at market. The farm belongs to King Astyages and I have no right to use his resources for my own purposes."

The farmer made it sound like a point of honor. The boy did not know his father was a criminal. Also, Paithi never questioned his father about how the animals came into their possession in the first place. The boy trusted his father without question.

In recent raids Mitridates had amassed a large volume of stolen materials he needed to sell in Ecbatana. He told his family, "We must load our camels and herd our sheep to market."

He packed his son and wife on the King's donkeys. They began the slow trek to the capital. It was the boy's first visit there. He was seven sun cycles into his life and Mitridates wanted to see how he handled himself among the crowds, the noise and the expanse of the city.

Paithi was very excited by everything he saw. He heard people other than his parents speaking Greek and other languages. He spent time standing near total strangers listening to them talk. He made it a practice to talk to them just to say new words he was learning. He was a favorite with the wives of merchants who appreciated a small boy with an inquisitive mind. When he saw something he had never seen before he asked questions about it. Sometimes Paithi asked these questions of his parents; at other times he questioned strangers. He was not afraid of anyone. He trusted foreigners to talk to him like an equal. The city teemed about him. There were colors Paithi had never seen. People had round eyes, slanted eyes, various skin pigments, unfamiliar shades of hair, and some wore clothes made of fabrics he loved to touch. Artisans made trinkets, weavers made rugs and metal mongers made metal objects of all kinds. The strange smell of spices he had never experienced before filled the air. The noise should have upset Paithi but he took it in stride. The world was interesting without being overwhelming to the boy. Mitridates was surprised at Paithi. The farmer wondered how his son could come from a quiet, isolated farm into a city marketplace without becoming frightened or confused?

On the first afternoon a very large man covered with hair and dust who sweated and stank bumped into the boy. The man roared at Paithi and shoved the child aside. The man was too large for Mitridates to confront in the defense of his son so he did nothing about it. The boy stumbled a bit then without flinching he stared back at the giant unafraid. It was as if Paithi was waiting for the man to apologize to him for the insult. Mitridates was as ashamed of himself as he was proud of the boy.

On the second day of their visit Paithi spotted a boy his own age stealing a dagger from a metal monger. It was brass and had a neat, well-designed sheath. The boy just strolled away after picking up the knife. Paithi ran after him shouting for him to stop. His noise caught the attention of the crowd. Paithi tackled the boy as the thief started to run. They fell in a heap to the ground. The dagger slid away. Paithi got up holding the thief. They struggled until the city youth realized he could not escape from this country-bred strongman. Paithi gave him a solemn lecture on honesty. People in the crowd began to snicker. Paithi picked up the dagger and dragged the robber back to the metal monger. Paithi made the boy apologize to the craftsman for stealing. Then Paithi let the boy go and passed the weapon back to the man. The craftsman tried to give Paithi a little knife as a reward, but he refused to take it. Paithi just walked away having done his duty.

Mitridates set up his booth to sell his wares, thinking it might take several days to get rid of everything. The Greek was not very effective at haggling over the price of items he had for sale. His unusual sense of value gave him a tendency to refuse to sell if he did not get his price. He had to learn to negotiate in the public market. His

213

inexperience kept him feeling edgy most of the time. Zav came up to Mitridates one day to look at his wares. The minister nodded to him then passed on. Neither spoke a word. Zav was satisfied that they appeared to be strangers to anyone who might have observed this encounter.

Mitridates was pleased that Paithi and Spaco were wandering in another area of the market. If the boy had spotted Zav the child would have called the minister by name. That would have been a mistake in this market, because the royal family wandered about aimlessly, and out of boredom watched whom the merchants dealt with. For a boy of the country to be seen speaking first in familiar fashion to a minister of the King would be a breach of respect, and any nobleman would wonder why the boy knew the minister. It could have meant trouble.

One prince who came frequently to inspect the farm saw Mitridates and asked, "Where do these goods come from?"

"They belong to Rusundatu," Mitridates promptly lied.

"Who is he?" asked the prince.

"He is a farmer who lives near the Great King's farm who pays me a small commission for what I sell for him."

The answer satisfied the prince who wandered away. Mitridates felt his heart beat fast for several minutes before he calmed down again.

Spaco shopped among the vendors who sold household items and foods she normally did not have available to her on the farm. She enjoyed learning little things when she was watching other women weaving, sewing, cooking and using face paints of all colors. She felt dowdy among all the finery available for sale. Her hair was plain compared to the fancy spirals and curly twists worn by the city women. These strangers wore fragrances that made them smell like a garden. She loved the city, but realized she could not be happy living in it. Too much happened all at once. Sometimes she got dizzy from the commotion.

When the family was ready to return to the farm they climbed onto the King's donkeys for the ride home. The city had been a great success for all concerned. Mitridates had sold everything, and except for the few things Spaco had purchased the donkeys were lightly burdened. Bringing Paithi had been smart also because the child had fun discovering the city. Mitridates enjoyed the boy's chatter about his adventures. Mitridates wondered if he might try putting his son to work selling their goods the next time his family came here.

When the farmers arrived home Rusundatu was there. He took Mitridates aside to inform him that the band was ready to travel again to intercept another caravan. They rounded up the others on the way to their next adventure. At the site where the robbery was to take place some of the robbers hid behind rocks waiting for the camel train to arrive. The rest went up the trail, around a corner to stop camels that might run in panic. Mitridates was in this latter group. It was safer there where he could begin inspecting items on the animals as soon as they were caught. All the men wore clothing usually worn by nomads. They hid their faces behind a face pall. The men behind the rocks each had a bow and arrow. They used these to scare the camel riders, not kill them. When the caravan approached it was Rusundatu's task to look over the entire group of animals to ensure there were no military guards. Zav only gave them information about caravans without a protective escort; however, sometimes the lead driver hired guards if he could afford it. Rusundatu gave the signal that all was safe. The band began to shout and shoot arrows above the heads of the camels throwing them into confusion. The inattentive, half-asleep riders began to scream at each other; some fell to the ground as their camels bolted. The camels snorted and the riders shouted. The noise augmented the confusion to the advantage of Rusundatu's men. No one was hurt. Rusundatu supervised the theft of booty as Mitridates declared what was worth taking. They did not steal the camels or take prisoners, hostages, or all the goods. Enough merchandise was always left with the caravan to make it worthwhile for the camel drivers to travel on. This made it safer for the robbers because if the caravan returned to Ecbatana military guards of the city might come searching until they found the plunder and beheaded the whole band.

The strategy was designed to rob caravans leaving Ecbatana, not the ones going into the capital. Most likely each exiting caravan got robbed numerous times before it reached its final destiny. The second robbery would probably be more vicious than Rusundatu's assault. If these camel drivers ever returned this way it was unlikely for them to identify the place of Rusundatu's attack to the city guards.

Mitridates sequestered his portion of loot in his secret hiding place as he looked forward to accumulating enough to take Paithi back to Ecbatana. He had enjoyed his son's first experience in the city; the father learned his son was fearless and inquisitive among strangers.

Paithi was also a leader. On the farm the boy enjoyed walking down the mountain to play with the children of the slaves. These boys and girls were trained to be submissive to his orders without question. He told them he was the general as they marched up the mountain into the forest where they helped him scare invading birds from the brush. When the birds flew away Paithi tried to bring them down with an arrow. He shot birds his mother could cook for a meal, never inedible fowl. He made certain that the first bird shot went to the slaves. Sometimes he made his soldiers help scare up squirrels. He liked their gamy flavor. He never tried to kill a deer, even if he snuck up close enough to one for a hit. Instinctively he knew his bow was too weak to deliver an arrow with enough force to kill such a large animal. If his Greek father was more like a Parsian the bow might have had more striking force, but that was a detail Mitridates missed.

Once the children had stumbled onto a wild boar. It was large and dangerous. The hog gave a menacing snort, lowered its head to aim its lethal horns as it charged one small boy, lumbering its dangerous bulk right over the child. The boy was hurt but not killed. Paithi stood firm and shot an arrow at the boar. His arrow just barely pierced the dusty hide. The angry animal turned to charge straight towards Paithi. Drool hung from it mouth and loud strange grunts seemed to leak from its entire body. Paithi nocked another arrow and this time with a lucky shot he hit the boar in the eye. It swerved away crashing through the woods snorting in pain and anger. Paithi ran to the injured boy shouting, "Come over here and help me. We must carry him down the mountain to his parents. Hurry!"

The scattered children come running. He said, "Stop screaming," although he did let the girls cry. Paithi led the way out of the woods. After a few days of rest the little boy was fine.

Locally, Paithi was creating a tiny legend for himself. He was described as fearless, kind and loyal to his playmates. When other farm managers came to visit Mitridates or Spaco they brought their children. Paithi always challenged the visitor to selected games of skill. He got to know which games other boys played better than he and those were the games he chose to play. Paithi always gave praise to others when they won, but he was competitive enough to know he had to improve himself if he was to win the next contest.

Frequently Paithi pestered Mitridates to take him to visit other farms. He enjoyed having to meet a rival on unfamiliar property because it gave an advantage to the child he visited. If he won at games there he knew he really was the best. He did not brag about his wins; he just expected to win because he tried so hard. He knew bigger boys could do things he could not, but he wanted to get as good as they were before he reached their age. Mitridates had explained the competitions of the Greek Olympic Games to Paithi. The farmer told Paithi the games were held every four sun cycles. The games included foot racing, chariot racing wrestling and boxing. This information caused Paithi to make everything a competition. He tried to climb trees faster than anyone else. He tried to get into the stream in the summer by running down the hill faster than his playmates. He tried to see the first rabbit in the woods.

He was developing into a fellow with a strong desire to win while being fair. Although he was always willing to give credit to others he never accepted that their superior performance was unbeatable. Paithi tried assiduously to beat the best competitor. This intensity never got in the way of his sense of humor or his happiness at just playing.

As he got older Paithi had specific chores to do around the farm. The child got up before daylight, walked down the hill to clean stalls, spread hay or sometimes milk a goat or a cow. The King kept a few camels on the farm that transported wool and crops to market. Paithi tended the camels. The princes of the court came to transact sales when the camels were loaded for market. It was Mitridates' job to load skins, wool, fruits, vegetables and meat on the camels then lead them to market, but the princes carried out the final bartering or outright sale of the King's goods. Paithi had to help his father loading and leading. He was allowed to go to the local market, but not always because sometimes he had to stay home to be schooled by his mother in specific lessons. He was getting better at reading and writing. He could do a little arithmetic too. When the market in Ecbatana was the goal he went now that his father saw how well the boy handled himself in the big city. Paithi was obliged by his father to do arithmetic to calculate value between different objects, which the child attempted but he had no zeal for the math involved. Paithi preferred activities that required physical energy not mental energy.

27.

Harpagus was feeling uncomfortable about his relationship with the Great King. After he returned from Bactria with his tired, wounded army he requested an audience with King Astyages. He had to wait for several days before being admitted into the great presence. King Astyages spoke in a booming voice to ensure no one present missed his performance. He said, "So you let Bactria escape from my kingdom. You let King Arsames assume independence from my authority. You shamed me before all the great kings of the world. What do you have to say for yourself, Harpagus?"

Harpagus took a deep breath and said, "Sire, I conducted the attack with my full force. I had both Parthia and Pars with me. We were outnumbered because the country of Gedrosia had already arrived to help Bactria."

The Great King roared, "You mean I have lost King Kauklia too! I sent you to keep one nation but you lost two? You imbecile, you child with a pretty horse! I should take your head."

Imparting complete humiliation was the King's tool. Harpagus fought to steady his nerves and answered, "Sire, maybe you should talk with the Parthian general or with King Cambyses. They will shed light on the situation we encountered. We attacked the citadel, but it was impregnable so we bypassed it to attack the city. It was fully protected by an army several times our size. We decided…, that is, I decided to leave before we were slaughtered. The defeat is my fault."

King Astyages said, "I have already heard from my spies in the city of Bactria. They confirm what you say. At least you are man enough to accept the responsibility."

The insulting outburst by King Astyages was a test to see if Harpagus tried to lie his way out of this defeat. So far the King had depended on this man to be forthright, honest, and once again the officer was true to his King and Astyages was pleased. The King was not pleased with the losses but at least he still had one man he could trust.

In a quieter voice King Astyages asked, "Harpagus, do you think I should send a larger army to Bactria? Or should I send an army into Gedrosia?"

The soldier said, "Sire, to storm the fortress in Bactria would take a full scale war. Our army would have to surround the entire citadel to starve it out. We would need a massive military force just to encircle that fort. There are five different gates we would have blockade just to confine the resources inside the citadel. It would be very expensive for you. It probably would cost you more than you would ever get back in tribute, Sire."

King Astyages was quite surprised at this assessment. He had expected Harpagus to see war as such a personal opportunity, leading him to suggest leaving with an army immediately. He next asked, "Harpagus, I want a complete answer. What about Gedrosia?"

Harpagus said, "Sire, we could fare better against Gedrosia. We could win a victory there with very little effort. The march to get there and return would take more time than the battle. From what I hear from caravan drivers it has no strongholds like the citadel in Bactria. The fight would be in open fields or in the desert. King Kauklia does not have weapons that are as good as ours. We would win, sire."

The King asked, "Is it worth doing? Would it cost me much?"

Harpagus said without hesitation, "You will have to ask Zav, sire. He is the only one who knows if the tribute to you justifies a military campaign."

Again the King appreciated Harpagus' answer. The soldier was willing to fight a war but leave the decision for making war up to others. The King looked toward Zav and bellowed. "Well?"

Zav jumped to the center of the audience room and bowed. The King chided, "Up, up. Answer me, you fool."

Zav began to tremble and he stuttered, "Ssssire, thththe tax is 200 talents each sun cycle from Gedrosia. King Kauklia has only paid his tax a few times. There is no true impact on the treasury when King Kauklia refuses to pay his tribute to you. The war will cost you the equivalent of a sun cycle of tribute just to come and go. It will be hard to make a tax burden on Gedrosia pay for a war. The tax from Bactria is much higher. It is 600 talents. We could increase the taxes on Bactria. That could make up much of the expense, sire."

The King waved Zav back into the crowd of onlookers. He turned his attention to Harpagus again. He said, "I have decided we will let both countries remain separated from us for the moment. We will not wage war on either of them," and glaring at Zav he continued, "and we will not increase the taxes on our own family farms to make up the tax losses, in case you are planning to, Zav.

"Harpagus, you have given me honest answers without attempting to shirk the responsibility of failure in Bactria. I am promoting you for being the kind of soldier I need. You may go."

Harpagus left the audience chamber exhausted. He plunked down in the first alcove he saw. He ordered a servant to bring him wine. The soldier needed to recover from the stress of having just offered his own life for the defeat he suffered in Bactria.

Prince Zatame came out of the audience chamber and sat down beside Harpagus. The prince said, "Harpagus, you did a fine job of advising the King. I am impressed with your well rounded capacity to judge the expense of war."

"Thank you, your highness," said Harpagus, a little out of breath.

The prince said, "You seem to understand important business aspects of war as well as you understand its military significance."

Harpagus said, "Your highness, we all know war is a burden. If Zav understood that we would have less fighting I think."

Prince Zatame asked, "Yes, but shouldn't we continue to fight Bactria now? Isn't it likely to become powerful enough to attack us? What are your thoughts, Harpagus? I can always get King Astyages to bring up the topic of war again if you think it is critical."

The soldier said, "No, Bactria is not an important adversary. Everything I saw there was defensive in nature. They are not developing offensive herds of horses. They are not making large fleets of chariots. Their camel herds are just large enough to support their caravan trade. The warriors we encountered in the city were foot soldiers. They were not ready to pursue us nor were they ready to attack our capital. They had no military offense at all. Their citadel is a massive defensive structure larger than anything we have around Ecbatana, except for this building and its seven walls."

The prince was impressed with how astute this officer was. Prince Zatame said, "Harpagus, I am amazed that you would be able to take all that in while you were engaged in battle. How do you do that?"

Harpagus answered, "I circled the city with our army before we entered it. We could see their large defensive force inside the city. We knew before we hit them that it would be trouble for us. We picked the spot to enter where we could retreat if necessary. If they were

221

developing an offensive capability we would have seen it. An offensive force would have chased us. It is my business to see these things, your highness."

Prince Zatame said, "You make it sound so easy, Harpagus. I have never fought in a war. My experience is in managing a city, not fighting in it." Prince Zatame thought for a moment and continued, "You know, the last big war Media engaged in, where economics and fighting had an intimate association, was many sun cycles ago. It was before the reign of King Astyages. That war made an enormous difference in the Median economy, far more than the expense to conduct the war."

Harpagus said, "Ah, you mean when Media joined Babylon to destroy Nineveh. I wish I had been old enough to be a soldier in that battle. It was a wonderful, decisive victory for us. Nineveh was a great military power at the time."

Prince Zatame retorted, "Nineveh was a great commercial center. We were able to shift the caravan route away from it making Ecbatana what it is today. We even took their craftsman as slaves to ensure they could not develop a decent trade capability again and it worked. Nineveh has almost disappeared."

Harpagus said, "Well, Bactria is not Nineveh. We can live in peace without worrying about Bactria or Gedrosia, but because we allow peace in the world, our empire is getting smaller. Countries that used to need our protection are showing us they can be fully independent. I am not sure I understand how King Astyages can hope to sustain a wealthy and feared empire as these countries decide to stop paying tribute to him."

The prince thought for a moment and said, "You are a very perceptive man. I worry about that too, but I don't think Zav is smart enough to give us a good answer. All that is important to him is his own power and status."

Harpagus was quiet for a moment because what he wanted to say was no compliment to the Great King. Finally the officer added, "As you indicated, Bactria and Gedrosia have armies that are defensive forces. They will develop independent economies with non-Median alliances. I hope the Great King knows that he is becoming less great."

"We will have to help him see it," said Prince Zatame, "but, Harpagus, I have another far less significant concern than the King's. You might be able to help me with it. There seems to be an organized group of robbers on the caravan route going west which is creating a minor problem for traders leaving Ecbatana. It is up toward Arbela someplace that they strike. Could you look into it for me, please?"

Harpagus said, "Let me know when the next caravan is leaving. I will supply guards for it as far as the Euphrates River, if necessary."

They chatted for a while then went their separate ways with both men feeling more respect for each other.

Harpagus arranged for guards to accompany the next caravan just before it left the city. Zav was unable to get word to Rusundatu warning him of the soldiers. Zav feared his source of profit might be finished. He could even encounter personal problems if the guards took prisoners who revealed him as their source of information. He was capable of lying his way out of any difficulty, but this could be precarious.

//

Everyone was in position when Rusundatu saw soldiers riding with the camel column. He got scared and almost ran when he remembered that all he had to do was wave off his compatriots. They hid among the jagged rocks until the column passed by. Mitridates disappeared around the turn into a clump of trees covering a dusty hill. When he saw Harpagus he almost ran in panic. The robber recognized the soldier from long ago. Instantly, the farmer was filled with dread. It was fortunate for him and all the others that he stayed petrified in place. He had guided his camel behind a boulder among the trees waiting for the danger to pass. Mitridates returned home praying that Harpagus would not come into his life again because this time it might be perilous, if not fatal for him.

When the farmer got home he decided to sell all he had stored up from previous robberies. He also resolved to quit his life of crime for the welfare of his family. Mitridates decided to barter away all his booty turning it into tokens or precious metals without telling Rusundatu, the consummate thief, until he had hidden his valuables in a safe place.

Since Zav had not come to the farm for quite some time Mitridates had a huge store of goods he needed to sell in Ecbatana himself. It would take him several days to get rid of his goods because it was difficult to barter for gold and silver in Media. Not many peasants were inclined to deal in precious metals. The common people did not hold gold or silver as bartering commodities because they were ornamental metals more than trading tools. That did not matter to the farmer. He would eventually bargain for what he needed.

Mitridates knew King Croesus was using gold and silver on a regular basis as a medium for exchange. This king was developing coins of gold and silver as money, but people were reluctant to accept them. A goat or a pig had real value. Most peasants distrusted the irregular value of tokens as well. Mitridates mellowed over thoughts of how wealthy he was going to be with his accumulation of precious metals in Sardis where King Croesus ruled. He dreamed of a farm outside Sardis where he could enjoy being well off with his wife and son.

Spaco and Paithi helped Mitridates get ready to go to Ecbatana. Paithi asked, "Father, where did all this jewelry and bronze come from?"

Mitridates lied and said, "It belongs to the King. It was left by another farmer who runs a large house the King stays in when he wants to get out of the city."

The boy asked, "Why doesn't the other farmer sell it for the King?"

Mitridates said, "The King believes I can get a better price than the other man, because I have you to help me."

Paithi knew his father was teasing about the latter point. The boy hardly helped sell anything when they went to the city. He did some physical work, but mostly he played in the market. It was his time of adventure to learn languages or see new crafts. He liked to observe experts making rugs and metalware. He liked to watch women weave dyed yarns because the colors were so interesting.

In Ecbatana Paithi was free to go off on his own. He had proved himself to be dependable and careful. He knew how to stay out of trouble. He always returned to his father when he was supposed to. He never complained about accompanying his mother when Spaco demanded it. Paithi carried her purchases and watched her bargain for household utensils. He never interfered when Spaco was negotiating with vendors. The boy was respectful of his mother's need to do her own shopping.

One day he spotted a pot that he knew his father could fix. He said, "Mother wait here, please," as he went to inspect the copper pot to make certain he was correct. A handle hung loose that had ripped from the side of the pot. Nothing else was wrong with the pot. There were no dents. He checked to ensure the cover fit snug. He returned to his mother and asked, "Is that pot useful to you, Mother? Father can fix it."

She was delighted that the boy had spotted it. She began to haggle with the vendor. It took her a while to barter an exchange. She was carrying a dried sheep's stomach containing a quantity of rice. The merchant said, "I will take your rice, plus the stomach it is in for the pot."

She ended up getting the pot for one quarter of her rice, without giving up the stomach container. When it came to supplying her kitchen she was always frugal.

On this trip Paithi decided to find a scribe magus to ask if it was allowed to look that the record-rooms. Paithi hoped to read a cuneiform clay tablet. He spotted a magus wearing a dark brown cloak over a brown toga. The priest had a full beard and uncombed hair that fell below his shoulders. Paithi noted the man needed a bath. His beard was crusted with food drippings. His moustache was speckled with an unidentifiable dried crust and his hands were covered with a reddish residue. The boy was not too self-conscious to speak to the magus. Paithi asked in a decisive tone, "Sir, are you a scribe magus?"

The magus looked at him a little surprised and a little amused. He answered in a weak voice, "No. I am a surgeon magus. You will find a scribe magus in the hall of records."

"Where is that, Sir?" the boy asked.

The magus directed Paithi to an untidy building that the boy entered, walking on powdery dust until a scribe magus saw him and asked, "What do you want, boy?"

"Sir," the boy said in a clear voice, "I would like to see the records you keep. I would like to see if I can read some of them with your help."

"You can't read. No one as young as you can," the magus said. "Go away, I have no time for your foolishness."

"Please, sir," the boy implored without hesitation, "I can read some and I need practice. You have a lot of writing in this place. I would like to see script that is not written by my family. My father is Greek. He teaches me to read."

The magus was amused by the boy's enthusiasm. There was no harm in showing the child the tablets. If he was unable to read it didn't matter if he saw government documents. The magus made a gesture for the boy to follow him. The building was undecorated. It had been designed for record keeping, nothing else. They passed a room where men were molding clay tablets. The whole room appeared to be covered with a reddish-gray dust. Paithi stopped to watch for a moment. The men were covered with slick paste used to make rectangular tablets. They stuffed muck from a pool of soggy clay into wooden molds arranged side-by-side on carts. The scribe magus said, "The workers pull these wagons into a courtyard where the clay is dried in the sun. Then the dried tablets are stacked indoors for later use."

Further down the corridor the boy saw more men in a room, sitting at benches. There were twigs piled in front of each man. Each magus had a bronze hand-knife he used to cut the twigs to about the length of a man's foot. One end of the twig was shaped to a point. The other end was shaped broad and flat. The scribe magus said, "The flat end makes triangular cuts and the pointed end makes straight cuts in our cuneiform writing with a single stroke. Like this," and the magus demonstrated the technique.

Paithi was impressed with this clever device. He said, "My father gouges the triangular shapes using several strokes. He could use this tool to make that cut with a simple twist of the wrist."

In the record room there were chips of clay all over the floor. There were shelves and shelves of clay tablets stacked to the ceiling. Ladders leaned against the walls, which made it possible to get to records in the higher places. Several benches were scattered about the room caked with clay debris.

Paithi noticed a pile of dried lambskins of various sizes in one corner. He asked, "Sir, what are the skins for?"

"When we have to send a message by camel caravan we have to presume it might rain," the magus said. "Rain will melt the clay destroying the message. We write on the skins with ink made of charcoal and oil. The rolled up skins are buried deep inside cargo that is being shipped to protect the message."

"Do you always do it that way, Sir?"

"No. Sometimes, nothing is written," the magus said smiling. "We memorize many messages that we recite to the receiver because the person sending it sometimes does not want a permanent record of a private communication. Then we can only deliver the message by a magus who has to go on the camel caravan or ride alone if speed is required. It costs quite a bit for this service; only the government or the rich use it. Sometimes the military has a secret requiring our verbal delivery service."

In childish innocence the boy asked, "Sir, do you ever forget a message? I sometimes forget what my father tells me to do."

The magus laughed, "No. We never forget. We are trained to remember. We are able to pass a message through several magi who keep the information exactly as it was originally told to us."

The boy was impressed but not surprised. There were legendary stories about great warriors that were only repeated by mouth but neither the heroes nor their exploits ever changed.

"Where do you live, boy?" the magus asked.

"My father manages a farm for the Great King near Arbela."

"What is your father's name?" the magus asked.

"He is Mitridates, sir."

The magus thought for a moment before climbing a ladder to a shelf that had the name of Arbela on it. The boy pointed and exclaimed, "Arbela!"

The magus was so amazed that the boy could read the shelf label he jerked almost falling off his ladder backwards. The magus lifted a tablet down and laid it on a table. It was too heavy for the boy to hold. The magus announced, "This is a record of your father's productivity. The tax minister keeps it even though no tax is paid on the King's farm. Read it."

Paithi began to trace his forefinger over the clay. The magus shouted, "Never touch the writing! If you rub the clay the record will disappear, never to be seen again. Just read, boy."

227

Paithi read what he could. His identification of the syllabic sounds the writing represented was sporadic. He read about the listing of the amounts of new calves and lambs born. He read a list of the slaves by name. Since Paithi knew all the people on the farm his father had taught the boy to read their names. Paithi read aloud his parents' names. He could not read what was said about them on the tablet. The magus stopped him and said, "That is enough, I am too busy right now to spend more time with you. It is impressive that you can read a bit, but you must leave now. Come back if you wish after you have learned to read better."

Paithi thanked the magus as he left the building elated at what he had accomplished. Walking away it occurred to him that he had not seen his own name on the tablet. Additionally, he had not seen the names of several little children of the farm. After reflecting on his experience in the record hall, he came to the conclusion that the tablet was old. It was a record of a time when he and other children had not been born. The thought intrigued him. Paithi thought if you could keep a record of occurrences by writing them, then the memory of another person was unimportant. Retelling the tail of the event would be more accurate because everyone would know the exact same story.

As he walked he noticed some buildings had pictures on them. He wondered why. The picture on one building was of a man harvesting barley. It was a public building with a guard standing by the front door. Paithi went up to the guard and asked, "What is this building being used for?"

The guard said, "It is a military barracks."

Paithi asked, "Why does it have a picture of a man harvesting barley?"

"Oh," said the guard, "is that what that is? Well, I am told this building used to be a granary long before I was born. Now it is a barracks."

Paithi had just gotten a history lesson from a picture and from a man. The man did not know he had helped a boy understand something quite significant. As Paithi looked about him the city was beginning to take on a new meaning, the pictures on the buildings identified what buildings were used for at one time, maybe even now. Then the boy thought that if a man performed some great act a stone picture could be made of it so the world would remember the deed forever. The experience gave him incentive to try to do his lessons better from now on. Paithi hoped to please his father with what he had learned today.

Paithi described his accomplishments to his mother and father on the way home and he pestered his father about returning to Ecbatana, because the boy was anxious to revisit the magus and read again.

28.

The sun was hot and the air was dry. Paithi sat in the dirt leaning against the cool, stone wall in front of the palace. He was thrilled to be back in Ecbatana even though the heat of the city air was far more oppressive than the country air on the Arbela farm. He watched mobs of strangers pass by. One woman drove a pair of oxen up to the gate in the palace wall. The animals pulled a flatbed wagon loaded with what looked like old rags tossed over wine amphorae. The rags were stuffed between the containers to keep the clay jugs from breaking against one another as the wagon jolted over the pavement ruts.

The old woman had humped shoulders. Her hair was unkempt, and she was covered with dust. She wore a dress that was in no better condition than the rags on her cart. Paithi guessed she had been travelling with her load most of the day because she looked very tired. The guards at the gate examined the contents of her cart before allowing her to disappear through the gate.

Soldiers passed in or out of the gate constantly. Some marched in precise formation; others strolled in casual clusters chatting. The boy saw that they wore dark woolen skirts tied by a leather belt at the waist. A bronze sword hung from the belt. The scabbard was tied to the thigh opposite the side of the sword handle. Paithi liked how most soldiers wore a sheaf of arrows and a bow over one shoulder. Some carried lances but they all wore a jerkin made of leather flaps with bronze fasteners holding the flaps together. The shoulder piece of the jerkin was a large, loose fitting, epaulet of leather. A protecting piece of bronze was fitted over the epaulet. The soldiers wore a hat of leather that was round and tall. Their long hair hung straight down to the bottom of their beards. They wore leather boots extending to mid-calf.

Paithi thought the soldiers looked smart. They were muscular and walked with great confidence. He admired the way officers wore an animal skin over one shoulder. It gave the men a fierce, impressive appearance. Paithi wanted to be like them. He began to dream of having easy access to the palace where the Great King lived.

Paithi noticed women coming out of the palace gate dressed in fine silk veils and delicate flat sandals. He liked the way they wore face makeup that accented their eyes, cheeks and lips. Even their toes were painted! He thought they must be the women that belonged to the King. They looked happy talking together as they walked toward the market. They were obviously going shopping. They were the most beautiful females in the vast crowd swarming slowly among the merchants. No one rushed in the hot sun.

A small boy sat down in the shade near Paithi. He wore a bracelet that indicated he was a slave of a Mede. Paithi was naturally genial and he said, "It is a fine day to sit in the shade and watch people busy with their chores. I am Paithi. Who are you?"

The slave was surprised at a freeman talking to him in such a familiar way as he said, "I am Oebares. I am a slave to a magnate of Media," and the boy held up his arm to display his bracelet to Paithi. The slave said, "My master governs a section of the city to the south. My master sent me here to watch the stone mason."

Paithi looked along the wall but did not see anyone working stone. The slave boy pointed to a man carrying a ladder. He was approaching the wall. Oebares exclaimed as if to explain himself, "My master has commissioned the mason to make a relief of King Astyages on this wall. I have to ensure the man comes to work every day. If he does not I have to tell my master, who has the man whipped."

Paithi inquired easily, "Why does your master want a relief of the Great King?"

"It is a gift. The Great King is a selfish tyrant who expects people working for him to give him gifts," the slave said. "If I could I would give him a bag of my night soil."

"Why do you hate the King? What has he ever done to you?" Paithi asked.

"He has done nothing to me," Oebares answered. "I just hate him because of the stories I hear of him from my master. Well, my master doesn't tell me, but I hear him tell others. Once, King Astyages had a mason whipped almost to death because the man made a statue of the King that was too short. My master says the King insists on being a giant in everything. Now I have to watch this man. If the picture he is cutting takes too long my master may be whipped."

231

Paithi took a drink from his goat stomach bag of water than handed it to the slave saying in a contented sigh, "Drink. It is hot today."

The slave took the container and hesitated for a moment before drinking because no freeman would ever be so nice to him. Oebares asked, "Who are you? Where do you live in the city?"

"I am the son of Mitridates," Paithi said. "My father and mother take care of a farm to the northwest for the King. We tend the King's land and his animals. We do not live in Ecbatana. My father is selling merchandise. We will go home when all his goods are sold."

"Come over here," Oebares said as he stood and pointed away from the wall. They went out into the sun to look back at the wall. The start of a wall picture in the stone was quite visible and Paithi was surprised he had not noticed it before he sat. A large section of mud-brick wall had been removed so a hard, white stone wall could be erected in its place. A profile of a very large man wearing a crown was being shaped in relief on the new section of bright stone. The mason had cut the figure from the top of the head down to the chest. Paithi asked, "Do you know what the finished stone picture will finally look like, Oebares?"

"There will be a king from the country of Pars and one from the country of Aria who are giving gifts to the Great King. They will be smaller than that figure," the slave indicted as he pointed to the King's image.

Paithi loved the King of Kings because of the magnificent stories he heard about his grandeur and power. The farm boy said, "I think the Great King should be the biggest because he is a wonder. Princes tell us how dignified the Great King is when they come to our farm. I want to be like him some day. He wins wars all the time too."

"No, he doesn't! He lost a war with Bactria and they will never pay his taxes again," exploded Oebares. "He is weak and contemptuous. I do not know what that word means, but my master says that word when he talks about the King."

Paithi had never heard anyone say such things about the King. He felt he had to defend King Astyages against this boy. He bragged, "Well, we think very highly of him on our farm, err.. his farm. He never comes to whip us." Then thoughtfully Paithi said, "He never comes to the farm himself. He is too busy running his enormous kingdom for us. We would fight to the death for him."

"You may have to some day if he doesn't change the way he acts toward his minor kings," said Oebares, giving one more jab at the King, as he pointed and continued, "See how the mason cuts the stone with his bronze tools? They get dull fast. He wastes a lot of time sharpening them. Making that picture is going to take forever to complete. I will burn up in this sun."

"That picture of the Great King will be there until that wall crumbles to dust. My sons will be able to look at it and I will tell them I saw the man make it. I will tell my sons that you were here but you did not like the greatest man on the face of the earth. They will feel sorry for you, Oebares," said Paithi, using his newfound awareness of the permanence and historical importance of stone pictures.

The boys sat back in the shade to have another drink of water. Oebares swallowed and thought how different this boy acted towards him compared to other freemen. Paithi said, "I am going to walk around the city for a while. I hope to see you again, Oebares. Maybe you will be free some day. Then we can walk together. Goodbye."

They waved to each other as Paithi disappeared into the market. As he passed through the crowds he decided a slave like Oebares probably did not appreciate a king the way free men did. Personally, Paithi still believed the Great King was grand, a man to be admired and emulated if that was possible.

The farm boy came upon two men who were arguing about the ownership of a goat. One man claimed the animal because the other man had given him rancid meat for it. The other was saying he had negotiated a fair barter trade agreed to by both of them.

The loud complainer shouted, "You gave me meat that made me ill. Take the rest of this garbage back. I want my goat," as he tossed a stack of meat at the man.

"No," hollered the other man who looked scruffy and smelled like rotting flesh, "you saw the meat, smelled the meat, even poked it with your finger before we agreed on the exchange. The goat is mine. You must have left that mess in the sun and it went bad."

The complainer said, "Your meat made me vomit. I just wanted something edible and you cheated me. I want my goat back!"

Innocently, Paithi said, "You should give the goat back if you gave him bad meat for it. It is not fair to conduct business that is not equal for all involved."

The smelly man looked savagely at Paithi and said, "Go away, boy, this is not your affair. He knew what he was accepting for the goat and he took it. Go away."

The man turned his back to Paithi and they continued to argue. Paithi felt the man with the bad meat and sick stomach had a right to a fair exchange even if he had received the opportunity to examine the meat before the deal was concluded. This sense of fair play was characteristic of Paithi and he got in trouble for it occasionally. Straightforward honest dealings between people were not always as clear as he wanted them to be.

He saw Prince Zatame and Zav walking together arguing. He stole up behind them to listen. Prince Zatame said, "You have to be reasonable. We can not accept a tax increase on royal properties just to make up the amount no longer received from Bactria and Gedrosia."

"The general taxes have been reduced again by the King's order," Zav retorted. "You were there at the audience; you brought up the subject of tax changes. Now I have to make up these deficits somehow. If the noblemen will not support me, I will have to see if the King will. There must be an increase in the tribute you and the other princes pay to the King."

"We can cause his properties to make more by increasing the pressure on our managers. We can add slaves to cultivate more of the fields," the prince suggested in an anxious tone. "Raising more crops will provide more to sell. We can make them increase the number of calves, lambs and ponies born each year. The camel herds can be increased so the King can expand his own caravan expeditions. There are many ways to maintain the King's wealth without taxing us."

Zav did not appreciate the way the prince was arguing back so he responded in a sarcastic tone. He said, "The Great King does not have to have his properties work harder to get rich. He just has to command you to pay more. His command! Do you understand, Prince?"

Paithi knew both men and decided to enter their conversation. "Sir," the boy said to Zav, "the prince has the best idea. The King's farms can produce much more than they do now. I know. My…"

Zav partially turned his face in the direction of Paithi without actually looking at the boy and he exploded with anger. Zav's rage blurred his sight keeping the minister from recognizing the boy. He shouted, "How dare you! How dare you! I should swat you into the desert for interfering. Get away from me."

"But, Sir," Paithi continued with his bravest demeanor, "my father runs a ..."

"Shut up! Get away from me, or I will have you trampled under a camel," shouted Zav as he swung his closed fist at the boy and missed.

Paithi saw that Prince Zatame was smiling. He recognized the youth and understood what the boy was trying to say. He nodded politely at Paithi then waved him off. The two men walked away from the boy continuing their discussion. Paithi wandered alone along the street, crushed at not being able to make Zav listen.

This was a peculiar day for him. Everyone argued with his standard of decency and his sense of fair dealing. Paithi knew there were fundamental principles here that had to be respected. In his innocence the boy had interfered in circumstances he had no right to be involved in. He felt very passionate about the ethical codes Mitridates had instilled in him. Paithi wanted everyone to act according to his rules because Mitridates had convinced his son they were correct.

Paithi reviewed in his mind his love for the King, contrasting it with what Oebares had alleged. Paithi believed the goat should have been returned because of the bad meat, and taxes did not need to be increased because the productivity of Mitridates' farm could be improved. His father had convinced him that dignified actions made an uncertain world stable. Morality gave meaning to life. Three of his principles, loyalty, honor and hard work, had been challenged today. Paithi was unset.

Paithi thought of how fables invented by a Greek man named Aesop were a favorite teaching tool his mother used. These short tales reflected the unchangeable nature of animals that did not always seem fair to Paithi. He was forced to accept that it was the nature of the lion to devour the wolf. It was the nature of the wolf to trick and devour the sheep. So maybe it was the nature of a slave to hate the king who allowed slavery like it was the nature of a freeman to love the king who allowed slaves to do the difficult work. Paithi pretended that today he had been the partridge arguing with the gamecocks when the gamecocks preferred to argue with each other. He thought about his farm duties. Paithi had confidence his father could make improvements there. All the family had to do was work a little harder. This fit Paithi's personal desire to improve. There was plenty of fertile land with grassy fields for camel herds, cattle feeding or sheep grazing. Paithi decided to ask his father if they could try to increase the yield on the farm, because the child agreed with what Prince Zatame had said. He liked Prince Zatame. Paithi was going to ask his father for help in ways to make production improvements on the King's farm by increasing the volume of everything! Paithi tried to think of what he might do himself to increase the farm's worth as he sauntered through the city.

Gradually, he became distracted as he wandered into an unknown part of Ecbatana. He was not afraid of strange neighborhoods. He loved to stumble across foreign languages so he could figure out what their words meant. He wished he could go to other cities to wander through them as well.

Today Paithi found himself in a very old section of Ecbatana. The houses were made of sun-dried bricks and stones. The rough rocks were eons old. No stone mason had smoothed the surfaces of the boulders used in these buildings. The street was dirt. No one had laid stone walkways anywhere. He knew this area turned to mud in the rain. Some windows had pieces of rough wood covering the opening. A few were covered with rags, but most windows were uncovered to let air blow through the house. The boy saw sheep and chickens in yards having almost no grass and one small girl was milking a goat. She looked about without seeing anyone and squirted the teat into her own mouth. Paithi chuckled because he had done the same thing many times.

He had the wanderlust of a nomad, except he preferred to wander in established, organized places. He liked large clusters of people around him that he could watch, talk to and learn from. He did not know he was developing the characteristics of an adventurer that he was going to exhibit for the rest of his life.

29.

Zav was feeling disappointed about his failure to convince Governor Pagakanna to make Babylon attack Pars immediately after the war with Judah. The governor had said that King Nebuchadnezzar would prefer to rest his army. Even with a worn out Babylonian army, Zav told Pagakanna that King Nebuchadnezzar could vanquish Pars in a short time since neither citadels nor walls defended Susa or Anshan. Also, Zav had advised the governor that King Astyages would never come to the aid of Pars even though the Great King had forbidden Nebuchadnezzar to attack there. After securing the safety of his daughter, King Astyages would even let the Sythians take Pars just to make an example of his minor king. Zav also advised that the Great King was becoming more willful, letting his own royal image be his only priority these days. The welfare of small countries in his kingdom had no priority. Zav had tried to get all that across to the Babylonian, but he did not care. Their army was tired of fighting.

Zav had visited Bactria too only to discover that the trail across the salt desert was becoming more established and busier with each passing day. Caravan traffic in Bactria was now substantial with trade from the north, south, east and west helping it to flourish, cheating Ecbatana out of enormous trade volumes. There was no way Zav could stop or interfere with this trade. He could not demand that King Arsames cease this commerce per the order of the Great King. Bactria was successfully independent and no longer answered to the Great King.

Zav was unable to convince King Arsames to stop trading with Cambyses, who was now a strong trading partner for Bactria. As Pars increased its wealth Zav wanted more than ever to hurt Cambyses and Mandane. His hatred of this royal couple was growing stronger, driven by the realization that he could not find any country willing to go to war with Pars. Additionally, up till now the Great King prevented him from over-taxing Pars, and Zav could think of no way to publicly insult King Cambyses.

Zav wondered if hurting trade to Pars was his best way to get at Cambyses. The minister knew only cargoes that did not spoil in the heat of the desert could be transported between Pars and Bactria. This meant that Pars still had to market meats, fruits and vegetables in Media. Milk products like yogurt and cheeses were sold by Pars to Media as well. That was it! He could smother Pars in its own pomegranates and citrus fruits. He could drown them in their own camel milk.

He waited for a season when the weather favored the production of all vegetation in Pars. He refused to deal with Pattmenidu, the chief merchant of Pars, in the trade of melons, figs, dates, lemons, limes, vegetables, cheeses, yogurt or meats of any kind. The scheme started to work just as Zav hoped. Pattmenidu was unable to find an alternative outlet for these products. The merchant tried to ship from Anshan to Susa, but Susa already had warehouses full of fruits and dairy products that they could not trade either.

However, Pattmenidu was more resourceful than Zav realized. The Parsian ordered figs, dates and meats to be laid in the sun to dry. This preserved them for consumption later. Dried strips of meat were not just suitable for eating later they transported in caravans well too. Pattmenidu bartered these dried products in Bactria and had them sent to the east to markets of the Chin people. The drying cut down on the volume of the foods making more room in the warehouses for grains. Since citrus and melon products rotted easily Pattmenidu had them sent to farms as fertilizer. If nothing else the soil could be enriched.

Zav had created hard times for Pars during a period of enormous plenty. King Cambyses was furious with Zav. There was nothing the minor king could do to force Zav to relent, but Pattmenidu's ingenuity had at least reduced the negative economic impact that Zav had contrived. The Tax and Materials Minister of Media was gradually increasing his power to control commerce, an area he normally could only influence with tax controls or shifts in materials storage. He also used the Great King's lack of interest in the business welfare of his subjects to illegally shunt valuables into his own possession.

//

Cambyses was aware of the hard work put in by his peasants to enjoy a crop of remarkable abundance. The peasants counted on the enlarged crop to help in the future when their output might not be as prolific. The merchants of Pars began bartering to give excess produce and meats to foreign customers without immediate payment, under a promise from the customer that Pars was to get other kinds of products in return later, such as cloth, raw metals, furniture and oil. These extended payment contracts, covering two to three future sun cycles, gave the peasants of Pars partial economic relief. The series of reduced taxes that King Astyages had decreed for Pars had expired. Zav planned incremental increases in the tax obligations to Cambyses above all previous levels. Cambyses sent noble emissaries to the Great King trying to stop these burdensome increases, but they were not successful. In most instances the Great King refused to even receive the princes Cambyses sent. The King of Kings threatened at one point to keep them prisoner if Cambyses sent more. Cambyses did not want his nephews and uncles placed in jeopardy by an unfriendly emperor so he stopped sending them. Cambyses was frustrated by the threat. He was no longer able to use the murder of the servant girl at Ecbatana against Zav. No one seemed to remember her death. Implicating Zav at this late date was impossible because of the way Cambyses had handled the discovery of her body. The minister had committed murder and escaped punishment. Zav had won and they both knew it. Zav seemed to be in a position to tax Cambyses at any level he wished. The minister started scaling Pars taxes so high that stealing large portions was not noticed in the Great King's records.

At the moment the combination of reduced national revenues and higher taxes were so unusually burdensome Cambyses was depleting his treasury to honor his obligation to King Astyages. There was no way to defer the payments. The Great King demanded homage from his subjects more than he required prosperity from them. He mistook the anguished look of suffering on the faces of the taxed as increased reverence to himself.

Within his family Cambyses had resolved one crisis but continued to live with another. On the first matter the king had met with his cousin, Prince Warohi of Susa, and they talked extensively about the issues that had bothered the prince. The king said, "Pattmenidu, tell my cousin of your conversations in Babylon."

The minor king saw to it that both Pattmenidu and Mandane attended the discussions with Prince Warohi.

"Governor Pagakanna introduced me to King Nebuchadnezzar's court, where I told the king that Pars was increasing weapons production," the merchant said. "I promised King Nebuchadnezzar that King Cambyses would make the weapons available to Babylon in case of war. Nebuchadnezzar took my comments to mean that we would use the weapons against him, and I was delighted that he did not kill me."

"I deserve to be beheaded for my thoughts of insurrection against my own king. Sire, I am sorry," Prince Warohi said. His face was draped in anguish. "Zav tricked me. I was too dumb to see it. It will never happen again."

As they reviewed the details of Zav's involvement it became clear to Prince Warohi how easily his naivete had made him act foolish. The prince said, "It feels good, yet humiliating, to admit my guilt to you, sire."

Cambyses let the prince feel the insult of his own thoughts and actions. The king wanted the severity of the infraction to be clearly understood and remembered.

"Smarter men than you have been duped by that man, Warohi. You know you should have communicated with me instead of committing yourself to go along with any suggestion of Zav's. You know I exonerate you from any blame. Your confession to me is enough. We will forget this."

Mandane was sitting in the room relieved at how this family was able to talk openly without deception or accusation. She said, "Warohi, it is the sign of a good man when he faces his errors and admits them to others. We are comforted by your honesty."

Her respect for the prince grew. She did not cry during the talks, though she wanted to as she observed the prince's pain when he admitted his errors. Mandane had to remember her lambskin that told her to be a lioness and not a peahen. She was becoming the queen of a nation that made mistakes and had its difficulties, yet these errors made her appreciate the compassion Cambyses had for Pars and its people.

Unfortunately, Mandane was the second problem that Cambyses could not resolve. She had become more despondent over not bearing children as time passed. She accused herself and Cambyses of being the source of the problem at odd times. She tried going to a magus who used all his mind travelling skills to help her, but nothing worked. She had gone to Ecbatana to talk with her parents and their Chief Magus. She felt something mystical had happened to her after the death of her son. She questioned whether someone could have put a curse on her. She demanded that her father investigate to determine if any of the midwives that had accompanied her during her birth delivery was an evil, daeva-like spell caster. It all came to naught.

Mandane wanted children more than anything. She became resentful of princesses in the palace who were having children. She began to lose friends in the palace and many residents of her *andarun* began avoiding her company as much as possible. One friend she retained was the beautiful Princess Ispitamu. This princess was very pleased with herself. She was preventing an heir to the throne from being born by simply adding a little silphium liquid to the queen's wine cup when no one was looking. Zav was able to provide her with sufficient quantities of the silphium bush to keep her 'poisoning' of the queen on a regular schedule. The princess had ceased introducing peculiar servant and slave difficulties into the life of the queen as Mandane created her own problems. Mandane argued with princesses, servants and began ordering the punishment of slaves. She accused magi of casting spells on her. She ordered them punished, but Cambyses refused to allow it.

Mandane wanted to sacrifice the newborn children of palace princesses to placate the gods who could remove the spell she suspected someone had placed on her. She tried to make live animal and human offerings to the gods common practice. Sacrificing was an accepted sacred ritual performed by a magus. The magi only made a human sacrifice at specific holy times or for special requests made by the rich to the divine. Cambyses adamantly refused to let Mandane make a human offering. Each time she demanded the life to a royal child Cambyses had to spend long hours talking to her. He had to tell her that human sacrifice was a sacred offering. It could not be used as revenge on another woman for having a baby.

Mandane knew her personality was changing yet she didn't care. She certainly had changed from being the caring woman Cambyses had married although she knew he still loved her very much and she loved him. But sometimes her behavior displeased him enough to cause him to reprimand her making her more embittered. Once the queen said, "Cambyses do you remember the shooting star we both observed in the sky during our time of bidding, before the marriage. I wondered then if it was a good or bad sign. Now I know we should have recognized it as an evil omen, which should have prevented our marriage!"

Her comment hurt the king. Mandane resented it when Cambyses recommended that she sleep in the shade of a fig tree because it was believed that the sweet, succulent fruit could mellow the mood of a troubled person while they slumbered. Mandane managed to retain her queenly image to the peasants and the noblemen who came from other parts of the country to seek favors of Cambyses. To them she was still the beautiful paragon who could do no wrong. She hid her mean disposition from them. Cambyses began worrying that her personality might be permanently changed, preventing her from ever returning to the perfect woman he used to know.

On a couple of occasions Mandane had even gone so far as to agree with Zav in the audience chamber. To Cambyses that was the most serious challenge he could expect from her. He had been shocked enough to spend time alone, reconciling for himself the problems produced by her anxiety and public behavior. There was another adversity that was helping to change Mandane's character that her husband was not aware of.

Princess Ispitamu had stopped sleeping with Zav. Long ago she became aware that he wanted to enter the royal family by marrying her. Firstly, she could never tolerate the prospect of being his wife and secondly, she could not abide the idea that he might ascend to the royalty within Pars through her. She was diplomatic about no longer inviting him to her bed. She suggested that one of her royal cousins was making advances, suggesting marriage, and it was an invitation she could not ignore. Zav got petulant, but he stopped expecting intimate association with her. They still met in private to talk about their success with Mandane's sterility but sexual isolation from this remarkable beauty caused the frustrated Zav to suggest another poison. A medical magus had described the effects of the oleander bush to him, which he decided the princess could use it as a second way to trouble Mandane. This bush could change the way the chest worked. He did not know how it happened, but a person could feel changes in the pulsing or beating of the chest. Princess Ispitamu needed more information so she questioned a magus. Again she pretended that she was more interested in the antidote than the poison. She learned how to prepare an oleander potion she could administer in water or wine, just like the first poison she had used for so long.

The princess was careful to use the oleander just once every three or four moon cycles because of the severity of its action. Queen Mandane never spoke about what happening to her after she ingested the 'gift' the princess gave her, but Mandane got nauseous and vomited a lot. She clutched her chest as a horrified look raced across her countenance. The princess sat holding the queen, pretending to comfort her when all that the princess really wanted was to observe the extreme pain the queen was experiencing. Somehow the oleander made Mandane's chest thump, and what she felt was a dramatic discomfort because of this strange sensation. It was frightening to the queen, and sometimes the visible change in her during these episodes scared Princess Ispitamu too. The princess gave the queen the oleander potion in her wine when they were alone. It was a very dangerous poison, which the princess knew was a sacred gift from the beneficial ahura spirits, because the queen did not die on these occasions.

The princess was delighted that Mandane said it felt as if she was being visited by death each time. It petrified the queen so much that she could no longer stand having people around her making minor mistakes. The princess also liked that Mandane began to believe the stupidity of others was the cause of this peculiar distress. Princess Ispitamu made a point of always talking about the blunders of the servants or slaves when she administered the oleander to Queen Mandane. The princess believed this excited the queen and helped the oleander work its magic agony. The queen began to relate the bumbling of her dumb help with her chest pains and nausea. She believed the servants were her source of physical discomfort. She never suspected she was being poisoned. Mandane never mentioned her symptoms to another person. The queen felt alone confiding in no one except Princess Ispitamu. The only comfort Mandane had now was her dreams of having a child. The queen did not know her child lived outside Ecbatana and enjoyed a very healthy life.

//

Paithi was now ten and the leader of play and work with the children on the Great King's farm in Arbela. He made the slave children responsible for all newborn animals. He taught them to watch the births, house the newborn and see to the feeding of the young animals at weaning time. He had the children build pens with feeding troughs. Paithi designed the pens. At the bottom of each he made the children put logs or boards close together to prevent wolves and other predators from entering. One adult on the farm said, "You're using too much wood. You're wasting material."

Paithi explained, "Many little animals die, because they get injured or eaten by scavengers as small as foxes. If our pens are built to keep predators out more animals will grow up giving us larger herds and flocks."

The adults were impressed with his logic when they realized it actually worked the way he said. They let him do as he wished.

The boy had the children take care of the grains that were fed to small animals. Paithi made them keep the grains dry so the animal feed did not rot. The grains were also rotated so the kernels did not shrivel up losing their nutritional value with age. The adults began to see that the way he guided the children was beginning to show results. The herds and flocks got so large that they began to make a real economic difference to the farm. There was more wool from sheep and more milk from more camels, goats and cows. The areas on the farm where the milk was processed to make cheeses and yogurt had to be enlarged.

Mitridates and the adult slaves began to improve on the changes Paithi started in such a way that the farm became a model of productivity visiting princes bragged about at other farms. Managers of other properties that belonged to the King visited to see what Mitridates was doing. They began to copy his techniques elsewhere. Mitridates became the paragon of efficiency. His son had started it all!

Spaco continued to teach Paithi what she could. There were Greek travelers who came through their area who stayed at the farm. Spaco always asked her Greek visitors about the man, Aesop, who traveled around Greece and Lydia spreading the fables he fabricated to teach common sense and wisdom. Spaco enjoyed repeating these fables to

Paithi. She enjoyed using animals as the model in her instruction, even if one had to make the animals sound human. She had learned that was what fables were all about; they were exaggerated pictures for the mind to implant morals and understanding of how the world worked. Paithi loved them. He tried to apply them to his own experiences. There was the fable of a dolphin that drowned a monkey who lied. Paithi understood that lying was a punishable offense, but no one knew what a dolphin was so that story was promptly forgotten. With the slave children he told of the meeting of the hares and the lions. The hares claimed everyone should be treated as equals by the lions. The lions said that sounded fine, except the words of the hares did not have teeth or claws like a lion. One of the slave children asked, "What does that story mean?"

Paithi said, "Freemen are the lions with all the powerful claws and teeth. Slaves like you are the hares subject to the vicious strength of the lions."

One thing confused Paithi about this latter fable which he did not bring up with the slave children. He knew slaves could be made freemen by purchasing their own freedom or by having an owner release them from slavery. These were two ways slaves could 'change their nature.' The lions and hares in the fable could not change their own nature. He wondered if the fable did not apply to individuals, but did apply to the stations of freedom and slavery. His education had allowed him to comprehend this deeper understanding of these two conditions. He did not try to evaluate if these two different states of living were justified or not. Slaves were the spoils of war. Their existence was natural.

As the self-declared leader of the children on the farm Paithi was never challenged. He not only assumed the authority of the highest rank; he also assumed the responsibility of the highest rank. If anyone got hurt in a game he took over to see that they were cared for by the others or by adults. He ordered his playmates around without being mean or without picking on the weaker ones. There were boys on Paithi's farm older than he was who were either slaves or visitors. When he was in charge age did not matter to him or them.

Once the son of a nobleman came with his father to inspect the farm. The boy was a prince, older than Paithi. The chores for the day had been completed when Paithi invited the prince to play. Paithi suggested playing the sports of the Greek Olympics. They started with foot racing in a field. The prince beat Paithi in three straight races. Paithi congratulated him on being so fast. Paithi suggested racing in the forest. Since the prince was a city boy he was not sure-footed on the forest floor and he lost. He got angry and accused Paithi of cheating. The farm boy ignored the prince's incidental complaint. Paithi suggested they try wrestling next. He knew it would be a struggle to beat a boy so much taller and heavier than himself. Paithi had learned to toss larger boys to the ground by using their own weight and forward motion. He could get the larger boy down easily but not keep him down. The prince became frustrated at being tossed first every time so he punched Paithi. Paithi immediately began to box back since it was just another Greek contest. Paithi was quick, but not as powerful as the prince was. They both ended up tired. Again the prince was frustrated at not having a clean win. They stopped challenging each other and went to find the slave children. This was Paithi's domain. He organized a game where he was king. Paithi respected the Great King very much, and he loved to play at being the King of Kings in games. The prince objected, but all the other children clamored to play the game. Because the other children were only slaves the prince refused to follow the rules. He began to disobey the orders of the king so Paithi jumped on him giving him a sound thrashing. Even the larger size of the prince did not help in this circumstance. Because Paithi was a king asserting his rights he found new strength in his assumed nobility. The beaten prince cried and ran to his father to complain. His father chastised Mitridates for having a son who had no respect for a royal prince. Mitridates got very upset. He knew no good could come of this. He beat Paithi for his transgression. Paithi accepted his punishment but refused to admit he did wrong. A prince had no right to refuse the commands of a king even if it was only a game. The rules had been clear to everyone. The farm boy had allowed the prince to remain a prince in their play with authority over the slave children. That should have been enough for his visitor.

Several days after the noble contingent left the farm a messenger arrived ordering Mitridates and his family to present themselves at the palace in Ecbatana per the order of the Great King. Mitridates was petrified. He knew he was about to die with his wife and son. Spaco was so nervous she could not be comforted. Paithi felt guilty because he knew all this was his fault. The Great King was going to kill them all. The boy wondered if the King killed people himself. Paithi felt it was the last thing he would discover about kings, and he was despondent over its ugly reality.

30.

Zav had a choice of going to the Great King's audience chamber today or not. He had no business to report and the King had not summoned him. The minister felt good. He was improving his relationships with the noblemen of the court. He was not increasing their taxes by much, which made the princes grateful. Zav told them he accepted their farming improvements as enhanced value in lieu of tax revenues. This value increase was made possible by procedures developed at the royal property in the northwest, near Arbela. Zav passed through the crowd outside the royal audience chamber to see who was there. He noted several princes he knew by name. He greeted them with a smile. They nodded to him, which was the best he could expect from them in public. Royalty seldom held conversations with him in a crowd; if he aggravated them the princes did not hesitate to confront him no matter where they were. The absence of conversation with the young princes did not bother the minister a bit.

Zav saw a family of three standing together away from the crowd. At first he did not pay attention to them. In the back of his mind, however, something told him he knew who they were. He continued surveying the waiting crowd when the doors opened to admit the royal attendees first, then the merchants and peasants. Also, all persons who had been officially summoned were admitted. At that instant he remembered the family was from the King's farm. The only time the King ordered his managers to appear was when there was trouble. Since a farm involved commercial materials, Zav decided to go into the audience chamber to find out what was wrong. He feared that the caravan robberies might be the reason these farmers were here. Upon entering the great hall he saw Harpagus was already in the chamber, standing alone against a wall. Zav also saw the farmer flinch when he observed Harpagus. Zav noticed the farmer's wife edged closer to her husband when she looked at Harpagus. Their boy moved as if alone, coming to see his King. The youth looked a little excited but somewhat fearful. Zav did not realize the boy believed he was here to die.

The business of the day began with a magistrate bowing before the King to report that a statue of the Great King was not going to be completed on schedule. The artisan had broken a limb on the statue forcing him to start over with new marble stone. The King had developed the new habit of punishing the bearer of bad news as well as the person who was the source of bad news. He ordered both the magistrate and the artisan whipped. Zav knew this was a bad way to start the day's proceedings. He backed up behind a support column to hide from the sight of the Great King.

An emissary from King Arsames of Bactria came forward and bowed. King Astyages ordered him to stand. The man began to give his compliments to the Great King from his own king. Astyages barked, "Harpagus put this thing in prison."

He was from a seceded state which made him an enemy of Media; the Great King decided to make the emissary a prisoner for an indefinite period of time. The man's face fell, and he trembled with fear. He knew the possibility existed that this might happen so he had prepared a pretty speech to prevent being imprisoned. He never got to deliver his statement.

Next King Astyages beckoned to one of the royal princes and said, "Come here." The man came forward and knelt with his forehead on the floor. The King ordered, "Rise. I hear you have a complaint about one of my farms. You had better be certain you have a good argument, or I may ignore your family connection to me and whip you too."

The prince was tentative in his response as he described how he had gone to inspect the running of the King's farm in Arbela with other noblemen. He said, "Sire, I brought my son along to your farm to teach him the responsibilities of reviewing the operation of royal farms. My son went off to play with the farmer's son," and the prince pointed to Paithi and said, "That is the boy. His parents are there," and the prince pointed at Mitridates with a menacing glare and said, "That boy beat my son and made him bleed. Is that any way for a peasant to treat a prince of your court, sire?"

The Great King looked at the three people crowded together and waved them forward. King Astyages felt mildly protective of these people because they were part of his extended family as his farm managers. He noticed the child walked with more self-control than his parents did as he approached the throne. The family bowed and the

King let them stay bowing as he said to the prince, "What would you have me do?"

The prince said, "Sire, they need to be punished. All of them."

The King sneaked a mischievous smile and said, "Your son is older than this boy. He is even larger, is he not?"

The prince answered, "Yes, sire. But this boy beat up a royal relative of yours."

The King ordered, "You, boy, stand up, look at me."

Paithi rose and looked directly into the eyes of the Great King without flinching. The boy stood erect, unflinching. He was ready to accept his punishment like a man, not a child. The King was impressed with the boy's bearing. King Astyages ordered the parents to rise. Mitridates and Spaco rose but slumped in fear. The contrast in posture between the child and his parents was startling to the King. This boy was different from this man and woman. The King thought the boy was a man-child. King Astyages commanded, "Tell me, boy, what is your name. How old are you?"

"Sire, I am Paithi, and I am ten sun cycles," answered the boy with a respectful voice.

"Did you beat my nephew as his father claims?" inquired the King.

"Yes, sire, I did," answered Paithi.

"Why?" demanded the King.

"Sire, we were playing, and I was the king." Paithi began with a steady voice, "I was pretending to be you. This prince refused to obey my commands so I beat him. I could not ask my subjects to do it."

"Why couldn't the slaves carry out your beating for you?" the King asked.

"Sire, they are slaves in life and they were slaves in our playing. It is not fitting for the king to order a slave to beat a prince."

King Astyages was almost entranced by the answers he was getting from this boy. The King continued, "My nephew is a prince in real life. Was he a prince while you were playing?"

"Yes, sire. I designated him my royal relative. We had agreed to that."

"I should have you beaten now for striking a member of my family!" the King roared. "I could have you killed. Do you understand that, boy?"

Paithi jerked at the force of the King's outburst, but he was not upset by what was said. Paithi answered, "Yes, sire, if you think a king should punish another king who has been disobeyed then I am ready."

King Astyages was completely taken aback by the self-assurance of this child. He could not take his eyes off the boy, but he demanded, "You, the father, is this your son?"

Mitridates whimpered, "Yes, sire."

The King said, "You manage my farm, do you not?"

"Yes, sire."

"You are the one who made the improvements in my farm?" the King asked.

"Yes, sire."

"Who had the ideas to improve the farm? You or a slave?"

"At the beginning, sire, they were my son's ideas."

The King had almost expected that answer. He rose from his throne and said, "I want this family to come with me. No one else," as he left the chamber.

Mitridates and Spaco walked behind Paithi as they followed the King. They entered a small room with one chair. The King sat in it. A guard closed the door but stood outside ready to enter at the least noise. The King looked at his subjects and said, "This boy is not yours. Who is he?"

Mitridates looked at Spaco; they both went weak in the knees. "Sire," said Mitridates, "Paithi has been our son for ten sun cycles."

"If he was your child he would not be so obviously different from you. Everything about his behavior is unlike your own. He is not yours. I demand the truth! Who is he?" bellowed the King.

Mitridates realized the truth was all that could serve him now and he said, "Sire, our natural born child died at birth. One of your soldiers delivered this boy to us and ordered us to kill him in the woods. We could not. We did not."

Mitridates took a deep breath trying to calm himself. Paithi looked at his father stunned by this admission. The boy did not say anything; the King had not addressed him.

"Sire, we put our own child in the forest as the soldier commanded before adding sheep's blood on the baby's clothing,"

Mitridates continued, "The soldier came back for the clothes. We brought Paithi up as our own son, sire. That is the truth."

Mitridates almost fainted when he finished speaking. His wife was paralyzed with fear and could not have spoken if the King demanded her to do so. Her mouth was dry; her eyes were bulging. She gazed at Paithi begging for forgiveness without speaking. The child saw the hurt in her face; it filled him with pity. Tears fell on his cheeks, but he did not cry out loud. He felt great love and sympathy for his parents.

The King looked at them for a few moments noting that the boy still stood dignified, tall and still, even after this remarkable confession from his father, who was not his father. The King demanded, "What did the soldier look like who left this boy with you?"

Mitridates took a deep breath and said, "He is in the audience room, sire."

"Which soldier?" asked King Astyages, but he knew full well, it was Harpagus.

"Sire, he stood against the wall. He was not a guard. I think he is an officer. He stood on the left mid-way down the room."

Now the King knew it was Harpagus because that was where he always stood when he was in the audience chamber. From the middle of the room Harpagus could see who came into the audience room and observe the faces of those who left. He looked for men with anger in their eyes who might need to be watched in case their wrath became a source of trouble.

The first thought the King had was that Harpagus had disobeyed him ten sun cycles ago; he had lied to his King! King Astyages resolved that Harpagus would pay dearly for those crimes.

The Great King stared at the boy while the family waited in silence for his next order. He now was assured that this boy was his grandson, Mandane's baby! His first impression of the boy was so favorable he had trouble keeping himself from leaping from his chair to embarrass the boy. Inside, the King was shrieking with delight, but to his audience he was the composed Great King. King Astyages marveled at how the gods had saved this child, his heir, for him all this time.

The King of Kings left the room and entered another small room. He ordered the Chief Magus into his presence. They spoke of the two dreams the King had experienced long ago and the boy's game.

"You were never much help to me when I was troubled by those dreams. I wonder if I can trust you now that I need counsel for this new situation," said the King.

"Sire, I am perplexed by your willingness to accept this child as your heir. What makes you believe he is the son of Princess Mandane...err, Queen Mandane?" asked the Magus.

"You never miss an opportunity to fail me, do you? Did you see his demeanor in the audience chamber? Did you observe his likeness to Cambyses? I am the Great King! I see and know things your mystical powers miss. Believe me his is who I say he is."

"Then we must concentrate on his place in your empire, sire."

"If my dreams predicted a challenge to my kingdom by my daughter's son he would have to be a king," the King concluded.

The Chief Magus said, "Sire, the boy has already been a king in his play. He did not endanger the empire then. His kingship is over. He is no longer a danger to you."

"Yes, he was a king but now he is only a prince. He can't harm me or my empire," the King agreed.

King Astyages returned to the family, believing his danger was eliminated. He looked fixedly at the boy for a moment. Finally, the King said, "Boy, do you know who you are?"

Paithi looked into the eyes of his King and answered, "No, sire. I thought these people were my parents. I thought I was Greek. I'm confused by what has been said of me. These people have always been my parents."

"Well, boy, I will tell you who you are. You are my grandson. Your mother and father are the king and queen of Pars!"

Paithi did not move. He continued to stare into the eyes of the King believing every word because the Great King said it. The King was pleased that the boy did not react except with quiet dignity. Paithi looked with love at Mitridates and Spaco knowing that he was about to be taken from them; he said, "Father, mother, you have given me all the love a son could wish for; I will never forget you. I will come to protect you for the rest of your lives. I will always need you to call me 'son.'"

253

With that Spaco was so overcome she rushed to the boy and swept him into her arms. She cried and Mitridates cried where he stood. The King watched them act out their anguish for a moment then stood and said, "You may remain in this room to say your good-byes. The boy is to stay in the palace with me. You two will return to my farm and continue your work there. I will provide you additional slaves to run my property.

"Boy, your name is no longer Paithi. Your mother and father wished to name you 'Cyrus' after your grandfather who was a king of Pars before your father, Cambyses. Your mother is my daughter, Mandane," and he left the room.

The farmer and his family huddled together in a tight cluster as they all tried to speak at once. Finally, Cyrus said, "Mother, father, I am proud of the love you given me. You will always be my parents in my heart. I feel I still belong to you."

Spaco cried. She couldn't speak. Mitridates said, "Son, we did not mean to deceive you. We only meant to save the life of a small baby boy and bring him up as our own. Can you forgive us for the lie we have lived?"

Cyrus answered, "It was not a lie to cherish me as you did. I have nothing to forgive."

Then speaking in the terms of a fable Cyrus said wistfully, "It seems I have been a calf hiding under the pelt of a lamb and the bull-king has unmasked me," and he smiled at his parents. They continued to talk until Prince Zatame came into the room beckoning to Cyrus. The goodbye was over. Spaco and Mitridates left with broken hearts. Now they had just each other; their son was lost to them forever.

Prince Zatame was beaming. "So, King Astyages tells me you are our Cyrus, the son of my friends in Pars."

Cyrus looked at him with a tinge of warmth because they were already well acquainted. The boy knew he could trust this prince. Cyrus remembered Prince Zatame from visits to the farm and the market place.

"Yes, your highness," Cyrus answered.

Prince Zatame said, "You and I are going into the audience chamber. King Astyages wishes to introduce you to his court. All you will have to do is stand still. I will stay with you. We will leave the room together when I tell you. Do you understand, Cyrus?"

"Yes, Sir, and thank you for…"

The boy lost his breath. The excitement of his confused day finally caught up with him. When they entered the audience chamber King Astyages had his royal family assembled in front of his throne. Queen Aryenis was on her throne beaming at the boy. She had to restrain herself from charging at the lad to hug him. The princes and princesses were buzzing with curiosity. The young prince that Cyrus had whipped was standing in the group with a smirk on his face. His father was beside him, fidgeting. King Astyages waved Cyrus to the throne beside him. The King put his arm around the boy announcing in his most authoritative voice so none could misunderstand, "This is my grandson, Cyrus. He is the son of my daughter, Mandane. You will all accept him and treat him as a member of our family. All of my empire will honor him as my grandson."

The King looked toward the Chief Magus and said, "Send a message to Cambyses and tell him to come here to collect his son!"

Everyone in the room looked shocked. They all knew the son of Mandane had died. They wondered if this was a trick. The young prince who had been beaten up scowled. The King looked at Harpagus and said, "You, Harpagus, tell my family I speak the truth."

Harpagus was taken by surprise. He wondered how the farmer had the courage to deceive him so long ago. He had seen the farmer and his wife come into the audience chamber, but he never thought this would be the result of their visit. All he could say was, "Yes, sire, it is true. The boy is your heir."

Harpagus began to plan the end of his life. He had always known he had disobeyed the direct orders of the Great King by not placing the child in the forest himself. For that his penalty would be death. He would never see his wife or son again. The soldier was convinced the Great King was about to order someone to cut off his head; Astyages might even do it himself.

Harpagus looked at the young lad and thought of his own son. His heart ached. No apology to the Great King would be powerful enough to suffice. No admission of guilt could bring exoneration. Only one path was available to Harpagus and it led to death. As a soldier he might welcome the end of his life if he had been able to fight in a battle attempting to prevent it, but now Harpagus knew the insult of death was going to smother him without a struggle.

Before this announcement Zav had remained in the audience room. He was surprised by the initial response of the Great King to the young boy. Zav had seen the happiness in the King's face when he returned to his throne. Zav wondered what had happened in the room where the King had taken the farmer and his family.

When the King came out of the room alone he ordered his family to come forward, and he commanded eunuchs to search the palace to summon the rest of his family to the audience chamber. Zav knew something big was happening so he stayed to see what it was. He saw the King whisper to Prince Zatame. Zav saw the startled response, followed by an uncertain smile on the prince's face. Were the King and Zatame both happy because a family execution was to take place right here in the audience chamber? Zav let his imagination exhilarate him. The King was going to kill a robber who was a threat from Zav's past.

When the King announced his grandson, Zav went weak in the knees. All these sun cycles of collaborating with Princess Ispitamu had been for nothing. All the laughing and reveling at the misfortune of Cambyses and Mandane had been for naught. Zav could not believe that an heir had come out of the northwest to be presented as the future of Pars. The minister told himself there must be a mistake. There had to be some mystical cloud hanging over King Astyages, which the Chief Magus had to remove with his priestly magic. A curse must be hovering over the kingdom. The entire tribe of magi needed to conjure a release for the empire from this spell so this child could be revealed as an imposter.

There had been several occasions when Zav and Princess Ispitamu had talked of killing any child that was born to Cambyses and Mandane. Could this child be murdered? Was this child to be so protected that such a crime was impossible? Could he or Princess Ispitamu use the oleander to kill the child without detection? Zav wondered if he could get away with murder a second time? He wanted to rush from the room to plan the death of this boy before the child had time to experience the privileges of royal living, but Zav was fixed in place by stunned disbelief.

The Great King introduced Cyrus to his family. The boy nodded with remarkable poise and elegance to each person the Great King gestured towards. His demeanor just made the King more excited and more committed to accepting the boy as his heir. Prince Zatame was also enthralled with the boy. He was smiling so broadly that his face appeared to have been slashed by a sword. Prince Zatame finally took Cyrus, who believed he was a Greek, from the room to begin a new life as a Parsian prince.

31.

"You traitor! All this time I thought you were the one man in my kingdom I could trust. You betrayed me! You always said you did my bidding to perfection. You lied! You always reported that each task was completed, no matter what I needed done and I believed you. You are useless to me!"

Harpagus said nothing. He just looked at the infuriated King. The soldier's mouth was so dry; water or wine could not take away the dusty feeling in his throat. The skin on his face felt tight. His eyes felt pinched and tense. He would not feel this helpless facing a lion. What could a dead man say that was meaningful or important? How could he justify his dishonor? Harpagus kept his mouth shut while the King raged.

"Your deceit is an utter failure to me," the King blurted. "You lied to me! You disobeyed me! Now I wonder how many times you have repeated these dishonorable crimes against me. I trusted you above all men in my kingdom for two reasons. You appeared to obey my commands without question. That made me confide in you. Also, because you did not have the power of royalty, you had nothing to gain by deceiving me. Now I discover you deceived me in the most important assignment you were ever given. You embarrassed me before the entire court, before the entire world! How do I begin to explain away our mutual conspiracy, Harpagus? The outcome makes you look more honorable than the Great King. I lied to my daughter and my wife. I said the child died in my own hands. I had a magus executed for nothing. Ah, Harpagus, you will pay dearly for this."

Harpagus had experienced scenes like this before when the King got so worked up over a perceived affront that he had no recourse but to take a life. The King never took the blame for mistakes. Two things were at risk in this room, the King's reputation and the soldier's life.

The King's face brightened. He exclaimed, "I have it! You, Harpagus, brought me the wrong child. And it did die in my hands. Yes, you conducted a conspiracy to have the real prince brought up in secret by a farmer. You abducted him yourself with covert mischief. Why would you do such a thing? Let me think," whispered the King as a faraway stare settled over his eyes. Harpagus wondered if the

King was trying to save his life or was the King trying to save himself from an egregious embarrassment. The soldier decided it was the latter.

"You had a dream, Harpagus, that the child was a threat to me. You wanted to save my kingdom. You took the child out of the palace to hide him on my farm. Yes, I am making you a hero, Harpagus. That is what happened!"

The King looked hard at the soldier and said with a menacing hiss, "I should kill you! Instead, I will make you a hero. However, you will give me a gift; I will take your son. He is to live in my palace. Maybe I will make him a companion to Cyrus. They are about the same age, and Cyrus has missed a lot of instruction by living on that farm. Your son will help him learn much of what he needs to know. You will be allowed to visit your son if I permit it. Your wife will never see your son again. That is the start of your punishment. Go bring your boy here, immediately."

The King waved the soldier away. Harpagus wished that he had been beheaded because that was a lesser punishment than losing his boy, his precious joy, and his wife was going to be unbearable to live with from now on. She was to lose her only child through no fault of her own. Her only reasonable response was to make Harpagus feel guilty for the rest of his life. Harpagus would have an unbearable home life, and he had no close friends to talk this out with to make the pain less hurtful.

While walking out of the palace Harpagus physically bumped into Zav who was also deep in thought. They looked at each other in surprise. Zav realized whom he had encountered and asked, "Well, young soldier, why did the King ask you to validate the truth of his grandson's existence?"

"It is a long, sad story. The Great King will reveal it, and there is punishment for me now that is even sadder."

Zav asked, "Are you to be executed? The King likes to cut off heads these days," and he chuckled.

Harpagus said, "No, my punishment is worse. My son is to live in the palace away from my wife and me."

Zav became quiet. He whispered in a sinister hush, "What did you do to deserve this? What did you do that relates to this Cyrus? Tell me. I can keep a secret."

Harpagus waved him off and proceeded home. He gathered his son and wife together and said, "Kiss your son goodbye. He has been ordered to go to the palace by King Astyages. We must leave now."

His wife beamed. She wondered what the occasion was and asked, "What great feat of our son's has caught the attention of the King? It is such a privilege to be presented to the King."

Harpagus answered in a pained tone, "The King has discovered his grandson lives and our boy is to meet him."

His son looked surprised and his wife said, "Something is wrong. The King's grandson is dead. I heard that child died ages ago. You told me yourself. Who is this child? Where did he come from? Is it really the King's grandson?" she asked, not believing what Harpagus had said. The soldier just shrugged and said, "Yes, my dear, something is strange about this. The King will announce what happened."

His wife looked at her boy beaming. She said, "But, son, you are to be honored today. You are called to the palace and that is no fiction. You must rush home and tell me what the mysterious grandson is like."

She hugged her son and kissed his cheek. Harpagus gazed with undisguised sadness at them both and said to his wife, "Give the boy a lasting kiss. He will need it. So will you."

His wife look a little perplexed, but she could never kiss her son enough. She happily sent him off with his father. Harpagus decided not to tell his wife of their fate until he returned. Waiting made it easier now to get the boy away from her. She had no idea she was kissing her beloved boy for the last time.

At the palace Harpagus told his son what the King had ordered. His son did not know whether to be happy or sad, but the boy thought living in the palace should be a great adventure for him, then he realized that his father had said that they might never meet again. The boy clung to his father and Harpagus said, "Son, you might be allowed to see me again, but the King has decreed that you will never see your mother again. I want you to understand what is happening.

"So you can understand the power of the Great King, I must admit something to you, son. A long time ago I disobeyed King Astyages. Now, our family must suffer for my dishonor, but you will have a comfortable life in the palace. You must learn to be happy on the path the gods have placed you. Go, boy," and with that he sent his son off with a palace eunuch. Neither of them knew the boy was to be a prisoner who would never meet the grandson of the Great King.

If Harpagus had known how to cry he would have. His mind was awash with pain, guilt and extreme unhappiness. He felt powerless. He might as well be a slave to the King. The hardest part was yet to come. He had to go tell his wife about the unexpected misery of her future.

Elsewhere in the palace, Zav was in a fit of confusion. He also had no one nearby to confide in. He called a scribe magus and sent a message to Princess Ispitamu telling her all he knew about the new grandson, which was very little. He asked her if she had ever heard the king or queen of Anshan speak of a soldier named Harpagus. Zav wondered what this soldier had to do with the boy he had seen living in Arbela. Was there a conspiracy separate from his? Was there another person or group who also hated Cambyses as he did? The possibility gave him hope.

Zav knew the grandson, that very boy, came from a farm belonging to the King, but he did not know the details of how the boy came to live there except to presume he was the natural son of the caretakers. If only he had known who that child was, he could have killed him on many occasions. Zav felt he had missed a great opportunity. The minister could have eliminated the heir with a single swipe of his blade, and that boy would not be living in the palace at this moment under royal protection. Ah, how the gods worked to frustrate those who deserved more in life!

Zav told the princess they must meet soon if they were to steer the future of Pars and possibly Media. The minister was anxious to go to the Arbela farm to question the farmer. Zav decided he could make the farmer give him details about the origin of this boy.

Meanwhile Zav decided to start spreading rumors about the fake prince. He told people he met that the boy had not lived with those people at all. Zav said the boy was found in the mountains. The woman from the farm was named Spaco and that word meant 'bitch' in the Median language so Zav decided a good rumor easily placed the boy as a foundling who had been discovered being raised by wolves in the forest and a bitch-wolf was his mother. Zav thought it was creative to make the boy appear as a wild, foraging beast. Zav wanted to think up more stories to make the boy appear foolish and unworthy of the Great King's attention.

//

Outside the walls of the palace Mitridates and Spaco huddled together crying over the loss of their son. They tried to comfort each other between fits of grief. The boy had said he would protect them forever, but as Mitridates and Spaco examined the forbidding massive walls surrounding the palace they admitted to each other that they had seen the last of their Paithi.

When they finally felt strong enough to travel Mitridates arranged for them to return to the farm. On the way they talked of the misery of their future. Mitridates said, "Now we have only each other, and we must plan to leave this country. We will return to Lydia."

Spaco asked, "Do we have enough stolen goods to live on in Sardes?"

Mitridates answered, "Yes, my dear."

Then Spaco noted, "The Great King will not let us leave. He will have us hunted down and killed."

Mitridates said, confidently, "We can hide from King Astyages until we are safely out of Media and forgotten. We can obliterate the pain of the past by going back to Lydia to a new farm. Our own farm."

At home they discovered everything had been ransacked. Many of their possessions were destroyed. Mitridates went to the hiding place where his gold, silver and tokens were sealed away only to see it was empty. It must have been Rusundatu who had raided his house to steal his cache.

Now it was final. Their golden future had vanished. Mitridates and Spaco could do nothing now but work for the Great King until they died. Their lives could never change. Instead of becoming free independent landowners they were essentially slaves. Looking around him all Mitridates could see was hard work without happiness.

//

In the palace Prince Zatame was showing Cyrus the rooms he was to live in. Cyrus asked, "Sir, am I to be free or am I a prisoner here?"

Prince Zatame became quite serious and answered, "Cyrus, we do not know. It appears that the King is pleased with you and he is convinced you are his grandson. It will make him happy if you continue to act with tact and intelligence, as you have done so far. You are allowed to roam about the palace for the time being, but you will not be allowed outside the walls until your mother and father arrive here."

"Do you know my mother and father, your highness?" asked Cyrus.

"Yes, your mother is beautiful. Your father is tall and straight, like you will be. He is honest. And he loves your mother more than anyone in the world. You will be pleased with your parents."

Cyrus thought for a while and asked, "Am I expected to live in Ecbatana or with my parents in Pars? I would like to live with the Great King. I have heard many wonderful things about him. What is the name of the city my parents live in, please?"

"Again, I do not know if the King will keep you here or send you with your parents. They live in a small palace in the city of Anshan in Pars. It is on a fertile plateau among the mountains. You father rules a poor country but he works hard to make it modern. They have very little that is artistic there because the peasants work hard just to survive."

"My mother and father...err, the Greeks who took care of me worked hard all the time. I worked hard. I will be pleased to live in a nation of people who are not afraid of labor."

"I suspect, Cyrus, that you will never work again in your life," Prince Zatame said. "You will have to learn to use weapons and fight, but you will never have to feed the horse you ride or grow the food you eat. You are royalty now. We will teach you what that means."

"I read. Will I be allowed to continue reading?" the boy asked.

"Yes, if you wish, Cyrus."

"I also can speak a little in four languages. Will I be allowed to practice them?"

"That I do not know. We could try to find people who speak those languages and make them talk to you if you wish. If the Great King says you are to speak exclusively Median then you will have to convince him to change his mind. And that is very hard to do."

"Am I to be a king after my father?"

263

"I expect you will be," Prince Zatame answered. "We will have to begin teaching you to be a king, but before that there will be a lot of instruction to make you first understand what it means to be a prince. The king part can come later."

They walked through a garden lit by the sun to a room larger than the entire house Mitridates and Spaco lived in. It had a small table with cheeses, breads and fruits on it. There were linen drapes beside the windows. The windows were opened, but thin mica shields could be pulled closed if necessary. There was a couch with cushions and silk blankets on it. Prince Zatame said, "Cyrus, your suite starts here. There are seven rooms just for you. They surround the garden we just passed through. That is your garden. You will be assigned three eunuchs as personal guards. They will stay with you to ensure you are always safe.

"Tomorrow you will begin your lessons. I will help you for a while. You must be quick to learn what is expected of you so you can be responsible for your own daily schedule. A certain degree of freedom is given to all the princes. However, we will monitor your progress, and we will discipline you if you do not put adequate effort into learning. Do you understand, Cyrus?"

"Yes, your highness," Cyrus responded with conviction. He intended to be better than they expected. He was determined to work very hard in the palace to be as good as the best of his princely peers, just as he did on the farm. To Cyrus this palace was only another place to try hard. It was special because everything was so valuable, and it all belonged to the Great King, but that had nothing to do with his own development and attitude.

"We have several young princes your age who will help you. I expect some of them will resent you at first. They may tell you incorrect things that will lead you to trouble. In a palace those kinds of tricks are very ordinary. It will be part of your education."

"I will be fine, thank you, your highness," Cyrus said. "You are being very helpful to me. I appreciate your attention."

Prince Zatame was astounded at the self-confidence of this farm boy. The prince said, "I have to admit that you are a very special young man, Cyrus. You are the only prince in the palace that everyone will know is going to be a king. You might even become the

King of Kings. I say this so you can be prepared for strange, unwelcoming behavior from people you meet in the palace."

Cyrus nodded and was silent. He roamed through his suite of rooms and returned to where Prince Zatame was sitting on cushions that rested on the floor; the prince was eating fruit and drinking wine.

"Your highness, I have no clothes, except these," and Cyrus tugged on his shirt.

"Do you think the Great King can't provide garments for his relatives? You will be provided far more than you will ever need," Prince Zatame said laughing.

Cyrus was beginning to relax in his surroundings after inspecting all the rooms. A hint of loneliness struck him as he thought of Mitridates and Spaco.

"Will I be allowed to visit the people who were my parents for so long, prince?" Cyrus asked.

"I do not know," Prince Zatame said with a frown. "King Astyages has sent for your real parents and when they arrive they will have to decide. As I said before, you can't leave this palace, or Ecbatana, until they see you."

"But, your highness, the city is so interesting. My Greek parents let me roam anywhere I wished in the capital. Can you help convince the Great King I should be allowed to go into the city, please?"

"Let us wait and see how your daily activities develop. You will have to join other princes in learning sessions. You have many topics to cover such as the history of Media which you probably have never heard before."

"Father told me a little," Cyrus answered. "I know of King Cyaxares who freed Media from the Sythians and who joined Babylon to destroy Nineveh. Father said King Astyages took over an established kingdom and all he has had to do is keep it together. He has lost Gedrosia and Bactria. But you are correct, your highness, beyond that I do not know much of the history of Media."

Prince Zatame was amazed at how easily this information flowed from this farmboy. The Greek must have been a very unusual man to teach so well. Cyrus already understood the current situation of Media as much as some palace princes who were twice his age.

"Cyrus, there is one important thing you must begin to do immediately. Stop calling me 'your highness.' You need not call any palace prince 'your highness' or 'sir.' You are a prince like the rest of us. You are our equal. You may and must learn to speak to us by name. I am Zatame to you. You are Cyrus to me. Understand?"

"Yes, sir," answered Cyrus, and they laughed together.

"You must learn to call me Zatame, just as some day I must learn to call you 'sire.' You may never become the Great King, but one day you will very likely be the king of Pars. Learn to feel like royalty. Learn to act like royalty because it is your future."

With that Zatame told Cyrus he must be ready in the morning to be presented to the King. King Astyages intended to instruct his princes that they better help his grandson. Cyrus was left in his seven rooms alone until a eunuch and a male servant entered to wait on him and instruct him on how his daily bath was administered. The servant laid out a soft, camel hair costume for Cyrus to wear the next day.

Cyrus looked at his new garments fingering them as he compared them to his simple peasant clothes. He looked at the servant busy fussing with arranging pillows. The boy surveyed the food on the table. He recalled standing outside the walls of the palace wondering what it was like inside. Now he was about to find out.

32.

"Get him! Get whom? Our son died," said the perplexed King Cambyses. The message from King Astyages said they had a living son in Ecbatana they were to come for. Mandane was confused yet hopeful. Maybe her boy Cyrus was really alive and protected by some mystical notion. She said, "Cambyses, is this a trick or a gift from the gods? Maybe all this loneliness and longing will be vindicated with the miraculous appearance of my son... our son!

"Have the gods smothered us with a lie only to lift their cloud of deceit so my dreams of having a son could be realized? Have the evil daeva spirits played a trick on us? Cambyses, maybe the good, ahura spirits finally won a struggle over evil. Are the good gods pealing back some cover of iniquity for us to see under? Should we get the Chief Magus?"

"Not yet. This might be a hoax," advised Cambyses.

Mandane was more than willing to let hope capture her heart. Mandane made a valiant, self-deluding effort to pull herself out of ages of dark despondency into a new sunlight of optimism. She allowed maternal exuberance to fill her with joyful expectation, and she began to feel healthier than she had felt since the loss of her son.

Instead of ordering a travel cavalcade to be readied, Cambyses decided he needed time to think. He remembered the old order from King Astyages when Mandane was pregnant. It was worded as a suggestion, but Cambyses had known better. The Great King wanted his daughter returned to him for the birth of the child and Cambyses had sent her alone. Cambyses recalled his fear, after moon cycles of waiting, when the arriving message reported the illness of his wife and the death of his child. He had hastened to Ecbatana to find his wife more ill than he had expected.

Cambyses recalled how Prince Bagindu had personally spoken with Prince Zatame to learn the details of his son's death. Cambyses was told the child died in the hands of King Astyages. Prince Zatame had confirmed it. All the sadness and heartache that followed came back to Cambyses. It struck just as hard now as it originally did. Cambyses began to recall his own feelings of uneasiness about the peculiar details of the baby's death. Something had been wrong. What was it? Prince Bagindu had told him they could not interview the magus who had conducted the funeral rite because the Great King had executed him. Cambyses had never been comfortable with that excuse. Where did Astyages get the temerity to kill a holy man? Cambyses had wanted to ask that magus how the dead body came into his care for the funerary rite.

There had also been a soldier involved. Prince Bagindu had not interviewed the soldier. Cambyses could not even recall if the soldier's name had ever been mentioned. Had that soldier been involved with some covert activity that Prince Bagindu had missed?

Cambyses had serious suspicions about the sudden appearance of this child. Was the boy the right age? Did he look like a Parsian or an ugly, long nosed Sythian? Did he act like a Parsian or a vulgar, self-important Median? Was the boy intelligent or an imbecile? Cambyses knew what he wanted in a son. Could this child measure up to his royal expectations? Cambyses wondered if he was even capable of accepting this half-grown stranger as his own boy?

Cambyses looked at Mandane and said cautiously, "I wonder if we might not expect too much of this message from your father. He is prone to deliberately misleading minor kings with false information. He gives us false hope sometimes just for sport. Remember, my dear, when we went to war with Bactria and King Kauklia told the Great King his country of Gedrosia would also be independent? Your father told King Kauklia that he would forgive him. He even promised to exonerate him from paying taxes if he sent a delegation of royal emissaries to Ecbatana to negotiate an agreement. King Kauklia sent his closest cousins and uncles, and your father did not even speak to them. He just made them prisoners and has never released them.

"If your father is annoyed with us for some unknown reason this message could just be part of such a trick. He knows what it takes to make us rush to him. Only the gods know what mischief he might be up to."

Mandane shouted, "Oh no, Cambyses, father means what he says in the message. He has discovered our son is alive! I know it. I feel it. We must hurry to Cyrus. Let us leave today. Please…"

The queen's entreaty was so earnest the minor king did not try to dissuade her. He allowed her this trust in her father. Cambyses ordered the guard and carriages they needed to get to Media and to return with his son, or the boy claiming to be his son. The minor king remained unconvinced in his own mind of what they were about to confront.

Princess Ispitamu became very distressed at the news of the live son. For such a long time she had lived with the understanding that the baby was died. The possible appearance of Cyrus filled her with dread. She got so panicky her cousins had to calm her. They wondered why she was so upset over such good news. The princess took the announcement as a personal insult. She thought the gods were harassing her alone with this cruelty. She began to wonder what she could do to make this horror go away. She was anxious to invalidate it and make it a lie. But in complete frustration she knew there was nothing she could do. Somehow Princess Ispitamu had lost and innocent Mandane had won. All this time the princess' craftiness had begun to work in her favor, as Mandane became more irascible and mean. Now all that effort was lost.

In Ecbatana the word spread about the prince. People in the streets were perplexed at the story. They knew there was no live prince from Pars. They thought this was some sort of hoax. They were ready to believe any derogatory rumor that was passed around about this mystery boy. The Zav-story about the wolf-bitch was a very popular tale that spread. People in the streets joked about seeing the hairy, wolf boy brought before King Astyages. Some expounded on the size of the den the wolves had needed to raise a child in. Some described the size of the pointy-snouted wolves that escorted the boy to the palace. He had been accompanied by all his four-legged brothers and sisters. Some joked that the Great King had ordered a meal of raw rabbit and squirrel for them. The celebration banquet had included mounds of uncooked gristle from the palace kitchens.

A second rumor, completely different from the first one, spread just as fast. It was reported that a mountain dweller who lived near the Sythian border had brought his own son to the King claiming the boy was of royal origin. The son in the palace came from the lowest scum on earth being a mixture of Sythian filth and mountain dwelling stupidity. Some claimed to know that the mountain man was a murderer of honest farmers. He also taught the boy to eat camel meat raw!

Other people claimed that the Great King was so desperate to have a grandson that he searched for a mountain criminal who had a son. The father was to be made a prince himself who could murder anyone he wished, just as long as he left the Great King's family alone.

The stories were ridiculous but the citizens loved spreading them. Many variations of these stories appeared since no official cuneiform record could be found about the original Cyrus.

Cambyses and Mandane finally made haste to leave for Media. There was a protective guard in their train, plus an honor guard that a royal person warranted, just in case Cambyses did accept the boy as his legitimate son.

While Mandane and Cambyses were making gradual headway over the mountains to their son, Cyrus was being introduced into palace life. He was made to ride horses. He did it poorly because he misunderstood the temperament of horses, which he had never ridden before. He expected horses to be like camels, which he did understand. He was surprised to find horses far more intelligent and far more agreeable than camels.

He became acquainted with his Median family by following Prince Zatame's instruction to call them by name. They were surprised that a boy raised in the outskirts of Ecbatana exhibited authority with such easy grace. The Great King was delighted. The King knew this boy had to be his grandson, because the child had such a fearless, commanding demeanor.

One day Cyrus said, "Sire, I wish to walk about outside the palace. I enjoy being in the city."

Some of the princes did not want Cyrus to have this privilege so they suggested fictitious rumors that implied danger to Cyrus. The King agreed with them. Then Cyrus requested to see the sculpture of the King that was being engraved on the outer wall. This flattered King Astyages who permitted this visit provided armed eunuchs escorted him.

Outside the seven walls Cyrus spotted Oebares, the slave, and waved to him. Oebares had been sitting in the shade of the palace wall and waved Cyrus over. Then Oebares realized how different his acquaintance looked and even worse, he spotted the enormous eunuchs. Oebares was about to run away, but he was held fast by his fear of the eunuchs. He did not have time to react before Cyrus was beside him. The prince sat against the wall and said, "How much longer will you have to watch the mason, Oebares?"

"Maybe forever, Paithi. I expect to die here in the shade. He works too slow," Oebares said trying to relax.

Cyrus sat for a moment and Oebares observed the new clothes the prince wore and said, "Are you the new prince they talk about, Paithi?"

"Yes, Oebares, and my new name is Cyrus, not Paithi. I think I am the same person you know though."

"Not if you were raised by wolves, as they say. Here let me see if you are covered with hair," he said and made a playful tug on Cyrus' collar. They were still young, energetic boys who were easy in each other's company. A eunuch stirred and Oebares flinched. Cyrus said, "Be careful, Oebares, I have not learned how to control these monsters yet. He may slice you up and I will have to talk with you through the crows that eat you."

They both laughed. Cyrus got up and said, "Come show me the sculpture, Oebares. What has the mason cut?"

The figure of the Great King was now cut to the waist. A second figure with a bearded face was visible. This figure wore the flat cap of Pars and looked at the Great King.

"It is very pretty, Oebares. It must be the king of Pars. He is my father, so they say."

"If he is a king then you will be a king some day. I have no right to talk with you, sire," and Oebares turned away. Cyrus grabbed his arm saying, "But, Oebares, I will need friends to help remind me of my previous life. I will come out of the palace every few days so can show me the progress the mason makes in the picture."

They sat in the shade and talked for a while, drinking water Cyrus had a eunuch carry. Cyrus thought he must remember to bring food for Oebares the next time they met. Finally Cyrus rose saying, "I have to go learn to be a prince. I will see you again, Oebares," and he entered the palace gate.

Later during his training sessions the princes discovered that Cyrus was already skilled at shooting a bow. In archery practice he was as good at target shooting as many of the older princes. He aimed well, but he had trouble pulling large bows. Mitridates had not seen that the boy's arm strength matched his size and age. The princes

271

were surprised he could shoot as well as he did. Cyrus was able to make friends by talking about how he used to shoot birds and rabbits in the forest. He told them of the wild boar he had once scarred away. Not all the princes believed him. They had not learned yet that he never lied.

The princes were not taught to box or wrestle because there was no one who dared fight them even in sport. Cyrus tried to teach a couple of the princes how to wrestle but they were so clumsy they did not find it interesting. He thought he could wrestle with Oebares some time just to practice, but to do that he would have to wear wool clothing and not silk. He would also have to make the guarding eunuchs understand Oebares was not to be beheaded if he won the match.

Life in the palace was comfortable for Cyrus now that he didn't have to do any real work. However, he began to miss herding, feeding, smelling and hearing farm animals. He began visiting the camel and horse barns. He tried feeding the camels and mucking out a stall one day to the horror of a keeper who ran up and took the rake out of his hand and began apologizing for the dirty stall. The keeper began to work with feverish haste to complete the cleaning Cyrus had started. It was evident to the prince that he might never personally care for an animal ever again. It made him feel a little empty inside.

Sometimes the prince rested on the grass in his private garden that was surrounded by his seven rooms the way he used to in the pasture. He tried to remember the sound of Mitridates and Spaco talking. He grew lonely when he realized he was forgetting what their voices sounded like. He missed all the comforting country sounds that were in the pasture. He longed to listen to the birds singing, crickets chirping and the rustling of scurrying squirrels among the leaves.

He wondered if his new mother and father were going to hide him in a palace the way his grandfather did. The noblemen here never had to do any physical labor; it was a punishment to be called to do any. They never gave a struggling servant a hand lifting something heavy. The princes never cleaned up a mess they created. They did not seem to even see such things. Cyrus saw it all, and he had to restrain himself from the inclination to pitch in and work.

It bothered Cyrus to have no responsibilities or obligation to do anything labor-related. Even the poor slave, Oebares, had a job to do when he swept up the chips of stone that fell from the wall carving. Cyrus missed the pressure of having to complete work. He felt useless. He began to wonder how so many princes could be satisfied with just wasting time following their whims. What bothered him more was that he would have to fit into that kind of listless life unless he could create activity for himself.

Once he tried to care for his own private garden. A slave told a servant. The servant told a prince or princess, in turn the King was told. Then there was trouble. That incident suggested to Cyrus that getting the King mad might be the diversion he needed. However, he was not able to make himself an annoyance to the King. It was partly out of love for the Great King but more because he was not a troublemaker. He always controlled his actions in a deliberate, well-behaved manner.

When the adult princes or the magi were teaching him the history of Media or the world, Cyrus asked more questions than there was information available. Written records contained the barest minimum of details. The names of some kings were recorded. In wars the countries fighting were written, and sometimes the winning general was recorded. When Cyrus asked for the name of the loser no one knew who it was. The names of most princes and princesses were not listed unless they did something of historical importance, like kill a king.

Cyrus discovered that he was very interested in the matters of warfare. He asked how armies were supplied when they traveled so far from home. The princes did not have much information to share with Cyrus on these topics. None of the adult princes had ever fought a war that lasted more than a few moon cycles. This was not because King Astyages loved peace. The princes said he was indolent. Cyrus did not like hearing them say such things. They told the new prince the Great King believed the welfare of his subjects and their property was their own affair. When his borders were pillaged by nomads, or by small armies, he usually told a magus to inform the attacked settlers to handle it themselves. He made an exception when his royal property was attacked. Most warlike conflicts just annoyed King Astyages. His major concern was being safe inside his seven walls. As long as his kingdom was large enough to make the Great King appear powerful, he was complacent and satisfied. Personal safety and self-image were his whole life. Willfulness and self-gratification in all things consumed his attention, and these were the personal attributes that weakened him as the Great King, which Cyrus did not see. He only noticed the grandeur of the Great King, his palace and his court. The King always praised the prince. Cyrus was influenced by that limited, favorable contact. The prince had not yet seen how self centered and mean the King could become. For this reason Cyrus never let anyone say derogatory things about King Astyages. The younger princes at first thought Cyrus was acting like a sycophant. They had seen many people appear this way before the Great King seeking his favor, but soon the princes realized his loyalty was real. Cyrus was truly devoted to King Astyages.

A member of the Parsian honor guard arrived dusty and tired one day to announce that King Cambyses and Queen Mandane would arrive in Ecbatana in two days. King Astyages planned a celebration.

33.

Normally when Cambyses came into the Median capital he was without his wife, and he resided in a quiet section of the city. He preferred to commute to the palace to ensure he had some degree of freedom. He also needed an isolated residence where he could think. This time he rode in the front of his retinue rushing his caravan through the outer gate of the seventh wall, without stopping to allow the guards to inspect his carriages or his entourage. The palace paladins made no attempt to stop him. It was common knowledge Cambyses was coming with the King's daughter. The guards did not dare to stop her.

Cambyses opened the carriage door to fetch his wife, and Queen Mandane stepped out looking resplendent in a purple toga with broad bands of gold filigree on the neck and sleeves. Her waist was cinched with a yellow sash having neat, gold tassels hanging from its ends. Pink embroidery of flowers and animals adorned the full length of the sash. Her hair was twisted in an attractive spiral beneath silk veils on the top of her head.

Several princesses that had gathered at the front of the palace to greet Mandane could not believe how stunning she was after traveling so far. She could not have looked more royal or appear more prepared for an audience with the Great King. Mandane was beaming with maternal anticipation. Cambyses looked tidy but thoughtful. He was not desperate or gullible like his wife. Mandane was prepared to believe any story to have a son. She could not rush into the palace fast enough. Cambyses followed her with one hand on her arm to ensure he stayed near his wife if some serious disappointment should be waiting for her. He did not trust her father.

In the audience chamber the Great King sat on his massive throne with Queen Aryenis beside him. The room was filled with the royal family and guards to protect the King. Zav and other ministers had not been allowed into the room. Queen Aryenis had decided this was to be a family gathering with only royalty present. The King and Queen were both smiling. There was an atmosphere of joy in the room. Cambyses bowed touching his forehead to the floor. Mandane just ran forward to hug her father and mother.

King Astyages ordered Cambyses to rise at the same time Mandane said, "Father, mother, where is my son?"

The King attempted to make small talk with Mandane, and she grew more and more agitated. Cambyses saw what was going on and started to get angry. He was beginning to feel that something was amiss. He reached out touching Mandane's shoulder. At that moment the Great King snapped his fingers. An enormous double door opened. Standing in the middle of the opening, looking small but confident was Cyrus. He stood erect with his head held high. He wore purple pantaloons, gathered at the ankles. His blouse was a lighter shade of purple and the sash about his waist was a rose color. It was decorated with geometric designs of gold and silver threads. His thick black hair was cut and neatly combed. Cyrus wore gold shoes. He stepped forward with slow, careful steps into the audience chamber and approached his new parents.

His young beauty and handsomeness transfixed Mandane. She was so overjoyed she almost swooned into a faint. She tried to speak but could only weep. This magnificent boy was hers. She tried to rush forward to take him in her arms but she could not move. She was seeing a small Cambyses. Her life was complete in that instant.

Cambyses was amazed at how handsome the boy was. The minor king began to think that if this was really his son, the boy he had dreamed about, he had been blessed by the gods. As the boy approached Cambyses recovered first and asked, "What is your name, son?"

Still walking with a firm gait the boy answered in a clear voice, "Cyrus, sire," and he stopped before his mother.

Mandane, with tears that clouded her vision, leaned to the boy; she hugged him to her breast. The gesture made her burden of guilt flow out of her like a river spilling into the sea. The Great King was exuberant. Queen Aryenis was weeping, smiling and fidgeting in her seat with happiness. She could not decide whether to look at her husband, her daughter, or Cambyses as her head swiveled trying to see everyone at once. A spontaneous roar rose from the people in the room. The princesses cried. The princes, young and old, cheered the wonderful scene. Mandane was one of them. They were thrilled at her joy. They wanted to surge forward to embrace her, but they stayed at a distance and reveled at the exultation in her face. There was never a more beautiful moment in Ecbatana.

When Mandane finally released Cyrus just enough to hold him at arms length he asked, "You are my mother?"

Mandane almost fainted again at a voice calling her mother. She wept, "Oh yes, my son, yes! I am your mother."

"And I am your father Cambyses, king of Pars, Cyrus," said Cambyses with proud surety that this was his son. The minor king was completely captivated also by this boy and his regal composure. Cambyses wondered how a boy of ten sun cycles, in this circumstance, could be so calm. As a first impression Cambyses wondered if he was meeting a king instead of a boy.

King Astyages announced, "We will all celebrate this historical event. I decree my grandson and his true parents are united. I have made this possible for them. You will be thankful that Cyrus has been safe with me."

During the celebration Mandane did not allow Cyrus to be more than a couple of cubits away from her. She needed to touch him constantly to ensure herself this magnificent child was not a dream. Mandane could not speak in complete sentences. She thought of nothing but Cyrus. What a brilliant joy he was for her and every few moments she wept with happiness then laughed at herself for crying. When Cambyses hugged her she felt like a bride again. A wonderful, more complete love was blossoming in her, and Mandane thanked the gods for this reunion over and over. Cambyses was happy for Mandane and for himself. He was convinced he was the father of this boy. Everyone who came up to congratulate him told him how much Cyrus resembled his father. That made Cambyses very proud. All the happy dreams Cambyses had experienced when Mandane was pregnant could be fulfilled now, and the minor king could start to make the next king of Pars a reality.

Cyrus grew more comfortable around his new parents during the banquet. He was a little surprised at how much his mother fussed over him so he tried getting away from her for a few minutes to talk with one of the young princes he was learning history and riding with, but his mother kept her son beside her. Instead of being embarrassed he just accepted it. His mother was very pretty, and he was glad she was so pleased with him.

Cyrus noticed that his father talked extensively with Prince Zatame. Cyrus wished he could be near them, but with his mother commanding his time it was not possible. Mandane kept Cyrus involved in conversation with herself. She asked questions of almost anything just to hear Cyrus' voice, but she did not want to hear of Mitridates and Spaco. Mandane stopped listening when Cyrus spoke of them. She did ask what the boy thought about growing up on a farm. He tried to tell her he did not like living in the palace as much as living on the farm, unfortunately, as he began to express these opinions and speak of his foster parents her face told him she had stopped listening to him again. He changed his tone shifting the topic to talking about the clothes he was given in the palace. She was listening again. Cyrus decided he had to discover what topics made her comfortable so he could restrict himself to those subjects.

Cyrus saw Prince Zatame nod his head in the affirmative. He and Cambyses had agreed on something. Cyrus wondered if they had been talking about him. He intended to ask his father when he got the chance. King Astyages came over and patted Cyrus on the shoulder and pronounced, "It is fitting for my daughter to have such a handsome son. You will be a credit to the family, my boy. Mandane you must take the time to speak with your mother. She has been very lonesome for your company."

Mandane took Cyrus by the hand to Queen Aryenis. Cyrus had little opportunity to speak with the Queen before his royal parents arrived. He was always tied up with princes or looking for men's business to stay busy. The Queen smiled just for him and said, "You are a handsome young man, Cyrus. It feels wonderful to be your grandmother. You will be a fine king some day if what I hear of you from our noblemen is true. But is it true that you can't ride a horse yet?"

"I can't, your highness, but I get better each time I try."

Mandane advised, "You must improve rapidly, son. In Pars it is a major responsibility of all men to ride well."

"I do shoot the bow well," he said with confidence.

"You will have to shoot the bow well while riding to be a respected man in Pars. They take the two more seriously than our Median men do, is that not so, Mandane?" asked Queen Aryenis.

"Yes, mother," said Mandane as she looked at her son. She continued, "I will enjoy watching you learn, son. Can you do tricks shooting with the bow yet?"

"No, mother, but I can hit flying birds sometimes," he stated emphatically without bragging.

Mandane loved to hear him call her mother, and she encouraged him to talk to make him say it again. She asked, "What is it that you want the most, son?"

Cyrus was not prepared for that question. He had not thought of wanting anything. He was thoughtful for a moment before saying very sagely, "I wish you to be happy, mother."

"That is far too diplomatic for such a young boy," said Queen Aryenis.

"Do not underestimate this young lion," said King Astyages who had been listening to the women talking to his pride and joy. "Already he charms all our young princesses and makes their mothers wish he was their age," laughing at his own rude joke.

Cyrus glanced at the Great King as if he had no idea what he was saying. Cyrus was not aware of the effect he had on people. When they praised him he was surprised because on the farm Mitridates seldom praised him. Spaco did praise Cyrus but only about obvious physical accomplishments, like when he helped a ewe give birth or when he made a strong repair on one of the barns. The prince was not used to people bragging about his abilities in general. It made him uncomfortable to hear personal compliments. He tried to avoid praise.

Cambyses came over and said to King Astyages, "Sire, I am confused about how my son was hidden from me for all this time. I also wonder why."

King Astyages drew the new family and his wife aside, away from others in the room and began to explain, "At the time of the birth, Harpagus had brought me the wrong child who died in my arms. Harpagus was plagued by a dream. He believed his visions told him that Cyrus was a danger to my empire at the time. Under his own initiative my soldier sequestered the baby on the farm in the care of the Greeks to protect Media."

King Astyages did not mind lying again. It even sounded believable to him as he told it. He was pleased with himself for thinking this story up alone. He found it easy to confuse reality with

279

his fabricated new facts. He said, "I discovered Cyrus was alive myself!"

Queen Aryenis and Mandane believed it all. Cambyses asked casually, "Why did you have the magus executed who took care of the dead child, sire?"

The Great King looked at him with a fixed stare that almost accused Cambyses of treason. The King decided to embellish his lie and said, "I was so angry at the death of my grandson I wanted revenge against the gods. How better than to execute one of their representatives?"

Cambyses said, "But to kill a priest, sire, is a grave offense against the gods. Are you not afraid of their retribution?"

King Astyages said, "My Chief Magus agreed that I had done wrong. However, it was the gods who deserved my retribution for killing my grandson, at least that is what I decided at the time."

Cambyses said no more. Killing a magus was an egregious sin Cambyses did not want to discuss. Let the gods decide if King Astyages was ever to be forgiven. Cambyses had other things on his mind. He and Prince Zatame had just agreed to visit the farm together so they could ask the farmer, Mitridates, to describe what he knew of this story. They hoped they could trust the farmer to tell them the truth.

Cambyses wanted to believe what the King said about the whole incident, but Cambyses knew if such a set of events had occurred as the King told it, then Harpagus would be as dead as the magus. Just a moment ago Prince Zatame had told Cambyses they should speak with the soldier before going to the farm in Arbela. Zatame arranged the meeting.

Cambyses let Mandane suggest staying in Ecbatana so she could visit with her mother. There was no need to rush off to Anshan now that they had their son in their care. Mandane and Queen Aryenis salved their loneliness for each other with long conversations every day. The two queens had much to share about family life and the future now that Mandane had her son. Over the next few days Mandane tried to keep her son with her all the time. She drew him into her mother's *andarun* where mother and daughter caught up on gossip. It was better than old times for Mandane because the presence of Cyrus gave her a sense of intimacy that the *andarun* had never provided before. Cyrus preferred to be off with males of the palace and his father, but he patiently stayed with his mother. She had a need he did not understand. Yet he knew he was responsible for her gay mood.

Prince Zatame took King Cambyses to see Harpagus in a private room in the palace. Harpagus was a little nervous, hoping to say the same things the King had said to them. The soldier was not afraid of the prince or Cambyses because they were just men. He understood men. Harpagus said, "Sire, I do not know any more about your son than what the Great King has related already."

"Harpagus, tell me all you know. Leave nothing out," Cambyses commanded. It was both the order of a king, and the plea of a father. Harpagus understood the yearning of this man. The soldier decided to spare the details to avoid contradicting the King's version of the facts.

"I had a dream that made me believe your son was a threat to Media. I took your son from his royal crib and hid him. I got a second baby from a peasant to show King Astyages, and the baby died while the Great King held it. Your son was taken to Arbela ten sun cycles ago, and that is all there was to it."

The officer did not describe the details of his dream or the nature of his interpretation of it. Dreams were very real to these men, and they understood that dreams could portend the future. The prince and the minor king presumed that Harpagus had a magus unlock the riddle of his dream.

Prince Zatame asked, "Harpagus, were you involved in killing the funerary magus?"

"No, I was delivering the prince to the farmers when that occurred. I have no knowledge of how that happened. It scared me when I heard of it later," the soldier said.

"According to your dream, Harpagus, is my son still a danger to the Empire now that he is back with his proper family?" asked Cambyses.

"No, a magus has confirmed that the danger is past."

Cambyses was looking for discrepancies, but none were evident. So far the facts seemed to match. That night when Mandane and Cambyses were alone in their rooms he said, "Prince Zatame and I are going to visit the farm where our son grew up. I want to see it. Would you like to come along, dear?"

"No!" Mandane said emphatically. "Why would you want to see a farm? You own so many. Stay away from that place, please," and she shivered with fear.

"I have to go for my own curiosity," the king said, "When I see where Cyrus lived I will understand how to care for him without making too many mistakes. I intend to bring Cyrus with the prince and me."

"Please do not do that," Mandane pleaded, "He is mine... ours. Keep him away from his past. Please, Cambyses."

Her husband was firm but compassionate as he said, "He will accompany me. I must see him with these other people. Cyrus might think that you and I are afraid of who he was. We must show him we are not."

Cambyses did not tell her he was still investigating the circumstances of Cyrus' delivery from the palace to the farm. This was the last connection he had to check before finishing with this fateful kidnapping investigation. Prince Zatame had promised to help Cambyses as much as possible. He thought two men would be more effective asking questions.

As their horses trotted out of the city, Prince Zatame asked, "Cyrus can you lead us to the farm?"

"Oh yes. I know the way. I rode a camel there many times," said the prince, thrilled to have a responsibility. The little prince took the lead even though he did not ride his horse well. Cambyses watched his son's riding technique to note if he controlled his horse with the pressure of his gripping legs and gave signals with his heels the way a Parsian should. Cambyses was pleased to see that he had much to teach his son.

Cambyses made light conversation with Cyrus, and Prince Zatame judiciously refrained from joining in unless they addressed him directly. It was a very pleasant ride. Cambyses liked the way the boy described the sights they were about to see around the next bend or over the next hill. This told the king his son paid attention to details and to nature. It was an important characteristic for a Parsian. Cyrus would have to learn to like the rocky ruggedness and inhospitable terrain of Pars as well as the quaintness of its cities and the unsophisticated manners of its peasants. For Cyrus to appreciate details of landscape around him was essential. Cambyses thought the boy had started well.

At the farm Mitridates ran to the house to tell his wife he had seen Paithi coming with two men. They stood outside the door in silence hoping he was coming back to them, but they knew it was a foolish desire. Cyrus leaped from the horse and ran to the Greeks. Spaco jumped forward to meet him. They both fell to the ground laughing. Mitridates picked up his wife then hugged Cyrus. Cambyses and Prince Zatame let them have their private greeting together. Cambyses was touched by the love he saw.

"Please, sire, come in out of the sun," Mitridates offered.

"We wish to tour the farm," Prince Zatame said after a light conversation and a cool glass of spring water.

"I can take you!" shouted Cyrus.

"Stay here and talk with Spaco. We will return soon, Cyrus," said the king.

Cambyses wanted to be alone with Prince Zatame and the farmer; the farm did not matter. As they wandered through the pastures and gardens Cambyses concentrated on the questions he needed to ask ignoring the production details Mitridates recited. Finally Cambyses asked, "Mitridates, when the soldier came to deliver the baby to you and your wife, did you have previous information about what your responsibilities would be toward the boy?"

The farmer got very nervous. Mitridates knew he was in trouble and might die here in the pasture so he decided to be perfectly honest. After all, truth would add honor to the advent of his death. He answered, "No, sire. The soldier just appeared. He said to tie the child to a tree in the forest until it died."

The prince and Cambyses looked anxiously at each other. This was a detail they had never heard. Harpagus had lied to them or left out this remarkable fact. Prince Zatame asked, "Why did the soldier want the boy killed?"

"He only told me what to do. He did not explain himself to me," said Mitridates.

"You did not follow his instructions. Why?" asked Cambyses without accusing the farmer of anything.

Mitridates told them of the death of his own child and how he had placed his own child in the woods. He described the way he added

283

blood to the clothing because the soldier expected to see blood when he came back to claim the garments. Then Mitridates described quite innocently how he and Spaco raised the boy. He told Cambyses of some of the heroic feats the boy had performed to protect the farm and the slaves.

Cambyses was pleased with what he heard from the farmer. The king thanked Mitridates with a pat on the back. Cambyses asked, "Mitridates, what would you like most in the world, other than the return of Cyrus?"

Mitridates said, "Sire, Spaco and I have always dreamed of returning to Lydia to buy our own farm."

Without saying anything, Cambyses vowed to himself to send Cyrus here one day with enough tokens and gold for the Greeks to do just that. He wanted to let the boy they loved fulfill their dream.

34.

"Can you tell me more about the circumstances of the prince's disappearance, Harpagus?" Zav asked.

"You have heard what King Astyages said on the matter. That is all there is," answered the officer. Zav had searched desperately for Harpagus. He was convinced the man knew more details about the disappearance of Mandane's baby or this new prince than had been revealed so far. They had spoken briefly after the King's announcement, but that was not enough for the minister.

"But you played much more of a part than we were led to believe, I think."

Harpagus said, "I have nothing more to add, Zav. You know all there is to know."

Zav was not ready to give up. Any new scraps of information might be useful to either himself or Princess Ispitamu in their campaign against Mandane. Zav knew he could make Cyrus into a fraud if only he could glean the slightest detail that contradicted the King's explanation, and this man was the most opportune source.

"What about the dead child? Who did he belong to?" asked Zav.

Harpagus hesitated before saying, "That is private information from the *andarun* of the queen. She will have to answer that."

"Is this Cyrus fellow really the son of Mandane?" asked Zav.

"Yes. I took him to the farm as the King said. I left him there to be brought up by the farmer. Now the prince is back with his parents so there is nothing more to say," said Harpagus who then turned and left.

Zav felt Harpagus was hiding something, but he had been unsuccessful in getting the soldier to convey more about the incident or the boy. There were no apparent contradictions in what the officer said that could be twisted into a lie. Zav wracked his brain trying to develop some story for Mandane to make her disown the boy.

There had been too much comfort for Zav at the union of the child with Cambyses and Mandane. Zav did not understand how after all this time the three of them could come together acting so family-like without obvious discomfort with each other. They seemed to meld together as a unit without hesitation. Zav believed most of their easiness resulted from the demeanor of the boy who was so controlled. Zav tried to resist a feeling that began to haunt him. He had a premonition that this child would grow up to be a danger to him personally. Therefore, he needed to invent a destructive rumor for Princess Ispitamu. He would refrain from telling her it was a lie. She would be more effective if she thought she knew the truth. She hated the queen so much her gullibility would let her believe anything that hurt Mandane.

Zav was aware that everyone in Media knew about the farmer who had brought the prince to the city. Since Zav organized the caravan attacks near Arbela he decided to use that information in his story. He added a twist to the prevailing story of the mountain murderer. The more he thought about his new fiction the easier it was to use true details. Mitridates was a thief; the boy was the child of this caravan highwayman. The robber part was accurate. Should he have Mitridates arrested to be charged for his crimes just to add credence to his story? No, Zav realized he would be at risk since he was the source of the caravan departure information, and Mitridates might tell on him. The farmer also knew that Zav bought stolen property.

The next point to cover was how to suggest the boy was truly the son of Mitridates and Spaco, not Mandane. The only proof that this boy belonged to Cambyses and Mandane was the story from the Great King and Harpagus. No other person had knowledge of the original events. Zav decided to tell Princess Ispitamu he had seen the magus who conducted the funerary rite carrying the dead prince to the Tower of Silence and had asked the magus what he was doing. Zav could claim the magus showed him the dead child and the royal robes. The dead body had to be Mandane's prince. The magus was dead so there was no one to contradict him. It was a good lie, a good deception. He called a scribe magus and sent his message to Princess Ispitamu. He used very positive statements. Zav was careful to not use terms of speculation. He needed her to be convinced, without question, of the peasant origin of Cyrus. The writing magus thought the misinformed minister was just passing on another false rumor. He paid no attention to what Zav told him to write because the priest had heard the King's proclamation, which was truth enough for him.

//

When Cambyses and the princes returned from their visit in Arbela they sent Cyrus off to his mother. Prince Zatame said, "Well, we have a new version of this strange tale, Cambyses. I don't want to conclude anything that puts suspicion on the parentage of Cyrus. What do you think?"

The king said, "I believe what the King and Harpagus said. The soldier did bring my son to the farm. I believe Mitridates when he says Harpagus brought him a baby. That child is my son and he is back in my life.

"It is strange that Mitridates adds two pieces to the tale. He says that Harpagus told him to kill the baby and save the robes. Harpagus picked them up and rode away with them. Why? Where did he take the clothes, for what purpose? It is strange. I want to believe Mitridates. He has no reason to lie."

Prince Zatame thought for a moment and then said, "You are right, Cambyses. Mitridates' details are peculiar. Something is missing in the story told by the King and his soldier. What does it mean? I doubt it changes the identity of Cyrus. He is clearly your son."

Cambyses asked, "Should we speak to Harpagus again? Will he be willing to tell us any more than we already heard from him? I don't believe the information about the garments will scare him. He will just say the farmer lied. Those bloody clothes imply to me there is some sinister and unspoken aftermath. What do you think, Zatame?"

Prince Zatame said, "He might go back and kill the farmer if the clothing is a significant clue. Why jeopardize the peasant? We have the legitimate future king of Pars. There is no doubt of his parentage. It is possible the soldier ordered Mitridates to kill your son. That only means we must not trust Harpagus in the future, but I prefer we find comfort in the information we are convinced is real and forget the rest."

Cambyses, visibly relaxed, said, "Yes, thank you, friend, you are correct. We must put the past behind us while I concentrate on returning to Anshan. You are a great help to me. I appreciate your support, Zatame."

They spoke for a while and parted. Prince Zatame went about his business and Cambyses went to his wife. Mandane was having a lively conversation with Cyrus when he came in. She said to her husband, "Oh, darling, you were right to let Cyrus go to the farm. He had been missing the animals and the slave children very much. He has been telling me all about the chores he had. He used to be as busy as any man."

"Yes, dear, we saw the places where he worked. The slave children told us how industrious he was. They even said he developed ideas that increased the productivity of your father's farm. I'm very proud of him. Do you remember, dear, Cyrus said he could not ride a horse well?"

"Oh yes, how did he do? Did he outrun you?" Mandane asked with a chuckle.

"He did just fine going to Arbela. He even led the way for us. He is going to be a fine horseman."

Cyrus sat in dutiful silence listening to their exchange. He was delighted that his father was pleased with him. Each day they made him feel more like a son. Without realizing it, Cyrus was beginning to love his new parents.

The trip back to Anshan went well. Cambyses let Cyrus ride at his side for a while as well with the military guard. He made Cyrus eat at least one meal each day with the troops. It was imperative that they get to know their new prince. The men began teaching Cyrus how to spot the trail in the mountains when the boulders and trees obscured it. They taught him how to control his horse on the crumbled rock surface of the hillside. They explained techniques to keep himself and his animal safe in treacherous terrain. Cyrus was solely responsible for the welfare of his horse on the trip. He appreciated the responsibility.

There were many places on this trip the prince was not allowed to ride because of the danger. He rode in the carriage with his mother where they talked constantly. It was a great adventure for him. He was having the time of his life. He became familiar with Mandane's servants and the young women could not help him enough. They spoiled him as much as he allowed them to.

One day a squall came up. Cyrus was intrigued with the way the soldiers tied ropes to the rings of his mother's carriage then to themselves to hold it in place. It pleased him to know these men risked their lives for his mother. He made it a point to thank them when the storm passed. His gesture endeared him to them. Cambyses was happy to see his son melding with the guards as if he had spent time with soldiers all his life. The king knew that in the near future he must place Cyrus in charge of these men. The boy had to learn how to gain the confidence of battle scarred, trail-hardened soldiers.

Coming into Anshan was a great triumph. Cyrus rode at the head of the caravan with Cambyses. Mandane had made certain he wore royal purple and his gold shoes. She wanted him to look as handsome to the peasants as he looked to her. The caravan stopped for Cyrus to clean and curry his horse. He combed its tail and mane. When he mounted the horse they made a lovely sight. Cambyses led his entourage through the city, weaving through the streets to ensure the citizens got a chance to see Cyrus. Cambyses did not want to race straight to the palace even though he knew his wife was very tired. This day belonged to his subjects as much as it belonged to his son.

Cyrus waved smiling like he was already the friend of everyone he passed. Each peasant took his smallest gesture as a personal salute. His mother had insisted on riding on a palanquin, carried by four eunuchs, so she could see the peasants cheer her son. The jubilation of the crowds made her sob with joy. She was so pleased for Anshan and for Cyrus. Being back in the city reminded her of her past behavior. She recalled her cruel demanding outbursts. She remembered having slaves whipped for the smallest mistake. Her past rudeness to the princesses and to her husband shamed her. She resolved to change completely. She might even make a general apology to her staff in the *andarun*. She was ready for a new beginning. She decided to stop talking with Princess Ispitamu about the failed childbirth, for there had been no failure. She resolved to make friends with other princesses the way she had done with Princess Ispitamu. It was going to be nice to have other women with children near her. She could brag to them about the accomplishments of her son.

This small tour of Anshan gave Cambyses an opportunity to view the condition of his capital. The main market place was crowded. There was no room to expand the number of stalls to allow room for an increase in local trade. He spotted an adjacent building used by his officials that took up quite a bit of ground space. Cambyses decided it should be razed and rebuilt elsewhere. Its removal would expand the business center nicely. He saw several very old buildings that were being used by vagrants. The condition of the structures was not amenable for a family with children to live in or a man with a craft to open a shop. The king decided to tear those buildings down also thus doubling the size of this marketplace.

Cambyses needed to tell Pattmenidu to be thinking of ways to increase the size of this central area or add new markets throughout the city that could be enlarged later. He would put Pattmenidu in charge of developing commerce, not just conducting business. He decided to make Pattmenidu his minister of commerce. Prince Bagindu was the nobleman Cambyses would assign to work with the merchant in completing these plans. Cambyses saw that his caravan was having trouble making its way through narrow streets designed for the passage of a single camel and nothing more. He had no city layout plan. He must assign a prince to develop one with his palace as the focus of the design.

He wondered why he had not noticed these things before. He thought he was a good king but maybe he spent too much time in his palace and not enough time in his cities. Maybe he should visit his mountain subjects more too. It was a time of peace. He did spend his energies on strengthening the defense capabilities of his army; now he must think of improving the life of his people, not just protecting what they had. He smiled at his son. Cambyses realized he had to instill these ideas into Cyrus. The boy should not have to discover this responsibility later when he became the king.

Cyrus saw the remarkable difference in the smallness of Anshan as compared to Ecbatana. He noted many crude old buildings constructed of unshaped rocks. The structures he saw were simple rectangles that probably contained only one or two rooms. The prince wondered if the peasants on the flat roofs ate and slept there in the hot summer. He saw windows covered with wood inserts or rags just like the hovels he had seen in Ecbatana, except here he did not see shaved mica windows anywhere. Many homes had no doors. There were dogs everywhere. He asked his father, "Why are there some many dogs about, father? They were not this common in Ecbatana."

"Dogs are our friends, son. They will protect a man at the expense of their own safety. We appreciate their loyalty so much that we keep them well fed and close at hand as our most trusted safeguard. You will find our people think of them in a spiritual way. Dogs are almost as sacred as the gods, and they have a special function in the funeral process which I will be sure you see when the time is right."

In Ecbatana the Great King's palace was very prominent within the city. It was easy to spot even when one was far from it. It sat on a small hillock. So far on this vast flat plain Cyrus could not see any sign of a palace. He began to wonder if there was one. Cyrus was not going to be bothered by living in a simple house because he always had. Still, he thought the king of a country deserved some kind of special residence.

Finally, they came around a corner and Cyrus saw the palace standing across from a large park that had flowers blooming everywhere. There was no wall or gate around the palace. It was quite large compared to the buildings Cyrus had seen elsewhere in the city, but compared to where King Astyages lived it was tiny. Still the first impression Cyrus had of the palace was that it was integrated into the city. The market was accessible from it. He saw how he could go from the palace into the crowds with no trouble to blend among his father's subjects or encounter foreigners that spoke other languages. The palace looked inviting and homey. The prince was pleased with what he saw.

The royal family was standing in a large semi-circle in front of the palace. There were palace guards strategically placed along the streets to keep the growing crowds from crushing forward. Cambyses waved and a roar lifted like a flock of ravens filling the air. He turned on his horse and smiled at Mandane. She was weeping. It felt good to be home.

35.

Cyrus was easing into a schedule of training that Prince Bagindu arranged for him. The prince had heard from Cambyses and Mandane about the history of work the boy had handled on the farm. Prince Bagindu was surprised that Cyrus could be proficient at doing hard labor at his tender age. It was not until a boy in the palace was declared an adult at fifteen sun cycles that he even came close to responsibilities like those Cyrus had already taken on, but a prince never actually did physical work.

Prince Bagindu made Cyrus fully responsible for the care of his own horse. This was a direct order from King Cambyses. Cyrus had to clean and feed the animal as well as muck out the stall. The boy was excited to get a job he loved after thinking he could never do it again. Other princes laughed at him when they passed the stall of his horse seeing him work, but inwardly they wondered if he was learning more about horses than they were. Prince Bagindu made Cyrus carry the sticks used to practice hand-to-hand warfare before and after each training session. Prince Bagindu began to worry that he was making Cyrus look more like a slave than the next king. Cyrus gave no inclination that he was offended or that the joking of the other princes bothered him at all. He even took on simple tasks on his own just to keep busy. Because of Cyrus' example some of the older princes began to be more serious about their training. They were impressed with how hard Cyrus tried to improve his performance in every activity.

He was fast but not as strong as the oldest boys were. The stronger princes soon learned to control their energy when they were paired in battle with Cyrus so he was always pushed a bit harder, but never overwhelmed. His spirit along with the gracious way he congratulated them when they beat him made them respect him. They were all anxious to help him achieve the improvement he obviously demanded of himself. He never bragged about a win. He always helped a loser get off the ground or said encouraging things to boost the spirits of the defeated. He encouraged every prince to try harder. He always tried to convince them they could do better.

Cyrus had a sense of fairness the princes had never experienced before. They were trained to look upon each other as competitors for position and rank, but Cyrus had all the princes believing that improving performance was more desirable than just winning. All the princes began to exert themselves more than they had ever done before. Prince Bagindu was stunned at the influence this young boy had on the whole family of princes. The boy may not realize it yet, thought Prince Bagindu, but Cyrus was training his own army.

//

Princess Ispitamu was tormented by not being able to isolate Mandane. Women and children surrounded the queen all the time. Mandane no longer acted like a special friend to her. The queen's attitude had also changed toward several women she had been jealous of previously who had children when she didn't have a child. Now the queen associated with these women so she could compare her son's feats of heroism with those of other children.

Princess Ispitamu was also annoyed because the queen had spent a day assembling her slaves, servants and princesses to give them a very heartfelt apology for all previous indiscretions she committed against them. Mandane had also promised to change her behavior and be more considerate.

To Princess Ispitamu this was a disaster. Her mind was filled with a torrent of miserable possibilities to punish Mandane. She hated the way *andarun* residents warmed to Mandane so eagerly. The princess had a magus re-read the message from Zav again so she could get his facts straight in her mind. It was essential to begin making disparaging comments about Cyrus to emotionally harass the queen. Unfortunately for her the prince impressed Princess Ispitamu as much as he did the other women. She began to regret that the boy was so young. If he was just a little older she could seduce him then tell Mandane he had accosted her. She could make it sound like rape. No mother wants to hear *that* about her son. The princess could spread rumors of this new wily beast that had only one thing on his mind whom every woman should be on guard against, but Cyrus was not of an age to allow that kind of story to be credible. The princess needed to get Queen Mandane under her control again. Spreading stories seemed to be the best strategy.

As time went by Princess Ispitamu began exploding with personal invectives against several princesses. It angered her that they would not believe her secrets about Cyrus. On a couple of occasions she became so frustrated that she threw a fit when the queen refused to see her alone. The princess wanted to tell the queen what she knew of Cyrus' parentage. Later, when Mandane and Cambyses were alone in his bedroom Mandane said, "I am concerned about Princess Ispitamu. Normally, I would not say anything against your family, but she has changed since we returned with Cyrus. I am afraid something is bothering her but she has not asked for my help. Can you do something for her?"

Cambyses thought for a moment and answered, "I will speak with her. Do you think she needs a magus to send her mind away?"

"I can't tell, dear, she just gets so nervous and angry around me and the princesses."

Cambyses smiled and said, "Well, for quite some time you were upset frequently too. But since our son returned you have become my bride again."

He lifted her gown. She helped him remove it easily. She reclined on his bed, naked and said, "I feel so different now that Cyrus is with us. I am truly sorry for the heartache I gave you for so long. Can you forgive me, dear?"

He leaned over the bed, himself naked, and kissed her lips softly. She pushed herself up to meet him. He said in a whisper, "I always knew you still possessed the sweetness we shared in our wedding bed. I just had to wait for you to share it. And now you have. I will always love you above every other person. You are my life."

She sighed and reached behind his back to pull him to her. Their lovemaking was as tender and as inventive as it had ever been. They squandered the night making love, enjoying rapturous satisfaction in each other's arms.

The next day Cambyses made it a point to search out Princess Ispitamu. He politely asked her, "Is there anything you need? I understand you have been upset. I want to help you with any problems you might be having."

His personal attention surprised her. It was unusual for him to search her out for a private conversation. She decided this was her moment. Since she could not tell her story to Mandane, she would tell Cambyses. She said, "Cambyses, I have information about that boy Cyrus."

Cambyses was surprised and disappointed by her manner of speech. He had not expected her to refer to his son as 'that boy.' He was not annoyed at her for calling her king by name since she was his cousin and had shared his bed before his marriage. She still had the right to talk with him in a familiar vane. Cambyses asked, "What have you heard, Ispitamu?"

"I know he is the son of a farmer. He is not yours. Your son died at birth and this boy is an imposter," she said in a voice that was both an accusation and a challenge.

Cambyses looked directly at her and saw not only belief, but also hatred in her eyes.

"Where did you get this information, please?" he asked carefully.

"I know for a fact that the father was a thief who has tricked you and everyone else to accept his tainted hatchling as your own," she said with a complete loss of caution, pleased to have his attention.

"Who gave you this information, Princess Ispitamu?" Cambyses demanded.

"It was Zav," she blurted out. "He knows all the details. He has first hand knowledge from the father and the magus who conspired in the funeral of your real son."

"Whom have you told this to?" Cambyses asked in a low strained voice, annoyed at where this vulgar tale came from. The source automatically made the whole story a lie to him.

"The princesses won't believe me, and your wife is never available for me to tell her," she answered with haughty insolence.

Cambyses took a firm grip on her arm to lead her to a guard in the hall. Cambyses said, "Go and find Prince Bagindu! Bring him here, now."

The princess misread his actions as she thought she had just convinced the king with her story; he was going to end Mandane's happiness by dismissing the boy. Prince Bagindu came in a rush. Cambyses ordered, "Princess Ispitamu, tell the prince what you just told me."

With prodding by Cambyses all the details came out. The prince was transfixed with disbelief. He knew the story of Cyrus from his king and from information sent by Prince Zatame. The prince thought she must be unbalanced to lie so. Cambyses said in a firm and regal voice, "Bagindu, take the princess and explain to her the details you know about my son. Then ask the queen for permission to enter the *andarun.* Help Princess Ispitamu prepare to leave for Susa. I will have a magus send a message to Prince Warohi that she is coming. From this moment the princess is banned from Anshan. Do you understand? She is to talk with no one in this palace before she leaves."

"Yes, sire," answered Prince Bagindu.

The prince led the distraught princess to her suite. Prince Bagindu allowed one servant into her rooms. He said, "Ispitamu, point to what you want sent to Susa without speaking to this servant. She will arrange for its safe delivery for you."

As Princess Ispitamu moved about her rooms she remembered the two poison liquids, one silphium to prevent pregnancy and the oleander to cause mysterious chest discomfort. She furtively picked up the oleander vial hiding it in her gown. She asked with a sob, "Bagindu, may I enter the queen's chambers to get a piece of jewelry I believe I left there?"

"Yes," said the prince after assuring himself the rooms were empty. He sent the servant to check and miraculously nobody was there. Princess Ispitamu hastened in and pretended to look for her jewelry. The Prince stood by the door not watching her quite as closely as he should. She opened the oleander vial as she moved to the table where Mandane's cup sat. She poured the entire contents of her vial into the cup already filled with wine, hoping the queen would drink it and die. Killing the queen this way was to be Princess Ispitamu's last act of vengeance. She turned to Prince Bagindu and said, "I apologize for my mistake. My jewelry must be elsewhere. I will look again in my rooms."

The princess had to make certain she took the empty oleander container, plus the silphium liquid with her to Susa. She also needed to take the bushes of each poison she had hidden away. While Prince Bagindu watched the princess, she removed two bundles from the vase and laid them with the things she was taking with her today. He had no idea of what was in those silk rags. The princess knew he did not care. Princess Ispitamu did not want to leave evidence of her past crimes behind, particularly if her attempt to kill Mandane worked. Prince Bagindu had her out of Anshan before the sun began to fall from its highest point in the sky.

//

Cyrus came into his mother's room with her flock of women and children late in the afternoon. Her suite had become a playground for children since she returned to Anshan. There was almost always some little girl playing with dolls or dressing up in adult clothes. The women liked to weave or sew in Mandane's suite while they gossiped in a gay babble. Cyrus leaned over a young lady to watch her weave and said, "The knot you Parsian women use in weaving is different from the one used in Media."

"Cyrus, how strange that you would notice such a detail and take our humble work seriously," the princess said as she smiled gratefully.

"How do you manage to get the design of the pattern so perfect when it is all done in your head?" he asked.

"It is simple; we just do it," the princess laughed as if embarrassed by his question.

"We are taught as children to weave and that as all there is to it."

He continued to compliment them on the weavings he appreciated the most. One woman went to Queen Mandane's table and picked up the queen's drinking cup. The woman said, "I get to drink from the queen's cup because I am the prettiest."

All the women laughed. She took three slow gulps and the cup fell from her hand to the floor. Her face twisted as her hand grasped at her chest. She was experiencing the same effects the queen had felt many times before only this time the reaction was more severe due to the volume of poison the girl drank. Everyone stopped what they were doing to look at the woman who had now fallen to her knees with a face as white as mountain snow. She tumbled forward dead.

The women began to scream, afraid to go near the victim. Cyrus rushed out just as a eunuch raced in to investigate the reason for the commotion.

297

"Fetch a medical magus now!" Cyrus commanded. "This is an emergency! Get a magus as fast as you can."

The eunuch looked towards the queen for his orders. She nodded her agreement to her son's commands. The eunuch obeyed. Mandane walked on tentative tiptoes to the body on the floor and knelt beside the fallen princess. She asked Cyrus to help her turn the woman on her back. Mandane touched the woman's face and nose, feeling for breath. There was none. She touched the woman's chest. There was no heartbeat. To the queen that was not a conclusive sign of death because her own heartbeat was seldom perceivable. The other women looked at her with admiration for having the courage to touch a dead person. Mandane gazed at the tortured grimace on the girl's face and felt a pang of sympathy for her. Mandane wondered if this woman had died of fright from the chest trauma Mandane herself had felt so many times before.

As the queen stared at the sorry face she realized this was the heroine who, ages ago, had saved her from drinking the sacred draught of homa that only men are allowed to have. Mandane was not aware that this woman was once again a heroine, but this time the princess had unwittingly given her own life for her queen.

The magus came to remove the woman to the Tower of Silence. Later Mandane was discussing the death with Cambyses she said, "I suspect the princess suffered the kinds of chest pains I suffered several times in the past. She grabbed at her chest the way I used to."

"Why did you never tell me of these pains?" he asked with an alarmed voice.

"They passed. I was only in pain for a short time and someone was always with me when it happened."

"Who was always with you?"

"I believe it was while I was having private meetings with Princess Ispitamu," she said after a thoughtful silence. Cambyses said nothing, but he suspected the princess had attempted to poison his wife. He wondered if Zav was behind it. It could not be connected with his son, because Mandane was describing events that occurred long before their boy came back into their lives. The next day Cambyses had a food taster assigned to the table of every member of the royal household until he could have Prince Bagindu complete an inspection of the rooms Princess Ispitamu had occupied.

"Did Ispitamu enter the queen's chamber and touch her cup?" the king asked Prince Bagindu.

"I took her there to search for jewelry that she could not find. Ispitamu moved throughout the rooms and went near the table where the queen's cup was, but she did not pick up the cup or touch it. I am certain of that."

"I want you to look for any signs of poisons in the rooms Princess Ispitamu occupied," Cambyses ordered. The prince took several princes with him, plus a surgical magus who might recognize medicines or poisons. The magus instructed them to look for weeds, herbs, dried plants and dried bushes. He also had them search for unfamiliar containers of powder or liquid. They found nothing.

The queen's drinking cup that had contained the fatal potion had been washed. There was no way to determine if it had contained something dangerous. One prince added a small amount of water to the cup and poured it into a saucer to let a cat drink it. Nothing happened to the cat. He did it again with a second aliquot of water and still nothing happened to the cat. This was their most effective method for ensuring that the cup was suitable for a person to use again. The queen never drank from it again; Cambyses had a new cup made for her. She let the princesses use the old one.

Prince Bagindu, his princes and the magus inspected the entire *andarun* without finding anything suspicious. He reported that to Cambyses. The king was determined to have food tasters continue their dangerous task until he was certain there was no assassin in his palace after his wife.

The cause of death was never discovered. Cambyses suspected Princess Ispitamu, but he had no evidence to implicate her. Princess Ispitamu had gotten away with murder; unfortunately for her she had killed the wrong person!

36.

When Princess Ispitamu arrived in Susa she felt humiliated. She was convinced that everyone in the palace there knew of her disgraceful banishment from Anshan. She was wrong. Only Prince Warohi knew of it and all he said to his family in Susa was that the princess was coming to live with them. His family did not question him even though he offered no reason. She was family, which was reason enough.

When Princess Ispitamu arrived he said to her, "All I know is you are to live here. I have been forbidden to allow you to return to Anshan. I am suspicious of why, but that is your business."

She cried and answered, "And I can't tell you. Please don't ask me."

She was still confused over why Zav's information differed so radically from what Prince Bagindu had told her. She wanted to believe Zav. She also wanted to believe her family in Anshan was living in a dream world that suited their boldest fantasies. In Susa the first thing she did was to get rid of all the poison materials she had brought with her. She even threw away the silk cloths she wrapped the bushes in. There was no residual evidence of her crimes lying about. After being in Susa for a few days she asked another princess to send a message to Anshan to inquire about the welfare of her friend the queen. Although they heard the queen was fine, they were both shocked to learn of the death of a princess right in the queen's own suite of rooms. They reminisced about how charming the young princess had been.

Later when Princess Ispitamu was alone in her rooms she struggled with a fit of anger at having failed to kill Mandane. Princess Ispitamu had little remorse for having killed her cousin. Her heart was hardened like a black lump of flint now that she was restricted from her home. She began to feel as if she had to spend the rest of her life as an outsider no matter where she was. She even prepared her mind to emotionally accept her fate.

Princess Ispitamu invited Zav to visit her in Susa when his business took him there. He did not write back to her, but that did not bother her. The princess knew Zav had to contact her eventually, because she was his only ally in his fight against Anshan.

//

Prince Warohi had kept contact with Governor Pagakanna in Babylon since the invasion scare stirred up by Zav. Pattmenidu, the merchant, had convinced Cambyses to develop a cache of catapults, bows, arrows, axes, lances and armor just as he had promised the Babylonians. It was never delivered. No one in Pars expected it to be delivered. The Parsians were keeping it as defense in case King Nebuchadnezzar decided to attack them. Most of these war implements were stored in Susa because that city was the lead defense between Babylon and Pars. These weapons were the responsibility of Prince Warohi.

Zav was talking with the Rice Rodent in Susa when he saw a load of the weapons was being delivered from Anshan to Susa. The Rice Rodent said, "Zav, Pattmenidu made a deal with Babylon. He agreed to send them weapons if they agreed to leave us in peace. Those armaments you see are the very items in question. We naturally store them here in Susa to protect ourselves against war."

"Do you intend to send them to Governor Pagakanna?" Zav asked.

"I don't know. I am not so close to our local royalty that they confide in me with such information."

"I think we both know Babylon will only see the sharp end of those weapons in battle. They are for Parsian use, not King Nebuchadnezzar's use. You stay here. I want to see where those wagons go."

Zav followed the wagons to a warehouse, and he was amazed at the vast store of armaments he saw. He wanted those weapons! Media did not need them for defense or offense and he did not want Cambyses to be so well armed. There had to be a way to get them from Prince Warohi.

Later, in the palace of the Great King, Zav tried to construct a rationale for taking the weapons from Susa, but since no war threat existed on any Median border he had no good reason to confiscate the armaments. Zav wondered if he could convince King Astyages to order Prince Warohi to ship the weapons stored in Susa to Sardes.

Have King Croesus receive them as a sign of friendship from his brother-in-law. Zav remembered that the fight King Croesus was waging was a naval battle. He fought ship against ship. There was very little land fighting. The islands of Lesbos and Rhodes fought King Croesus on the sea, and there was no land fighting in Lydia or on the islands. Their war interrupted naval commerce. King Croesus did not need close combat axes or lances, which were used in land battles. The Lydian could use bows and arrows because of their effectiveness over long distances. Hundreds of flaming arrows shot in a naval battle could set fire to the sails and decks of ships. King Croesus needed modest sized catapults that could be mounted on ships to hurl missiles at the masts and hulls of enemy vessels.

Zav felt that if he could talk King Astyages into confiscating some of the weapons, then Zav could change the order to take everything, leaving the Parsian war chest empty. Cambyses would be weakened. Also, the cost of losing all that equipment without payment would be prodigious. Zav had to know the location and approximate quantity of the armaments. He would use Princess Ispitamu to get that information for him. He intended to rob Cambyses of his strength.

//

Cambyses decided to take his son and a few of the younger princes to the buildings where arrowheads and lance blades were produced, then to where arrow shafts and lance handles were made and finally to where the metal heads were attached to the wood shafts. The first thing the young men noted was the heat and the noise in the metal shop. There were open coal fires every few cubits. Hot lumps of copper and bronze were being hammered into the shape of blades. The workmen were sweaty. The whole building stunk of smelly bodies. There were two stories to the building. The heat got fiercer when they climbed to the second floor and the visitors began to sweat too. Cyrus noted this and asked, "Father can you have windows or an opening cut in the roof or in those walls to either let this heat out or let cool air in?"

Cambyses said, "This building had always been enclosed this way. No one has ever suggested changing it."

The more the king thought about it the more reasonable the suggestion sounded. He called to a foreman and said, "Assign some men to break holes in those walls. Let this heat out. Make holes in the walls on both floors where the strongest winds blow."

"The breeze will take heat from the annealing fires, sire," the foreman protested mildly.

"Make large holes high up on the walls and then fill them in until the men are more comfortable and the fires are not affected," advised the king. The man nodded and turned to do as he was told. There were plenty of fires to keep the building warm during the winter.

Cambyses was pleased that his son was so astute. It took a keen observer to pick up on such a simple detail. Cyrus had no corresponding recommendation in the wood working building. All the princes were intrigued with how rapidly the men worked the wood and attached the metal arrow and lance heads. Cyrus said, "I used to make my own arrows on the farm. It took me a lot longer than this," and he waved his arm toward the craftsmen.

"My quality was terrible compared to these professionally made arrows." Cyrus said as he picked up a lance and tried to pull the head off. It was rigid. The man who had just attached the head smiled to himself proudly when the prince nodded with approval towards him. Cyrus knew that if a boy of ten could wiggle the blade or jerk it off its shaft the lance was useless for battle. Cambyses was delighted that his son had a way of honing in on the most critical work and inspecting the battle worthiness of the war implements. He had a son of ten who thought like a man.

"Father, why are we making so many weapons when there is no war?" asked Cyrus.

"For two reasons. First, I want to be prepared in case Babylon makes good their threat from long ago to attack us. King Nebuchadnezzar was angry with me for not fighting in Judah with him. Second, if we do not use the arrows for war we can have Pattmenidu barter them for our royal family in exchange for food from our peasants in the mountains. It will feed the palace, and our subjects in the hills can spend less time making hunting equipment and more time hunting."

Cyrus saw the logic in that. He turned with an inquiring nod to the other princes to see if they were satisfied with the answer. Because

Cyrus was so direct with all his inquiries they were becoming braver too. One prince asked "Sire, will we be allowed to return to this building and work with these men making arrows? Cyrus is the only one of us who has ever made an arrow. We would like to do it also."

"Yes," answered the king.

Cambyses was pleased at the interest the prince showed about expanding his skills. The king was also surprised that palace training did not include this task. He considered this a serious omission he must rectify. He hoped that all young peasant boys still made their arrows and bows. He had to investigate this also. A prince would be limited in his effectiveness, as a leader, if he did not understand the ability of his peasant soldiers to arm themselves during wartime.

Until Cyrus arrived in Anshan, Cambyses had not spent much time with these royal youths. The king worried that he had been making a mistake by ignoring these boys who were the future leaders of his country. Cambyses had to look more closely into what they were being taught. He intended to assign Prince Bagindu the task of itemizing not only what they learned, but what they did not learn. Some day these boys would assume the same responsibilities throughout his kingdom that their fathers did. Cambyses needed his princes to be properly prepared.

As King Cambyses spent more time with his son he realized he himself was becoming a better king. In the past he had spent too much time waiting for problems to come to him. Now that he went out into the streets, businesses and villages near Anshan he was noting ways to improve many things that had been overlooked. The expansion plans for the marketplace were developing well. The training of the princes began to improve. Pattmenidu was contacting tribal leaders to see if the arrows, axes and lances being made in Anshan could be bartered for meat or produce from distant farms. Cambyses began to make arrangements with tribal leaders to have all his princes Cyrus' age invited on hunting trips in the mountains to improve their riding and shooting skills. It also was a way to teach them how to live in the open and make a camp that was protected from prowling lions or other dangerous nighttime hunters. It also forced these privileged youngsters to associate directly with peasants. They needed to know and respect each other.

Some of the princes older than Cyrus needed to be sent out to make their own lion kill. On such an excursion the princes went out alone using close encounter weapons. Cyrus learned that a sling shot or a bow and arrow were looked upon as weapons of a coward in the lion hunt. A lance could never leave the hunter's hand; a knife or a sword was the defense of a true man. To get a lion was an essential commission every royal prince had to complete. Cyrus was most excited about this obligation when a young man came back from his lion kill injured but victorious. Cyrus congratulated the men who achieved a clean kill who did not get hurt. It proved they had superior hunting and fighting skills. But an injury meant the man had been in obvious physical danger and had not been a coward; these were the bravest men. Cyrus did not forget who they were. For Cyrus the best fight was to win when your foe had the upper hand. When you had to force yourself to continue with courage and maximum effort to succeed. He respected the underdog who was able to push his strengths to the limit to vanquish a superior foe.

Cyrus had been brought up caring for camels and needed no training with them. He acted as educator for the other princes when they were obliged to ride camels. However, they all needed training in riding tame bulls and oxen. It took skill to make these animals behave. Cyrus was becoming more confident at riding horses. He began to develop a clear love of this animal. He admired their speed and intelligence. He began to pick a different horse each day. He learned that if he rode the same animal day after day, they became used to each other and riding was no challenge. Everything he did had to be turned into an adventure.

He loved going into the mountains with his father, travelling several days, catching their food, or finding water to drink. Other princes his age always accompanied them. The princes learned to track animals just as they learned what they could eat that grew on bushes and trees. All the princes became stronger. Many of the younger boys began to lose their baby fat as they developed new muscles. They were delighted with the changes in their bodies and preened before the young princesses to the amusement of the adults.

Cyrus had natural leadership that he used carefully. Often he assigned another prince the job of leading them for a day. It honed their confidence when them learned to pay attention to someone else when they might be inclined to selfishly focus on themselves. Cambyses never interfered with these exercises. He was proud that Cyrus was so aware of the training needs of others. Cambyses was happy to let Cyrus participate in the improvement of his princes. The king recognized his son's unexpected leadership and supported it.

Cambyses had given Cyrus his old throne chair so the prince could sit in the audience room at a place of his own. Cyrus was grateful his father had given him such an important gift. It had once been the throne of the first Cyrus of Pars. The chair was made of ebony wood with silver inlay covered with animal and geometric engravings. It was not placed on the dais where the gold thrones sat. It was placed on the lower level off to one side so Cyrus could see the faces of the people who addressed his parents. Cambyses told Cyrus, "Son, it is time you began to understand my duties as king. I will have you sit in council with us when important emissaries come."

"May I greet them, father?"

"No son, you will say nothing at all in my public audiences."

Emissaries from other kingdoms who visited solely to extend greetings or keep up contacts showed Cyrus the importance of courtly manners. Business visitors taught Cyrus that Pattmenidu was not always the best candidate for the king to call on to improve or retain commercial enterprises. Sometimes circumstances required royal authority. Military visitors and Parsian tribal leaders always were interesting to Cyrus. They initiated discussions about defense weaknesses, arms supplies or requests for Cambyses to send troops to protect a border from nomadic invaders. Cyrus enjoyed the talk that was centered on mountain fighting. He had wonderful dreams at night that took him to unfamiliar places. In his dreams he saved villagers from mud covered cowards who came sneaking among the rocks, stealing and killing before they ran away to hide from the sword of Cyrus, protector of the weak.

His obedience kept Cyrus silent in court during public receptions, but the prince always had questions for his father or mother after each audience was completed. He asked about the families or history of their guests. He asked his father about the geography of foreign places. He asked about the size of the armies and the quality of the fighting skills of foreigners. He asked his mother about their art. He was not disappointed that there was very little art in Pars. He just wanted to know where the best ornaments or decorations were made like the ones he had seen in Ecbatana.

Cambyses did not invite Cyrus to Reconciling Day audiences yet. The boy was too young to be introduced to the judicial system and the vague complexity of Parsian law. Reconciling Day could get confusing so Cambyses kept Cyrus from becoming disillusioned by uncertain legal philosophies. The boy was responding well to his other training so far.

One feature of Cyrus' development that pleased Cambyses was the way the boy made Mandane so happy with his stories of his experiences. The prince never failed to include her in any new adventure he encountered. Cyrus had a strong sense of family that kept him from ever alienating himself from his parents. Cyrus never talked about Mitridates and Sparo to Mandane. Cambyses was grateful for that. The king had noted himself how upset Mandane got when these Greeks were mentioned.

The first sun cycle of their family relationship progressed at a smooth, comfortable pace.

37.

At the end of the first sun cycle that his son lived in Anshan, Cambyses wanted to be certain he was teaching Cyrus as much as he could about Pars. While sitting in the shade on a roof of the palace Cambyses said, "Son, the tribes throughout our country were very different from each other. We have nomads that move frequently just for the adventure of wandering. Several tribes, including our own Pasargadae people, are settled in specific places and only migrate when crowding forces them to move on. In both stationary and migratory tribes the family-connected clans have their own chiefs. Local leaders encourage loyalty within each clan. This helps keep peasants together when rivalries develop."

He continued, "Disagreements develop frequently over geographical boundaries separating our clans, just like nations fighting on common borders. Sometime I worry about these fights because larger battles could grow from small hassles to jeopardize the safety of many of our people.

"Our tribes are very large. When they fight it is a major problem for me, however, serious wars seldom occur in Pars at this level. My leaders understand the enormous destructive force such battles have cn our commerce and national security. Between tribes I encourage men to call each other cousin to preserve their sense of national unity."

"I have noted how you always tell men of authority to give your greetings to your 'cousins' in other tribes," his son said. "They usually smile or nod when you say it. I have never seen a man refuse. It helps keep peace doesn't it?"

"Yes."

"Father, tell me about our tribe."

Cambyses smiled and said, "Our Pasargadae tribe lives mostly in a congested circle around Anshan. I am our tribe's leader as well as the king of our nation. All our clans have noblemen of our family included in their ranks. I keep many Pasargadae princes around me in my palace. There were many more noblemen I have delegated administrative duties to throughout our lands. For instance, Prince Warohi in Susa has the duty to protect royal properties in and around that city. He has to administer law and assign punishment for crimes. One problem we have is that our laws are not written down, like the ones Hammurabi of Babylon wrote so long ago. Scribe magi kept records of my Reconciling Day conclusions but that is my only written legal text. I rely on a code of morality more than I rely on formulas. I trust our Parsians to be fair."

Cyrus said, "It seems to work, Father. At least I do not hear as much arguing in the markets as I did in Ecbatana."

"Yes, son, but my judgements only get disseminated throughout our lands by word of mouth. When I change my mind our moral code appears to change as well. Sometimes this causes local decisions to be contested. We have leaders who enjoy making me face contradictions I have caused by sending confused people back to me as the final arbiter. In this way I create my own problems sometimes," and he chuckled. Cambyses continued to explain Reconciling Day and its significance to the peace of Pars. He was pleased Cyrus listened so intently.

//

In Susa Prince Warohi held his own Reconciling Day sessions to settle arguments and confusion arising over personal issues or contract disagreements. He also managed the construction and maintenance of every public edifice used to run the government's local business. Because Susa was the closest city in Pars to the major west to east trade routes Prince Warohi had to maintain numerous storage buildings as warehouses for commercial goods that came to or left the country. He observed that the warehouses he was filling up with bows, arrows, animal harnesses, saddles, catapults and other war related equipment were having a negative impact on his ability to manage household implements, lanterns, farm equipment, grains and other items of value to the caravan trade. He often thought it might be much better to get rid of the armaments so he could use the warehouses commercially, but military preparedness was important, and his king had ordered it.

Prince Warohi talked with Princess Ispitamu often to help her relax as she settled into a routine life in Susa after her insulting banishment from Anshan. He did not understand that she was having trouble accepting the notion that her world was shrinking because of her own foolish actions. He held numerous small dinners to introduce her to distant Pasargadae relatives and to foreign emissaries coming through the city. She responded with genial sociability but something deep inside her kept her aloof. He had no idea of what it was that made her this way.

Princess Ispitamu could not release the hatred in her heart for Mandane. She was even resentful of Cambyses. Her cousin had acted with such abrupt superiority by sending her away it took a while for the shock to subside. She did not forgive Cambyses as much as she just shifted her attention to other matters. The princess needed to adjust herself to a new life and a new living atmosphere.

The princess enjoyed participating in plots with Zav. He had a delicious, twisted mind when it came to revenge. She learned to appreciate his evil ways and his capacity to be vindictive. The princess felt her royal life was monotonous, but Zav added excitement to otherwise undisturbed palace dullness. If only he would come with an adventure to share! She was ready to participate.

//

In Ecbatana Zav met with the Great King and asked, "Sire, is there any information about the war King Croesus is carrying on with Lesbos and Rhodes?"

Zav did not want to be too obvious about wanting to take weapons from Pars. King Astyages queried casually, "Why do you ask, Zav? His war has nothing to do with me. Even as my wife's brother, I am not worried about him. He's in no personal danger. Those island states will never attack Sardes."

Zav said, "Sire, I thought you might wish to send him supplies to speed his victory."

The King grew pensive and asked, "What do you have in mind, Zav?"

"Sire, the Parsians have built a substantial arsenal of weapons. You could send some to King Croesus as a gift," said Zav.

"King Croesus doesn't need a gift. His streets are paved with gold while mine are paved with camel droppings," King Astyages said in a contemptuous tone.

"Sire, I have seen some of the warehouse storage in Susa and it's surprising how well equipped the Parsians are. If you remove some of their weapons you can change their military preparedness from an offensive posture to a defensive one."

"You don't know about military offense or defense. Pay attention to your own matters!" the King ordered.

Unfortunately, this suggestion caused the King of Kings to remember his old dreams. He was instantly haunted by his hideous reflections about his daughter in the rain and the threat that implied. He thought of the vine that grew from her over all his land. King Astyages' eyes searched for Harpagus, who stood at his familiar location half way down the audience hall and the King said, "Harpagus, what would King Croesus need for his war with Lesbos and Rhodes?"

"Sire, he would need bows, arrows and small catapults for his ships," the soldier answered. "He might be able to use swords and knives, possibly axes, for boarding parties assaulting enemy ships at close quarters."

"Zav, you will go to Susa and order a small shipment of arms, as stated by Harpagus, to be sent to Sardes," pronounced the King. "Tell my brother-in-law I wish him a swift end to his war."

Now Zav had the command he wanted even though King Astyages had ordered 'a small shipment" Zav could alter that detail. The Great King's command could not be disobeyed. Zav decided to deal with Prince Warohi in Susa instead of going to Anshan. As much as he loved to give Cambyses orders, he felt he needed to keep his action plan streamlined for maximum effect. Zav would enjoy it more if the shock of being defenseless could sneak up on Cambyses later when the king had no recourse to alter what had taken place. This plan depended upon being able to move all the armaments, instead of a 'small' quantity.

Zav sent a message to Princess Ispitamu and asked her to get the location of all the warehouses in Susa storing weapons. He refrained from mentioning to her that he intended to empty them all.

When the princess got Zav's message she was thrilled. He had not given her any details of what he was up to, but she was glad to have a task to do that was so unusual. She had to be careful. Wanting this

311

type of information was extremely rare for a woman. She did not want Prince Warohi to suspect anything was amiss.

Princess Ispitamu said, "Warohi, will you escort me in the city, please? Can you give me an administrator's tour of Susa?"

"You have been in our markets many times," the prince said, "I would think you know your way about by now. Didn't one of my princes take you around when you first arrived?"

"I need to see the city from your point of view so I can understand your vast responsibilities. In fact, Warohi, I wonder if you can give me three separate tours. On the first tour you can point out where the public buildings are that you use to control your administration. On the second tour maybe explain your plans to expand the city and show me where the expansion will occur."

"And the third?" asked the prince looked at her with suspicion.

The third tour was the least interesting subject for her, but the most important. She said, "I would like to see the defense structure of the city and your armory."

Prince Warohi thought this was a bit exaggerated, but he agreed. He wanted to help her accommodate to the life here. If this was what she thought she needed then he would do it.

The princess had to concentrate very hard to what Prince Warohi told her on the first two tours. She knew she had to get a good sense of the layout of the city. After their first two excursions were over she had to remember the location of the buildings Zav was interested in. She attempted to make a charcoal picture on a lambskin of her perception of the city. It was very crude but she needed something to help her recall details for Zav. It was exciting for her to invent her own way of recording what she saw.

"Do you really want to see the defense system of the city, Ispitamu?" he asked in an incredulous voice.

"Oh yes, Warohi, you have made this so interesting I am anxious to see all the wonderful things you are responsible for. You are so impressive. Cambyses is correct in assigning you to keep watch over Susa. You are brilliant," she said, using her most officious compliments.

The Prince took her statements as nothing less than the truth. As they moved through streets now familiar to the princess she was able to match her location in her mind with her shabby lambskin map.

Later, all she needed to do was mark the map with a dot for all the warehouses that the prince showed her and her job was done.

The prince said, "This building contains saddles and harness leathers for camels and horses as well as chariots for our army. Our stables are outside the city near pastures kept specifically for our mounts."

This was not information Princess Ispitamu wanted but she tolerated his thoroughness just to get to the more pertinent data. When they came to one structure Prince Warohi said, "This building contains war armaments."

"May I look?" she asked.

Prince Warohi was very surprised at her request, but relented. Inside the warehouse the princess partially recognized what she was seeing. The princess normally saw these items from a distance without paying attention to what they really were. She was amazed to see enormous piles of axes and arrows.

"The toys of men!" she laughed.

"Yes, they are." the prince chuckled.

Princess Ispitamu could not count high enough to estimate how much material she was looking at. If all the buildings they were to visit were packed like this, Zav was going to have quite a time counting, if that was what he wanted to do. The princess was afraid she might alert Prince Warohi into suspecting something was amiss so she said no more.

She counted on her fingers and toes the number of places the prince identified as having equipment of interest to Zav. Princess Ispitamu was able to remember the location of over half of them for her map. She knew Zav would be pleased.

After spending so much time with the princess, Prince Warohi decided to report to Cambyses about her. A scribe magus took a message that acknowledged to King Cambyses her banishment from Anshan, plus the intent of the prince to honor his king's instructions. The prince also mentioned that he found her interest in the defense system of the city amusing.

The latter information made Cambyses very suspicious. His first thought was of Zav. Cambyses sent out two messages. One was to Prince Warohi telling him that if Zav showed up making demands about changing the defenses of Susa to ignore him. However, the prince was to act as if he meant to follow Zav's orders then inform the king.

The second message went from Cambyses to the Great King. Cambyses reported the stores of armaments he had accumulated and asked King Astyages if he could help Media in any way with their defenses. The message he got back was upsetting. The Great King told Cambyses he wanted a small quantity of arms sent to King Croesus immediately. 'A small quantity' was open for interpretation, and the King had not made mention of any kind of weapons.

The most disconcerting part of the King's message was his statement ordering Cambyses to send Cyrus to Media to live with him and Queen Aryenis while the Great King trained the young prince in how to be a man. The message implied the boy was to receive Median training for several sun cycles before and after he became an official adult. It was a typical egocentric demand from the King. Cambyses did not want his son to be a Mede. Cambyses wanted to continue to train Cyrus the Parsian way. The boy was to rule this country some day. He needed instructions that related to Pars not Media. Cambyses deferred acting on this command as long as he could. He told Mandane, "My darling, your father wants our son to live in Ecbatana for a number of sun cycles. At least until after he is an adult."

"No!" she shouted, "He can't do this to me…to us."

"Easy my love," said Cambyses surprised at her outburst.

"But my son is being taken from me again."

The queen had been in such high spirits since they had their son returned to them, Cambyses worried that she might revert back to the disgruntled attitude she had displayed for so long.

"We will delay as long as we can. We will investigate possible plans of our own that might satisfy you father."

Cambyses began sending periodic messages to King Astyages giving excuses of why the boy could not come just yet. He was able to delay his son's departure for almost an entire sun cycle before the King demanded his grandson's appearance.

In that interval of time Cyrus continued his Parsian training. In a few short sun cycles Cyrus would officially be a man. He was now thirteen, soon to be fourteen, and the prince entered manhood at fifteen like every Parsian male. Cambyses did not want a magus to perform his son's inauguration into manhood while Cyrus was living in Media. Cambyses planned to allow the boy to spend one sun cycle in Media when he finally went. Cambyses was ready to argue with the Great King and force the issue if he had to. The Great King was not going to take over his son's life!

Cambyses continued his son's training by ordering the horse-riding instructors to begin having Cyrus shoot his bow from a trotting horse at a stationary target. Cyrus may have made arrows and bows before, but his bow-drawing strength was far less powerful than the strength of other boys his age. The Greek had not made Cyrus increase the pulling force of his bow as he got bigger. The boy's barnyard strength used different muscles than the bowman. Now Cambyses watched carefully to see that his son made faster than normal progress in developing arm strength. The boy took to the challenge readily. His progress was going well. Cambyses wanted him to integrate his riding technique with skillful bow shooting because a mature warrior in the Parsian army had to be able to hit a moving target, while galloping at full speed on a horse moving in any direction, relative to the target. There was a lot for the boy to learn.

Cyrus still had to make his own arrows and bows now that Prince Bagindu added that obligation into the curriculum of the princes. It pleased the princes when the archery trainers taught these techniques to everyone. They learned which tree or bush branch limbs were best for each weapon. They shot birds to acquire feathers to stabilize their arrows. They had to spin their own hemp to make bowstrings. The older boys had to learn to dry and shape animal gut to make stronger bowstrings. All the skills a warrior needed on the march were included, and because Cyrus loved it so much the other princes became infected with his enthusiasm.

The first time a boy hit a stationary target while riding at full gallop was applauded vigorously. They shouted cheers at the hero. Slaps on the back almost knocking the breath out of the celebrity. Cyrus was not the first to achieve this stunt, but he did succeed. He became more consistent with the technique quicker than other princes his age. It would still be a while before any of them were allowed to shoot at moving targets while riding a horse. They had to start by shooting from a slow moving camel first.

Cyrus did not spend much time with noblemen who were responsible for helping his father run the country. He was content to learn of their duties from what he heard in the court. He was satisfied with the information he got from questioning his parents after royal audience sessions. Cyrus decided he could wait until he was a man before he started interacting with administrators. Now he only wanted to take on tasks he could master.

Cambyses made a special effort to teach Cyrus his 'noble' Aryan heritage. Cambyses was personally proud of the first kings and their accomplishments that forged a country from such rough rock and harsh terrain. The natural nobility of Cambyses inspired Cyrus, and the prince loved hearing his father's stories that were told with such elation. Cambyses said, "Media, including Pars, was handed to your grandfather as an established, functioning empire. The Great King is letting it get smaller and weaker. The kings of our lineage in Pars forced their empire away from Sumaria and Elam. Over time our royal ancestors made continuous improvements that strengthened our unity.

"Unfortunately," Cambyses admitted, "Pars lost its independence to Media long ago. And I still have plenty to do to improve the general welfare of our subjects."

"I will help you, father," Cyrus promised.

38.

"I have come to Susa to help you, Prince Warohi. I have an order from King Astyages relating to your armament stores so I must view your military warehouses. We can get down to the details of the Great King's order as soon as you show me where all your armaments are located."

"Zav, why don't we enjoy supper before getting into that. Such an inspection will take so long it will tire you. You need a little relaxation after your travels," said Prince Warohi. The prince wanted to delay because Cambyses had warned him to be careful of Zav and his demands.

"How is my friend Princess Ispitamu? Zav asked, "Is she well? Does she still live in Susa? I would like to see her while I'm here."

Prince Warohi said, "She is here. I have decided to put on a large banquet and I invited many of my relatives, including Princess Ispitamu. You give me a good excuse to treat my family to a party."

When the banquet began there were several courses, and the meal lasted late into the night. Wine and salads were served at the outset. These were followed by a rice dish, then venison. A different rice dish seasoned with saffron, cooked with a stiff, browned crust on the bottom, was served next. Wild boar was next. Several spiced vegetables followed the meat. A light yogurt was next. The conversation between servings was lively to allow diners to partially digest the various courses they sampled. Wine flowed freely helping the guests keep up their spirits.

Prince Warohi was concerned at the amount of time Zav spent with Princess Ispitamu. The prince had placed her quite far from Zav, but the visitor deliberately moved to sit beside her.

There was entertainment between dinner courses. Jugglers, jesters and acrobats put on an exciting show. Their costumes were colorful and gay. Women belly danced and men fought mock battles with knives, swords and flaming torches. Musicians played constantly. Drums, tambourines, reed horns, lyres and harps could be heard all evening. The atmosphere was a credit to Prince Warohi. He was very pleased with the outcome when his relatives left exhilarated complimenting him for his hospitality.

Because of the noise and the close sharing of tables with the prince's guests Zav could not speak to Princess Ispitamu about the topics that were foremost in his mind at the banquet. The princess and the minister agreed to meet the next day, very late in the afternoon, when they both expected the headache and tiredness from the banquet to leave them.

During their meeting in her rooms, Princess Ispitamu showed Zav her lambskin map. She said, "It is a bit crude but you are familiar with the layout of Susa, and you can see approximately where these buildings are."

"You have done a perfect job with this," Zav complimented. "Thank you for being so thorough. I intend to remove everything I can from these warehouses because the Great King has ordered it. I want to leave Pars as defenseless as possible because I intend to tell Governor Pagakanna of Babylon that Pars is ripe for the picking if King Nebuchadnezzar is interested. That will be the end of the reign of Cambyses!"

"You what? Cambyses is my king; Pars is my country! You can't do such a thing. What have I done?" Princes Ispitamu asked, completely upset at the thought of having hurt Cambyses.

"The Babylonians will ensure that Cambyses is safe, but Cyrus will not inherit the country. The Babylonians will agree to give Pars to Prince Warohi."

That sounded better to her and she calmed down.

"Plans will be made for you to be protected in Ecbatana before the Babylonian attack," Zav promised.

The princess did not like the idea that Cambyses might lose his country but it was better than letting Cyrus have a turn at ruling. So once again they had a plan. For Princess Ispitamu, Cyrus and Mandane were to be dislodged. For Zav, so was Cambyses.

Zav had already made arrangements to move large quantities of stock from Susa to Ecbatana. He was prepared to do exactly what the Great King had ordered by designating the first shipments to go directly to King Croesus. The following shipments were to be directed to storage facilities he had emptied in the capital. Everything was planned in precise detail.

Cambyses had cautioned Prince Warohi that the Great King wanted arms shipped to King Croesus. Only a token quantity was to be sent. That was the only command the Great King had given, and it was the only order Prince Warohi was to honor, no matter what Zav said. The prince felt confident of his position. He decided to have fun with Zav by pretending to agree with everything the minister demanded.

"Your workers have been very busy. You have shown me much more than I expected to see," said Zav about the vast piles of weapons in the armories. It was obvious to Zav that the princess had not appreciated the magnitude of what she had seen.

Prince Warohi hid nothing. Finally, Zav said, "Prince Warohi, the Great King commanded me to have the contents of all your armories sent to Ecbatana. He wishes to help support King Croesus in his sea battle with some island states. You know you can depend on Media to always protect Pars. The Great King wants all these weapons under his control so his military supplies are at full strength before he engages in any combat enterprise."

Prince Warohi was expecting a story but not this. It almost sounded convincing enough to be believed. However, the prince only meant to do what Cambyses had ordered. Prince Warohi said, "I suggest loading a small caravan of armaments that you can take with you when you return to Ecbatana to promote your picture of efficiency before the Great King."

"Thank you," said Zav smiling gratefully at the prince. He liked agreeing to proposals that complimented his own image. Zav left Susa with his caravan of camels loaded with catapults, bows, arrows, and axes. He was quite pleased with himself knowing more was to come later. Now if he could get Babylon to attack Pars his enemies would be ruined.

//

In Anshan Cyrus spent much of his free time in the markets. One day he was walking in the market with two armed eunuchs in the brilliant sun enjoying the bustling noise around him. The boy was so well known in Anshan by now that he no longer needed their protection, but he kept them near anyway. Cyrus knew that if he were to come under any danger every man, woman and child in the city would swarm to his rescue. The prince saw a man approach him. He looked like a vagabond in his plain wool gown and worn sandals. The stranger smiled and said, "You must be from the palace, sir. Your guards are not the guards of a peasant."

Cyrus grinned genially and answered, "Yes, sir, I am. I am Cyrus," expecting everyone to understand what that meant.

"Are you the son of the king?"

"Yes, sir."

"I am Zarathustra of Media. I have heard many strange tales about you."

"Yes, so have I. They are interesting but incorrect," said Cyrus.

"I can see one fable is incorrect," said Zarathustra snickering. "You were not sired by a wolf, nor raised in a wolverine den. You are not covered with their silver gray hair, like I have heard."

"My mother, at least the mother who brought me up was named Spaco, and that is why that story about wolves started," Cyrus responded a little annoyed by the implied insult to his foster mother.

"Ah yes, the term 'bitch' in our Mede language," nodded Zarathustra. "That explains both the dog and wolf stories I have heard about you. You'll be a king some day, young man, and these tales may help make you a legend. Don't let yourself be too upset by them."

Zarathustra thought for a moment and added, "I met your father long ago. He is a good man. Is he a good king?"

Cyrus found this man interesting because he was a foreigner to Pars.

"Father is a very good king. He is careful to do only those things that help the people," said Cyrus as he swung his arm about signaling the people around them. Zarathustra liked the gesture. He believed this young man was already aware of the peasants of Pars, not just selfishly focused on his own personal royalty.

"Why are you here, sir?" asked Cyrus.

"As I told your father long ago I am travelling about the lands to talk with people to see what they believe in. Do you believe in one great god, sir?" Zarathustra asked.

"No. There are many gods," answered Cyrus giving the man a surprised look. "I'm not sure they all have names, but there are gods of water, gods of the sky, gods of the earth and gods of the fire."

"Why must there be so many, Prince Cyrus? May I call you Prince Cyrus?"

"Of course, sir. Why, sir, there has to be many gods. One god can't oversee the whole world. Just look at all these people. If they all pray at once one god could not hear their prayers."

Zarathustra responded solemnly, "I think there might be only one god, or at least one supreme god. He may be the maker of all we see and have. Angel spirits that surround him may help him. Do you think that is possible?"

"No. One god can't handle everything. I'm sure there are spirits though," said Cyrus. "There are the good ahura spirits and the bad daeva spirits. They fight for man's attention."

"If the spirits struggle for man's attention," said Zarathustra, "then man must have some say in whether he will be good or bad. Does man have this choice?" asked the dusty man.

Cyrus found this question intriguing. No one had ever asked him this before. "I am not sure, sir. We have the choice to make offerings and pray, but I am not sure. I can decide this moment to be good or bad, but I am not sure if I can decide my whole life will be good or bad."

"If you could make the choice which would you pick, Prince Cyrus?" asked Zarathustra.

"I would choose to be good like my father."

"You are wise, Prince Cyrus. And what do you pray for? How often do you pray for yourself?"

"I never pray for myself," the prince said. "I do not think it is permitted. At least I do not know anyone who does it. I pray for father, mother and my country. I pray for grandfather."

Zarathustra asked, "Is your grandfather the Great King, Prince Cyrus?"

"Yes, Sir, he is. He is the King of Kings; I am very proud of him!"

At that moment a man rushing through the crowd bumped Cyrus hard enough to make him stumble two steps. The two eunuchs reacted immediately to chase after the man. Cyrus easily lifted a hand to stop the eunuchs. Zarathustra was pleased. The boy had the power to have the man whipped for insulting a royal person, but Cyrus just ignored that privilege. Zarathustra continued the conversation, "Is your

321

grandfather a good or bad king. Is he a good or bad man? Does he have free will to decide how to run his life?"

"I never think of him as anything but the Great King," said Cyrus. "He decides daily how to run his kingdom. He has personal splendor and enormous power. I believe he is good; he does beneficial things."

Cyrus continued, "Yes, sir. He is so magnificent I'm sure he would prefer nobility and honor for his life if he had the choice."

"Well, Prince, we have made quite a serious talk out of our casual meeting. Where were you headed just now?"

Cyrus answered, "I want to visit the metal shop to see if they are making swords today. I like the feel of a new blade. The princes are teaching me to fight with swords. It is fun."

Zarathustra smiled benevolently at the boy. The traveler said, "You must realize that striking a man with a sword is an act supported by the daeva, not your ahura. Are you about to choose a life of evil, Prince?"

The prince was so taken aback he paused. Then he said, "No, at least I hope not."

They spoke for a few minutes more and in closing Cyrus said, "I enjoyed talking with you, Zarathustra. Please pass this way in your future travels so we can speak again."

Cyrus had enjoyed meeting a man who asked such penetrating questions so easily. Later the prince spent a little time sitting in his private garden reviewing the conversation with Zarathustra. He only had three modest sized rooms in Anshan, unlike the seven large rooms in Ecbatana. However, his garden here was much larger. There were vegetables; small plots of crocus and several fruit trees interspersed among the bushes and flowers. He thought of Zarathustra's question about his father. The stranger had asked if Cambyses was a good king. Looking at his garden reminded him of a statement his father once made. Cambyses had instructed him by saying, "Son, I am told you have been working the soil and weeding your garden. I would like you to leave that work to the gardeners. They are experts at getting maximum production from all our gardens. Every small amount of food we get on our own is just that much less that I have to demand from our people. They have so little to support themselves. Small changes in my demands for more crops from them make enormous differences to our peasants. You must help me make them richer."

Cyrus decided that was the advice of a good king. The boy thought his mother was a good queen. He envisioned her on her throne looking with a combination of sternness on her brow and compassion in her eyes at a supplicant on Reconciling Days. She touched his father when Cambyses made a fair judgement. Cyrus knew her touch was her complicity in a fair decision. He also knew she not only loved his father but she worked very hard at being a good mother. The prince thought of the many times she had told him how happy he made her. She said publicly that Cyrus even made her health better. Because of him her whole body was full of love and good feelings. She mentioned to Cyrus once that her chest no longer caved in hurting her the way it used to. Her headaches were gone. She said that she was able to appreciate everyone around her all because of him. Cyrus was skeptical about her latter claim.

Cyrus had never seen her in the long interval when her behavior was mean. No one spoke to him about it; so he did not really understand what she was saying. To him she was an excellent mother. A special woman. A fine queen.

Cyrus knew he was going to go back to live for a while with his grandfather. His father had mentioned it without specifying deliberate plans for the visit. As much as Cyrus enjoyed seeing King Astyages, he preferred to stay in Pars. He liked all aspects of his training especially the stories his father told him about past kings.

The prince was proud to be named after his father's father. Cambyses had personally instructed Cyrus in the family history. The prince cherished that teaching. The boy dreamed of how King Cyrus and his father before him had diligently worked to bring peace among the tribes in this country. Before King Cyrus tribes and clans used to fight viciously over a single pasture. They were so poor that a single field was worth more than the lives of dozens of peasants. The young prince envisioned King Cyrus teaching his peasants to respect each other when the great man set up the Reconciling Day court to provide a place for angry men to argue for a lasting royal decision. Since no written code of laws existed, the prince knew law was the judgement of the king, his father. The king's word was obeyed in the distant hills and mountains only because the peasants respected him.

Cambyses had informed his son that at first King Cyrus forced respect with military interference. Gradually the peasants began to see fairness in his decisions about their woes so they willingly obeyed him. Cyrus trusted his father's claim that the first King Cyrus made truth a national emblem of manhood. Cambyses now perpetuated that emblem because it kept peace between the tribes.

Young Cyrus knew his grandfather, King Astyages, never told stories of past glory such as this. He only told stories about himself. Cyrus longed to make his visit to Ecbatana short. However, the prince knew he had to stay as long as his grandfather decreed. If King Astyages insisted that he stay for several sun cycles, the prince was going to feel trapped. Cyrus preferred not to fret about the Great King's wish, instead he focused on more important issues here at home. He concentrated on what he heard in his father's court.

"Sire, the business of the city was doing much better because of the expanding market plaza. The salt desert caravan route continues to get busier and a greater variety of merchandise is being transported over that path, but at modest volumes," said Pattmenidu in King Cambyses' audience chamber.

"Good! I am pleased," said the king, encouraged by his good report.

"However, sire, Zav bothers me. The minister is mad because the trade coming directly to Ecbatana from Bactria is reduced in volume. It hurts his personal profits. He threatens to have the Great King send a militia force to close down the salt desert trail. Is there anything you can do, sire?"

"It is time I sent my son to Ecbatana," said King Cambyses. "The presence of Cyrus might distract King Astyages. I'll tutor Cyrus on what to say to the Great King about Zav's exaggerations on the significance of this trade route. It's an opportunity for Cyrus to become involved in the business of diplomacy for Pars. It will also be useful test for him."

"Zav has sent several messages to Susa demanding the shipment of all our armaments to Ecbatana," added Pattmenidu. "Prince Warohi is following your orders. Nothing has been forwarded to Ecbatana as Zav ordered."

Cambyses called a scribe magus. He smiled letting his message tell Zav that Pars had responded according to demand of the Great

King. A small quantity of arms had been sent. The issue was closed. Later Cambyses explained the situation to Cyrus. He had confidence in his son's intelligence. Everything was going to be fine.

"My son is being taken away from me again! Cyrus would be away at least for one entire sun cycle and maybe longer," moaned Mandane when plans for Cyrus to go to Ecbatana developed. She began fidgeting with nervous agitation. She wanted to keep her family together.

"My dear, why not go with Cyrus? You will enjoy seeing your mother and father," said the king. Cyrus was delighted. He said, "Yes mother, come so we can be there together."

It would make his stay more enjoyable with her near him. Realizing Cambyses did mean for her to go made her happier. She asked, "Can you come too, dear?"

"No. I have too much to do. I will miss you both."

Mandane was going to miss her husband too, but she was going to be with her boy!

No one rushed the travel preparations, but everything was finally in place. Mandane and Cyrus left Anshan in tears and sadness. Cyrus accompanied the military guard on his horse. He decided for himself each day if he should ride or stay in his mother's carriage. Actually, the military officer had been instructed by Cambyses to ensure the boy did not overextend himself. Along the hill or mountain paths Cyrus sometimes rode beside his mother's carriage and shouted through the shaved mica windowpane about what he was seeing in the forest or in the steep mountain cliffs. He told her when he spotted a village. When he sighted people he told her how they were dressed, their sex and his guess of their age. If he saw men that looked threatening he did not tell Mandane. He waited for his guards to take whatever action they deemed necessary.

His father had clearly instructed him in spiritual respect for water. The boy had been told there were gods for flowing and static water that no man was to defile. Magi confirmed for Cyrus that Parsians never bathed in a river or a lake. He was told that water had to be taken from a body of water in jugs so personal hygiene could be performed from the container. Cyrus observed how carefully the soldiers conducted themselves and their animals to observe this religious obligation. The prince was learning techniques with first hand experience on how to keep the holy rules.

At night Cyrus ate and slept with the soldiers. He grew fond of camping. He loved the smell of the campfire. The prince took small excursions in the mountains after a day's travel to hunt. Two or three soldiers always went with him. They stayed nearby to protect him. If he was lucky enough to kill a large animal, like a deer, they helped him get it back to camp. Mostly he killed birds or hares.

As the entourage entered the mountains of Media the soldiers became more alert. They had been warned that Mandane's carriage had been attacked once, and they were determined to not let that happen this time. Security at night was increased. Cyrus was forbidden to hunt at dusk. He understood the restriction so he did not complain. Besides, he wanted to be near his mother if she was ever in danger. He wore a bronze sword, tied to his leg, just like a real soldier. He always carried his bow and he kept his quiver full of arrows.

Every man was obliged to water his horse or camel before he drank himself. It was a rule of all travelling Parsian men. Cyrus took complete responsibility for his mount. He cleaned, curried, watered and fed his horse on the trail. This journey was excellent training for him. The soldiers did not treat him like a boy. They made demands on him as if he were truly one of them. Cyrus loved it!

As the cavalcade came close enough for Cyrus to see Ecbatana he realized he had never observed it like this before. The city was enormous. The prince knew it was large because he had ridden and walked through the city many times, but he had ridden on camels or donkeys from the west when he was younger, entering the city from the farm. Back then they came through a mountain pass and he never saw the full expanse of the city like this. He could see his grandfather's walled palace on its hillock. He felt proud of the grandeur his grandfather represented in this view. He was truly entering the capital of an important empire, and it belonged to his family, his King of Kings!

Cyrus never associated himself with the greatness of his grandfather. He did not think he deserved extra respect just because he was related to one of the most powerful rulers on earth. Cyrus wanted to earn accolades through his own accomplishments.

39.

Mandane and Cyrus went straight to the King's audience chamber without hesitation. Cyrus brushed grit from his garments as they raced through the corridors. Mandane rushed to kiss her father first. It was a formality that she knew he expected. Then she greeted her mother with a big hug. Cyrus bowed with his head to the floor. He was no different from any other visitor when he came into the presence of the Great King. King Astyages ordered, "Cyrus, stand. My, how you have grown!"

The guards of the palace had not removed the weapons from Cyrus that he wore. However, they kept a careful eye on him to ensure he approached the Great King with slow, cautious steps and no suspicious moves.

"You look like one of my own soldiers with your bow and sword, boy," the King said, very pleased.

"Sire, I am one of your soldiers if ever you should need me," Cyrus responded with conviction and love.

The Great King was delighted. This prince always said the correct thing and always sounded as if he meant it. Mandane leaned toward her father and said, "Cyrus is going to be the best soldier in your empire, father. He is already the most handsome one," and she laughed.

"Cyrus, it is so refreshing to have you here. Later, you will have to tell me how my daughter has been treating you in Anshan. And I expect the truth from you young man," Queen Aryenis said, laughing with happiness.

It was a joyous reception. The King had ordered a banquet with music and entertainment. Mandane was happy to be among the princes and princesses that she had grown up with. She loved the opulence of this palace. She felt at home here as she settled in her suite. Cyrus returned to the familiar seven rooms he had occupied previously.

Zav stood in the reception chamber resenting everything he saw. Mandane looked beautiful after so long a trip, but all he saw was an enemy he wanted desperately to destroy. The boy was growing too fast, acting too much like a man. Zav thought of murdering him but that was wishful dreaming. The boy had too much protection here.

At the banquet Zav stayed away from the visitors. He was angry because Cambyses was not obeying his order to ship the Susa defense materials to Ecbatana. Zav's warehouses were still empty. He had nothing to put in them. Even worse, Pars still had adequate defenses, so he could not go to Babylon yet to claim they were easy prey. He needed to approach the Great King again on the subject to receive a regal order that allowed him to weaken the military strength of Cambyses.

Food, music and laughter filled the air. Women danced together in their hop-and-skip fashion to the delight of the men and specially the King. Astyages enjoyed seeing their breasts bounce when they danced. Mandane danced while the King and Queen applauded her with parental vigor. Cyrus laughed and tried dancing when the men danced. Their dance steps were less graceful than those of the women. The men made higher jumps and twirls as they hopped or skipped with energetic lunges. Some men jumped so high they had to be supported by other shouting men when they came back to the floor. The banquet lasted late into the night. Everyone agreed it was a great success.

Getting on a regular training schedule was difficult for Cyrus. At home the prince had made himself a vigorous sequence of activities for his training. Here in Ecbatana he had a problem getting involved with the princes who preferred to dally and procrastinate. The training of Median princes was too casual, too inconsistent. It aggravated him that he had nothing at all to do for long periods of time, but since his mother was here he spent time with her. He was still young enough to be allowed to roam in the Queen's *andarun* as he wished since it was permitted for children, including the young boys.

He loved his grandmother. He enjoyed spending time talking with her as well. She doted on him making him feel special. What he appreciated most was her innate kindness toward everyone around her. She was a likable queen.

King Astyages ordered Cyrus to attend court every day he held it. The King wanted Cyrus to see how Media operated. He wanted the boy to see how important his grandfather was because King Astyages was very proud of himself. The presence of Cyrus added new vigor to the announcements the King made. He grew more pompous, more self-righteous with each audience session. He could not show off enough for the boy. Gradually, the Great King realized he was getting a bit ridiculous so he calmed down, but only a little.

Cyrus was impressed with the military reports the generals gave of the Median army. They talked of thousands of camels and horses. Cyrus thought of all the leather needed to harness such a massive herd. He could not imagine how many leather workers it took to make the saddles and reins; he wondered how many oxen or cattle hides it took. When the military leaders talked about tens of thousands of soldiers Cyrus looked at the leather breastplates of the guards in the room with the shiny brass couplings that held the leather strips and epaulets in place. This had to take many metal workers, but not as many as it took to make the weapons the soldiers needed. There were chariots that made up another form of mounted soldier. The prince wondered how many carpenters it took to cut wood just to make the spoked wheels of the chariots? Cyrus began to marvel at this enormous city with all its soldiers and their families, plus the workers and craftsmen needed to support them.

Gradually, Cyrus thought he was beginning to understand how vast the Median Empire really was. The market places had always felt huge to him, but from the perspective of the palace and the Great King's throne, size took on an entirely different proportion for the prince. Anything King Astyages undertook was complex, requiring gargantuan support systems. Cyrus had not developed this sense of enormity in Anshan. The colossal majesty of his grandfather grew in his mind as he sat in the audience chamber day after day. Cyrus tried to analyze the well-established organizational systems that helped this empire work without serious problems. His father was part of this huge operation. Cyrus developed a new respect for Cambyses who helped the Great King run his dominion.

When Zav gave business and commerce reports the numbers were even larger. The royal grain storage facilities were in numerous locations throughout the kingdom. The facilities to handle produce were just as ubiquitous. Cyrus had always thought the farm Mitridates managed was large. This new perspective made him understand just how small that farm operation had been. He was glad the experience of living with Mitridates and Spaco helped him understand details of the farm so that now he was able to comprehend the magnitude of what Zav reported. Cyrus knew Zav and his father did not get along well, but the young prince began to see Zav in a different light when the Taxes and Materials Minister gave his reports. Zav was a smart man who could read a little as well as be mean.

Cyrus wanted to practice his reading so he talked with the King's Chief Magus. Cyrus asked, "Can I go to the hall of records and have a scribe magus help me read better, please?"

The Chief Magus knew Cyrus had been to the hall of records before, but the priest was not in favor of such visits. It was not good for royal family members to learn too much about reading. It might weaken the advantage of his priests who relied on this special craft to keep royalty dependent on them. It was how they supported their tribe throughout the empire. The Chief Magus was afraid to say Cyrus could not go to learn reading, but he did not encourage it.

"The magi are extremely busy with their work," the Chief Magus said. "Also the records they keep are so fragile they break easily. If you were to destroy a record we would never be able to recreate it, Prince Cyrus."

"Your magus protected the records the last time by insisting that only he would handle the tablets I read. I was allowed to hold one just to see how heavy and bulky it was. We can place the clay on the bench like before. I will keep my fingers off the writing," Cyrus said simply, without being too defensive or overly aggressive.

"Of what use can reading about property deeds or food storage be to you?" the priest asked, finding it difficult to discourage the boy's enthusiasm. "You need to spend your time learning about military matters or the diplomatic issues your grandfather has been exposing you to. Reading is a waste of time for you, Prince."

Cyrus did not like challenging a man of such importance, but he was anxious to read again. "Sir," he said, "I can read a little Greek and a little of the Mede language. I can speak Pars and Aramaic but I can't read these last two. I would like to learn."

The Chief Magus relented. He offered to have a magus bring clay tablets to the palace. That way he could decide what records the boy saw. If Cyrus just went into their building and pointed to any clay tablet he chose to practice on the magi would not refuse him. They could place something the prince shouldn't see in front of him.

Cyrus was anxious to get out of the palace to wander the city again the way he used to, so he declined the Chief Magus' offer. They were at a stalemate; Cyrus eventually got his way. The prince irritated the Magus but he did not alienate him. It took several wistful days before Cyrus could get to the hall of records; during that interval Prince Zatame had noted how inactive Cyrus was so he scheduled several military training sessions that kept the boy busy.

//

News of Mandane's trip to Ecbatana reached Susa. Princess Ispitamu wondered if she should try to travel there too. The princess had destroyed her supplies of poisons that she used long ago to plague the queen. Maybe Zav could get the plant that caused abortions just in case Mandane had gotten pregnant after the princess was exiled from Anshan. She thought the queen should still be pleased to see her. Princess Ispitamu had no indication she shouldn't. Cambyses had only put one specific restriction on her travel; maybe it was allowed for her to go to Ecbatana. She spoke to Prince Warohi about her desire to travel there.

The princess had a scribe magus send Zav a message asking about the supply of silphium that must be acquired from Cyrene. She did not request him to order the plant. There was no need to rush. If Mandane were already pregnant again it must have occurred recently since no news had come from Anshan about her being with child again. The princess expected Mandane to stay at her father's palace a long while, and pregnancies lasted a long time. Princess Ispitamu decided she needed to be very deliberate about the actions she took against the queen.

//

News spread to King Croesus of Mandane's visit so he decided it was a good time to visit his sister and his favorite niece. He was not concerned about his war with the island states. King Astyages had forwarded his message to King Croesus promising arms support. King Croesus did not need his brother-in-law's gift, but he decided to pick up the supplies himself. Getting a present was a good reason to travel.

He planned a smaller contingent for this trip than the one he took to attend Mandane's wedding. That had been a special occasion when he brought the most expensive wedding gift the world had ever seen. This time his gifts were to be far more modest because he knew the gift he would receive would be paltry.

//

Mitridates and Spaco heard that Mandane and Cyrus were in Ecbatana. The farmers made plans to leave the farm for the market with the hopes of seeing their 'son.' They both missed his company. They admitted it would be a pure accident if they saw him, but they were willing to try. Mitridates felt he was forced to travel with the thieves again in hopes of building a new fortune. He always suspected that Rusundatu had robbed him, but he had no proof of it. He made a new hiding place in the woods he knew Rusundatu could not find. He resented the thought that Zav had probably profited from the goods previously stolen from the farm too.

40

Cyrus was anxious to practice reading. He was afraid that if he did not go when the Chief Magus agreed the priest might change his mind. Cyrus walked through the city to the record building and this time the prince approached the scribe magus with a specific question. Cyrus asked, "Do you keep records of the Great King's audience sessions? I have noted men are always in the audience chamber writing without stopping when the Great King speaks."

"We try to take down the important decrees the King makes," the magus said. "The issues of international significance are the most important."

"Do you ever go back and have to read them to help resolve arguments over what was ordered or agreed upon?" the prince asked.

"Yes, sometimes, but it is infrequent. When the King gives orders they are obeyed."

"There was an order my father was given by the Great King to send weapons to King Croesus," the prince volunteered. "Would it be possible for me to try to read that clay tablet?"

"When was this?" the magus asked.

Cyrus and the magus discussed the details Cambyses had instructed his son on. The magus was not certain if the clay tablet was stored in the vault relating to Pars or in the vault relating to Croesus and Lydia. He asked several soiled men if they recalled the topic in the audience chamber. One priest said he thought he had been a member of the scribe contingent that wrote that day. He took them to a vault deep inside the building, lit by candles; he located a tablet he thought they wanted. The magus climbed a ladder then passed the slate to another man who placed it flat on a table. The magus admonished, "Remember, Prince Cyrus, you are to keep your fingers off the surface of the clay. Now try reading what you see. It is in our Mede language."

Cyrus began stumbling over the images and only picking up a word here and there. It did not seem to be what he was after and he asked the magus to find the correct line for him. The magus peered over his shoulder and pointed. "Read from here."

Cyrus read, "Zav, you will …. Cambyses to …. ship a small …. of …… to ….. for King Croesus from the Susa …..I do not want you to…… it is my gift to my brother-in-law."

The magus pronounced the words 'order, immediately, caravan, military weapons, Lydia, warehouse, delay' as the words Cyrus could not read on his own. It was a very thorough record of what the Great King ordered. Some of the clay had been obscured, which was common, when the tablet was transported from the palace to the record hall, and that made it hard for Cyrus to read it. However, this was the precise record Cyrus had hoped to find. He continued to read the tablet. It was important to see if the King ordered all the remaining armaments sent to Ecbatana. There was no such command. Cyrus asked, "Sir, is there some way to identify this specific tablet if I wanted to refer to it later?"

The magus said, "No, there is none. We don't number or code these records. However, I would have not trouble recalling it because your presence here today is so unusual, prince. The tablets are stored in the sequence they are written and separated by a vague system of categories. Beyond that we have no way to track information. We spend a lot of time hunting real estate deeds, grain sales, Parthian emissary visits or the like, when necessary. However, that is extremely infrequent."

Cyrus tried reading other miscellaneous tablets in Greek. He asked to see Aramaic writing. It was a common language and the magus started to teach him to recognize the syllabic images of that language. Cyrus soon began to tire so he left the building after thanking the magus for his patience. It was more than a significant achievement; it was truly a gift of the beneficial ahura gods the prince gave thanks to because of what he accomplished.

On his return to the palace he came across Oebares, the slave he considered a friend. The slave did not recognize Cyrus. The prince had grown. Also, he was now wearing unfamiliar Parsian clothes, not the elegant silks and flowing capes of Media.

"Well, Oebares, how is your mason doing?" Cyrus asked as he gazed at the wall. The Great King image was complete and the image of the Pars king making an offering was almost complete. There were three more images in various stages of completion. These included another minor king, a bull and a lion. Oebares recognized the voice and tentatively asked, "Paithi? Is that you?"

Cyrus smiled and held out his hand as a greeting, "Yes, it's me, but I'm Cyrus, remember? I have returned to see my grandfather. How have you been? You're getting bigger. So you still watch the mason."

"Yes, he likes to sleep in the shade and I'm supposed to report him when he stops working. What do you think of the picture?"

"It's quite nice. There's nothing like this in Anshan. Our people don't have time for such luxury."

They talked for a while. Cyrus asked, "Oebares, do you still have your poor attitude towards the Great King?"

"Of course and I'm more hateful than before," Oebares answered. "The magnificent King gets more foolish every day. He has forbidden slave owners from freeing their slaves. I'll never be free no matter how hard I try," and he held out his hand to show his slave bracelet.

"At least before we had hope of freeing ourselves. My magistrate promised to free me after I had worked long enough to more than pay for his expense to purchase and keep me. He was even going to pay to send me away to a place where I could make a new life. That will never occur."

Oebares continued, "Also, my master has had his properties penalized with higher taxes, but we don't know why. It was a direct order from King Astyages."

Cyrus listened without commenting. He did not appreciate what Oebares was saying, but the prince refused to talk against his grandfather. Cyrus changed the subject, which allowed them to talk like friends again. After they ate and drank in the shade, Cyrus got up to enter the palace.

In the audience chamber of the Great King an emissary from Babylon came to give greetings from King Nebuchadnezzar. The emissary said, "Babylon is ready to go to war with Egypt again, because Pharaoh Necho was still causing problems in Judah. This time King Nebuchadnezzar intends to stifle Judah by putting Jewish leaders into slavery. The troublemakers will go back to Babylon to build his Hanging Gardens, plus large new buildings my king wants. We are going to stop influential Jews from conspiring with the Egyptians. This collusion led to the downfall of King

Nebuchadnezzar's control over Judah, and he doesn't intend to let it happen again."

"I wish him success. His fight has gone on long enough," said the Great King.

"King Nebuchadnezzar requests assurance that you will help him, King Astyages."

The Great King had no intention of helping, but he chose to play a game before giving his answer to the Babylonian. The Great King looked in Cyrus' direction and asked, "What would you do, Cyrus?"

Cyrus was startled to be included in the conversation. He hesitated before saying, "Sire, I would not offer military help, but I would confirm my intention not to interfere by helping Judah either. This is not an issue for Media. You gain nothing from this war, sire. Caravans directed between us and King Croesus will not be affected by the Babylonian war."

King Astyages waited for more but the boy was silent. The King was surprised at how clear the boy's thought process had been. It complimented his inclination to be passive. Going to war for someone else was inconvenient and took energy. He looked at the emissary and said, "You have heard my grandson. His answer is my answer. You are dismissed."

Cyrus was shocked that he had just made a significant decision for the entire empire of Media. He wanted to tell his mother immediately so she could have the joy of bragging about him. It was his first international decree!

The Great King called Zav forward and asked, "Is my gift to King Croesus ready?"

"Yes, sire. I have it ready to send. I will get it into a caravan in a few days."

"No you won't! You'll keep it here. King Croesus is coming. I'll give it to him myself. He can take it with him when he leaves for home."

Zav decided this was the time to get authorization for having Susa transport the contents of all their armaments to Ecbatana. He said, "Sire, Pars has vast stores of axes, lances and other useful military materials. We should have those stores moved here."

"Is it reasonable for us to do this, Harpagus?" the King asked, looking in the soldier's direction.

"We have no need at this time for more weapons. There is no war. Let Susa keep what they have. Why clutter up our warehouses, sire?"

"But, sire, you ordered me to retrieve weapons for King Croesus and take all the armaments in Susa as a precaution of war," Zav said, not willing to give up his campaign to weaken Cambyses.

Cyrus recognized the lie and spoke up at the risk of a severe reprimand. The prince said, "Sire, you only ordered the gift for the Lydian king to be removed from Pars. You did not order the entire supply of stored arms to be sent to Ecbatana."

Zav's eyes flared as he swung his head to glare at Cyrus.

"Sire, this prince doesn't know what he's talking about. He wasn't even here when your insightful decree was ordered."

"Sire, just this morning I read the record of the magus on this. You limited your instructions to the gift," said Cyrus with all the boldness he could muster.

King Astyages laughed and said, "Cyrus can you read that well? Magus, show my grandson what you have written today. Make him read it for us."

The magus placed his clay tablet on Cyrus' lap who said, "Sire, I think this is Aramaic. I speak it, but I can't read it yet."

King Astyages laughed in a loud, satisfied cackle believing his grandson had just played a trick on Zav. The King would have been suspicious if he knew that Cyrus had actually read the correct record earlier that day. Also, because the prince had helped him with the Babylonian, King Astyages decided to yield again to Cyrus.

"Zav, if I have my gift for my brother-in-law, I am satisfied. Let Susa keep its weapons," the King ordered.

The topic was ended. Zav could not believe the boy of the hated family had now foiled him in such an important scheme. How he hated those people!

After the session was over Cyrus decided to walk in the market before visiting his mother to tell her how he had helped both his father and his grandfather today. He was surprised to see Mitridates and Spaco setting up to sell goods. The boy thought the merchandise must belong to his grandfather. He ran up to them, and they all had a big cry between hugs and kisses. Mitridates said, "Oh son, we have missed you so. Everyone misses you."

337

Spaco asked, "Can you come to the farm to visit us now that you are in Media? I want to cook for you again."

Cyrus told them, "I am visiting with my mother, but I do have plans to see you at the farm. Maybe I will be the official prince my grandfather sends the next time to inspect you."

Spaco said, "If he does please bring your mother. I would like to see what the queen looks like. I hear she is very beautiful."

Cyrus said nothing. He could never let Mandane see this couple. His mother's jealousy could get them killed. He also did not tell them his father had provided the fortune they needed to return to Sardes. That was his surprise for later. He spent the afternoon with them swapping gossip.

"Are the slaves I used to know still living on the farm?"

"Yes, I believe most of them are. Some might have died since you left," answered Mitridates.

"How is your output of goods for the King. Do you still make improvements?"

"Yes, we have made additional changes, based on suggestions you made while living with us, and so we continue to please the royal inspectors. Everything is going well. You must come and see."

Mitridates sold most of their goods that afternoon just because people came by to see Prince Cyrus. Some peasants were bold enough to speak to the prince who chatted with them in a familiar fashion that made them proud to have spoken personally with a future king. Cyrus made it a day many peasants never forgot.

While eating supper with Mandane that night Cyrus made a big story of how he helped her father make the decision about Babylon. He spoke without vanity, just enthusiasm. He said to her, "Mother, I hope grandfather allows me to help like that again. It was fun to make a suggestion he took seriously."

Mandane said, "Son, your grandfather is enchanted by you. I am sure father will let you help him again, because it is his way of training you for important diplomatic work."

Cyrus smiled remembering his other success over Zav and said,

"Before I left Anshan, father told me how Zav had ordered Prince Warohi to send military equipment to Ecbatana under the guise of an order from grandfather. Today I read the original record of the magus.

I was able to keep Zav from stealing from father by quoting what I read to grandfather."

The queen asked, "How did you do such a thing? How did you know where to find such important information?"

Cyrus gave her the details of his past exposure to the hall of records and his reintroduction to it today. He explained, "I asked for a specific clay tablet which a magus found. In grandfather's audience session today, Harpagus agreed with us but for different reasons. The whole day was successful for us. Father got what he was hoping for."

Mandane hugged him. She glowed at his intelligence as well as his dedication to both his father and his grandfather. She resented Zav's antics, and she was happy Cyrus had foiled the minister in a trick she did not understand. Mother and son spent the rest of the evening talking about various topics. Mandane sent a message to Cambyses to let him know how smart his son was. She had a hard time keeping the message short. She loved to brag about Cyrus!

41.

King Croesus needed his companions to plan well for his trip to Ecbatana because it was a tedious undertaking. His servants had to anticipate every possible problem along the way. First, they had to decide which route to take. They knew whatever trail they chose would split sprawling landmasses occupied with migrating nomads and semi-nomads, not cities. They would move across vast spans of earth without being able to rely on seeing other people for days, if not weeks. Therefore, if something went wrong in the king's caravan, like a wheel broke on a wagon, or a supply carriage falling off a cliff, they would find no help nearby. They had to supply the king's caravan with skilled workmen to service all his needs. Also, the route chosen had to provide a plentiful supply of water. Food for the entire contingent of people and animals also had to be available as it was needed.

Additionally, the king's servants knew their travel was to be limited to the distance a healthy man could walk during daylight, which was five or six farsangs unless everyone rode in his cavalcade. King Croesus knew that moving his caravan several hundred farsangs took many moon cycles. If, however, he had his entire travelling party mounted in chariots, carriages, camels, donkeys, mules, or horses the distance could be covered in a much shorter time. Moving through mountains the way King Croesus had to travel was not just difficult because of the inhospitable terrain; the distance covered each day was reduced compared to flatland travel. Mountain roads required more time, burned more energy, used more supplies and strained everyone's patience. The journey through gorges or passes could be dangerous because rocks might fall on his travelers. Often there were marauders hiding among the rocks of these places waiting to steal the possessions of richer, more industrious individuals. Nature was an adversary, like severe weather, or predatory animals that robbed his caravan of goats and sheep to make his travel more difficult. His servants had to bring many objects they could barter to get essential consumable provisions needed along the way. A poor man might end such a trek with little more than the animal beneath him and the garments on his back because he consumed or bartered away all his original resources.

When King Croesus chose to travel from Sardes to Ecbatana he undertook the task of travelling about three hundred farsangs, over unforgiving hilly, mountainous trails, with occasional pastures and fertile vistas, but that distance was as the falcon flew, not the wandering path of a man. The entire sojourn, from kingdom to kingdom, would take over three moon cycles. Kings sent messages when they made decisions to visit, not when they began their journey. Therefore, the message from King Croesus telling King Astyages he was coming was at least one moon cycle earlier than the actual departure from Sardes. The time of travel in a royal cavalcade was slower than a commercial caravan because the king's companions required comforts along the way that camel drivers could not even imagine. For these two kings to visit each other required almost an entire sun cycle for the round trip. It was a very important commitment and King Croesus knew he was paying his host a huge compliment.

This time King Croesus chose to be more frugal about his travel. It was more for convenience than expense. He was so rich that cost was never a consideration in any decision he made especially if it involved his family. He did not want to waste unnecessary time on the road so he took only a few wives and concubines. He left his musicians at home this time too. He did take a large contingent of soldiers sufficient to protect himself and the gifts he carried for his sister's royal family, which were unpretentious. This time his gifts were not as splendid as the golden thrones he had brought when Mandane married. That had been his last trip to Ecbatana almost fourteen sun cycles ago.

When King Croesus entered Ecbatana the mood was more subdued than on his last arrival. Previously it was not so much his presence as the wedding of the princess that created the happy atmosphere. Then he only added to the festivities with his pre-arranged pomp. This time people looked, waving as they went about their business. Their lack of enthusiasm reflected the fact that not many of them expected to profit from him on this trip. The lack of excitement for King Croesus in the crowds was more energy conservation than a sign of disrespect. He arrived at the palace with a minimum of fanfare. He passed through the seven gates without complications because the guards had been warned of his coming.

Inside the palace was where all the appropriate exuberance awaited King Croesus. His sister, Queen Aryenis, and Mandane were waiting on the terrace in front of the royal entry to the palace. The entry door was a mammoth structure twenty cubits high. The wood was as thick as a man's foot was long. Bronze hardware with beautifully cast animal decorations secured to the wood sparkled in the sun. The balance of the double doors had been meticulously gauged to open at the push of a small child.

After the emotional greetings outside they entered the palace, and music wafted over them everywhere they went. Flowers brightened every corner and alcove. Princes and princesses were gaily dressed who bowed with elegant grace to the visitor. This is what King Croesus was used to. He was gracious in his acceptance of their homage. King Astyages was expansive in his greeting also. "Welcome, my brother. I have gone to a lot of special trouble just to make you comfortable. I have made very expensive preparations just for you. I hope you're pleased." He thought he could impress the richest man in the world. He could not.

King Croesus almost shouted his greeting when he noticed his sister. He said, "Ah my dear, you get more beautiful every time I see you. Here, I have a small gift for you."

Queen Aryenis said, "Oh it is so grand to have you here. I miss you very much," as she quickly unwrapped his present.

"Oh! It's a gown made of gold thread. It's the most elegant garment I have ever seen!" she exclaimed.

King Croesus knew there was nothing like it in the world. Queen Aryenis was so overcome with surprise and flattery that she promised to wear it every day. Mandane laughed at her mother's glee. Mandane accepted a gold ceremonial sword on behalf of her husband with the dignity of a queen. She was given a superb gold footstool to match her throne in Anshan. Cyrus was given a gold and silver saddle. King Astyages received a gold scepter with a magnificent star sapphire that had come from across the Indus River, far to the east.

The initial days of the visit passed, and King Croesus began to relax. As ceremonial and social banquets slowly tapered off, he asked,

"May I accompany you to your court as you conduct your business, Astyages?"

"Of course, my friend. It will be a great event to have two kings in attendance to stand in judgement of the legal problems of my Empire. As a courtesy I may even ask you opinion, Croesus."

But it was understood that the visitor could not make decisions in the kingdom of another ruler. If he could the richest man in the world might cost his host a small fortune, just to amuse himself.

During one audience when Zav was reporting on the tax and materials status of the kingdom. King Astyages said, "Brother, I have a gift of armaments for you. Zav you are to keep my gift to King Croesus where I told you until he is ready to leave us."

The Great King was referring to a small warehouse that would look filled to make the gift appear larger than it was. It was the Great King's way of pretending he was generous. Appearances were King Astyages' new realities.

King Croesus said, "May I view my gift so I can estimate what I will add to my caravan on the way back to Lydia? I may want to send it ahead before I leave here."

The Lydian king was not tricked by the small building. He recognized the modest scope of this cache of arms. It amused him. In his own kingdom he examined storage sites routinely. Nothing escaped his eye.

As they toured King Croesus said, "Zav, show me your commercial storage buildings."

The visitor quickly spotted which buildings were warehouses by their general outward appearances because there was a lack of imagination among the design engineers and planners of this city. King Croesus pointed to a building and said, "Let's look there."

He did this repeatedly to embarrass Zav because the minister could not refuse. The visiting king picked buildings Zav had emptied for the Susa armaments that never came.

Later in a public audience when Zav was present King Croesus said with royal politeness, "I wish to thank you, Astyages, for your gift."

He then suggested, "Brother-in-law, you need to get out of your palace. Inspect your warehouses. Half of them are empty. That is no way to get rich. You have to develop better plans to keep

343

merchandise, grains and valuable spices coming in and going out at a regular pace."

"Oh?" exclaimed King Astyages, looking with an angry glare at Zav for embarrassing him. "Have you spotted a weakness in our commerce?"

"Worse than a weakness. I will have to speak with you and that man," pointing to Zav, "and teach you how to run your business better. Empty warehouses are one thing, but not having a plan to refill them is a crime."

King Croesus had already demanded to review records of material receipts, exchanges and shipments, he easily spotted where Zav was stealing. He said nothing in front of Zav but when the family was alone King Croesus said, "Astyages, I examined records of your tax minister. He is stealing from you very blatantly. He steals supplies, sells them and keeps the proceeds. I realize all ministers steal a bit. I allow it myself, but your man is greedy. You need to watch him."

Cyrus listened with fixed intensity concerned about Zav's dishonesty. King Astyages did not listen. The feature that frustrated King Croesus most about his brother-in-law was the way Media depended on taxes and tributes from its subject nations. Astyages did not encourage minor kingdoms to enhance local wealth, as well as empire wealth, with hard work and the development of profitable commerce. King Croesus told King Astyages, "You need to make profit for your princes and merchants a significant facet of how you conduct your business. Change your philosophy, Astyages. Don't get your royal wealth exclusively from tribute burdens from your citizens."

King Astyages refused to listen or change his established method of operating. He said, "Ah, Croesus, you are in an unusual position. You make profits while we do all the work. There is nothing for me to change."

What King Astyages was really saying was the suggestion would require too much effort. Empty warehouses may be embarrassing, but the King of Kings was willing to forget this minor humiliation.

After King Croesus had viewed his gift King Astyages asked, "Harpagus, do you have military recommendations to give King Croesus about his island wars?

Harpagus answered, "No, sire. I have never participated in a naval battle or even seen a war ship. King Croesus, are there materials besides those in your gift that would be beneficial to your efforts?"

King Croesus eyed this soldier, liking his thoughtful answer. The king answered, "I could use straight timber for masts and oars. The catapults in my generous gift from Media are too heavy for my ships. Such large equipment will slow down our sailing speed."

King Croesus smiled at King Astyages and said, "It will be easy for my ship builders to reduce the excessive size of your giant slingshots. I will be able to put the cut-away materials to other uses. Nothing will be wasted. Your gift is more generous than you imagine."

One day in the audience chamber King Astyages decided to put Cyrus on the spot. He liked to amuse himself by embarrassing others. He believed without question that the best way to look good was to insult others. His ego kept him from understanding that making others look valuable was a more suitable way to increase his own image.

In the presence of Mandane, King Croesus and his entire court King Astyages asked, "Cyrus, who is the greatest king, your father, King Croesus or me?"

It was a tricky question but Cyrus said, "Sire, my father is the greatest king in Pars, King Croesus is the greatest king in Lydia and you are the greatest king in Media."

Croesus laughed because he knew King Astyages had just been beaten at his own game. "You have a prince in your family who is ready to be a king, Astyages. You should make him a regent. Give him a kingdom!"

King Astyages felt his own joke had gone wrong, but since it involved Cyrus he accepted it. He said, "Yes, you are right. He is clever enough to rule somewhere. Bow Prince Cyrus. Since you came to us out of Arbela I make you regent of Arbela and my farms there."

It was all done in good humor, but in fact Cyrus now was responsible for Arbela and the farm of Mitridates. He did not realize that he was also going to face the knavery of Rusundatu some day.

Cyrus sat in the audience chamber every day and became more impressed with how King Croesus thought. He liked the active, energetic approach the king took toward everything that came up. Cyrus was able to contrast this with his grandfather's sedate, erratic approach to all issues. The prince could not help wishing he could spend time alone with this dynamic man to talk in greater detail about his way of developing trade. This foreign king had much to say that could help Pars.

One day King Croesus said, "You should think of doing what I am trying to do, Astyages. I am expanding the use of metals as a monetary system. It is my belief that more men could involve themselves in productive commerce if they only needed small, metal coins for conducting transactions. They could store tiny stacks of metal away safely without being threatened with the loss of wealth by storms or floods, by drought or fires."

King Astyages smiled dismissively without saying anything. King Croesus said, "It is a concept I have been developing for a long time. The major problem with my idea is getting more people to agree on a standard value for gold and silver."

He said as he laughed, "I am having trouble assigning agreeable worth to a specific weight of silver. Rather than use a small lump of silver or gold to pay for a herd of sheep, men prefer to drive herds across dangerous terrain to sell, or accept fist-sized tokens, shaped like an Egyptian pyramid. They still think gold and silver are only supposed to be decorations."

"Why do you fatigue yourself with such silly ideas, Croesus?" asked Astyages.

Cyrus was intrigued by what the king was saying. He did not comprehend the full meaning of it all, because he had never transacted a large barter exchange. He did understand the fundamental idea of bartering however, and this gave him a slight insight into what King Croesus was suggesting.

Cyrus decided to make a small simple coin for himself. He would make it symbolize his promise in an agreement. It would not be a souvenir for people to remember him. When he gave it to someone, it was to identify his agreement of a binding contract. Cyrus believed this was at least some of what King Croesus was suggesting. Cyrus visited several metal craftsmen until he found one who made jewelry. This man had molds of all shapes and sizes. He was a proficient artisan who handled gold and silver with skill. Cyrus was in no hurry so he began visiting the shop to watch the man cast and engrave the jewelry he sold. Finally, Cyrus decided that the man's cleaver designs were exceptional. This craftsman could design any figure in metal. After careful thought Cyrus said the man, "I would like you to make me a coin with my profile on one side to establish the identity of the coin. On the other side you are to engrave the sacred flame."

In his mind these two symbols represented the sacredness of his word and his dependence on trust.

"I wish the coin to be thin and square. Can you do that?" he asked.

"Easily, prince, but I have never been asked to do such a thing before. I have never heard of anyone wanting a square coin."

Cyrus had never seen a square coin that's why he wanted one. King Croesus had shown them only circular coins. Cyrus was pleased because now he had a symbol of his word that did not have to be recorded by a magus. No matter where he happened to be he could make an honest verbal agreement with anyone, even a peasant, by rendering his metal square.

Cyrus showed his mother his new treasure and said, "With these coins, Mother, I can make agreements with any man, anywhere, as a bond of honor."

Mandane was a little confused and asked, "But, son, why would such a thing be necessary?"

Cyrus said, "I will not always have a magus to write for me. If I am in the mountains obligated to commit myself to a contract these coins will be my promise."

The queen was a little confused by what he was saying. She wanted to encourage him so she just smiled. The ideas he was explaining were unfamiliar to her. If she said too much she knew she might spoil her son's enthusiasm. She chose not to mention the coins to Cambyses in her regular messages to Anshan. She did not want to make a mistake of misrepresenting their meaning to her husband.

Mandane was having a very enjoyable time here with her son and mother. They spent much time together and Mandane was pleased to see her mother take pride in Cyrus. He enjoyed telling his grandmother about his activities each day. He did not embellish his role in any important event. He just stated in factual language the part he played. His mother and grandmother did the exaggerating for him. Mandane could not tell King Cambyses often enough how much she missed him. Occasionally she allowed her language to get a bit lewd when she was feeling womanly. The scribe magi never reacted to her words, and she never blushed at her thoughts in front of them. To her scribes were fixtures rather than people. They were not much more than their clay tablets or lambskins. Mandane thought of the scribes as tools that prepared her thoughts for a trip over the mountains to her lover.

She was enjoying her uncle, King Croesus. In one meeting King Croesus said, "Mandane, your Cyrus is a very intelligent boy. I am happy to see a boy so young, so ready to be a royal adult when he becomes fifteen. Your son reminds me of my own two sons. They are exceptional youths too. One will be a great scholar and the other is going to be an accomplished warrior."

He made his boys sound so magnificent Mandane hoped Cyrus developed so well. King Croesus said, "Mandane, I encourage you to let Cyrus use his imagination during his training toward manhood. He shows signs of being like his father, a man I respect very much."

King Croesus was very impressed with Cambyses even though their contact had been minimal.

The king continued, "Cyrus is deliberate like his father. I have always liked the quiet, thoughtful approach to things that Cambyses exhibits. If it were not for the Great King, your husband would be a far more important man in the world."

When Cyrus heard this statement it made him proud of his father and of Pars. Mandane considered this a compliment to her husband, but for her it was not a family compliment. It sounded to her like an insult to her father. Within a family saying such things were touchy, especially within a royal family where wars could foment.

After a few moon cycles, King Croesus decided to return home. King Astyages found him tiring after a while. Queen Aryenis found him loving and as solicitous as ever. Mandane found his affection a comfort and Cyrus found him inspirational. Zav found him threatening.

42.

Zav profited by dealing with Rusundatu without putting himself in direct physical danger. He was content with this arrangement. No one could connect him with the crimes the peasants committed in the west unless the thieves revealed his complicity, which was unlikely. It was a near-perfect arrangement for him because even if they did, he could simply deny it and ask if the word of the King's minister was more valuable than a criminal's word.

While he was in Ecbatana King Croesus had come close to getting Zav in serious trouble with King Astyages. Croesus enjoyed visiting the markets and storage areas and reading the records of commercial transactions Zav was foolish enough to show him. The hawkeyed King Croesus easily saw where Zav had been taking illegal profits, but the indolence of the Great King saved Zav from losing a limb or his life. Zav now knew he had to modify his accounting procedures by finding a more furtive way to take his profit from the government without leaving such clear evidence. For now he just needed to get a secret message to Rusundatu about the next caravan to be attacked.

Rusundatu was a rich man. He had secretly stolen his first farm from a man who had not understood how to record his deed with the correct legal processing. The thief continued to accumulate farm properties with assets he got from attacking caravans and with goods he stole from his colleague, Mitridates. The latter robbery was philosophically satisfying to Rusundatu because he stole from a fellow thief, which did not constitute a real crime. To Rusundatu it was comical satire.

No prince or king owned the lands immediately adjacent to Rusundatu's farm so he negotiated to buy properties nearby to expand his holdings. His farm now supported sheep, oxen, cattle, camels, horses, goats and various kinds of fowl. He had planted orchards and planted vast expanses of pastureland with vegetables. He was a farm laborer by birth, but made himself an important man in Arbela. He began thinking seriously of replacing his illegal occupation of robbing caravans with a political position instead. Getting a nobleman in Arbela to assign him an administrative post might let him steal from public supply sources.

Zav said to Rusundatu, "Avoid robbing the great caravan of King Croesus leaving Ecbatana on its way back to Sardes; too many soldiers are guarding it. The one behind it is more suitable."

Rusundatu sent his slave to round up the men who helped with the caravan assaults. The farmer always gave them a decent cut of the booty to induce them to come back. The biggest concern Rusundatu had was with Mitridates because that man knew the value of goods better than the others did. Somehow Mitridates seemed to end up with more precious trinkets than the rest, but Rusundatu was not overly concerned as he took the greatest quantity every time trying to ignore the extra edge the Greek was able to finesse.

As they sat in their hiding places waiting for the camels to bring tonight's loot to them, Rusundatu was thinking that he should begin speaking with the Great King's family in Arbela about an appointment before stopping his association with this gang. It would be better to have a government position established before giving up such a lucrative avocation. Sitting here waiting to commit a crime made him feel cold. He was also dirty and feeling a little threatened by the risk of injury during the attack. Rusundatu was convinced he had to give this up soon.

The jingle of bells and grunt of camels made him peer harder into the darkening evening air to see his target. The camel drivers were mumbling together about stopping to camp soon; he wanted to hit them while they were still riding and logy. It was safer. He signaled his raiders to be alert. He did not see any armed guards accompanying the small caravan. The attack began in the usual fashion. The front and back of the train were sealed off so there was no escape. Arrows were shot over the heads of the riders until much shouting and whistling created confused chaos. Mitridates appeared from his safe hiding place to examine items as his fellow bandits opened crude wraps that held what they might steal. The camel drivers were searched. Usually the most valuable materials, like jewels, gold and silver were hidden on the person of the driver.

Mitridates was standing beside Rusundatu, holding a large sack of gems, while Rusundatu was searching a camel driver for loot when they heard the hammering of horse hooves on the road and yelling of a military guard. The troop of bandits was horrified. They all began to run to their mounts to escape. Mitridates pulled at Rusundatu leading him behind a rock into a small cluster of trees. Instead of making themselves running targets they became still shadows. Mitridates hid the gems inside his garments. If they escaped he could tell Rusundatu he had became frightened by the charging soldiers and dropped them.

Swords flashed in the setting sunlight. Screaming and shouting were all around the two hiding men. Mitridates knew how to disappear in the midst of close danger. He had escaped angry boars and charging bulls by stealth before. He held tight to his companion whom he did not trust to remain still.

Eventually, the mayhem was over and the caravan leader slowly moved on to find a suitable camping site. The military had killed several of the marauders. The wounded escaped. There were no prisoners. Mitridates and Rusundatu looked about and found one camel they could share. Rusundatu asked, "What did you save from the caravan, Mitridates?"

The farmer said, "Nothing. I lost it all when the soldiers appeared. I have never been so afraid for my life before. I am going to give this up. Do not call on me again."

Rusundatu said, as he feigned being solemn, "So many of our dear friends were killed that I doubt we will be able to continue anyway. Yes, this is the end. I will find some other way to get by, besides running my farms. We have nothing to give Zav. He will be annoyed when I tell him we are finished."

On the way home Mitridates resolved to give up his life of crime and the packet of jewels he concealed was his last robbery cache.

//

In the capital city of Media Zav needed some way to ingratiate himself with the Great King. Zav needed to come up with a new drama to make himself look valuable, before the King accused him of being useless. Attacking was the King's way of keeping his ministers off balance. Zav took them as personal affronts. His ego could hardly stand the King's insults but he had to tolerate them. Zav picked the ruination of the salt desert trade route as his new project to sell to the Great King. Zav studied shipping records from the east to describe in detail how the caravan shift to the south over the salt desert had hurt the trade in Ecbatana by reducing its volume. He would ask the Great

King to send a military force there to close that path. He memorized facts, figures and made up what he could not find. He developed a sound argument. His intent was to force the trade of Bactria back to Ecbatana. Additionally, his hatred of King Cambyses would be satisfied when profitable caravans stopped traveling into Anshan from the east. Zav was angry about the message from Rusundatu and even angrier at not knowing Harpagus had sent a guard behind that caravan. The soldier's sneaky move had put an end to the minister's near-perfect scheme.

Zav noted that King Astyages was allowing the boy Cyrus to take increased participation in the daily audience court. To Zav it was becoming obvious that the boy had intelligence. He wondered if Cyrus knew of the salt desert route or its significance in trade control.

"Sire," began Zav, "I have been examining certain records because of the astute comments of your brother-in-law, King Croesus. I have detected a disturbing trend that explains our empty warehouses. The movement of merchandise from the east to Ecbatana has reduced significantly. I believe King Arsames of Bactria is sending King Cambyses cargoes by a new route across the salt desert to avoid us. We are unable to collect taxes or profits from this trade."

He stopped for a moment to let that sink in. He did not want to rush his presentation. These discussions worked best when the Great King came to a desired conclusion, believing it was his own idea. Then the King would demand action no one could refuse. Zav continued giving numerical data of changes in volume of grains, hides, gems, gold and silver that no longer moved from east to west through the capital. He made the numbers sound enormous. Cyrus listened intently. He was familiar with this salt desert route. He had listened to Pattmenidu talk to his father about it on several occasions. Before leaving Anshan his father had made a point of tutoring Cyrus about it. The prince decided it was his duty to help his grandfather understand the nature of this trade route so the King could evaluate Zav's arguments with greater rationality.

"Sire," the prince said aloud, "that salt desert route is not as large as Zav indicates," as Zav began to fume at another interference by this pup.

"The only items father ever talked about from that source were sugar, tea, a little silk and bronze hardware," Cyrus continued.

"Sire," erupted Zav, "it is much more. Much more! We are losing vast sums because of that trade path. It is imperative that you send troops to seal it off and force the caravans into Ecbatana like before."

"Harpagus, what do you think?" asked the King.

From his middle-of-the-room vantagepoint the soldier said, "Sire, the army is not accustomed to controlling trade. We do use the army to protect trade, but I have not heard anyone here say that bandits are involved. Are we to waste our time directing traffic in the desert with our army?"

He made Zav's suggestion sound foolish. Cyrus asked in his innocence, "Sire, is it reasonable for you to ask my father to send his merchant Pattmenidu here to report on the salt route trade? Pattmenidu will give a complete and honest rendering, I am sure."

The King thought for a while and decided the whole business was just so much inconvenience. The King of Kings said, "Zav, this business is a trifle. Tell me of the problems we are having with Babylon."

This change of subject drew no conclusion about the salt desert route; Cyrus had not won but neither had Zav. The King just moved on to a new topic, as was his privilege.

The next day Cyrus prepared to visit Mitridates and Spaco. It had taken quite a while to get the Great King to authorize him more liberal movement than just close walks outside the palace. Now that he had a regency Cyrus was free to go where he wished; he could travel to Arbela to present his father's gift to his foster parents.

"Harpagus, I wish to go to the Arbela area. I would like you to have guards attend me when I travel there."

"Well, Prince, since you are the regent of that area now we trust you will inspect it on a regular basis like other princes have. Of course I will protect you," said Harpagus.

"Harpagus," said Cyrus, "you had something to do with delivering me to that farm in Arbela originally. My father believes there was some mystery about the events. I would like you to tell me what you know some day."

"Prince, the only facts I can give you are the ones the Great King told when we discovered you alive. I have nothing more to say."

Harpagus looked at the boy thinking of his own son. He had not seen his own boy since the day his child entered the palace. He had not even heard stories of his son. Harpagus wondered what had become of his boy. Harpagus had once asked Cyrus if he had met his son after the prince had been in the palace for a long time. The prince had not met the child. For some reason the Great King had the soldier's son hidden away. Harpagus hoped his son was well and happy.

Cyrus dropped the topic of how he was hidden on the farm. It was obvious that this perfectly controlled man was not going to reveal any new information. When Cyrus arrived at the farm in Arbela it was a surprise to his foster parents. He acted like an investigating prince reviewing the King's property. His air of authority mystified Mitridates and Spaco. He did not act like the boy they had raised and loved. His sharp questions about various aspects of the products produced were easy for Mitridates to answer, who responded with the same formality he used with older noblemen. Finally, Cyrus burst into laughter, hugged them both and made fun of his own behavior. He had put them so much on edge with his arrogance it took a while for them to relax.

"I am regent of Arbela now and of this farm," Cyrus said.

"Oh what happy news, Paithi...err, Prince," said Spaco.

"Yes, I will be obliged to come this way to visit you periodically. And call me Cyrus, mother."

This made Mitridates both happy and sad. He would love to see Cyrus frequently, however, he and Spaco knew they were going to leave as soon as they could afford to go. Mitridates would escape from service to the Great King of Media. In Lydia no one would bother to find him to send him back to King Astyages. All the couple had to do was slip away from Media safely, but now they also saw themselves deserting their son who might have the responsibility to search for them. Mitridates thought the gods were far meaner than necessary at times.

Cyrus and his stepfather walked over the farm engaging in easy conversation. Cyrus asked, "How are the slaves?"

"Fine, we have added new ones, sent to us by the Great King just as he promised."

Cyrus felt a twinge of pride for his grandfather and asked, "And the gardens, are they yielding as much as they used to?"

"More. With the extra help we were able to plant more trees."

Their conversation was casual, and they laughed at old experiences they had shared. Mitridates was pleased his son had not forgotten a single detail about the farm while the prince appreciated that the continued efficiency of the operation was a credit to Mitridates and his management. Cyrus entertained the slaves with stories of Ecbatana and the palace. He encouraged them to ask questions. He was having fun with his old friends. The slaves laughed at humorous stories he made up for them that were part fact, part fable. He made certain his exaggerations were so outlandish that they were beyond being lies. His descriptions of the palace, the rooms, the gardens and the meals the royal family ate were beyond the ability of the slaves to comprehend. The lives of the slaves were frugal and simple; he spoke of exotic objects they had never seen, nor would ever see. For instance, the elaborate sconces burning olive oil that lit corridors and rooms in the palace with their fancy designs were completely different from the simple cups of oil the slaves used.

It was impossible for these slaves to envision the images Cyrus described. The prince said, "When the Great King burns oil in his palace at night the dark is chased away by the glow of the lamps. His rooms shine like the day when he has banquets and parties."

"So much oil!" one slave said.

The slaves lived in shadows and darkness after the sun went down. It saved oil. After dusk was also when they rested, slept and released the aches of a hard day's work. The dark of night was not the time for them to sing or celebrate. Cyrus' words added new enchantment in their minds about the Great King and his life.

Mitridates had often explained to the slaves what the city looked like. How large the crowds were. Cyrus talked of the pictures on the buildings that identified what the structures were used for. The prince said, "There are seven walls that surround the Great King's palace, and on the outside wall I have watched a stone mason make a carving on a specially built white-stone section. It is where all the people who pass can see it. The images of the Great King and my father, the king of Pars, are on that wall. My father is as handsome in the picture as King Astyages is."

Cyrus was delighted when their eyes lit up at the suggested majesty of his father.

"There is the bull of Media and the lion of Pars in plain sight too," the prince said.

"Is the lion alive?" asked a small boy.

"No. It is carved on the wall," laughed Cyrus.

He told them about Oebares and embellished the importance of the slave's responsibility to keep the stonecutter working. They were encouraged that a slave could oversee the work of an expert stone worker and keep him busy at his assigned task. That was certainly different from their responsibilities.

The slaves could not help noticing that everywhere Cyrus went his guards went with him. It did not intimidate them, but it gave them a new respect for their friend. He was so important now that other men protected him with their lives. The slaves were proud to be able to talk to the prince so intimately under such circumstances.

In the house Spaco prepared Cyrus' favorite meal. This was a special night so Mitridates lit extra lamps. Cyrus' guards camped outside in the dark. After supper Cyrus went to the door to tell a soldier, "Bring me the bundle on my horse."

The man placed it on the table indicated by the prince and left. Cyrus looked at Spaco and said, "Open the bundle with care, mother."

She was nervous because she was not used to receiving gifts. On top was a rose colored toga with violet embroidery. She squealed and ran to hug Cyrus. He laughed at her antics as she held it in front of her dancing in circles.

Spaco said, "This is far too beautiful for me to wear on this farm. Maybe I will find a special place to wear it someday," then she blushed at the thought of their plans to escape. She was too cautious to say that she would wear this garment in Sardes.

There more personal gifts for both of his foster parents. They were very grateful for his thoughtfulness. Finally, he reached into his pack and pulled out another bundle. He placed it before Mitridates and said, "My father appreciates all that you did for me when I was living here. He wishes you to have this. It will keep you rich for the rest of your life."

Mitridates tentatively opened the bundle and out fell tokens and gems. He jumped back to stare. It was like a king's ransom. He picked up one token he knew was worth one hundred cattle. That was all the wealth any man could want, and it was only a portion of what was there. He began to cry. Spaco sobbed. Cyrus said, "You have been good parents to me. You have spent your lives as honest farmers. Now you can live in comfort."

The farmers both sobbed as they said, "Thank you, son. We do not deserve what you have given us."

"You can build a larger home near here and buy slaves to serve your own needs," said Cyrus, which made the farmer and his wife cry even harder.

Mitridates thought of his crimes, and was admonished by the boy's innocence. His foster-son did not know anything about that part of his life. Mitridates' conscience almost made him confess, but he held his tongue. He made up his mind that as soon as Cyrus left them he and Spaco would leave for Lydia. The time Cyrus took to return to the palace was going to help get them just that much farther away. Mitridates intended to send a message to Cyrus later in Anshan to apologize for abandoning him.

In bed that night Mitridates said to Spaco, "Make your final farewell with Cyrus tomorrow, dear, but be careful of what you say. We must leave for Sardes as soon as he leaves us in the morning. We have the rest of our lives in that bundle. We are rich!"

Confused with happiness and sadness she sobbed herself to sleep.

Their parting was touching. Cyrus talked as if meeting again was inevitable. They had trouble letting him go from their arms. After Cyrus was out of sight Mitridates decided that taking one camel from the King was not stealing. He thought of taking horses that could travel faster, but he decided he preferred a camel the more he thought about the terrain that they had to traverse. The uncertainty of both his route and available water made the camel the better choice. They would stop less often with a camel. Mitridates decided that taking the animal was his bonus from the Great King, his reward for the improvements he had made on the farm. The runaways were lucky to intercept a caravan going west. Mitridates was happy to pay the asking fee to join its protection. They arrived in Sardes dirty, tired and rich.

43.

"Alright, you may go to Ecbatana. I will tell King Cambyses I have allowed it," said Prince Warohi.

"He will not care as long as I do not go back to Anshan."

Prince Warohi finally gave in to Princess Ispitamu. He was tired of her constant glares as well as her snide remarks about his manhood. She castigated his city management skills. She did not intimidate him. She just wore him down. The princess had no plan of action other than to see Zav when she arrived. She was going to need new poisons she could administer furtively to Mandane in the Ecbatana palace. The princess speculated about killing Cyrus with the substances the minister might acquire for her. She was just not convinced she could do that, but she intended to be alert to the opportunity if it arose.

When she arrived at the palace the princess made her first stop the chambers of Mandane. She needed to re-establish her old familiarity with the queen. Mandane saw Princess Ispitamu and her heart skipped a beat as she said, "Ah Ispitamu, welcome."

The queen looked about the room to make certain there were plenty of women about. She was not sure she wanted to be alone with this princess she greeted with a cautious smile. The princess noted the large crowd of children and women in the queen's suite.

"My, are you ever alone these days? Can we ever have a cozy chat together like we used to?" she asked.

"Probably later," the queen said. "I so enjoy the children and these women have been my friends all my life. You must get to know them also."

The princess bit her lip to remain patient. Becoming acquainted with these women and their offspring was not the reason she was here. She planned to visit Zav the next day.

In the palace Princess Ispitamu was talking with Zav in private while they had lunch. She had not heard from him in a long time. She wondered what lethal materials he might be able to get for her. She said, "Zav, I can get the chest pain poison myself in the gardens, but the bush that prevents pregnancies has to come from you. I have thought of poisoning Prince Cyrus with the oleander or some other substance if you have a suggestion."

"The silphium is here. I can give you a new supply of it, but since the prince exists new pregnancies seem unimportant. I will talk to a magus about different poisons if you think you can give it to the boy without getting caught," Zav volunteered.

They talked about that possibility. Zav was trying to avoid admitting his disinterest to Princess Ispitamu about her efforts to make the queen sterile. Killing the prince was more to his liking. There was a time when he thought he could have the prince killed, but now the boy was so well protected it was impossible to plan such a feat. The princess complained, "Prince Warohi is so aggravating. He keeps me a prisoner in Susa, and if it were not for your ideas, Zav, I would die of boredom."

Zav felt she was becoming too much of a liability. Her moods were unpredictable. In spite of her beauty, he felt he must stop seeing her. He tried to smile and commiserate about the grievances she made sound so petty. He decided that he needed a new ally because this one had lost both her effectiveness and her enthusiasm. She was nearly useless in Susa, and she admitted she could never go back to Anshan where it was possible to feed poisons to the queen in her home. Zav came close to asking Princess Ispitamu to leave. Her royal rank prevented him from being so insulting; she could cause trouble for him if he was not careful. He took a deep breath and let her rave on.

Finally he lied and said, "You will not be able to prevent Mandane's pregnancies using silphium in the future because I can no longer get it for you; the Cyrene plant is no longer allowed to leave that country, per a decree of its king. What I have on-hand is the last of it. Besides, living in Susa has its drawbacks, no?"

The princess screamed, "Ah, everything has gone wrong for me. I've had trouble seeing Queen Mandane alone, but you're right!"

In a fit of anger she left him; he was much happier than she realized.

Elsewhere in the palace Cyrus was busy with his royal education. He was no longer able came to Mandane's rooms often. The Great King had ordered Harpagus to take personal charge of Cyrus' military training, horse riding and archery. It was a task the soldier appreciated and he kept the prince busy for long hours each day. Cyrus was hard working yet pleasant. Harpagus wondered if his own son might have a personality like this prince. The soldier had been disappointed that he never heard a word about his own son from anyone in the palace, and he regretted his past deceptions to the Great King. The officer decided King Astyages was just showing him how powerful the King could be as well as how stupid it was for a soldier to disobey orders. Thinking of his own son left him with a hollow feeling deep inside.

At home his wife had never recovered from the shock of losing her son. She held it against Harpagus but she refused to talk to him about it; she resented her husband's right to be free when her son was a prisoner for something he had never been a party to. For a long time she had ceased being a loving wife to Harpagus so he began seeing other women for comfort. Gradually she relented, and they reestablished a degree of family togetherness that never quite returned to the intimate life they once had. His most cherished comfort now came from his military duties. Harpagus said to Cyrus, "By Median standards I am considered an expert shot with the bow from a horse or from a chariot."

Cyrus observed how Harpagus hit targets with great consistency from the fast moving chariot the prince drove. Cyrus said, "Am I driving too fast for you, sir?"

"No, but keep a steady line as you drive so I have time to aim well. I will let you know when I am ready for you to change direction," Harpagus advised.

Cyrus learned the responsibility of driving carefully while another man launched arrows, lances or axes from a chariot. Harpagus drove later. As Cyrus prepared his bow he began to understand not only the importance of shooting but also the true value of careful control of the horses. Harpagus was very skilled at watching the archer and horses at the same time. Cyrus said, "You drove well, but I missed. Please turn so I can try again."

Harpagus was encouraged at the intensity of the boy's concentration. He advised, "Prince Cyrus, relax. Pretend you are playing when you shoot. Keep your grip relaxed but firm. Allow your arms to pull with a strong smooth draw."

"Why do I get more accurate when I don't try so hard?" the prince asked as his shooting got better.

"You are relaxing your muscles. The reduced tension places more control in the muscles you really need for aiming," Harpagus said. "I noticed also that you are using a stronger bow. Relaxing is helping you to pull smoother."

Cyrus continued to make good progress with archery. Harpagus also had the prince using heavier pieces of metal attached to sticks when they practiced hand to hand combat. The extra weight tired the prince's arms, but it only made him try harder. Harpagus knew when to call a halt so Cyrus did not hurt himself or get discouraged. The prince had a vital intensity that the soldier appreciated.

One day Oebares was outside the palace in the shade, half-asleep, when Cyrus crept up on him and placed his two eunuchs in front of the slave. Then Cyrus gave an order in his most commanding voice, "Beat him for his laziness!"

Oebares jerked awake and could only see two mountains of flesh standing before him. His eyes popped. He froze in horror. Cyrus laughed as he waved the eunuchs away. When Oebares got control of his breath and stopped trembling they laughed together. Finally, Cyrus said, "The mason makes good progress. I hope he does not make a mistake now. My grandfather will probably kill him if he has to start over. Grandfather has told his whole court to come out here to see his image. He has not seen it himself but he likes people to tell him how majestic he looks on this wall."

Oebares said, "Prince, I wish your grandfather was as noble as that picture. If I were a mason I would give him the eyes of a snake."

This criticism annoyed Cyrus. He did not appreciate anyone making fun of the Great King. Cyrus decided to change the subject and he said, "Oebares, I went to Arbela and visited the farm I grew up on. I spoke with the slaves there I used to play with." The prince described his visit, leaving out any mention of the gifts. Oebares felt comfortable with Cyrus, and their conversation took on the simple expressions exchanged by friends. Eventually the slave returned to his favorite topic. He said, "I resent the King's decree which makes men slaves for life. I have lost my dream of freedom, and my life tomorrow will have to be exactly like today. Your friends in Arbela have no reason to work hard anymore since efficient labor will never set them free. We slaves cannot expect to be rewarded with freedom for hard work anymore. I never work hard, prince. I do far less then I used to. I watch the mason, but I did not report him to my magistrate when the stonecutter stops his work."

Cyrus noted that Oebares had changed. His attitude was calloused. Cyrus missed the old Oebares who used to care about life. Nothing the prince said changed the slave's demeanor. Cyrus promised, "I will free you some day."

Oebares smirked. The prince said, "I do not know how or when but someday it will happen, I promise."

Cyrus got up and went to the King's audience chamber to listen to the various requests for the Great King's judgement regarding contract complaints. One feature Cyrus did not appreciate was the lack of consistency in the decisions made by his grandfather. It was always a mystery how a final decree might end up in his court. The King, more often than he should, decided an issue based on favoritism or on his dislike for a man's garments or the shape of his beard, which upset Cyrus. If the King told his audience the color of a man's cloak was abhorrent to him the poor complainant knew he had lost his argument. As rumors spread of the King's follies, men tried to guess which colors were most acceptable or which fashions were the best to wear. Cyrus worried that the erratic nature of his grandfather's temperament made a mockery of his regal decrees. The Great King was seldom drunk during the audience sessions, but when he was Cyrus knew the audience always ended in disaster because some poor creature was bound to end up maimed or dead.

Cyrus learned when to keep his mouth closed. He moved as little as possible when the King was drunk. The prince drew a minimum of attention to himself. His grandfather might love him when sober, but the boy knew he too was in jeopardy of losing a limb due to the homa or wine his grandfather drank. Cyrus would rather die in war than die because of a glass-of-nonsense quaffed by a powerful man who should know better. Cyrus felt his respect for his grandfather slowly slipping away, but he had not yet developed the acute disrespect Oebares had. The Great King was still the most powerful man the prince knew, and most days the King's control of his empire was impeccable. The King of Kings had competent men supporting and advising him. When the King lost control of himself Cyrus was beginning to think of his grandfather as a fallible man who made more mistakes than he should make. There was one unfortunate aspect of the Great King that Cyrus did not understand. When King Astyages made an error he never admitted it; he seldom rescinded an unfair act. A man in Pars would be honorable enough to make amends. Cyrus hated to see his grandfather oblivious to such decency.

King Astyages truly upset Cyrus after his return from Arbela. The Great King heard that Cyrus' foster parents were missing. At first the King's reaction was laudable. He demanded, "Harpagus, take a prince with you to see if they are injured or even dead in the forest."

The prince who had gone reported, "Sire, we inspected the entire property but found no trace of the couple. I took an accounting of the livestock. I suspect the farmers may have stolen a camel or two, but I'm not positive. I questioned the slaves. They claimed that every time Mitridates left the farm he told them. This was the first time the farmer did not, and the slaves fear for his safety."

"Harpagus, hunt them down. They must be going west. That is where they came from. Bring them back alive!" the King demanded. "Cyrus, you will watch them die. It is time you learned about obedience."

Cyrus was stunned. He dared not say anything, but he prayed to the ahura gods of Pars for the Greeks to remain safe, wherever they were.

Harpagus had no stomach for this task. He obeyed by travelling slow without being too obvious about deliberately delaying his search. He ordered his guards to inquire about a man and woman who might be travelling alone together at every village they came to just to slow their progress along the west to east trade route. Harpagus knew it was futile to ask strangers such a question. No one paid attention to people in a caravan. A man and a woman would blend into the mass of animals and cargo like unseen spirits.

Harpagus returned and said, "I was unable to find the farmer and his wife, sire. We searched all the way to the Halys River at the edge of your empire."

King Astyages did not let the matter drop. Cyrus wondered what it was about his foster parents that upset the King so much. King Astyages spoke to his scribe magus and said, "I believe they are returning to Lydia. Send a message to King Croesus. Tell him I demand the return of the disloyal farmers he gave me. Tell him I intend to execute his gift."

Cyrus thought this was just petty revenge. His grandfather's attitude bothered him very much. No one ever saw Mitridates and

Spaco in Media again because the King of Lydia ignored his brother-in-law's demand. He was pleased that a rich, well-trained farmer had returned.

//

Mandane refused to see Princess Ispitamu alone because she was not sure if the princess could be trusted. The queen also thought her friend should get to know the children and princesses that spent their time in Mandane's rooms, but the queen's friends began to aggravate the princess. She had little fits of temper that surprised Mandane. The queen came close to refusing to allow Princess Ispitamu into her royal suite; instead she decided to try to pay more attention to the princess by talking to her more in the presence of others. This just seemed to make matters worse.

Princess Ispitamu's behavior became aggressive; she argued with everyone. The princess prepared her oleander poison to administer to Mandane but waited patiently. The princess did not want to take the chance of making another mistake like last time. She knew the precise way to administer an effective dose of the oleander; all she wanted to do was make Mandane suffer a bit and she prayed to the gods for the opportunity to perform her malevolence. The gods did not heed her cry.

Eventually Princess Ispitamu became so plagued by frustrated hate that she created a violent scene the queen could not ignore. While having a snack in Mandane's rooms the princess spilled yogurt on herself. Immediately she turned to a servant and shouted, "You clumsy fool. You spilled yogurt on my dress. You sloppy hag!"

The queen had seen what occurred and said, "Ispitamu, the girl did not cause that. You did it yourself."

Princess Ispitamu threw the dish of yogurt at the servant and began hitting her. Mandane looked to her eunuchs and called, "Come here and stop this fighting. Remove the princess from my presence."

Mandane's eunuchs were obligated to carry the screaming Princess Ispitamu away to remove her from her victim. The next day instead of letting the princess in to apologize, Mandane ordered her out of the palace. Once again Princess Ispitamu was banished in shame. Her hatred now escalated to where her only pleasure came from thinking of Mandane's death.

The King asked, "Mandane, why did you send Princess Ispitamu away? She was a beautiful woman, and I think she should be here for me to enjoy."

The Great King liked having beautiful women about him. He believed they complemented his virility. He asked this question in a public audience but Mandane was reluctant to make the princess look bad in this setting.

"I demand an answer!"

"There was a disagreement in the *andarun* and the princess got confused," said Mandane. "I think she was tired and lonely for her home. I decided it was best for her to leave."

That was a feeble answer but the best she could muster. The King did not look pleased. If Mandane had been anyone else the King would have pressed the point by using torture if necessary to find out why a lovely princess was removed from his court.

"Do not send anyone else from my kingdom without my approval. Understand?" shouted the King to his daughter and his audience.

Mandane gave a silent nod. Cyrus stifled the urge to defend his mother.

On another occasion the King's actions continued to undermine the confidence Cyrus had in him. It was an act of complete religious intolerance that shocked everyone.

Cyrus knew that in Pars people believed in the gods and prayed. They offered animal and human sacrifices for special occasions, and many times the prince had seen the magi use a flat rock or a constructed altar to make the offerings, out in the open on a high hill. Cyrus had never entered a temple in Media because in Pars they did not have temples of worship. Everyone worshiped in their homes or at the altars, but in Media they attended temples. The Chief Magus and his tribe of magi controlled these buildings. A Median prince had once told Cyrus that long ago in the past the priest clan was considered the ruling body of the nation because they assumed the right to rule as the intercessors between the gods and mankind. In those ancient times religion and government were the same entity. Later kings took the ruling privilege away from the priests. Cyrus had been told that the magi were determined to keep some degree of power so they established temples to make it an obligation for people to attend rites they controlled. Cyrus understood that visitors to a temple were expected to give donations to the gods via the magi. This practice kept the magus clan wealthy. It also gave the priests a privileged roll in society. The prince also knew that specific rites were created to bring both peasants and royalty to the temple. Sometimes these ceremonies were seasonally scheduled to ensure attendance every sun cycle. Other rites were designed to enhance family religious practices. Cyrus respected the magi who mystically blessed new homes; conducted the presentation of a newborn child to the gods and performed weddings. He respected the people of Media who believed all these practices were essential. There was always a fee that had to be paid to the magus. It might be a sheep, a container of wine or a tanned hide from a cow, and the prince knew the Median people paid for their sacred services.

On the occasion that concerned Cyrus a grain merchant had built a new storage barn and asked a magus to dedicate it to the gods. He was willing to pay with several sheep. The magus ordered the merchant to commit to the magi a specific fraction of the grain the building could hold for the next two crop cycles. The man thought that was too expensive and appealed to the Chief Magus, but the Magus agreed with the suggested 'offering.' The merchant appealed to the King in public audience. That day the King was drunk enough to not be religiously inspired so he ordered the Chief Magus to dedicate the building himself at no cost.

It was imperative for the Chief Magus to challenge this to keep his religious authority intact. He refused with a long discourse. The King became incensed at the argument made by the head of religion in Media. The King decided to show his power over the priests, and even the gods, by ordering the destruction of the temple run by the magus who had ordered the original payment. Such an offense against religion had never occurred before. The King demanded immediate action. His princes and his army refused to comply. They feared the Great King but they were willing to risk his wrath before they risked the anger of the gods, for to insult the gods with such a terrifying act was to completely forsake the happiness of the afterlife.

King Astyages tried to enforce his decree by killing a few military officers. When he saw his soldiers were not intimidated, he reverted to ordering slaves to destroy the temple. The slaves did not respect the religion of their owners and gladly insulted the gods that held them prisoner.

This act was so sacrilegious Cyrus was sure the gods would destroy Media. The young prince feared his grandfather had lost his place with the ahura gods in the afterlife. The prince wondered if the Great King was now a compatriot of the evil daeva spirits. Cyrus had trouble maintaining his respect for his grandfather to the extent of questioning his honor. Cyrus vowed to himself that if he were ever the king of many nations he would always respect the religion of others.

44

"I understand how a farm works. My concern is the operation of Arbela. I do not know where to start to inspect or evaluate the efficiency of a city," said Cyrus.

"Just ask other adult princes to go with you to Arbela. Invite them to review the grain stores, business operations and animal farms for you until you begin to recognize how and where important problems arise," suggested Prince Zatame.

Cyrus was concerned about his Arbela regency. His job was to oversee all the royal properties there, plus the administrative processes that controlled the peasants and public services. Cyrus said, "I am only thirteen, well, almost fourteen, but this is a vast responsibility. I don't know how to begin. Prince Zatame, will you help me please?"

The prince was amused at how serious Cyrus was about his responsibility. Prince Zatame offered, "Cyrus, you and I will make your first visit to Arbela together. First, we will inspect the water. It comes from wells and from channels coming directly out of the surrounding mountains. The peasants have cisterns in their homes that catch and store rain water. Next, we will inspect the grain and produce stores. After that we will inspect the meat shops that put chunks of goat, lamb and fowl in the meat markets. With just that much you will have inspected the water and food for the city."

"Zatame, you make it sound easy. Maybe being a regent is not too difficult after all."

"Cyrus, what I just described is the easy part," said Prince Zatame knowing he had to be cautious. He did not want Cyrus to think a city was easy to run. He continued, "Working with people is hard. You will need honest administrators and managers. You will have to decide who is forthright; who is not. There are as many thieves in the government of our cities as there are brigands on the roadways. We have minor princes in Arbela who might not steal from you. They will administer various functions of the city and the surrounding areas you are responsible for. They will hire people to do the work of running day-by-day operations. These latter workers are the ones you must assuredly look out for. Never limit your inspections to our royal cousins. You have to contact the factotums with the dirty hands. There lies your greatest difficulty, Cyrus."

"How long should I plan to make a visit last, Zatame?"

"You need to start just as we have been saying. You will spend a few days just traveling throughout the city. Observe big items first like water, food, and sanitation. On a second visit inspect two spheres of business, but evaluate them thoroughly. It may take you three or four days. Gradually you will realize what you must do. You will find people you have to remove from their positions. You can replace them yourself, or you can assign a trusted prince to do it for you."

"How will I be a good regent later on when I return to Anshan, Zatame? Can I govern from that distance?" Cyrus asked.

"Cyrus, you can certainly travel from Anshan to Arbela," Prince Zatame chuckled. His eyes beamed at the boy as he continued, "Most importantly, you can ask Prince Warohi in Susa to go for you, or ask him to go with you. He is an experienced city administrator who can give advice I can't. Prince Bagindu is another man who can help you. You must not worry too much about this duty. You will do fine for your first 'kingdom.' How do you think your father governs cities in Pars that are far from Anshan? He uses trustworthy surrogates."

This conversation was comforting to Cyrus. Prince Zatame was extremely helpful with his advice. Cyrus decided to speak with Zav as well. The prince was not sure he trusted the minister, but Cyrus recognized the magnitude of the Taxes and Materials Minister's obligations. The man might have information worth listening to.

//

Stolen merchandise was no longer coming from the Arbela area to Zav because Rusundatu had disbanded his robbers. To Zav calling it disbanded was generous. Most of the original men were dead and Mitridates had successfully fled the empire. Zav kept contact with Rusundatu to see if the criminal managed to secure a position in the Arbela government. He might be more valuable to Zav than in the previous business. In a public office Rusundatu could rob from the entire Arbela area at will, undetected. Zav thought, let the son of Cambyses be regent. The boy will mask my crimes with his figurehead of integrity.

369

"Zav, can we meet some time to talk about the city of Arbela?" asked Cyrus.

"Let's have lunch in my rooms, prince. Come with me," the minister offered.

Cyrus was impressed with the opulent suite Zav occupied, particularly since the minister had no royal heritage. Zav showed the boy his record rooms, which were extensive. Zav said, "Numerical records are essential to city supervision. Numbers can be summed or evaluated to assess general municipal welfare. You must review city inventories."

Upon seeing the tablets piled in Zav's record room, Cyrus asked, "Why are all these clay tablets here? I thought the magi kept them."

"These are only the current inventory records for the past three moon cycles," Zav said.

"So many!" Cyrus said, surprised. "Zav, I wonder if inventories can be faked. How does one check that?"

Zav answered pompously, "It will take experience for you to recognize when that occurs. Look at the goods in the warehouses first and then check the clay tabulations."

This was exactly the opposite of how Zav did his job. He always reviewed the tablet numbers first so he knew what to count in the storage areas. He reconciled what he saw against remembered lists of numbers. He intended to give the boy as much bad guidance as possible so he could rob from this prince later.

Zav advised, "There is a man in Arbela named Rusundatu. You must give him an important position. He has large farm holdings. He knows how to handle responsibility."

Cyrus thought and said, "I have met a man by that name before. I was not very impressed with him. He was not as straightforward as I like a man to be."

Zav said, "If you work directly with him yourself you will be impressed, if this is the same man."

Cyrus felt he was being misled. The more they talked the less sure Cyrus became of what he was learning. All that the minister said sounded fine, but his explanations seemed somewhat hollow. Zav's answers were neither complete nor clear like Prince Zatame's advice had been. Zav did convince Cyrus to assign Rusundatu to help run the city, but the prince was not sure that was a wise decision, yet Cyrus agreed to it.

In Mandane's suite the children were making their usual raucous noise. The chatter of the women added a low hum to the overall atmosphere. Cyrus had come in to talk with his mother. She was gaily showing two small girls how to blend a fruit flavored yogurt and diluted wine to make a sweet, creamy drink. Cyrus loved seeing his mother happy this way. He wondered if she could have been a better mother to him than Spaco. It was hard to imagine.

"Mother, I have had talks with Prince Zatame and Zav about my regency. They were both helpful," the prince said.

Mandane looked up sharply at the name 'Zav'. "Watch yourself, son, with that man Zav. He has the honor of a hyena. He will laugh with you in the daylight and steal you goatless at night."

Cyrus had heard Mandane talk like this of Zav before, but he thought he was able to detect bad counsel from sound advice. Cyrus had decided to follow some of Zav's suggestions to see where they led.

The boy and his mother were comfortable in each other's company. Both spoke longingly of Cambyses. It had been almost a full sun cycle since they left him. Cyrus was getting useful experiences in Ecbatana, but he wanted to get back to his father and Pars. The prince had observed differences in religious beliefs, in how the two countries applied themselves to hard work, and in the philosophies of royal rule. Cyrus preferred Pars where religion was more integrated into the hard work of daily life, and the people were more loving and forthright than in Media.

Cyrus was interested in his mother's problem with Princess Ispitamu. He asked, "What made you send Princess Ispitamu away, Mother? Grandfather was unusually upset over it."

"Ah, she was my first friend in Anshan. She helped me adjust to being away from home. I could not have commanded better help than she gave me, but she changed somehow. I can't explain it."

"I have heard she had a fit and had to be wrestled to the cushions," Cyrus laughed.

"Yes," said Mandane as she brightened to his mood. "She began throwing things and shrieking." As the queen said the last word her voice went up. "She attacked one woman and would not stop hitting her. It was awful. I do not know what disturbed her so much. I saw it all. Her actions mystified me."

"Maybe Prince Warohi can help us understand what's wrong," Cyrus suggested. "We should try to do something to help her if she was your first friend in Pars, mother."

She looked at her son wistfully. She said, "Unfortunately, son, I am no longer interested in seeing the princess. Our relationship has crumbled since her vulgar performance in my mother's *andarun*."

The queen never invited the Princess Ispitamu to visit Anshan after the banishment. Mandane was more comfortable with her in Susa. Mandane never discussed Princess Ispitamu in Anshan with her ladies of the *andarun*. Cambyses told her part of his reason for sending her away. She was not told how the princess had lied about Cyrus; the queen only knew Cambyses thought Princess Ispitamu was too close to Zav, and he wanted the princess away from his family. If the queen ever tried to convince her husband to rescind that order she would invite a vehement argument. Mandane's silence about the princess protected her from her husband's anger.

Mandane bounced on her couch like a playful elf and said, "Son, please let me have one of your silver coins. I want to make it into a pendant I can wear around my neck."

He handed her one from the leather pouch he carried them in. It was the first one he gave away. He looked at it closely to ensure the images of his profile and the sacred fire were sharp and clear as he handed it to his mother. She grasped his hand in pride and held it for a moment. They were so happy with each other. Cyrus asked, "Mother, when will we be going home? I would prefer to be with father when I become a man."

She smiled at this and said, "We should begin to suggest leaving to your grandfather. He will have to get used to the idea before he will permit us to go."

After departing his mother's rooms, Cyrus decided to wander in the marketplace for a while. He was not seeking anything in particular when he was tapped on the shoulder. He turned as his eunuch guards approached rapidly. He waved them away when he recognized the man who had introduced himself when the prince first arrived in Ecbatana with his mother. It was Zarathustra, the wandering man. Cyrus could not tell if he was a priest or a prophet. Cyrus knew the man's name meant 'camel driver.' It sounded like an apt description of the man's origins. Cyrus recalled the wanderer was seeking without knowing what he sought. The prince said, "Ah, it is you. I am glad to see you again, sir."

Zarathustra smiled at being recognized. He said, "My prince, you look as if you prosper in these surroundings. How are you?"

Cyrus answered, "Well, thank you, sir. Have you found what you seek?"

Zarathustra said, "Not yet. I am returning to my home to rest for a while. Then I will be off again. You live in Pars, if I recall correctly. When will you go back, prince?"

Cyrus said, "Mother and I were just talking of that. We both miss father very much."

Zarathustra appreciated a close family and he volunteered, "I am happy to be returning to my family. I get lonely for them."

Cyrus decided to joke with his acquaintance and asked, "Are you visiting your mother to get confirmation of your birth to a virgin?" and he laughed. Zarathustra was not offended by the prince's humor. He said, "If it was such a birth I have not yet discovered how it has set me apart from you or other men. Maybe in the afterlife the supreme spirit who I think holds the highest rank over all other gods will tell me. The Greeks believe this way."

"You are convinced one god dominates, sir?" Cyrus asked. "I prefer to believe there must be many equal gods. Think of how many kings we must have to run the world. It would require a lot of different gods, with various ideas, to create all this," and the prince waved his arm to signal all that was about them. Zarathustra liked this young boy. He was a thinker. He did not accept new ideas at face value yet he challenged ideas by comparing them to what he thought he already knew. It was a good attitude for a future king. Zarathustra decided to see if the boy could take a joke as well as he gave them and said, "You speak of my beginnings with mirth, but I keep hearing stories about the she-wolf that suckled you and chewed all your hair off so you could pass as a man. You no longer smell of the den as I have heard people suggest."

Cyrus was caught off guard. He never suspected that this serious man liked to joke. Cyrus blurted out a laugh that made people nearby stare at him for a moment. Zarathustra smiled, not at his own humor, but with amusement at the reaction of the prince. Cyrus was a fine boy and would become a strong, self-reliant man.

Zarathustra said, "Someday you will be a king. I will come to visit you then so we can talk again. I like your company, prince. Maybe the next time we meet I will know more about god or the gods. I may convince you of this one supreme head, if I have convinced myself by then."

With that he moved away. Cyrus continued his round of the market reflecting on this strange man who seemed to appear from nowhere periodically to challenge what was already known to everyone.

Later on, in the palace King Astyages was holding an audience Cyrus was obliged to attend. The boy rushed from the market to take his seat to wait for the King. When King Astyages entered everyone bowed. The King ordered them to rise with a wave of his hand. He gazed throughout the chamber as if to take inventory of those present. The King was quick to notice who was missing. Sometimes the Great King commented on his observations, which obligated the missing person to explain his absence at the next audience. It was the King's way of keeping everyone attentive to his interests.

Cyrus decided it was time to suggest that he and his mother prepare to leave. He spoke up clearly and said, "Sire, I have had the benefit of your teaching and your example for almost one entire sun cycle. Are you tiring of me? Should my mother plan to take me out of your sight back to Anshan?"

Cyrus waited without moving. He was hoping he had not offended his grandfather because the prince did not like being the source of bad feelings. The King looked at him in surprise and then started to laugh. "Cyrus, I intend for you to live with me until I die. You are the most pleasant company I have."

Cyrus did not want to hear that! Mandane decided to support her son now that the thought of them leaving was suggested and said, "Father, my son is right. We have troubled you enough. If we return home soon we can begin planning our next return with my husband. Cyrus could return so you could make him a man. An official man," and she giggled.

The King did not want to be reminded that his only daughter and only grandson belonged to another man and another country. He had ordered that relationship himself when he forced Cambyses to marry Mandane. It had been a time when he could not control his feelings about two strange dreams that had scared him, the flooding waters and the vine that covered his lands. Maybe having the boy so near was the threat that his dreams had so mystically suggested and the danger was just not obvious yet. The King did observe how everyone seemed to like this child. He could easily be the focal point of insurrection. Sending the boy away was worth considering. Distance might protect his empire. Instead of making a decision he changed the subject. King Astyages announced, "I am having a banquet!"

He looked at Queen Aryenis and said to her, "You and our daughter are to plan our largest feast since her wedding. We will enjoy ourselves, dear. I want all the minor kings to attend. Mandane, your husband is to come. Harpagus, you will attend also, and Zav you will give my Queen everything she needs for my banquet."

The soldier wondered why he had been specially mentioned. It must mean something. He wondered if he was to get his son back.

45.

Mandane and her mother made a celebration out of planning the banquet. They included as many princesses in the work as they could. When Mandane looked at the children in the *andarun* she tried to think of an active part they could play in the festivities too. She might have them sing or pretend to play musical instruments. The latter might be amusing.

Messages had gone out to all minor kings ordering them to attend the King's banquet. It was no invitation. Everyone knew it mean death to refuse.

Mandane told her mother that she believed it might be more romantic if they held the banquet in the same garden where her wedding was conducted. Queen Aryenis was enchanted by the thought. Why not let the women celebrate a small reminiscence while they reveled at the King's command?

This time the Queen was determined not to rush. She was going to take her time; she let the women of her *andarun* squabble over details. It helped the women feel important as well as actively involved. The Queen needed to feel that she was in control of something significant as well. She allowed the plans to be fully discussed and reviewed by the princesses, which occasionally led to explosive wrangling. The Queen began to ask various princesses what they appreciated most about a banquet. One always liked to have music playing. Another preferred to have the guests all facing the center of the room where entertainment took place; it made the activities more visible to everyone, and they could talk about the amusing performances they had seen. Another wanted a lot of fragrant flowers. The aroma added romance and enchantment as the evening wore on. The Queen liked what she was hearing so she incorporated as many of these ideas as she could into her project.

Queen Aryenis recalled the overhead shading banners that blocked the sun at Mandane's wedding. If she used those again the party could begin early in the day and continue until everyone was exhausted or fell asleep on cushions at the tables.

One princess was told to ask Prince Zatame for information as the women tried to estimate the size of the guest list attending their event.

The prince had an idea of the number of minor kings coming, but he could only guess at the size of the full audience. The Queen identified people from Ecbatana that were coming. Mandane got several princesses together to visit the courtyard to plan the arrangement of entire vegetation beds. In the interval since her wedding the yard had changed gradually but substantially. They needed to clear spaces to accommodate the revelers who would attend the feast.

As the plans for the banquet began to take shape the women of the *andarun* became more animated with hope, mutual support and anticipation. The Queen was very proud of her princesses. She found herself helping them as much as they aided her. Women complimented each other for the most trivial success.

"How are your arrangements for my banquet progressing?" King Astyages asked.

"We are doing very well," said Queen Aryenis. "Mandane and the girls are changing the garden we will use to make it comfortable. You only invited the minor kings and Harpagus. Do you have any other guests you want to have attend?"

"No, they will suit my needs," he answered.

Queen Aryenis wondered what 'needs' he had for a banquet. He said it so casually it did not sound important, and she forgot he said it.

The minor kings began to arrive. Small parties developed around these men and their companions. They brought wives, concubines, children, magistrates, servants and slaves. Some even brought their jesters and musicians. The entire city gradually became involved in the festivities of having every king of the empire in one place. These men brought varying sized troupes that had to be fed and housed. Hordes of animals needed food, water and bedding. Overloaded city stables eventually required the city managers to find pastures for horses, camels and donkeys a full day's journey outside the city. It was essential, since adequate forage grass had to be provided without crowding the animals.

Peasants migrated to the city to capture a small fraction of the wealth being spread about as large crowds of visitors came to the capital. With this gathering the visitors and animals spilled out of the city into the countryside. The peasants were pleasantly surprised to have the wealth come to them. Everyone knew about the big banquet that stimulated this confluence of the richest on the land, but only a few foolish people were upset by it. This was an economic boon that provided enough income to sustain some of the poor for many sun cycles.

Every homeowner tried to clear a room they called a cookshop for hungry visitors. The roof was a favorite lunch or dinner setting. Some roofs became living quarters for owners who rented out rooms. Unemployment disappeared. There was always a job to be had with a meat cutter, a stable or a granary.

Many of the magistrates who accompanied the kings brought large caravans of merchandise. This was a great opportunity to trade. New marketplaces began to appear where the visitors stopped their camels. Peasants pulled out useless junk to barter as they tried to improve the quality of their household accoutrements. It seemed as if everything was available for exchange. The excitement of shopping became infectious. Streets that had not been busy for ages became clogged with haggling masses of humanity that hardly moved all day. Animal husbandry farmers had to herd their pigs, sheep and goats into and through hordes of fussy tradesmen on the way to slapdash stockyards. The dirt-covered streets were piled with lumps of animal excrement that shoppers tried to avoid as they rushed to capture bargains or cheat each other. Mud created from every foul, rotting or slopping material coated the ankles of royalty and peasant alike. The stench wafted in the hot, sun-flooded air as sweat, smelly droppings, rotting swill and hanging dead carcasses exuded abhorrent vapors that diners tried to ignore.

Not all the arriving royalty were able to reside in the palace. As large as it was, there were hordes of people who had to find billeting beyond the city in the environs. Men with wagons tried to convince commuters their rustic carts were phaetons fit for a prince. Riding in a cart did keep excrement off garment hems.

Small fights broke out frequently over paltry misunderstandings. The number of languages spoken added to the daily confusion. There was a lot of arm waving and shouting. Pushing became the only cue to signal one's desire to move on. Noblemen did not take the jostling as an insult. If every prince tried to punish everyone that pushed him, mass slaughter would have to take place. Eunuchs assigned to protect the royalty in the streets were dumbfounded by the confusion. They simply could not do their jobs properly.

When the minor kings decided to move about the city they got the help of military guards mounted on horses or camels. These animals surged into crowds. Hundreds of people were injured. The medical magi were extremely busy providing services, receiving payments. They loved getting richer too!

The Chief Magus saw his opportunity to devise several new religious ceremonies requiring attendance at a temple. The temples filled several times a day where peasants deposited trinkets and animals as donations. These were all hidden away for the magi to drool over later.

City managers were powerless to suppress the chaos. They simply gave up and joined the hubbub as vacationers. Civic responsibility took a recess. Watchmen and military guards who normally were stationed throughout the city to prevent trouble only responded to problems if a fight or robbery occurred within their view. Shouting from a distance was ignored.

Many people were burned when fire pots of oil or charcoal were tipped over. No large buildings burned down because these structures were constructed of firebricks or natural stone. The gods had been generous with foresightedness with this blessing. The gods also seemed to protect the thousands of men, women and children who had to sleep in the streets. Peasants began to believe temple offerings were worthwhile after all.

46.

Cambyses arrived in the capital and fought his way to the palace after ensuring his escorts were securely situated. In the palace his arrival was hardly noticed, except by Mandane and Cyrus. Their meeting in her private garden was lovely. Cambyses held his wife a little too tightly. She grunted in his grasp. He slowly relaxed his grip on her then he gave her a long sweet kiss. It was a moment of pure bliss for both of them.

He reveled in the sight of her lovely face and the feel of her soft body. Mandane swooned when Cambyses whispered tender endearments to her. Cyrus stood behind his father proud of his parents' love for each other. Cambyses turned, with his arm still around Mandane to look at his son and said, "Well, my boy, you have taken fine care of your mother. Thank you."

Cyrus stepped forward and hugged his father. Cambyses drew the three of them together in a single warm embrace. Cyrus was overcome with happiness. A tear slid down his cheek. Cambyses saw it and was content that his son was still a boy who had not changed into a man during his absence.

"We have so much to tell you, father!" exclaimed Cyrus with enthusiasm.

"Ah, son, before we get into heavy discussions let me just look at you. You have gotten taller and wider."

Cambyses reached out to squeeze his son's biceps. The king said, "You are putting on muscle. Good. I am anxious to see your bow. We will have to shoot together soon."

They walked casually around the garden chatting about how they had missed one another. Being together as a family again came naturally to them. Eventually, the delicate pressure of Mandane's grip on Cambyses' hand became too much for him. He walked her to the door of her suite and said to Cyrus, "Son, please ask the women and children to leave us alone for a while. You should go to clean up for the evening meal. Your mother and I will come to get you later."

Cyrus was not disturbed by this dismissal. He did as he was asked and returned to his rooms.

Cambyses and Mandane tried to take their time to let the urgency of their long separation kindle slowly, but the gods were not letting lovers come together slowly today. Blushing heat rose like the glow of strong wine. They were naked in an instant. Clinging together, with desperate tenderness and aching need for love, they settled on the silk cushions beneath them and found perfect contentment in their passion.

Over the next few days Cambyses spent the early mornings riding or shooting with Cyrus. Harpagus watched the boy challenge his father in playful sport. His heart ached for his own son. Cambyses approached Harpagus to say, "Thank you for increasing the pulling power of my son's bow. He needed to be stronger. You have done well with him. Did he work hard enough for you at his training, Harpagus?"

Harpagus answered like the soldier he was and said, "Yes, sire. You have a fine young man who does his best. He never blusters or embarrasses the lesser skilled princes. All the young noblemen respect him. He has no enemies. The bigger boys love to challenge Cyrus because he tries so hard. They teach him how to avoid fighting mistakes, as a reward for his sportsmanship."

Cambyses could not have asked for a better report. As a father it made him proud. As a king needing warriors in the future Cambyses saw that Cyrus was not yet a strong archer in his long distance shooting. The prince still needed to increase his arm strength to improve his long-range shooting accuracy. Cyrus needed to increase the number of positions from which he could sit on a horse while still firing accurately. When he shot to his right or to the rear it was almost laughable. In fact it was laughable, because Cyrus fell off his mount once while trying to shoot to his right when he lost his knee grip. Three young princes rushed to his aid, and they all fell into a heap of laughter when they were convinced he was not hurt. Cambyses was going to enjoy helping his son become a warrior.

One morning Cyrus was telling his father about sitting in the Great King's audience hall learning how large the Median Empire really was. Cyrus told his father of the visit by King Croesus. "Father, Uncle Croesus is far smarter than grandfather, I think, but not as smart as you. He made fun of Zav when he viewed a large number of empty storage buildings. Zav tried to get grandfather to let him empty storehouses of arms in Susa to fill buildings here. Grandfather ignored Zav."

Cambyses said, "Yes, son, we managed to settle that issue without difficulty. It did take some effort on our part to stop Zav, however."

"Oh, darling," piped up Mandane with the hint of a song in her voice, "you would have been proud of Cyrus for how he protected the salt desert route."

"You sent me a message telling me about it, darling. What did you say to the Great King, son?"

"It was not much. I have heard you and Pattmenidu talk of the route, and I only related what you have said. The route is significant in neither the volume of products nor the variety of products it carries. Grandfather was not impressed with Zav's argument. Zav said it was taking a lot of trade from Ecbatana. He wanted military support to force the closing of the route, but Harpagus would not support the minister, and grandfather just ignored Zav."

"Well, son, that route has become far more important since you left Pars. From the viewpoint of producing an impact on commerce in Ecbatana it is very important now. Zav was correct. I am very happy with our relationship with Bactria, and I will be talking with King Arsames in the next few days to ensure our relationship is strengthened. You did well, but you argued with old information. We were lucky this time, son."

Cyrus listened carefully to his father's words. The prince learned that making suggestions and decisions with old data could be potentially dangerous. Cyrus began to wonder if there was some way to rectify the slow delivery of important information.

Mandane was proud of Cyrus' regency. She loved to brag about her son's importance. She said to Cambyses, "When Uncle Croesus was here he told father that Cyrus was ready to rule because our boy was so smart and diplomatic. Father gave Cyrus the title of Regent of Arbela. What do you think of that, dear?" she asked Cambyses.

Mandane had already sent a message about this to Cambyses, and the king smiled at the thought of his son being so important. It was a real responsibility and he asked, "Have you visited your regency yet, son?"

"Yes, father, once with Prince Zatame. He helped me review the major water, food and sanitation facilities. I still do not understand all he said about those operations, but I got an awareness of some very important places in that city. I plan to ask Prince Warohi to help me when I go to inspect Arbela from Anshan."

"Son, you are using two very smart men to help you. We will talk at home about running the city, and I may be able to show you parts of Anshan that will teach you about Arbela. I am pleased that King Astyages thought so highly of you and honored you this way." Cambyses was very proud.

Cyrus smiled at his father's promised support. They continued to talk of family matters, while Cambyses waited to go to lunch with other minor kings.

King Arsames of Bactria and King Kauklia of Gedrosia both invited themselves to the banquet. Other minor kings had told them of the event. They had no obligation to King Astyages and were not invited, but they wanted to show him they retained a certain level of respect for a man with a kingdom far larger than their own. King Astyages understood the reason for their presence, taking no offence when he received them. Their presence complimented the Great King's ego.

King Arsames, King Kauklia and Cambyses met in a small dining house Cambyses was familiar with. They had used the military to force a path for them through the crowds of the city. The proprietor liked serving Cambyses because the king was generous with his compliments and his payment of the meal. The building had a rooftop area behind high walls that blocked street noises, which kept their conversation from being overheard. The open topped roof let refreshing breezes cool the men.

King Kauklia bragged, "I have come to Ecbatana uninvited! Look how safe I am after I seceded from Media with impunity. I pay the Great King nothing! I owe him nothing!"

King Kauklia felt proud of his cockiness. In his excitement his bulk jiggled. He smelled of nervous sweat and dirty clothing. He was almost enough to ruin the meal for the other two kings.

King Arsames said, "Let us talk of our businesses."

He was very aristocratic looking and his large frame would normally be imposing and commanding. However, Cambyses was his equal in dignity and authority. King Arsames continued, "Cambyses, my cousin, what new products do you want to improve our commerce?"

Cambyses did not want to make radical changes, just slight modifications that would improve the overall efficiency of the system. He answered, "We can handle more tea. We have developed a true taste for it in Pars. There seems to be a wide variety of tealeaf flavors, and we have become interested in these taste differences. We could use more sugar as well. We like to get sugar damp and let it harden and after we break it into chunks we hold a small hard lump of sugar between our teeth while sipping tea through it. We find this the most satisfying way to drink our tea. Also, our women have made a cherished ritual out of reading the future in the teacup among the leaves. I will have Mandane read your tea leaves one of these days."

Cambyses returned to the discussion of business by saying, "Of course just about any type of spice that can be kept fresh will do fine in our markets. What we can't use we have a market for in Babylon, or beyond. My contacts with Babylon are very good right now."

King Kauklia asked, "Cambyses, what is there from my country that you can use?"

There was not much, but Cambyses did not want to upset this mass of royal yogurt with an accidental insult. He said, "I can use all the copper you can afford to send me."

King Kauklia smiled at being useful because he knew his country was never going to be rich and important, but it pleased him to be more than just the end of a minor trading trail.

Cambyses suggested dealing in specific volumes of several products from numbers Pattmenidu and other ministers of Pars had given him. The three kings had a very productive and agreeable discussion and King Kauklia ate sumptuous heaps of all the various foods placed before them.

"My friends, are your countries at peace?" asked Cambyses.

"Yes," answered Kauklia, "except for the usual skirmishes, but those are easily kept in check."

"I wonder if King Astyages has us all in Ecbatana to declare war against us or some larger nation," Cambyses said. "No one knows why we are here."

Neither King Arsames nor King Kauklia had any rumors or facts about this gathering. King Arsames suggested, "The Great King does not have to make war against any of the minor kings; he can make us all prisoners right now, if he wishes. The Great King's army is here, but we only have token defensive guards. We are extremely vulnerable."

47.

The women continued to make efficient progress with the banquet. They were frequently interrupted by the turmoil caused by their visitors, but they concentrated carefully on their various tasks. This was a women's event that they wanted to be perfect. The outside court had been completely changed. A small orchard of citrus trees was moved from the middle of the yard. New flower and vegetable plots were planted. Poles for oil lanterns were carefully situated so aisle space was not obstructed. A place for the Great King was identified. The central entertainment space was marked off. Small balconies were raised to reduce the courtyard area musicians would otherwise take up. This left more space for servants and guests to move about.

The women ordered two additional gates to be cut in the surrounding walls. These openings provided separate entries for guests, food and entertainers, which added improved control for the activities during the feast. The princesses organized the entertainment as well. They planned to have a chorus of children sit on the top of the wall to sing in their soprano trills to create a gay, innocent mood early in the festivity well before the tots went to bed. Mandane and her friends wanted as much funny entertainment as they could get. The day was going to be one great laugh that they would remember from now on as the happiest party the royal women ever created. In the *andarun* the princesses prepared themselves and the youngsters for the party. They dressed boys and girls in funny costumes made just for the feast. Silly hairdos were propped on top of the heads of innocent children who thought they were having loads of fun, and they were. Elegant new gowns and pantaloon suits made of vibrant silks were floating about as women laid out several changes of clothing for the day. The women planned to bath and change several times as they got hot during the day's activities. They helped each other with fanciful coifs. There were many women wearing diaphanous turbans that covered beautiful swirling hairstyles.

Mandane had Cyrus wear a new outfit made just for him. It had a blue silk top with loose, blousing sleeves that fell below his elbows. His collar opened wide to accent his long, straight neck and handsome head. The hem of his shirt fell to about the tips of his fingers, but it was cut at a sharp angle dropping away from left to right. His purple silk trousers were tightly gathered at the ankles. He wore a yellow sash with gold tassels. His leather shoes curled up at the toes while gold tassels hung from the tips of his footwear over his instep. His black hair hung straight to his shoulders. There was a natural curl at the ends of his locks. His beard had not yet started to grow. Mandane lightly painted his cheeks with her rouge face makeup, against his wishes. She laughed as she applied it. He tolerated her joking.

Mandane wore a pink sheath with embroidery of rose colored thread. Her eye makeup was red. Her cheeks were painted far brighter than her son's cheeks. She wore gold shoes with upturned toes and gold tassels too. She had dozens of thin, gold bangles on each forearm that jingled when she moved her arms. Cambyses wore a plain undyed linen toga and leather shoes turned up at the toes, but he refused to allow Mandane to add tassels. He did not follow his wife's suggestion to wear gay colors with flashy gold decorations. He was a simple man, a simple king.

They entered the garden about mid-afternoon. The crowd had already begun to congregate earlier making a loud festival noise. On the walls overhead musicians played harps, lyres, tambourines, drums and reed pipes. There was also the delicate sound of bells, plus wood hammers hitting hollow pieces of wood. All the sounds were cheerful.

The family found a place to sit near the center ring so they could see and hear the entertainment when it started. The Great King's table was to their left. He had chosen a select few minor kings to sit with him. His son-in-law was not one of them, but Cambyses was satisfied, not insulted, with the arrangements.

Mandane noted one place directly across from them that had a canopy over the table. It was not something she remembered the princesses discussing or setting up. She wondered about it for a moment then forgot it in the interest of looking about the yard. She was pleased that the gaiety the ladies had hoped for was materializing. There was laughter everywhere. People were moving about joking, chuckling and talking together with the sole intent to have fun.

Cambyses waved to King Arsames. He got up beckoning Cyrus to follow him. Cambyses announced, "Son, this is my cousin, King

Arsames from Bactria. He is the man who sends us trade over the salt desert."

Cyrus bent at the waist politely. King Arsames said, "Cambyses, this is a fine looking boy you have. Does he sit on a horse well?"

Cambyses laughed and said, "If he is not shooting to the rear, yes," remembering the time the prince had toppled off his mount. Cambyses wanted Cyrus to see this man. His business was more important each day to Pars. Someday Cyrus would have to deal with this side of the family. They talked of general topics related to the current party. Finally Cambyses decided to bring business into the discussion. The king of Pars said, "I have been wondering if the people across the Indus River should start a southern caravan route across the bottom of Gedrosia, through Utia into Pars. It could skirt the coast of the Erythraean Sea bringing goods directly to my southern provinces. Now Susa and Anshan have to transport goods to the south. It might reduce the trade I conduct with you, but I do not want to start using new routes that will make you lose profit."

"Cambyses, I can't imagine your changes will entail much trade; how much merchandise do you expect it to be and what kinds of goods would be transported?" asked King Arsames.

"I am not sure yet," answered Cambyses. "It would be minor to start. I doubt it would grow much, but it would reduce what I get from you though."

The king of Bactria said, "Well, my friend, do what you will. We can keep track of its impact. Have your Pattmenidu report to us both about it, and if we decide it needs to be changed we can adjust the merchandise it carries easily. Do you agree?"

Cambyses nodded; glad that his son saw how reasonable King Arsames was about dealing with his own family. It was an important lesson for the boy. They talked for a while before Cambyses excused himself and Cyrus.

The next person Cambyses wanted his son to see was King Kauklia of Gedrosia. There was a mountain of dark blue silk bundled on a mass of cushions a few aisles away and they approached it.

King Kauklia said, "Ah, Cambyses, you have your son with you. He is far more handsome than you are. Come sit for a moment so we can make as much noise as everyone else."

Cambyses introduced Cyrus and they sat. Cyrus again was silent. Cambyses asked, "I have been thinking of having the merchants across the Indus River start a new caravan route across the south end of Gedrosia into Utia and Pars. Do you think it is worthwhile, my friend?"

"It can't hurt anything but it might not be profitable," said King Kauklia, then he added, "What would be transported?"

Cambyses answered, "I am thinking we might get that red iron ore from the Indus. I hear they have mountains full of it, but my metal workers can't process it correctly yet though I suspect they will learn some day. The iron will be harder than the bronze we use now. Swords will be stronger and our metal household goods will last longer, I think."

King Kauklia said, "We are getting older. Why do you want anything to last a long time? I have seen iron. It is dark, ugly and it turns a dull red eventually," he belched and continued, "The red seems to rub off on everything it touches. It will stain your pretty white linen gown, my friend."

They talked amicably and agreed that a new trade route could work if Pattmenidu was able to encourage the tradesmen across the Indus River to send their goods along a novel route.

Cambyses continued wandering around the yard as he introduced his son to people he knew. They both made new acquaintances, feeling secure in each other's company. It was good for the father and son to conduct casual business together in this gathering. Mandane also wandered about the crowd congratulating her friends from the *andarun* for their obvious success at organizing the arrangements of the banquet. The shrill tinkle of women laughing could be heard everywhere. Children played in the aisles and in the center area. They dutifully vacated that spot when a juggler or acrobatic group entered to perform.

Food was being served constantly. There were servants carrying jugs of wine, jugs of water and trays of crackers, bread and fruited yogurts. Large platters of fruits floated like clouds over the guests. Everyone shared the food and drinks. The people knew this was to be a long day so they ate lightly.

Mandane noticed eunuchs were now standing by the table with the canopy over it. They were keeping guests from sitting there. Mandane wondered who had made the arrangement for that place. The queen decided her mother must have set it up. It was interesting to guess who the mystery guest was going to be. Mandane joked about it with the other princesses. The table was so prominently placed it was visible from everywhere in the court. Mandane decided surprises were always nice.

The sun was bright, unobstructed by clouds. The dry air was clear. Banners high overhead cast a flowing shade across the court as they billowed in a soft breeze. Queen Aryenis had ordered several different colors of banners, and as one looked to the sky the banners appeared to mimic the brilliant hues in the garments of the guests.

As the day wore on the noise got louder as the throng grew bigger. Part of the loudness came from those who had chosen to drink a lot of wine too early. Since Harpagus had been singled out by the Great King to attend he arrived with his wife in the late afternoon choosing to recline near a table against a wall. It was a suitable vantagepoint to see the full expanse of the yard. If anything untoward were to arise, beyond the playful pushing that always occurred at such a fete, he was in a perfect position to keep control for the King. There had been rare occasions in the past when knives had been drawn after punches had been thrown. He intended to prevent violence tonight. He specifically arranged for a substantial contingent of armed guards to be waiting a short distance outside the gates leading into the yard.

A blare of music announced the entrance of the King and Queen. This was a time when all in attendance had to bow to the ground. Everyone bowed in the direction of the King acknowledging his presence. The noise dropped to a hush. The gold crowns of the royal host and hostess glistened in the sunlight as they came through the gate. The King waved at the visitors expansively; they rose to comfortable lounging positions. The King grinned. The Queen appeared to glide weightlessly beside him with a smile for everyone she passed. She received numerous compliments on the decorations, the food, the entertainment and the weather. This was her triumph. She had planned it. She had made it splendid. The King walked about as if this were his doing. King Astyages was the only one in the court who was not aware that this was his wife's success.

The King had ordered the kings of Parthia, Hyrcania and Armenia to be present at his head table, but until he allowed them to sit they had to roam about the crowd. These were countries that the west to east caravan route passed, and the Great King wanted to show everyone he supported that vital link across his empire. Zav was attending the party, but he was only allowed to sit at a place where other ministers were placed. It did not offend him, but he hoped that some day when he married someone, anyone, of royalty he could be elevated to sit among noble guests at a dinner such as this. As it was, he sat against a wall with other administrators who were also restricted from mingling among the noblemen.

The King and Queen roamed about greeting and hugging their guests. They took their time. The King made certain everyone knew who was important tonight. Except for music, all entertainment stopped until the King had finished circulating. His extended entrance was the new entertainment. The regal couple maintained a convincing exuberance as they greeted their guests. Their presence increased the jubilation that had been filling the air. It seemed as if nothing could ruin this lovely event.

The Queen whispered to the King, and he nodded. She needed to sit because she was getting a little tired. He took her arm as they made their way to the royal table. Their chosen table-guests could not sit until the Great King settled in his place. It was his privilege to begin the seating at the head table by decorating it with his illustrious presence. Once in his place others of the head table graciously bowed to him and took their assigned position as the King pointed to where each person should sit. It was these small signs of power that made his presence so overwhelming.

In his place King Astyages took time to gaze about the yard. He saw the table with the canopy and smiled privately to himself. He waited a while before he took the action he intended for that spot. He suspected there must be a bit of interest in what that table meant and whom it was for.

Mandane's family settled down to drink half-filled cups of wine while eating in sparing nibbles. Prince Zatame sat near them to share their carafe of diluted wine and tray of fruit. Prince Zatame asked, "Mandane, who is to sit there?" as he pointed to the canopy.

She shrugged saying, "I don't know. None of the princesses planned that place. Maybe mother has contrived a surprise for us."

391

Dusk turned to darkness and the olive oil sconces throughout the yard were lit. There was almost no difference in the brilliance of the light from midday to nighttime. The women had planned for enough lamps to keep shadows from hovering over the festivities.

Finally the King raised his hand and those who saw it shushed those who did not. As the yard quieted the King announced with a strident voice, "Harpagus, come sit here." King Astyages waved toward the canopied table. Harpagus got up with the deliberate ease of a well-conditioned soldier. He helped his wife rise from her reclining position. She appeared startled at her husband's obvious award. It was different from every other table. It must be a place of honor. They walked to where the King had directed them, and they reclined with simple grace. The eunuchs stepped aside but remained behind them.

A busy buzz began to stir the air. Comments rushed through the guests.

"So this was the surprise."

"The military was being honored."

"Does it mean war?"

"Does it mean the King will announce he has an enemy in the crowd?"

"Is Harpagus going to be ordered to take a minor king prisoner?"

The meal progressed with fruit following the cheese trays as the fuss died down. A rice dish seasoned with several spices followed uncooked vegetables. Yogurt with cucumber came next; then nuts and sweet candies were served. A new rice dish was served that had brown spices not usually found in rice but it was very appetizing. Neither the serving nor eating of each course was rushed because the social aspects of the gathering were far more important than having a filling repast. In between each course entertainers performed in the center area. Jugglers tossed flaming wooden clubs. Jesters jounced about with hilarious antics. Acrobats bounded about performing what appeared to be impossible jumps, twists and single-handed catches.

King Astyages was drinking heavily as if trying to catch up with the most drunken visitors. Finally, a meat course was served. Every table was served from a silver platter. Even the royal table was served on silver. The single exception was at Harpagus' table. He and his wife were served from a gold platter covered with a gold dome. They each took a small amount of meat and ate it. Then new rice, yogurt and fruit dishes were served.

Later another meat dish came on silver platters for everyone, except Harpagus and his wife. Again their portion was on the gold platter. This time the meat was flavored with light, green spices, and King Astyages asked in a loud, drunken voice, "Harpagus, can you tell me what type of beast that is?"

Harpagus tasted it, as did his wife, and they could not agree on what type of meat it was. "No, sire, I don't know what it is," Harpagus answered. "It could be lion, leopard, hyena or any other beast of the forest."

The meal and entertainment continued. Mandane was curious why Harpagus was at the table of honor. She asked Cambyses, "Do you know why they are there, dear? The women certainly didn't arrange that. Obviously mother didn't either."

"I have no idea, my love. It must mean there is some special military event to be revealed tonight."

A third meat course was served just as before only this time the golden container was placed on the table in front of Harpagus, covered. The King asked again, slurring his words in his inebriation, "Harpagushsh, tell me the kind of meat you have been eating. Tell us all."

Harpagus was tentative in his response and answered, "I can't place the taste, sire. My wife is unable to identify the meat, and her ability to detect tastes is superb."

All eyes in the court were on the gold salver. The King rose to his feet and waved to the servant standing near Harpagus. The servant lifted the cover and stepped aside. Sitting on a pair of human hands and feet was the head of the son of Harpagus. The soldier and his wife had been served the flesh of their son!

The King roared, "Ah, Harpagushsh, how dare you disobey me. Everyone, see what punishment is possible for those who refuse to do my bidding. See there," he said pointing at Harpagus, "the man who lied to me. I made the man who disobeyed me eat his son!"

The King swayed in drunken uncoordination. He blinked to keep Harpagus in focus. As it struck the soldier what both he and his wife had done, Harpagus vomited retching in violent surges. His wife shrieked and vomited. She then mercifully passed out. Harpagus tried not to look on the face of his dead son as he doubled over gagging. The entire court was struck dumb by this vicious, cruel trick played by the Great King. Women cried. Many passed out. Men vomited. Those who had just been drunk were sober and powerless to move. Cambyses hid the face of Mandane on his shoulder as she shivered in fright shocked at her father's heinous trick.

Chaos erupted! People trying to escape the yard slipped on vomit and rolled in its slim. Disbelief and revulsion were rampant. The King continued his tirade against Harpagus. He roared, "Come on sholdier. Tell them your crime. Tell them how I ordered you to kill that boy," and King Astyages pointed to his right at Cyrus. Queen Aryenis screamed in disbelief. She looked at her husband agonized with the possibility that he had lost his mind. She could not believe what he was saying.

Cambyses squeezed Mandane as she turned her head from the wife of Harpagus to her father who was pointing at her own son. Every muscle in her body went taut. She could not look away from her father. Terror filled her mind. She could not cry or scream. She was petrified. Cyrus sat stunned. He could not believe his grandfather had ordered his death. The prince looked at the agonized expression on the face of his father realizing he had just heard the meanest confession of his life, and it must be true.

King Astyages raged on in his drunken insanity and said, "Go on, Harpagushsh, tell them how you hid the boy I ordered you to kill when my dreamshsh told me he was a danger to me. Tell them..." he shrieked as he fell to the ground exhausted lying on the cushions panting. Queen Aryenis moved away from him. The courtyard was emptying fast. Harpagus was carrying his unconscious wife toward the gate. He was still retching in agony.

Two minor kings sitting near Queen Aryenis guided her out of the courtyard to be attended by a medical magus. The King attempted to enter the *andarun* but his wife refused to see him, and her eunuchs rebuffed his attempts to enter. It was the world of the women and even the Great King could not enter without the approval of his wife. The Great King ceased threatening the eunuchs, conceding his isolation from his Queen. He left her alone.

Cambyses picked up Mandane and carried her out the food service gate, through several hallways to their rooms. Cyrus walked with a slow, unsteady gait behind his father. His knees were so weak they hardly held him up.

Zav came up behind Cyrus and said in a harsh voice, "Well, prince, tonight explains many things. You are lucky to be alive. Be careful in the future. Others may try to kill you."

The family spent the night together, huddled in confused disbelief. Cambyses ordered meals to be brought to them in their rooms over the next few days. He did not permit anyone but a single servant into his rooms. His guards, hearing of the tragic episode, prepared to travel back to Pars at their king's command.

Slowly Mandane regained a slight degree of her normal sensibility. She had been in a mind-altering daze. Cyrus was just as stunned at what he had heard. His loving devotion of his grandfather was crushed. Several times he reached out and patted his father. Cambyses squeezed his son's hand trying to smile at the boy. They all knew there was no comfort for them until they were away from this place.

King Astyages sent a eunuch to Mandane's rooms ordering her family into his presence. The minor king refused to allow his family to go because if Cambyses stood before the Great King now, the tyrant would die.

Prince Zatame came to visit. Cambyses let him in because the minor king needed to talk with someone about the event. Cambyses asked, "How could he think up such a heinous trick to play on that soldier? Or to do such a thing to his own daughter so long ago?"

Prince Zatame was not as impressed as Cambyses was. "He did not think up what he did to Harpagus, Cambyses. The Greeks tell of a man that ate his sons long ago. King Astyages probably heard the same tale I did. I was told that a Greek family got confused by a complex series of events that included a murder, the theft of the Golden Fleece, a family seduction and a couple of forced exiles.

"Long ago it seems a man named Atreus and his brother Thyestes killed their half-brother, Chrysippus. Their father forced them into exile at Mycenae.

"Atreus became the king there. Thyestes got jealous so he seduced Atreus' wife and stole the ram with the Golden Fleece that had been a gift to Atreus from the god Hermes.

"Later Atreus discovered what his brother had done, and he invited him back from exile to Mycenae to feed Thyestes the bodies of his own two sons. The idea of preparing such a meal is not new with our Great King, Cambyses. He is just a vicious copier."

Cambyses nodded, impressed with the mythical Greek story. Prince Zatame said, "I have spoken with Harpagus. He regrets his complicity in the King's crime against your family. He begs your forgiveness. I asked him about the bloody clothing he retrieved from that farmer, Mitridates, and he said it was to show King Astyages to prove that Cyrus was dead."

Cambyses in a broken voice said, "Harpagus did not intend to do good with his deeds, but he inadvertently saved the life of my son. And after what he just suffered how can I refuse to forgive him?"

"He explained the garment bundle we heard about from the farmer," Prince Zatame said.

"Well, after what we just saw, I can't hold Harpagus responsible for any of the past. Guilt resides with the Great King alone," Cambyses said.

Cyrus volunteered, "I have prayed to the gods that Harpagus' wife can get over the ghastly experience she has had to endure. Maybe I even owe Harpagus my life. I am not sure I owe grandfather anything," as he looked at the people in the room.

Cyrus continued, "I am not sure if I still love or respect my grandfather any longer. Maybe the only people I really need to share my love with are in this room. I feel confused," and he sadly hung his head and whimpered.

48.

The emotional wounds of Cambyses' family were slow to heal. It was a special gift from the gods that they had each other and found strength in their mutual devotion. Before leaving Ecbatana Mandane spent long hours with her mother. They did not say much. They just held each other crying. Words were not necessary. They suffered together over the evil behavior of the Great King. Neither said it, but the magnificent party the women had planned and organized was going to be remembered for a very long time but for the wrong reasons.

King Cambyses showed the judgement and compassion of a marvelous king and family patriarch by keeping his family isolated from the Great King's court. He knew Mandane would suffer more if she had to face her friends. Cyrus kept to himself. He was not morose or depressed. He was carefully evaluating his grandfather's actions without jumping to conclusions or ridiculing the man too quickly.

After several days, King Astyages sobered and ignored the activities of his daughter and her family. The Parsian royal family made a quiet, safe trip back home to Anshan. Had King Astyages prevented their exit, Cambyses would have sent word to Prince Warohi through royal contacts to wage war on Media.

In Anshan the prince could not help recalling the fable of Aesop that Spaco had told him about the burden men carry. She had said that at birth a man is given two sacks to carry. The small one hanging in front is easy to see and contains the faults of other men. A much larger one hanging over his back is difficult to see, which contains the faults of the man carrying the sacks. Cyrus decided he had to be cautious about finding fault or blame in another man, yet he could not find love in his heart for his grandfather right now.

The prince had dreamed of living with pride in the shadow of the great man. That dream had crumbled. Now Cyrus would have to build a new dream based on the dignity of his own father and the noble country of Pars.

Cyrus could use the exposure he got in his grandfather's court with its huge control over massive quantities of people and goods, plus multiple countries, to get a better perspective of Pars. Listening to Zav had made Cyrus realize just how large the world really was. Zav may be a problem for his parents, but the man did business on a scale that could not be equaled in Anshan and that was important. Cyrus might use Zav's experience some day to his own advantage. The thing that bothered the prince most about Zav was the comment the minister made to him as he left the banquet. Was it a threat? Was it a suggestion that Zav knew of enemies who wanted him dead? Did Zav know of a specific plot against him, which already existed?

The questions developing from Zav's hint were secondary to the problems the prince had about his grandfather. The prince had to determine the kind of relationship he could tolerate with the Great King.

Cyrus was still the regent of Arbela. That was both an honor and a responsibility he would not forsake. He knew he had to go back there periodically to protect the Great King's properties. Cyrus concluded that protecting the estate of the empire was not the same as protecting the King of Kings. He could easily do the former, but he was confused over what he should do about the latter. Only the passage of time would enable the young prince's mind to settle on a comfortable compromise about his grandfather.

Cyrus began to daydream about the horrific banquet. He focused on how his own grandfather had ordered his death long ago. Cyrus let his mind wander over the details the banquet revealed. He became concerned that the Great King might some day resurrect his original fear of Cyrus and try to either imprison him or kill him. Cyrus decided he had to be ready for that eventuality so he committed himself to becoming a man who would always be prepared to protect himself.

As the next sun cycle developed, Cambyses oversaw the boy's training. Cyrus was allowed to sit in his father's court to watch the routine business of running their small, poor country, including Reconciling Day audiences. Most of the Parsian people who came to Reconciling Day wore rags. If they brought farm implements with them into the court as part of their argument about a contract, the materials were frequently broken, and they were always crafted from some ancient design that hardly eased the labor required for using each tool. Cyrus could only envision extreme hardship related to every piece of equipment that he saw. These Parsian farmers and peasants were not greedy people. They wanted fairness, and they were glad to share all they had. He began to love the open dignity of his father's people. He wanted to be a man among these noble men. They were worth so much more than the richer population of people in Ecbatana.

Cyrus was to be a man soon and some day the king of Pars. He committed himself to being a more decent, more compassionate man than his grandfather was. He had to start working hard now to be worthy of this nation of Pars and its stalwart people.

THE END

C.J. Kirwin

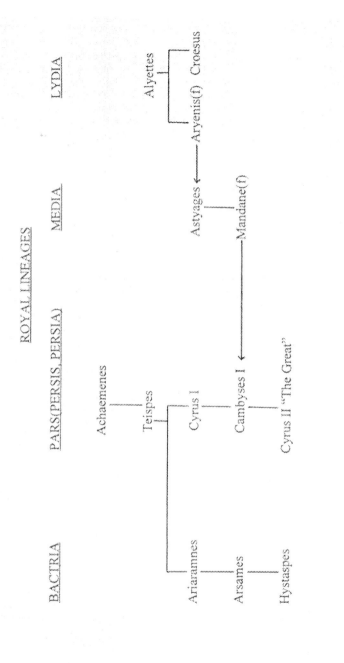

ROYAL LINEAGES

BACTRIA   PARS(PERSIS, PERSIA)   MEDIA   LYDIA

Achaemenes

Teispes

Ariaramnes   Cyrus I

Arsames   Cambyses I

Hystaspes   Cyrus II "The Great"   Mandane(f)   Astyages ← Aryenis(f)   Croesus

Alyettes

(f) – female
N. B. - Female—marries→Male

400

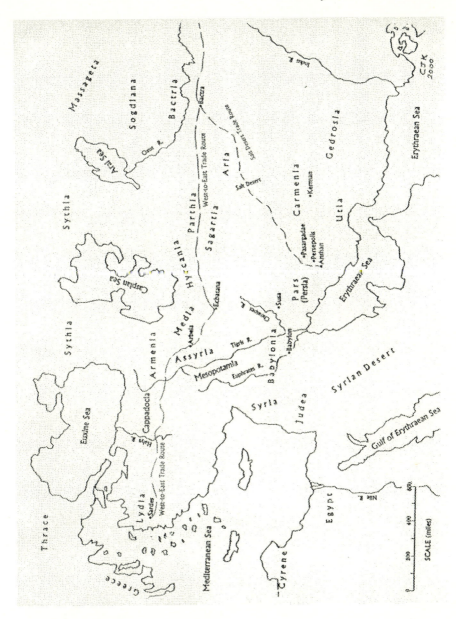

About the Author:

C.J. Kirwin retired from a career as an industrial toxicologist. His extensive travels led him to take an interest in ancient history. After a family member introduced him to Cyrus the Great, Mr. Kirwin was surprised to find Cyrus so prominently represented in important segments of the Old Testament, which he had never read. After years of research he decided to integrate historical inconsistencies about the childhood of Cyrus into a fictional novel.

Mr. Kirwin lives in Oklahoma with his wife, three daughters and four grandchildren.

Printed in the United States
50289LVS00008B/74

9 781410 764782